CERTAIN RICH GIRLS

Three girls from posh Fairfield County, close
friends to each other, but mavericks to their classmates, grow up in the 60s and—courted by power,
fueled by ambition—become members of that
restless Manhattan sorority of new women in the
70s for whom the answers of the past are not
enough.

This is their story.

CERTAIN RICH GIRLS
Ann Pinchot

For J. Walter Kennedy

CERTAIN RICH GIRLS

*A Bantam Book | published by arrangement with
Arbor House Publishing Company*

PRINTING HISTORY

*Arbor House edition published March 1979
2 printings through March 1979
Bantam edition | September 1980*

*Bantam Books are published by Bantam Books, Inc. Its trade-
mark, consisting of the words "Bantam Books" and the por-
trayal of a bantam, is Registered in U.S. Patent and Trademark
Office and in other countries. Marca Registrada. Bantam
Books, Inc., 666 Fifth Avenue, New York, New York 10103.*

PRINTED IN THE UNITED STATES OF AMERICA

0 9 8 7 6 5 4 3 2 1

PROLOGUE

LOCUST RYSE: 1967

The morning sun had burned off the mist drifting in from Long Island Sound, and before noon the sky had turned to a clear, watercolor blue.

"Thank heaven," murmured Phyllis Merritt-Jones, headmistress of the Locust Ryse Day School for Girls, as she looked out of her office window at the brilliant day. The sweep of emerald lawn stretching to the rocky beach was set with rows of folding chairs that would accommodate several hundred guests. On a raised platform were placed a semi-circle of seats and a lectern equipped with loud speakers that Georgio, the gardener, had attached to cables that went to the white stucco Main House, now dazzling in the sunlight.

Seated at her polished desk, bare except for the dozen diplomas stacked in a flat wicker basket and the school yearbook open to a picture of the graduating class, Mrs. Merritt-Jones prayed for the day to go well. So far Graduation Week had lived up to the Locust Ryse tradition—except for the shocking incident that had occurred the previous night. Georgio and Miss Caswell, who taught ethics and athletics, had come to tell her about a bundle they had found in the bushes.

Mrs. Merritt-Jones closed her eyes, the blood draining from her bold-featured handsome face, as she remembered the scene. *Put it out of your mind*, she told herself. *Don't ruin your day. Only an hour more to the ceremony, and afterward—afterward, you are finished with them. The responsibility is no longer yours.* But suppose the police were to discover . . .

I

How could they? Georgio wasn't apt to talk. Certainly not Miss Caswell. Mrs. Merritt-Jones wondered why the two of them were together when they found the bundle, but she had no time to ponder the young teachers' indiscretions.

Who was it? she asked herself. Who was the guilty one? She was probably a senior, who would soon be walking with a lovely measured tread on the red carpet, head held high, arms cradling a sheaf of scarlet roses. This was a difficult class, the headmistress knew. She scrutinized the glossy photographs of the students. They were well brought up girls from affluent families, the best Fairfield County had to offer—barring the three mavericks. They had been her cross to bear. Exasperated, she had turned for guidance to the chief of psychiatry at a local private hospital.

"One is the only daughter of the Towle family," she told him. "The other is the daughter of Bonnie Rob Roy, the singer. The third is our scholarship student—" She couldn't very well say, "our token underprivileged student." "Oddly enough, they cling together. They do not meld with the others."

Just talking to the doctor had helped. He seemed so calm, as though he thought mavericks should be taken in stride. And she had needed this sort of advice during the past semester, with the tensions of preparing for the College Boards, waiting for college acceptances, and dealing with mothers who were edgy because their daughters hadn't been accepted at the Seven Sister Colleges. . . .

As Mrs. Merritt-Jones stared at the photo Miss Caswell strode in, a graceful young woman with short, curly blond hair crowning a pretty face that glowed with natural beauty. She wore a classic white linen shirtwaist with a navy blazer set with gilt buttons. Like the headmistress, she believed that life demanded a certain protocol.

"The guests are arriving," Miss Caswell announced.

Mrs. Merritt-Jones closed the yearbook and stood up. She was a lean woman who had a contempt for curves or superfluous flesh. She still wore the pastel woolen skirts with matching pullovers and tailored shirts of her Wellesley days. "I'll go and get ready." She paused and ran her fingers through her thick, artfully retouched red-gold hair. Then her eyes met Miss Caswell's. The younger woman looked sympathetic, but remained silent.

"Problems. I'm not sure how to cope with this one," the headmistress admitted.

"Perhaps if you ignore it, it'll go away."

"I wish it were that easy. I'm afraid I'll have to report it to the police. But what will happen? How can it be hushed up? Whom shall I ask for advice? Caswell, we're due for trouble—"

"People know these accidents happen—even in the best schools."

"That doesn't comfort me. It's never happened before. Tell me, frankly, who do you think it was?"

Miss Caswell, who had her private suspicions, didn't answer. "Put it on 'hold' till later," the younger woman suggested. "What shall I do meanwhile about the photographers?"

"The photographers?"

"From the New York papers."

"But only the photographer from the Stamford paper is allowed."

"They're here to cover Bonnie Rob Roy. They say she's due here for her daughter's graduation."

At the mention of Bonnie Rob Roy, Mrs. Merritt-Jones's blood pressure surged wildly. "I won't have that scandalous creature here. Nobody told me she was coming."

"Evidently Cristina sent her an invitation. It's natural to invite one's mother to one's graduation."

The headmistress thought, *I can't cope,* and hurried out into the hall, up the curving staircase to her private rooms.

Fifteen minutes later, a calmer Mrs. Merritt-Jones greeted the ceremonial speakers in the intimate reception room, its windows open to the translucent blue day. There was the Reverend Donald McBride, the rangy red-haired Scot who would give the Invocation; Stephen Terhune, the tall, distinguished President of the Board of Trustees; and Dr. Constance Peake, a leader of the woman's rights movement who was disguised as a small, dowdy housewife.

Mrs. Merritt-Jones smoothed the dark processional robe over her shoulders and arranged her long, flat body and still youthful face to give the impression of academic style. Stephen Terhune caught her glance and smiled. She had always got along well with him. Why, she wondered, did he allow his former wife to come for graduation? Surely he knew what the other parents' reactions to Bonnie Rob Roy would be. They might applaud her in a garish nightclub but they wouldn't want her to participate in this occasion. But then, Mrs. Merritt-Jones reflected with rare tolerance, he probably had no more influence on her than on their daughter. Willful, hyperactive and insolent, Cristina Terhune was one of her Trio of Sorrows in the class of '67.

Outside the open door, on the private flagged terrace, she could see the girls gathering in their filmy white dresses. She thought they looked like strangers, nervously staring at each other in their graduation finery. When Mr. Beamus, the Yale Fine Arts instructor who came once a week to teach music to the upperclass girls, played the first majestic notes of "Gaudeamus Igitur" on the organ, Mrs. Merritt-Jones fell into line behind the speakers for the procession. She was followed by the graduating students, the faculty and the guests.

The front row of seats was reserved for the families of the graduates. The mothers—youthful, slim, tanned by the golf course and tennis courts—were elegant in the latest Pucci silk dresses. The older women wore pastel linens with cashmere sweaters dyed to match, pearls and picture hats. Grandfathers in white suits and Panama hats looked as though they belonged in the Reading Room at Newport, and the younger men— proud fathers in navy blue blazers and gray flannels— were equipped with the latest Polaroids and Kodaks. The photographer from the Stamford paper lounged discreetly in the rear, in the shadow of the stunted Australian pines that made a windbreak for the flowering shrubs, jeweled with honey bees and butterflies.

Mrs. Merritt-Jones walked slowly along the strip of carpet, a scarlet division between guests and graduates, and up the three steps to the raised platform. There her eyes focused on the twelve girls of assorted shapes and sizes who moved toward her. Their youthful, unformed bodies were exquisitely gift wrapped in white silks, organzas and chiffons. Endless rehearsal with Miss Caswell was reflected in their bearing—shoulders erect, chins up, stately gait (yet unsteady because of high heels). Mrs. Merritt-Jones reflected that just as all brides were beautiful, so were all graduates of Locust Ryse, the seminary that blended preparation for college with a gracious way of life.

Even pudgy Cristina Terhune, stumbling awkwardly on the first step, was adequate, though hardly attractive. Fortunately the triple tiers of organza skirt billowed out, diminishing her thick bodice. What a pity, the headmistress thought, that she hadn't inherited her father's elegant appearance. She took after her mother, a famous singer whose street waif looks had brought her world recognition and multiple miseries, but poor Cristina lacked her mother's talent and charisma.

The girls shimmered in the bright sunshine. Here among the daughters of account executives, top-ranking corporate officers, physicians and lawyers, Mrs. Merritt-Jones saw the other two girls who'd given her such a hard time for four long years. Marianna Ellis—thin, bony, her pale brown hair falling around her oval face—was marked by unusual self-control. Her scoop-neck dress was not flattering, although the headmistress surmised it was probably a costly gift from one of the other mothers.

Allegra Simon's dress was quite different from the others. It was simple, almost Grecian, with a bateau neck and graceful flowing lines, accenting her beautiful tan. Her glossy hair, black as anthracite, was a lacquered helmet framing the winsome face. *What a sly one*, the headmistress reflected. Allegra never looked at you directly—always sideways to show her remarkable almond eyes at their best. The girl's expression during the ceremony was cool, withdrawn yet aloof, almost bored. She'd gone through four years at Locust Ryse in much the same manner and had got away with it.

Mrs. Merritt-Jones felt her throat muscles tense with suppressed resentment. Herself from an impecunious academic family, she had respect for money. Money was the only power, she thought—the great silencer. Just look at Allegra's relatives—the Towle family—sitting with the poise and self-interest characteristic of the old rich. They behaved like American royalty, as if the scandal that had made newspaper headlines years before had not touched them. . . .

After all the speeches had been delivered Mrs. Merritt-Jones went to the lectern to award the prizes for the year. She unfolded the paper naming the winners and made certain that the prizes themselves—a Spanish-English dictionary, a thesaurus, a volume of great American poetry, the *Columbia Desk Encyclopedia*—were on the small table beside her, each volume wrapped in pretty paper, with a notation as to its content.

The first one, for excellence in English, went to Marianna Ellis. The girl's face was blank, but fury burned in her hazel eyes and the corners of her mouth were taut. As the older woman handed her the thesaurus their exchanged glances belonged on the battlefield. *Thank the Lord I am rid of her,* Mrs. Merritt-Jones thought in relief.

She called Marianna back for another prize, this time in history. The girl received a third in creative writing, a fourth for her contributions to the school paper and finally a fifth for her four-year scholastic record. Mrs. Merritt-Jones was offended by this display of excellence, stemming as it did from this one dreadful girl. If the other mothers were upset, she didn't blame them. But there was nothing to be done about it.

The headmistress then came to the prize for the girl who had shown the most self-improvement in the four years: Cristina Terhune, of course.

The last award went to the girl who had done the most for the school. The choice of the recipient had required less soul-searching than it had academic politics. When Allegra walked forward, her tunic folds undulating, Mrs. Merritt-Jones read the scornful humor in her expression. They both knew the reason for the recognition, just as Cristina knew why she had been singled out for the other: The school depended on the financial gifts bestowed by the families of these two students.

Next, the diplomas were distributed. Stephen Terhune gave each girl her sheepskin and shook her hand as the headmistress read off the names. When his daughter Cristina reached the lectern he took her hand, leaned down and kissed her cheek—and was rewarded with a cool, sullen look. The other girls accepted their diplomas with warm smiles for him; only Allegra kept her eyes downcast, which surprised Mrs. Merritt-Jones, for the girl was anything but shy.

The ceremony at an end, Mrs. Merritt-Jones stood in the receiving line, poised, gracious, her smile more brilliant for generous parents. She shook hands with Marianna Ellis's ebullient mother and looked with disfavor at the woman's headful of blond ringlets, her turquoise knit pantsuit (she was the only woman who wore pants) and her gaudy gold jewelry. The headmistress had to admit that the tasteless woman was astonishingly beautiful, although in a rather *mitteleuropa* way.

With her faint Gabor-sisters' accent, Marianna's mother said, "You have given so much to my little girl. But she has done well. I understand her four-year record is the best in the history of the school. Is that right?"

Then Marianna's mother turned to Allegra's mother, who stood behind her in the line, and smiled brightly. "Four years. It doesn't seem so long . . . since I brought Marianna to your house for the scholarship."

The headmistress felt her nerves crawl. But Allegra's mother, Mrs. John X. Lovell, nodded graciously and managed to bypass the woman without seeming impolite. She was followed by Stephen Terhune and his wife Rose Eileen, who was Cristina's stepmother.

Stephen said, "We'll be meeting before the week's over to go over the construction plans."

Mrs. Merritt-Jones nodded, but her mind was elsewhere, on the discovery in the bushes. Miss Caswell, aware of the older woman's concern, took her aside and said in an undertone, "There's no need to worry. It wasn't a full-term dead infant. It was a fetus, scarcely developed beyond the fourth month."

Mrs. Merritt-Jones moistened her lips. "How do you know?"

"Georgio took it to a doctor. Georgio has friends—"

"What . . . what was done with it?"

"The doctor disposed of it." Miss Caswell's well-scrubbed face was benign. "No cause for alarm."

"I wish I *knew*—"

"Do you really? Isn't it perhaps better that we don't know? I mean, under the circumstances—"

"It couldn't be one of the graduates, could it? They all look so . . . so healthy. If this . . . this birth . . . happened to one of them, I should think she'd be indisposed—"

Miss Caswell patted her arm. "Try not to think about it."

"I *knew* something was wrong." Mrs. Merritt-Jones turned back to the group to shake hands with Mrs. Towle, Allegra's grandmother. She was a tall, erect woman with a deeply lined face and wore a Liberty print cotton dress and wide-brimmed straw hat. Mrs. Towle was the matriarch of the family, and the amount of money the Towle Family Foundation would contribute to the school depended on her good will. The headmistress kept her face calm, impervious to inner storms; after Mrs. Towle continued down the receiving line, she moved away, inconspicuously, to regain her poise.

The graduates were behaving well, Mrs. Merritt-Jones saw—shaking hands, accepting compliments and congratulations with exemplary poise, signing the yearbook pages for the benefit of the undergraduates. Among the younger students she heard bursts of girlish laughter with the overtones of hysteria that seemed the mark of adolescent girls with ripening bodies and immature brains. *The idiots!* she thought, watching them flirt with boys as they passed trays of *petits fours* and punch—little girls yearning for sex to cover their ignorance of life, longing for something they didn't quite grasp.

How many virgins were there in the graduating class, the headmistress wondered. It was a question she didn't dare face. Values were changing. Earlier this year, there'd been a suggestion from some students that the seniors be given a more advanced course in sex education than the one Miss Caswell taught. Mrs. Merritt-Jones had conceded that some private schools were more progressive in sex education than Locust Ryse. Let *their* students experience Berkeley or UCLA, she'd announced, her voice biting with scorn; our girls are being prepared for a finer destiny.

Locust Ryse girls were not products of the revolutionary sixties with their lamentable breakdown in moral fiber; they were the end result of a private school that stressed Christian ethics. The problems that tormented the heads of other finishing schools—drugs, alcohol, fornicating—were unfamiliar to Mrs. Merritt-Jones. What was important to her and what she transmitted to the student body were morals, good manners, discipline and an appreciation of cultural interests —upper middle-class values in education. She fought against mediocrity. She dedicated herself to the making of fine character and refused to lower school standards. . . . Which brought her to Marianna Ellis.

Marianna had turned away from the receiving line and was drifting toward the edge of the lawn, where the narrow strip of flowering shrubs, grown in green boxes, made pointelles of elementary colors against the sunlight. Marc Finley, the English and economics teacher, was coming out of the Main Building. Pupil and teacher met and made a vivid picture, Marc holding out his hand, Marianna grasping it and looking up at him with a kind of rapture seldom revealed in her disciplined manner. Marc thought highly of the girl, Mrs. Merritt-Jones knew. He was responsible for at least two of Marianna's academic awards and had shown obvious distress on hearing that Marianna was going to find a job rather than attend college.

A strange sense of foreboding suddenly gripped the headmistress, clouding the sunlight, the laughter, the felicitous moment. For several months, she'd been aware of something wrong, something elusive, something threatening. Then, two months ago, in April, she had stumbled on a clue.

It was after nine o'clock on a quiet weeknight. Students and teachers had left at four o'clock; the kitchen staff was gone. Mrs. Merritt-Jones was in her upstairs rooms, working late on college applications, worrying about how to convince ambitious mothers that smaller junior colleges would be better for their daughters than the Seven Sister Colleges. Tension made her hungry, and she decided to forage for food in the school kitchen.

As she was going down the stairs, she noticed a pinpoint of light in her office transom window. She stiffened. Georgio sometimes checked the buildings at night, but the gardener was off today. She walked quietly and fearlessly the length of the hall, turned to her door, flung it open and switched on the light.

She thought she might encounter a man intent on stealing the money she kept in the file in her office. Instead she found a girl in a Locust Ryse uniform sitting at the desk.

The girl looked startled at the sound of the headmistress's voice. She stood up, her hair falling over her pale face.

"Marianna! What are you doing here?" Mrs. Merritt-Jones shouted.

No answer. There were drops of perspiration on Marianna's short upper lip and terror in her eyes.

"What were you looking for? I demand an answer."

Again the silence, the awful fear. Mrs. Merritt-Jones thought she'd never witnessed such terror: Marianna's heartbeat was disturbing the bosom of her white blouse.

Suddenly the headmistress saw that the lower right-hand desk drawer was open; a blackbound book had been removed and lay open on top of the desk. She thought that Marianna must have been searching for the questions and answers of the final exams. Perhaps the girl wanted to raise her marks even higher or to share the information with her friends—or even to sell them. Nothing was beneath her. *I knew it!* Mrs. Merritt-

Jones said to herself. She'd been right about the girl from the beginning. Marianna, with the smell of poverty about her, didn't belong at Locust Ryse. She had corrupted Allegra and Cristina; without her, they wouldn't have been nearly so troublesome.

"What do you want—the finals?"

"Oh, no!"

"You were looking for them, weren't you?" With rising anger, the headmistress added, *"Answer me!"*

"No—no, Mrs. Merritt-Jones. I wasn't—"

"What were you looking for?" The headmistress moved toward Marianna and saw with surprise that her address book lay open on her desk. The girl retreated, flinching; her hands were clenched in a frantic effort at self-control.

"I demand that you tell me the truth."

"It was a dare—a kind of dare." Marianna raised her anguished face, eyes closed, as though in a confessional. "A dare—"

"Who else is involved?"

Silence.

"Answer me, Marianna!"

"I can't. I promised—"

"I want the names of the others—"

Mrs. Merritt-Jones knew Marianna wouldn't answer, for at Locust Ryse students were taught contempt for anyone who tattled. She was relieved, and decided to regard the incident as a prank. But she didn't intend to let the girl off easily.

"I should suspend you."

"Oh, no. *Please* . . ."

In her anxiety, the girl approached the headmistress, her hands outstretched.

"You're not fit to walk in the procession with your peers—"

Mrs. Merritt-Jones usually had mixed feelings when it was necessary to punish a girl. She wanted always to create an image that her girls would admire and emulate. But she knew the importance of discipline: If she let down one iota, the little savages would devour her.

"I didn't mean anything—it was a dare," Marianna

repeated, her sobs muffling her words. Tears were cascading down her pale, stricken face.

"I'll think about it." The headmistress's voice was cold. "You may go."

"You won't keep me back. You won't suspend me."

"You may leave, Marianna."

In the morning, when she was calmer, Mrs. Merritt-Jones decided to do nothing. She would let the girl suffer. In the two long months to graduation, Marianna would be afraid to face each day, expecting the fateful summons to the headmistress's office.

When she returned to her own rooms the following afternoon, Mrs. Merritt-Jones found an envelope pushed under her door. She picked it up, curious, for even her private mail was sent to her office. The envelope was marked PRIVATE AND CONFIDENTIAL. The words weren't handwritten or typed; they were cut out of a newspaper and pasted together.

Without waiting to close her door, she ripped open the envelope. The message was on a single sheet of paper. Here again, the words were put together from a newspaper column: THINK. FORGIVE. YOU WERE YOUNG ONCE.

. . . So Marianna had marched in the procession and carried off almost all the school honors. And when, at last, the receiving line broke into small animated groups, Mrs. Merritt-Jones watched Marianna talking with Marc Finley and she knew in a flash of insight what the girl had been looking for the night she broke into her office. She recalled now that the address book had been open to the last page. There she had written the name of a Dr. Rapf, whose services she hoped never to resort to. Her own gynecologist had given the information to her, saying, "If you ever run into a problem with any of your girls, I'd recommend this fellow. He's a wiz. And much more accessible than the fellows in Puerto Rico."

"We've had no such problems."

The gynecologist had laughed. "There's always a first time."

Now, staring at the girl and her young teacher, Mrs. Merritt-Jones thought she had stumbled on the truth.

Perhaps Marianna had suspected, in a kind of desperation, that such a name would be available to the headmistress. The fetus was hers. No wonder she'd looked so
wan in the procession; no wonder she'd trembled when
she stepped forward to receive her awards. There *had*
been a first time after all.

And the man . . . could it be Marc Finley? Possibly.
He was so attractive; all the girls had crushes on him.
Mrs. Merritt-Jones had decided earlier in the year that
his presence at Locust Ryse was a disturbing factor.
The only kind of man who belonged in a girls' school
was someone like Mr. Beamis, who was asexual. Marc
drew the girls; his intensity and aloofness were a challenge to them. At the same time, they absorbed so
much in his class, because he was an excellent teacher.
She couldn't believe he'd been involved with Marianna,
gawky creature that she was. Not even Allegra, who
had been voted the prettiest girl in her class, had
aroused him to anything but academic interest. When
Mrs. Merritt-Jones had suggested that Marc's contract
not be renewed, Stephen Terhune had objected. But she
had prevailed: The young man would attend Harvard
Graduate School in the fall.

Turning away from Marianna and Marc, she walked
back to the receiving line, where she shook hands with
Allegra's stunning mother and eminent stepfather. She
bestowed a faint peck on Allegra's tanned cheek and
smiled, implying that all was forgiven and forgotten.

Then she bade farewell to Cristina. Taking the
girl's hand she said, "Now that you've won the award
for the most self-improvement, you must maintain these
standards, Cris dear."

Cristina Terhune bobbed her head, the dark hair
falling over her large soulful eyes, her full mouth spilling over with excitement. "My mother couldn't make
it. I guess she had an unexpected rehearsal, because
she planned on coming. . . ."

Mrs. Merritt-Jones looked up and met Stephen Terhune's wise, tolerant glance, and she thought, *How that
woman must have hurt him. I hope she doesn't get her
hands on Cris again. It will ruin the girl.*

And now for Marianna, whose mother was pulling

her in the direction of the headmistress. "We have so much to thank you for," the woman began.

Mrs. Merritt-Jones felt it behooved her to mention Marianna's future, considering the girl's scholastic achievement. "I wish you success, Marianna."

"Thank you."

No doubt Marianna, of them all, would need the good wishes and the help she could get—or take, Mrs. Merritt-Jones thought. Yet there was something positive about her. *She's a survivor,* the headmistress said to herself. *Of them all, she'll survive.*

Late on the night of Cristina's graduation, Rose Eileen—the second Mrs. Stephen Terhune—was suffering the spasms of guilt and sorrow.

That dear Stephen should have fathered only one child—a daughter who made no effort to hide her contempt for him—destroyed Rose Eileen's serenity. Her own love for Stephen was so all consuming, such a total commitment, that she had made the round of Manhattan's finest gynecologists, pleading for a miracle. But they had told her that no miracle was needed, since there seemed to be no physical reason why two such healthy specimens could not produce an offspring of their own—especially in view of Rose Eileen's Scotch-Irish heritage. Her mother had borne a dozen children, each more beautiful than the last, and her brothers and sisters had multiplied according to the good Lord's edict: Multiply. Fructify. Produce sons, so Terhune International would have heirs. . . .

The three Terhunes were gathered in the solarium to open Cristina's lavish gifts. Glossy boxes bearing Bendel, Bergdorf and Saks logos were partly open, the cornucopias of costly wrappings carelessly ripped, the air rich with each shop's individual scent.

Rose Eileen had spent a week shopping, debating with herself, asking advice of Stephen, listening to the flighty salesgirls recommending suede skirts for fall, nightgowns, silk blouses. Meekly, she had followed the suggestions until she was obliged to admit that she needed a size sixteen.

"Sixteen! We carry nothing larger than twelve."

So she had bought leather bags Cris probably wouldn't use, caftans that would moulder in her closets and sweaters that would be donated to Good Will.

Rose Eileen looked at her adored slender husband who was looking at his adored overweight daughter and she wondered for the thousandth time how Cristina could be so unkind to him. Yet she knew in her heart that it was not malleable Cris's doing. The source of the girl's vicious, unforgiving anger was, of course, Bonnie Rob Roy. Rose Eileen thought it was so unreasonable, considering how much Stephen had done—and was still doing—for his first wife. And for Cris, who wouldn't appreciate him until she was a parent herself.

Of all the rooms in the spacious New Canaan country house, Rose Eileen loved the solarium, even more than the greenhouse. The plants were tended with her rare brand of love and they produced specimen blooms. She glanced at Cris and reflected that her stepdaughter added little to the beauty of the room. Slouched in a white wicker fantail chair, her round cheeks flushed, Cris was pitiful. Yet she *could* be pretty—well, at least, attractive. Rose Eileen wanted to help her, but she wouldn't be able to if Bonnie Rob Roy took over once more. Bonnie, she knew, could be the destruction of her daughter.

Dear God, Rose Eileen prayed, let her stay with us, where she'll be safe.

"Cristina, have you made any plans?" Stephen asked.

For the summer or the rest of my life? Cris wanted to say, but she suppressed the urge. *Play it carefully,* she told herself. Mama had warned her to hold her tongue if he got strict. Stephen still exerted power over poor Mama; it was tied up with money, Cris suspected. Mama had no money sense. Her new manager was always fussing, "Bonnie, you act like money grows on trees. Even yours doesn't. The IRS isn't going to wait forever."

Poor Mama. She owed everybody—hotels, chauffeur services, designers, the many doctors she went to. But she was always good for the money; she always paid up with her next week's check. Once, Cris recalled, in Vegas Mama had demanded to be paid in greenbacks,

and when the hotel manager had arrived with the
strongbox she tossed the bills all over the place. She
was having such fun that after a while everybody
joined in and there was champagne. When Mama went
on stage that night, the applause was a tornado of
love and kisses to America's Songbird.

That was the part of Mama the world knew. But
few realized how much Mama longed for kindness and
love. Cris knew, because they were like sisters. She
knew about the long, black melancholy nights, when
Mama would pace around her hotel room like a wild
creature in a circus arena and swallow too many down-
ers and cry, "God, why don't you help me?" Cris would
say, "I'm here, Mama. And I'll always be here to hold
you. You can always count on me, Mama—"

That is, if *he* didn't separate them again.

"Cris—" Her father's voice pulled her back into the
present. "Rose Eileen has some ideas for the summer.
Would you like to go to Seale Harbor? Or a tennis
camp? Or have you and Allegra and Marianna come
up with anything else?"

"Allie's mother wants her to go on a student tour in
France—"

"Would you enjoy that, Cris?" Rose Eileen asked
eagerly.

"No, because Allie isn't going. Marianna's working in
the Piano Store for Miss Evalina in exchange for piano
lessons."

"Would you prefer to stay here?" Stephen asked.

Cris's full, glossy lips folded in a stubborn line.

"One thing we better have out once and for all,"
Stephen said. "You were a child of divorce. But you
were *not* an abandoned child. Ever. Your mother's notion of love doesn't coincide with mine. But in her way,
she loves you. And when you ran off on the road—
like some homeless kid—you hurt her as much as us.
There'll be no more of that. Is it understood?"

She met his icy challenge. His eyes were light, either
blue or gray; she couldn't remember anymore, because
it was so long since she'd looked him directly in the
face. Mama hadn't made such a fuss about her running

away. "So what," Mama had said. "I was younger when I ran away from home."

"I want your word, Cris," Stephen repeated.

· "Darling—" Rose Eileen sounded teary and muddled. "If you need a—a change from us, tell Daddy first. So he can arrange it."

"And it will save us an appearance at Children's Court." Stephen's voice was bitter.

He didn't understand, nor did Rose Eileen. How could she explain that sometimes she felt she could find escape from her pain only with roads and cars and crowds? How was she to know that the hopped-up kid was giving her a lift in a car that wasn't his?

Memories of Mama's pep talks gave her courage. "I'm eighteen. I'm my own boss now. You've got no right to treat me like a delinquent—"

For the first time, pain flickered in her father's eyes. "Then for God's sake, don't act like one," he snapped.

"Stephen, *please*." There was something healing in Rose Eileen's voice; she had more control over Stephen than Mama had. Mama deliberately goaded him until he was ready to explode. But Rose Eileen always somehow calmed him, and Cris liked, respected her for it . . .

Cris said deliberately, "I'm leaving tomorrow for Mexico."

"For where?" Stephen demanded.

"Mama is going to Mexico City first. Then we'll take off for some new hotel in Acapulco. I'll be with Mama until she comes East again." She was tempted to add, "Any objections?" but decided she'd said enough when she saw the sudden pallor of her father's face. Mama evidently hadn't warned him. She glared at Stephen, gloating inwardly as he pushed back his Brighton chair and stalked out of the room.

Cris had learned not to feel, not to get hurt. But she did care for Rose Eileen. "I have to go with Mama," she explained. "She needs me . . . Don't cry, Rose Eileen. I'm counting on you to understand. Don't cry, please don't cry—"

"I won't, my darling, if I know you'll come back. You've taken such risks, darling, and thank God, you escaped. But we read about such awful things in the papers—girls raped and murdered, innocent girls who believe the world is good—"

Cris was too old for these runaway bits now. She'd had some near-misses, which she'd never mention to Rose Eileen. But once she'd boasted about an escapade to Allie, who told her not to be a fool. "If you want to kill yourself," Allie had said, "there're easier ways than having some crazy hack you to pieces."

This time she really wanted to stay here with Allie and Marianna and Rose Eileen. She wasn't going to give in to him, though. *The bastard.*

She didn't know it, but she sounded, of course, just like her mother.

"I'll be back, Rose Eileen." Cris buried her face in her stepmother's shoulder. But she had her fingers crossed, the way she used to when, as a child, she was telling a lie.

The morning after graduation was fair. Allegra opened her eyes to sunlight, a zephyr breeze and happy canine yipping from the kennels in her mother's Greenwich house. Her nude body covered only with a sheet, she lay quietly, momentarily disoriented. She had awakened from a troubled dream, in which she had wandered through a bleak stretch of landscape, with monstrous rocks and the pitfalls of shell holes. She was searching for her father; he was always ahead of her, just beyond her reach, and she couldn't catch up with him. "Wait for me!" she had shouted again and again.

Allegra was sadly aware that not even in her febrile dreams could she see her father, who was gone forever. The only link she had with him now were the photographs in her room at Grandmama Towle's New Canaan house. She had hidden them carefully so that even the maid wouldn't discover them: There were newspaper clippings, of course, about the scandal, his trial and the sentence a very cruel judge had pronounced. But Allegra ignored these yellowed scraps of paper. What she looked at, when she longed for the sight of him, were the wedding pictures taken by a society photographer named Hal Phyfe. The pictures washed out all character and gave Mommy and Daddy the glamorous radiance of movie images; they were partly responsible for the press calling them the most romantic couple of the year. But the mementoes she truly treasured were the snapshots of her parents taken for an article in *Town and Country,* which was all about Prudence Towle of the Towle family and a Russian emigré named Pavel Simon who was something of a Wonder Boy on Wall Street.

How she'd wanted her father during yesterday's celebration! Closing her eyes for a moment, as she sat among the eleven girls of her class, Allegra had pretended he was in the front row beside her mother, pride, love and tenderness reflected in his face.

But it was John X. Lovell seated beside her mother —so proper, so self-contained. He was a well-known corporation lawyer with an impeccable background— proper schools, excellent family connections. He appeared a carefully preserved half-century, his hair combed back from his high, intelligent forehead, the expression in his eyes hidden by glasses, his mouth pleasant but disciplined—the proper match for her mother after her father had gone to prison. Everyone said John X. Lovell was the man she should have married in the first place and saved herself all the torment and her family all the scandal.

Lying on her bed, Allegra looked around the room, which she considered her halfway house. The furnishings were unlike the expensive Tudor, Elizabethan and Chinese clutter of the rest of the house. There was a white-and-gilt desk, chests and bookcases that held most of her childhood favorites, from *Pat the Bunny* through *Anne of Green Gables* and the *Nancy Drew* series. Her special loves—*The Russian Fairy Tales* and later *The Wilder Shores of Love* and other romantic books— were kept in her bedroom at Grandmother Towle's. But here at Mommy's house, the growing plants and the stuffed and ceramic animals were calculated to remind Allie that she was still a child, not a precociously sexy young woman, as she liked to think.

The trouble between mother and daughter had started before the divorce seven years ago. It had peaked after the second marriage, when Allegra came to live with Mommy and John X. in the Greenwich house. She didn't much like her stepfather—not that she had anything against him; he was unfailingly considerate and generous with her. But she hated him for taking her father's place.

Allegra's anger had assumed a peculiar form that puzzled even herself. She took to running out to greet her stepfather when she heard the sound of his car in the driveway. Sometimes she'd been dressed only in panties, and she'd rush down, neglecting even to put on a shirt. And one afternoon, when her mother saw the scene—ten-year-old Allie, all legs and skinny frame, but with flat pancake breasts marked by brown nipples —she had a bedtime talk with Allie.

"If you try that again with John you'll go to your grandmother's for good. Seducing your father was enough. I don't intend to allow it to extend to John . . ."

Allie was shocked. What did Mommy mean—seducing her father? She'd worshipped him. Was there anything wrong with adoring your father? The accusation still stung, a wound never healed, ready to bleed again at any moment . . .

Allegra sat up in bed and inspected her toes, which were tipped in pink enamel. She ran her palms along her thighs to her ankles, the skin reflecting a sun gloss. Her legs were better than her mother's, much more shapely—anklebones narrow, flesh swelling gently to rounded calfs. She was flat in the belly, too; her mother, for all her golf and tennis, had a round curve, suggesting that in spite of exercise and massage, age couldn't be entirely conquered.

No wonder she wants me out of here, Allegra thought. She moved slowly out of bed and padded to the windows overlooking the cutting and vegetable gardens. Flowers blossomed in early profusion. The gardener, trundling rich topsoil in a wheelbarrow, was an old man, sun-wrinkled, testy to everyone but Mommy. There were no longer virile, healthy young men on the house staff. Mommy had her obvious reasons, no doubt . . .

Turning on her heel, Allie felt slightly dizzy. She went to the bathroom, again decorated in what Mommy considered appropriate for a young girl—pale blue-and-white tiles, coy ruffles on the blue-and-yellow chintz curtains and shower. Digging into the top drawer of the wicker towel chest, Allie came up with a small silk makeup bag. From it she withdrew her most precious possession—a beautiful amethyst circled with gold filigree and black enamel. She took the jewel from the bag and admired the intricate work done by the artist Fabergé, who had created fabulous jewels for the Czar of Russia. Daddy had discovered it in an Eighth Avenue pawnshop, where it had been left for an unconscionable time. He redeemed it and tried to find the owner, but without success, and so he gave it to Allie. . . .

Feeling refreshed from a cold shower, Allie wrapped herself in a bathsheet. She blotted her skin, applied a lotion and inspected her breasts, noting their faint rounded shape. Touching the nipples to encourage them, she wondered if they would remain full. Her skin was burnished, its pigment deeper than her mother's. She ran her fingers over her flat hips and the gentle curve of her flawless belly. She used a tampon. Then she shrugged her shoulders into a white Jax jersey and put on tailored black pants, slid her long narrow feet into exercise clogs and braced herself for the inevitable meeting with her mother. She allowed the amethyst necklace to slide under the shirt.

Prudence Towle Lovell had spent the last hour in the kennels, absorbed in talk with a young woman handler who showed the prize Kerry Blues at various dog shows. Allegra's mother was tall—nearly six feet in height—and her body looked as if it had the strength and durability that was characteristic of the Towle women. Her dark hair, once almost purple-black in sunlight, was now liberally streaked with white, and its short locks made an attractive frame for her fine-boned face. Like those of her daughter, Prudence's eyes had strangely black irises and were outlined by a double row of black lashes. Clad in a white tailored shirt and pants, Prudence looked stunning; one couldn't imagine her with uncombed hair or spotted clothes.

A half dozen Kerry Blues were penned in the run. They bounced against the links, turning it into a wailing wall.

Allegra paused at the fence, slipped her fingers between the links, and received the dogs' slobbering adulation. She nodded to her mother, wondering if she could reach the garage without an unwanted scene.

"Good morning, Allie." Prudence dismissed the handler, who returned to the kennels.

"Morning." Allegra hitched her white canvas bag more firmly over her shoulder.

"I thought it went very well yesterday," her mother said.

"I guess so." Allie inched forward.

"Coffee?" Prudence gestured toward the vacuum flask and ironstone mugs sitting on a small white table in the nearby shade.

"No, thanks." She would make superficial talk until she could manage to escape without more questions, more pressure.

When her mother fell into step beside her Allie wasn't surprised. They made a striking pair. Most Towle women—Prudence included—displayed broader bone structure than Allie's. Their bodies were elegant, elongated in Prudence's case by discipline and exercise; in Allie's, by her English and Russian genes. The daughter's hair was similar to her mother's—black, somewhat thick and coarse. Where Prudence's face was rather long, with prominent, even teeth that gave her an obstinate cast, Allie's teeth were small and irregularly shaped, and her jawline, while good, lacked the strength of her mother's. The curve of Allie's small chin was accented by a faint indentation. Both mother and daughter had a sultry, brooding beauty, but what gave Allegra's face its unique appeal were her cheekbones, which were prominent, high and obvious and set her eyes deep into their sockets, allowing for alluring shadows—Slav cheekbones.

"Allie, have you finally decided where you want to go?"

"I haven't." There was no insolence in her voice, just indifference.

"Mrs. Merritt-Jones is quite disturbed. She expected your decision some time ago."

"Decisions, decisions."

"It's for the next four years."

"You forget. I wasn't accepted by a four-year school."

"Two years, then. You can't just *drift*—"

"I wasn't planning to."

"Will you tell me what you have in mind?"

When Allegra hesitated, Prudence followed up her advantage. "I don't intend to push you. But if your father were alive, he'd be bitterly disappointed. He believed in education. He worked nights to put himself through McGill—"

They were approaching the four-car garage, beyond the kennels and the gardener's preserve. Glancing sideways through her oversized dark glasses, Allie thought she saw a look of pain register on her mother's face. It struck an emotional response. With pride, Allie recalled her father's courage. But her response was cool. "He was a penniless refugee who had to make good. I don't have his character or his needs."

Her cool answer was calculated to remind her mother that she was no refugee, that she was independently rich—or would be in a few months on her eighteenth birthday—that she could arrange her life to suit her whims or her impulses with no interference from her family. She knew that not one of them gave a damn anyway. Her mother was too busy making herself into the image that she'd discarded after ten crazy, ecstatic years as the wife of that marvelous Russian emigré. Her grandmother—with whom she had lived for the past four years while attending Locust Ryse—disapproved of Allie, but with tact unusual in an elderly woman, kept quiet. As for the more distant relatives who sat on the board of the Family Trust, she seldom saw them and had no intention of allowing them to shape her life according to the family standards. She could very well take off for Europe and settle there like some of her cousins, who'd been Anglophiles since the time of the Depression. *I'm free, damn it,* she thought, hardly able to believe it.

Prudence's lips were set in a firm line over the strong white teeth. "Allegra, you must at least *start* college. If you're unhappy, if you don't adjust, well, you may drop out. I give you my promise."

Allie snorted, very unladylike.

"You have your choice of two schools. Mrs. Merritt-Jones managed it—a favor for which she'll surely extract her pound of flesh—"

"Mommy, why can't I take a year off and then decide—"

"If you're out of the academic discipline for a year, you'll never go back, Allie. I should call Mrs. Merritt-Jones—"

"Can't we talk about it another time?"

"There isn't much time left. You'll be leaving on that Student Tour—"

"I'm *not* going. I told you that . . . it'd be nice if you would listen to me."

"What's the alternative?" Prudence asked coldly.

Allegra felt the recent trauma, which she'd successfully weathered, now threatening to betray her. She felt weak, drained and frightened. "A couple of the Choate boys are driving out to San Francisco. They bought an old hearse and are fixing it up to sleep six—"

"Allegra!" Her mother was shocked.

"Or I could tag along with Cristina and her mother. Maybe I could be Bonnie Rob Roy's secretary or her hairdresser—"

Ignoring Allie's suggestions, Prudence said, "You spend altogether too much time with Cristina . . . And another thing, Allegra—I don't like the way you look. This vegetarian diet is robbing you of proteins. Yes, your tan is fetching, but it's deceptive, too. You look rather done in." She put her arm around Allie's resisting shoulders. Her voice softened. "I expect it's been a difficult year for you."

"Mommy, can't we *please* talk another time?"

They reached the garage and Allegra went directly to a red Jaguar XKE.

"You should do something constructive this summer. Have you considered taking courses at Columbia? Or doing some volunteer work at the hospital or the Girls' Club?"

"Oh, God . . ." She blew out her breath. *She can't handle me,* Allie thought with a surge of confidence. *She's defensive. And I'm damn well free of her. Finally . . .*

If she had still been the pre-graduate, tied by duty to the family, she would have done what was expected of her—drive to the New Canaan house, listen to Grandmama Towle and accompany her to Newport (where she would be sharing the shore cottage with a distant Towle relative) or take the dumb tour to France with a group of her peers, sharing marijuana and cocks, which would be the order of the day between trips to famous landmarks. But body and mind, she was now her own boss. What she had learned in the last few weeks, she thought, her roguish face breaking into a secret smile, could be useful in many ways.

The Jaguar responded to Allie's touch as she swung from North Street onto the Merritt Parkway and drove the smooth, landscaped road until she reached Route 123. But she didn't head in the direction of Grandmother Towle's place. She knew where she was going. The idea had taken shape in her mind even before she had left the Greenwich house. Her smile was pleased, and her eyes, behind the large, owl-round sunglasses, had the gleam of a wicked conspirator.

Marianna awoke at six in the morning. She was used to getting up then, because it was the best time to do her homework. Sometimes she would pause in her studies to fix breakfast for herself and her sister Darlis, since their mother was a late sleeper.

But this was the day after graduation. *I'm free,* she thought, flexing the muscles in her pelvic region, stretching her legs, enjoying the novelty of her condition. How would she adjust to it? Even the prospect of freedom of choice left her full of guilt.

She looked beyond the messy bedroom toward the small table desk by the window, crowded with Darlis's comic books, dimestore makeup and rock and roll records. Darlis appropriated whatever space was available, and last week, when Marianna had stacked away her Locust Ryse textbooks, folders and notebooks, in the attic of the building, Darlis promptly usurped the empty space.

Leaving Darlis asleep in her nearby bed, Marianna put on a seersucker robe over her cotton nightgown, ran her hands through her hair and went into the bathroom to wash and from there into the kitchen. The early sun lent an apricot mother-of-pearl luster to the sky. How she loved these summer mornings; every day seemed . . . a new beginning.

Beginning of what? she wondered. She recalled what her teacher Marc Finley had written in her copy of the Locust Ryse yearbook: "Live as though you intend to make your life a work of art." How would she accomplish that? Well, she didn't have to decide today. Today was her freedom day, to enjoy without any thoughts of tomorrow or the future.

She heated water for coffee, took out white bread for the toaster and opened the refrigerator to forage for butter and honey.

She was finishing her orange juice when Darlis entered, still in her babydoll nightie, warm, tousled, drugged with sleep, looking fresh from a tumbled bed shared with a lover. Like their mother, Darlis was candy-box pretty. She had blue eyes with milky white, heavy lids; a small, pert nose; full, pouting lips that promised much; and a body with a creaming of baby fat. Darlis was sexually precocious at thirteen, which Marianna thought quite shocking. But in some subtle, puzzling way she suspected her mother encouraged Darlis's behavior.

Brushing the blond hair out of her eyes, Darlis went directly to the radio on the windowsill and switched on a rock station. She was too young for David Bowie and Alice Cooper; Elvis was still her idol, and she kept time to his music, snapping her fingers, thrusting out her hips, humming to herself. Marianna watched her, suffering from the distance between them. Darlis and her mother communicated in a way that often did without words. Sometimes, when the three of them were together, Marianna would catch the glance between her mother and Darlis and suspect that they were silently criticizing her, her looks, her contrast with Darlis . . .

Now Darlis poured herself coffee. She held the cup with both hands, drinking in short gulps, wrinkling her small nose like a damn bunny.

"Well, you can say goodbye to your buddies." Darlis put down her empty cup and used her tongue to wipe the coffee from her full lips.

"What are you talking about?"

"Friendship, friendship," Darlis hummed, "School's over. They're outa your class, kid—and they're not gonna bother with you anymore—"

"Mama's been talking to you." Marianna felt the anger tighten her throat.

"Yeah, she's been gabbing—" Darlis looked at her older sister with a suggestion of innocence that softened the sting. "You wanna know something, Mari? You're a creep. All that grind, studying all the time, doing all those snotty kids favors. Mama figured you'd make real friends who would help you when you're going for a job. But you didn't make it—"

Marianna flushed. "So Mama thinks I'm a flop."

"You are, kid. Listen—what'd you get out of it anyway? All those trips with that Simon girl and Cris Terhune. Real buddies, huh? In a pig's eye. School's out. They don't need you anymore—not to help them with their studying, not to act like a slave. It's goodbye, Mari."

The combination of Darlis's toughness and her childish prattle unnerved Marianna. "You've got it all *wrong*. So has Mama. They've been my friends for *four* years, and they'll be my friends for life—"

"Ha." Darlis found a cruller in the breadbox and attacked it with her sharp little teeth. "That's what *you* think."

Marianna glared at her younger sister. They had never got along; whether or not it was her mother's doing, she couldn't decide. All she knew was that

Darlis parroted her mother's opinions. Marianna admitted to herself that her anger was fueled by her envy for Darlis's uncomplicated prettiness, which would some day blossom into a dazzling pink-and-white chorus-girl confection. Even though Darlis was only on the first rung of her teens, in her presence boys overlooked her older sister, which made Marianna feel even more inadequate than she usually did.

She got up to wash the few breakfast dishes, depressed by her sister's rough candor. Darlis went into the bedroom, and Marianna changed the radio to the news station.

"Hey!" Darlis came back, dressed now in denim shorts with frayed edges and a blue plaid outer bra that did more than suggest the roundness of her developing breasts. "Leave my music to hell alone!"

As she moved to switch back to her station, Marianna blocked her. "You're not the only one living here."

They were in the midst of a row when Jan Dietrich came in. His straw-colored hair and beard neatly groomed, his face fresh and youthful, he looked too young to be Darlis's father. He was rolling up the sleeves of his blue workshirt; his jeans were held tight over his lean waist by a belt with a heavy silver buckle.

He nodded, pleasant as always, as he separated them. "Why don't you get dressed?" he asked Darlis, pouring himself coffee.

"I *am* dressed." She giggled. "Don't you think I look good, Daddy?"

"You're not going out on the street like that."

"Why not?"

"You're not going into the store like that."

"Why not?"

"Because you look like a slut."

"For Pete's sake, Daddy, don't be so—so *European*—"

"Get back to your room and put on a shirt," he ordered. "Why can't you take a lesson from Marianna?"

"*That*'ll be the day."

"Darlis, you heard me." When she obeyed reluctantly he turned to his stepdaughter. "Marianna, can't you do something with her?"

"Mama likes her the way she is," she said quietly.

But not me, she thought. *Mama doesn't really like me at all. She thinks I'm a flop.* . . .

She couldn't explain to her mother that her friends wouldn't desert her. They owed her too much. And what's more, she thought with a momentary sense of power she didn't trust, or like, she knew too much about them.

CHAPTER I

MARIANNA

Few of the local Connecticut tradesmen and shopkeepers could afford to live in the village they served unless they were willing to settle on the outskirts.

The Dietrichs—Marianna, her mother, stepfather and half-sister—were lucky. They had the good fortune to meet a benefactress—a musician named Evalina Novak. She was a heavyset woman with round face, slightly protuberant eyes, a short neck and a powerful constitution. A graduate of Julliard, she had started her career as a concert pianist of blazing promise. Unfortunately, she had made a poor impression when she walked on the stage to perform, clad in modest, flowing black chiffon, her chin high, defying her audience to laugh at her. But when her stubby fingers had descended on the piano keys and the powerful chords of a Beethoven or Brahms concerto rose in heroic splendor, her audience answered with a wildly appreciative reaction.

A concert booking agency took her on, but she never quite fulfilled her own dreams or her manager's faith. Refusing to give up her ambitions, she developed an act of fractured classics, taking themes that were bastardized in pop songs. She went on a fast that nearly killed her but reduced her peasant body to a normal size. With her dark hair now bleached platinum blond, her new figure clad in draperies by famous designers, Evalina switched managers and started fresh. Her second debut was in a lounge of a Las Vegas hotel. She was successful for five years until her popularity was usurped by Liberace, who looked considerably more at home in sequins.

When Evalina retired she came to Connecticut, where she purchased a small white house just beyond the shopping district of New Canaan. She took a part-time job teaching music in a nearby college and started a music school on the main floor of her house.

Soon Evalina, always ambitious, bought the vacant two-story building next to her house. There she began a business called the Piano Store, which rented and refurbished pianos. The store lodged more than a dozen instruments, from a rare old Bechstein to a magnificent Queen Anne baby grand to several Steinway concert grands, Yamaha organs and Baldwin spinets.

She decided she needed a manager for the place, someone who could tune pianos and had a good working knowledge of musical instruments. She found the person she was looking for in Jan Dietrich, who had learned his craft in Vienna at a fine old school for piano technicians. His ear was as sensitive as a tuning fork, and he had an appreciation of the great pianists. He was unhappy with his job in a Bridgeport factory that manufactured miniature spinets for children. Evalina offered him the position, adding as an inducement a rent-free flat with the Piano Store.

Jan Dietrich was a quiet man, more at ease with the piano keys than with people. His brash and pretty wife, whom he called Liebschen, managed the store with the help of their two girls while he was out most of the day, bringing the right vibrations to the many precious musical instruments in Fairfield County, where skilled technicians were few. Jan soon acquired a good reputation, and his services were required every three months wherever a serous musician lived. When Evalina leased a piano for a concert he made it ready before the event and checked it afterward as his stepdaughter, Marianna, looked on in fascination.

Jan did well for Evalina, but she was close-fisted and he earned far less than he was worth. In spite of his wife's prodding—Liebschen was always running short of household money and complaining about it—he wasn't able to stand up for himself.

To be poor in a town like New Canaan was an exercise in depression and despair. Marianna, struggling into her teens, was acutely conscious of the family's relative poverty. Nevertheless she did find a few compensations. When Evalina had a class or private pupils, the open studio windows carried snatches of melody into the Dietrichs' living quarters. Music became an important part of Marianna's world, solace for so much of the misery that the life of her family inflicted on her.

That Evalina exploited her as much as she exploited her stepfather didn't upset Marianna too much. Here, also, there were compensations. Evalina had many dinner parties for old friends, and Marianna would serve the food and wash the dishes. She found it rewarding to listen to the musical talk and the piano duets and would refuse to accept money, a gesture that infuriated her mother. Marianna would also housesit when Evalina was away so that there was less danger of a break-in. She would water the plants, feed the cats, and pretend the place was hers. There was an ancient three-speed Capehart phonograph in excellent condition and a wonderful collection of old 78 RPM records, among them Schnabel, Horowitz, Rubinstein and Brailowsky.

Evalina often asked Marianna for dinner, and afterward she would play for the girl. From her Las Vegas days, Evalina had retained the bleached ash-blond hair, false eyelashes and heavy makeup. But her vast knowledge of music and her teaching talent brought her even more pupils than she could accommodate. Marianna, admiring, learning music from her by osmosis, thought Evalina deserved more than she got from life.

Evalina was philosophical. "To make it to the top in my profession, a woman must either be a genius or have a man to back her. Look at Maria Callas. She got her first big break from a man of strength and influence. You need one to sponsor you in any field—" Her painted mouth turned down at the corners. "I was never so lucky. The men in my life weren't givers. They were takers—and losers."

Evalina didn't care much for Marianna's younger sister Darlis. "You don't have to worry about that one. She'll make it. Her brains are in her boobs." She smiled at Marianna. "In your case, Cinderella is the older one. Take a lesson from me, kid. Cultivate men. Use them."

Evalina herself turned out to be a rabbit's foot for Marianna. Through the Piano Store, she met Cristina Terhune, who was to become one of her two best friends.

Cristina came into the store one afternoon to inspect a spinet. Marianna figured the girl wasn't really serious about a purchase, but was probably marking time until her next appointment. It was early March, and the winds were testing pedestrians, who braved the icy blasts. Marianna, cold and lonely, was delighted to have a visitor.

"Do you play?" she asked Cristina.

"Well, sort of. I've had a few lessons but I play mostly by ear." Cristina looked about fifteen, and under her quilted scarlet ski jacket and windproof pants baby fat was collected on her sturdy frame. Her knitted red hat reflected the high color of her cheeks. She had enormous olive-black eyes and a mouth with shapeless, moist lips that protected prominent, crooked teeth: a face easy to caricature, and yet with a wistful expression that Marianna found oddly touching.

Marianna, who was the same age as Cristina, felt a reaching out and responded to it. Her own shyness, compounded by her mother's constant criticism and her sense of not quite belonging anywhere, kept Marianna from making good friends among her classmates at the local junior high school. But with Cristina she felt strangely at ease.

The phonograph was playing a recording of Paganini. Marianna invited Cris to take a seat, since the visitor was clearly intrigued by the music.

Cris unzipped her jacket and pulled off the knit helmet, revealing a mass of dark brown hair. She half-sprawled on the easy chair. Marianna offered her coffee from the pot she kept warm, and they sat listening and sipping the fragrant brew in companionable silence.

The overcast pewter sky seemed to shut out the world, so that the big room with its massive pianos felt comforting to the girls.

"D'you live in New Canaan?" Marianna asked.

"Yes. We've just moved up here."

"You like it?"

"I don't know yet, but I'll get used to it." With a fetching giggle, Cris confided, "I've traveled a lot with my mother, so I'm used to new places. They don't bother me." She raked her fingers through her tousled hair, stood up, looked around and moved toward the spinet by the wall under a portrait of Beethoven.

"I guess I'd better pick out the piano. . . . This size, I think. It has to fit into my room."

Marianna couldn't quite believe it. The girl actually ordered the spinet, saying it was to be charged to Stephen Terhune at the Pan Am Building in New York, and asked when it could be delivered.

Evalina was pleased by the sale. She recognized the Terhune name. "He's one of the new millionaires—construction, I think. They bought the old Lorrimer place . . . I wonder if the girl's interested in taking lessons?"

When it came time for Jan Dietrich to deliver the spinet in the pickup truck, he hired a high school boy to help him. Marianna asked impulsively if she could go along for the ride. She couldn't figure out why she wanted to join them, although she did enjoy being with her stepfather when her mother wasn't around to stir up trouble.

Jan Dietrich was personable, with searching, bespectacled blue eyes and a sensitive turn to his mouth, which was nearly hidden by a thick, straw-colored mustache. He was, Marianna suspected, overqualified for his work. But she'd never heard him complain; nor did he ever mention his past in Vienna. As far as her mother was concerned, Jan Dietrich had come along when she needed him. A deserted wife, with a small child on her hands, Mrs. Ellis had been working at a newsstand at Idlewild Airport, and it was here that she met her future second husband when he arrived at his destination, with great hopes for a good life in America but few prospects.

Mrs. Ellis, who'd learned to make do for herself and Marianna, took Jan under her wing. Although her blond curls, prominent blue eyes and showgirl appearance suggested frivolity, she'd developed a strong sense of self-preservation. She found a room for Jan Dietrich and helped him direct his life. Through a newspaper want ad, she directed him to his first job, salesman in a new cut-rate appliance shop in Connecticut. Jan was grateful to Marianna's mother. He asked her to marry him, and together they moved to Connecticut.

Liebschen was shrewdly ambitious for her husband. She suggested he set up a repair shop since he was mechanically adept. But nothing went well for him in business until he met Evalina Novak and found a place for himself in the Piano Store.

Marianna liked her stepfather. She was rather sorry for him, without knowing the reason—perhaps because she so often read scorn and contempt in her mother's eyes. Jan was immensely kind to both Marianna and his own daughter by Liebschen, although honey-blond Darlis shared her mother's opinion of him. Marianna was more considerate on the rare occasions when they spent time together.

Once he said rather shyly, "I feel you are more my daughter than Darlis." She was moved; she understood what he meant. Darlis was all Liebschen.

Jan was pleased that she had asked to come along on the ride to the Terhune house. As she hopped into the pickup truck and squeezed between him and his helper, Marianna tightened her plaid scarf, buttoned her blue pea jacket and prepared to enjoy herself. They left the village behind and were passing the gracious old houses, with their elms and oaks that had been planted before the Revolution, their gardens protected from the winter's sere winds, their swimming pools drained. Lamps glowed in the early March dovegray twilight; the fading wash of gold reflecting the promise of spring.

The house sat well back from the country road, sur-

rounded by huge trees and a spacious lawn. Additional
wings had been added to the colonial structure, in har-
mony with the original pre-Revolutionary main house.
Jan Dietrich drove the truck around to the side entrance, got out and rang the bell to announce their
arrival. He and the schoolboy proceeded to lift the covered spinet onto a small trolley.

And just then Cristina ran out, followed by a big
long-haired shepherd that added its voice to her welcome. The dog sniffed the men, ignored them and
loped toward Marianna, still sitting in the truck.

"Don't mind her." Cristina was laughing. "She looks
ferocious, but all she wants is a little affection." She
grabbed the animal by the collar. "Gee, I'm glad you're
here. Come on in," she said to Marianna.

Cristina was dressed in black slacks, a boy's faded
green pullover and brown suede boots, and her hair was
more dishevelled than Marianna remembered. There
was a friendly warmth to her invitation, and Marianna
wanted to accept. She was curious to see the interior
of the house, and she wanted to be friends with Cristina
in spite of her own busy schedule. Her mother expected
her to help at the store, to start supper and to wash her
own clothes, which didn't leave much time to develop
friendships. Still, she said what was expected. "I think
they'll be finished in a few minutes and we'll be leaving."

"Can't you stay awhile? Please do. We'll get a chance
to get acquainted."

"I'd love to. But they won't wait."

"We'll drive you home. Can you stay for dinner?
You can telephone your mother—"

After Cristina turned the full force of her persuasion
on Jan Dietrich, it was arranged. Jan said Marianna
wasn't to worry; Darlis could do the supper dishes for a
change.

After he drove off Cristina led Marianna into the
house. The two-story center hall had a staircase on
either side, converging on a second-floor landing where
a window seat of multi-colored Tiffany glass served as
a showcase for greenery in colorful cachepots. The
white paneled walls were reserved for brilliant flower

paintings above old carved chests. The house was quiet, but not museum-quiet.

The shepherd, accompanying them, pulled at Cristina's sweater and barked joyously.

"Quiet, *quiet,* Miss Greta." Cristina nodded in the direction of the right wing. "Rose Eileen has a headache."

"Rose Eileen?"

"My stepmother."

This was the first link between her and her new friend, Marianna thought. "You have a stepmother, I have a stepfather. Isn't it *strange?*"

"Oh, everybody has seconds. I've had two, beside Stephen."

"Stephen?"

"He's my real father."

"Is your mother—?" Marianna didn't quite know how to phrase her question.

Cristina laughed. "Mama is alive and well. The last I heard she was going to perform in London—"

"You mean she's an actress?"

"Mama," Cristina explained matter-of-factly, "is Bonnie Rob Roy."

"You mean the one on radio and television—"

"And the Music Hall and the Palace and the Paladium. That's why I need the piano."

"For your mother?"

"Not exactly. But to practice the songs in her repertoire—in case she needs me." Cristina wrinkled her bumpy nose. "With Mama, you never know whether she'll love her new accompanist or hate him—so I have to be in the wings."

She opened the door to her own suite—a large bedroom, a sitting room and a bathroom nearly the size of the bedroom Marianna shared with Darlis. The furniture was wicker and bamboo in natural tones, its color and texture heightened by bright draperies, pillows and a print bedspread with bold, stylized scarlet poppies outlined by vivid emerald-green leaves on a white background. The low oval table before the deep-cushioned sofa was a block of cypress with a glass cover; it held movie and television magazines and a box of Plumbridge chocolates. A woven Indian basket was spilling over with large dog biscuits. Miss Greta helped herself, then retreated to her own tufted rug, from which she watched them.

The new spinet stood between two windows that looked out on a garden and a small reflecting pool, drained now until spring. Marianna surveyed the room, which was unlike any she'd ever seen before, and thought that it must be absolute heaven to live here.

They had dinner on trays in front of the television set. The middle-aged maid seemed delighted that Cristina had a guest.

"Where d'you go to school, Cris?" Marianna asked.

"No place yet. I just came to live with Stephen. I have a tutor for English, and then in September, I start at Locust Ryse. Do you go there?"

"No, I go to the junior high."

"Are you good at math?"

"Well—yeah, I guess so. My marks are pretty high."

"Then maybe *you* could tutor me in math. I'm *awful* at it. I still count on my fingers." She added, with no touch of regret, "I've traveled so much with Mama that I've missed a lot . . . of school, I mean. Mama says I've gotten a good education in what counts, but Stephen isn't satisfied. That's why I have to live here and get a *formal* education." Cris's face was suddenly solemn. "I'm so glad we've met, I don't know anybody around here. Of course I have loads of friends on the road—Mama's friends are mine—but it's kind of lonely here."

Why, Cris was lonely, too, Marianna realized—even amid all this splendor.

"I wish you were coming to my school," Cris said.

"I do, too."

"It'd be real nice, having a friend—even before school begins."

"Well, maybe we could keep in touch anyway."

"Definitely! We could study together—I mean, we'll probably be learning the same subjects, even if we don't use the same textbooks."

Before the evening was over, Marianna began really to appreciate Cris. She was forthright, blunt, but never unkind, and she had a contagious, bubbling laugh. Marianna felt they had taken the first step toward friendship, and she hoped, stifling a sense of anxiety, that they could continue.

Her spirits were still high when the Terhune house-man prepared to drive her home. She caught her last glimpse of Cris, framed in the golden fanlight of the doorway, waving enthusiastically, the shepherd barking goodbye. Sitting beside the servant in the station wag-on, Marianna thought it surely had been the nicest day of her life. . . .

The Piano Store was shuttered. She let herself into their apartment and found her mother in the kitchen finishing the dishes, which Darlis had evidently ig-nored.

Liebschen poured coffee, set the two cups on the table and questioned Marianna about the Terhune house, its furnishings, its people. "The Terhunes are rich and important," she said. "They're the kind of people who can do you a lot of good. Cultivate the girl."

The advice offended Marianna. She didn't want to be calculating in her newfound friendship. She only hoped Cristina would want to see her again.

The following Saturday Cristina stopped by the Pi-ano Store to report her satisfaction with the spinet. Darlis reluctantly relieved her sister so Marianna and Cris could go down the street for a hamburger and a milkshake. Afterward they dawdled, windowshopping, browsing in the bookstore and finally returning to the store, where they listened to records, sipped Cokes and chatted.

The two girls enjoyed being together. It wasn't sur-prising, therefore, when Cris followed up her sug-gestion and asked if Marianna would tutor her in math during the next weeks. At noon every Saturday there-after the Terhune station wagon picked Marianna up and drove her to the Terhune house. After lunch the girls settled down for three hours of study. Mari-anna met Cris's stepmother, Rose Eileen, who was friendly as well as beautiful, and her father, Stephen Terhune, a handsome man with an easy, warm manner.

During these Saturday sessions, Cris sometimes spoke of her own mother, relating stories about their travels whenever her mother went on tour. Marianna thought Cris was the luckiest girl in the world.

But it was only after she heard about the scholarship that Marianna realized how much her friendship with Cristina meant to her. She didn't learn about the grant through Cristina. Yet if not for Cristina's friendship, she'd never have applied for it.

Before her school closed in June Marianna had seen the notice on the corridor bulletin board: A scholarship for Locust Ryse was available. Meeting her at the bulletin board one morning, her English instructor said, "You should try out for it."

Marianna shook her head. "I'd never get it."

"You'll never know if you don't try."

She put the thought out of her mind, but it stirred to life as she grew closer to Cristina and she imagined how nice it would be if they both attended the same school. Before Cris flew to Switzerland in August for a month's vacation with her mother, Marianna confided that she had made out an application and was to be interviewed by the Scholarship Committee.

"Swell." Cris was delighted. "You're bound to win."

"I don't know what the competition is. But I understand it's narrowed down to another girl and myself."

"She won't be as good as you, no matter *who* she is—"

"I don't think I stand a chance."

"D'you want it badly?"

"Yes."

"Then you'll get it. You know what Mama always says: Be careful what you wish for, because you're bound to get it."

Marianna's mother woke her early the day of the interview.

"I'm a nervous wreck," Liebschen complained. "I just hope you don't make a fool of yourself."

When her mother went into the kitchen to make breakfast, Marianna got out of bed and looked out of the window. The sky was clear blue, the air was crystalline and the flowering shrubs surrounding Evalina's house were putting out their rich, colorful petals: a golden day, surely an auspicious sign. Please God, let me win, Marianna prayed. At the same time, the part of her that sometimes stood on the sidelines—watching, cold and critical—speculated, *Suppose you do win and they don't like you at Locust Ryse?*

"*Marianna.*"

Her mother's voice was shrill with impatience. Marianna put on a robe and went into the kitchen, blinking in defense against the morning sun. Both heat and humidity were building.

Darlis, in thigh-length shorts, ignored her elder sister. She was scowling at a plate of scrambled eggs and favoring a package of Twinkies instead.

"Eat your breakfast," Liebschen commanded. She poured coffee for Marianna. "We don't want to rush . . ."

"We aren't due there until eleven-thirty."

"It'll take a half hour to get to Greenwich. You've got to allow plenty of time in case we get lost. Some of those estates are hard to find. No street numbers—"

Darlis looked up. "I don't know why you bother." She bit into the Twinkie, letting her tongue ravish the crumbs on her lips. "They're a bunch of creeps at that school. They can't even play decent hockey."

"Mari needs that background." Liebschen scooped up a bite of egg on Marianna's plate with a morsel of toast. "She needs a good school so she can improve herself. If she were pretty, it'd be different."

You mean, if I had Darlis's looks, Marianna thought, feeling hurt. She knew her mother believed a girl's looks were her passport to success, which meant a husband of good standing and means. Liebschen took credit for Darlis's beauty—the poreless porcelain skin, the full, teasing mouth, always slightly open. She counted on Darlis to do well, convinced that even in the Piano Store, her younger daughter would score. Marianna was obviously doomed to an academic career, probably as a teacher, with little hope of the kind of success her mother valued.

The maternal eyes, trained to the beauty of blonds

in B-type television series, failed to appreciate Marianna's potential. Liebschen dismissed her as just an average girl, yet Marianna had the fine frame seldom seen in young girls padded with adolescent fat, and remarkable gardenia-pale skin. Her high, rounded forehead was balanced by a strong jawline, and her hazel eyes, amber flecked, were deepset and well spaced.

"What are you going to wear?" Liebschen asked.

"A blouse and skirt."

"Are they clean and pressed?"

"Yes."

"What about your hair?"

Marianna's hair was medium brown, baby fine and straight, and she wore it off her forehead and over her ears in a ponytail. "I'll wear it the way I always do. There's no sense in trying to be what I'm not."

"Well, you've got to make a good impression. You aren't the only one up for the scholarship, you know."

Liebschen inspected Marianna's plaid shirt and blue cotton skirt and decided against them. She rummaged through Marianna's clothes and chose a flowered dress with short, puffy sleeves and a full, gathered skirt. She had bought it on sale at Bloomingdale's, originally for Darlis, but she decided it would soften Marianna's angular lines. Her elder daughter seemed to be late in maturing, while Darlis already had an adorable little bosom.

"I look *awful*," Marianna objected, scrutinizing herself in the mirror. "Mother, that dress is *not* for me."

"It's more feminine than your shirts. Wear it. And do something with your hair. I don't want them to think we're beggars."

She herself dressed carefully for the luncheon, deciding on a three-piece black silk knit suit with a tiny band of ermine at the collar and slingback beige-and-black pumps that flattered her small, high-arched feet. Marianna sensed it was an unsuitable outfit for a meeting at which mother and daughter would be under the sharp scrutiny of two members of the Board of Locust Ryse and the school's headmistress. She wished she had been allowed to come by herself. But evidently the committee wanted to check on her mother's eligibility as a Locust Ryse parent.

"Well, I suppose you look as good as you can." Liebschen surveyed her critically. "Let's hope for the best." She picked up her white handbag and led the way to the battered Chevy.

Marianna followed, her lips set together, controlling her anger. Rather than face her mother's constant picking, she would often retreat into herself, where neither reproaches nor reminders could reach her. Her survival kit was her ability to tune out.

When Marianna took her seat in the car next to her mother, she too hoped for the best. But even as she prayed—hands clenched, eyes closed tightly—she suspected that it wouldn't happen.

As Marianna and her mother plodded along the highway in their old car, Phyllis Merritt-Jones, headmistress of Locust Ryse. was also driving to Greenwich. The Board of Directors of the school, heeding the recommendation of Mrs. Merritt-Jones, had decided to award a scholarship to a needy girl, preferably of a minority group. The headmistress felt that the scholarship would allow the school to show its awareness in a period of frightening social upheaval. Since there were few suitable candidates in New Canaan, the search for the recipient of the scholarship would include Norwalk, Danbury and, of course, Stamford.

Mrs. Merritt-Jones had suggested that Mrs. John X. Lovell and Mrs. Stephen Terhune judge the candidates —with the headmistress herself casting the deciding vote. Both women were rich and could wield potential power in the school. Mrs. Lovell, the mother of student Allegra Simon, was a Towle, which meant that her background was faultless, in spite of a scandal years before that had briefly tainted the family's reputation. The Terhunes were newcomers to New Canaan, and their daughter, Cristina, would be enrolled in the ninth grade in September.

Mrs. Merritt-Jones had met Cristina's father earlier in the year when he arrived at her office to discuss his daughter's academic future. She was surprised that he had come alone; she wondered about the girl's mother, but confident, wealthy Stephen Terhune was not a man one questioned. She found him extremely attractive and singularly youthful for the father of a fifteen-year-old girl.

Part of the headmistress's success with the Board was that she operated on two levels: first, as a competent executive who ran the school with the dignity its reputation deserved; second, as a good-looking woman who knew how to deal with a group of highly prosperous businessmen. Primarily because of her efforts, the school operated at only a minor loss, but that deficit would become major if her dream of two new school buildings materialized. The Terhunes were therefore important to her.

Her mind was clicking like a computer as she guided the school's Ford station wagon off North Street onto the private road that led to the Lovell estate. The committee had already interviewed the second scholarship applicant, a girl from Norwalk whose widowed mother was a practical nurse at Norwalk Hospital. The girl's scholastic record was outstanding, and she had even more in her favor: She was black. Mrs. Merritt-Jones planned to vote for her. She thought it was time the school took a stand; a token black would be a positive step forward in these troubled times.

The headmistress drove through the opening in the five-foot red brick wall sheltering thick glossy rhododendron and laurel and arrived at the Lovells' rambling Tudor house, half stone and half timber—architecturally authentic, she concluded with an appraiser's eye for quality. There was one other car in the space facing the multiple garage unit, a station wagon with initial plates that read, "RET."

Mrs. Merritt-Jones walked briskly to the main door and lifted the antique brass knocker.

The door opened and Mrs. Lovell came toward her, elegant in a simple sheath of black-and-white cotton tweed outlined in white piqué, blending in with her full, dark, graying hair. She greeted Mrs. Merritt-Jones pleasantly, a gesture the headmistress recognized, since she'd often used it herself, as doing her duty with grace.

"Mrs. Terhune is here," Mrs. Lovell said, ushering her guest into the spacious hall, paneled in old gleaming wood, with a carved oak table and two old Tudor chairs. "And the girl, Marianna, and her mother are on their way. I've asked Allegra to join us for lunch."

"Excellent," said the headmistress, with just the correct degree of warmth and deference.

Allegra Simon had successfully completed the eighth grade, her first year at Locust Ryse—a strange girl, the headmistress thought. There was an aura about Allegra that kept the other students at a distance, yet her manners were exquisite. She was courteous and obedient, really beyond reproach. However, her teachers and Mrs. Merritt-Jones felt they were not getting through to her. It was, the headmistress reflected, as if a great deal of hostility was penned up inside the girl, held back until the restraints might one day burst.

Prudence Lovell led Mrs. Merritt-Jones through the library into a small sunny morning room, the walls of which were covered with rare ancient Chinese paper. It was an effective setting for Mrs. Stephen Terhune, who sat on the sofa of Brighton wicker, a vision of extraordinary beauty. She was perhaps in her mid-forties, as the fullness of bosom and slight spread of hips suggested. A cloud of magnificent burnished red-gold hair, growing thick and unwaved from her forehead to wings on her temples, complemented her creamy skin and prominent blue eyes. She was wearing a white Chanel suit trimmed with blue braid to match her blue silk shirt, and all the glitter Chanel encouraged was looped around her neck. It wasn't costume junk, Mrs. Merritt-Jones decided; the gold and semi-precious stones were pure David Webb.

They shook hands and introduced themselves, and Rose Eileen Terhune moved over to make space for Mrs. Merritt-Jones.

"You are Cristina's mother," said the headmistress.

"I wish I were," Rose Eileen Terhune responded. "Unfortunately, we're related only by marriage."

"I enjoyed my interview with Cristina," Mrs. Merritt-Jones said. "She will be a great asset to our school."

An elderly maid in a striped summer uniform

brought in a tray of Bloody Marys, which Rose Eileen barely touched.

Watching her, Prudence Lovell was surprised by her obvious discomfort. She wondered how anyone so spectacularly lovely could suffer from shyness. Prudence found herself thinking that Rose Eileen probably gave her husband pleasure: A man would want to devour that rich skin, those sensuous, suggestive curves. This woman wasn't the least like the other mothers Prudence had met at the PTA. Locust Ryse mothers made vocations out of breeding dogs, showing horses or growing rare plants, for which they invariably collected awards and photographs in the pages of *The New York Times*.

"What rather concerns me," began Mrs. Merritt-Jones, wiping her lips after a swallow of her drink, "is the size of our scholarship." She sat erect, her left foot behind her right, her knees close together, gray skirt properly discreet.

"I don't understand," said Prudence.

"It is only for one year. Once the year is over, the student may be obliged to return to public school—which you must agree would be a difficult readjustment for her."

Rose Eileen looked anxious. "Isn't it possible to increase the amount of money so it covers *more* than one year?"

"That would be ideal—if we could manage," Mrs. Merritt-Jones explained, hoping her words would get back to Stephen Terhune. "But we have priorities. We cannot wait much longer for a new gym. This Quonset hut is obsolete—wretchedly cold in the winter. And we must give serious consideration to a new Lower School. We're overcrowded."

"What is our plan then?" asked Prudence crisply.

"Perhaps the Alumnae Association would consider expanding the scholarship—that is, if the girl's marks turn out to be outstanding each year, her tuition will be automatically renewed for the following year."

"That's sensible, don't you think, Rose Eileen?"

Mrs. Terhune nodded in the direction of Prudence Lovell. For a second she seemed about to speak, but remained silent until the conversation was interrupted by the ringing of the door chimes. Prudence excused herself to greet the new arrivals.

Marianna felt like a trespasser as Mrs. Lovell led her and her mother through the splendidly decorated house. Suddenly, she was intensely aware of what her mother was always talking about: the wonder of having money. She realized that there were certain girls born by chance to this rich life. Always before, she'd had a stoic resignation about her condition. Now, however, the desire to rebel took fire. *I'll get that scholarship,* she vowed. *I'll watch and learn and study how to be one of them....*

She had often seen the Locust Ryse girls after school on the New Canaan streets. They looked clean and scrubbed in their gray flannel skirts and blazers. The white cotton collars of their blouses peeked out of their wool pullovers with the Locust Ryse emblem. In the winter they wore gray knee socks, and their oxfords were always well polished.

You were either born into this affluent world or you reached it by wits and wile, Marianna knew. She would try to reach it by her wits. She kept sending her mother a silent message: "Don't talk too much. *Don't spoil it for me.*"

Mrs. Lovell was guiding her mother, offering a polite smile that was actually just a symbol of good manners. Marianna thought she was stunning, all black and white, with sun-polished skin and no makeup, not even lipstick. Her mother, Marianna realized in misery, was overdone. Mrs. Dietrich's smile and her mascaraed blue eyes flashed with too much animation, like the end man in a minstrel show.

They walked through the library into the morning room, where two women were seated upright on a wicker sofa so that their backs avoided the bright oriental fabric of the cushions. The contrast between the dim, shadowy library and the brilliant light blinded Marianna, and for a moment she couldn't make out the woman in white, although she looked familiar.

Rose Eileen Terhune exclaimed, "Why, Marianna, what a nice surprise!"

The woman was a friend—Cristina's stepmother, who'd been so kind to her whenever she visited Cris. In a burst of gratitude, Marianna longed to throw her arms around Mrs. Terhune. Instead, she found herself crying—silently but obviously sobbing. Her mother stared at her, horrified. The other woman on the sofa regarded her with disfavor.

"Something in your eye?" Cristina's stepmother asked. "Here, Mari, let me see—"

The poor child, Rose Eileen said to herself as she offered her handkerchief, a gesture to help her save face. She thought Marianna was a lovely girl and was touched by her obvious desire to please her judges. It had not occurred to her that Marianna was being considered for the scholarship, since the family name on the list was Ellis, not Dietrich.

Rose Eileen felt somewhat out of place on the committee, but she wanted to please Stephen and help Cristina's chance for success at Locust Ryse. Cris desperately needed the stability of a traditional school, after her gypsy existence with her wayward, careless mother. Locust Ryse had been delighted to enroll her, and it had been arranged that Stephen would be elected for a two-year term to the Board of Incorporators of the school.

Suddenly Rose Eileen felt the onset of a migraine. She seemed to have inherited the tendency to severe headaches from her grandmother, who had emigrated to the United States during the potato famine in Ireland, and had served as a second maid to a Yankee family in Boston, where Rose Eileen had grown up.

The slight pain in Rose Eileen's face was a warning signal. Next would come the blinding lights that doubled her vision, the pangs of nausea, the dry heaves. She wished she was back home in her room, her medicine taking effect, the promise of relief settling over her. But she was afraid that her departure would hurt Marianna, who sat rigid, like a prisoner about to be sentenced.

"Your grades are good—for a public school," Mrs. Merritt-Jones was saying to Marianna. "We do not mark so high. We expect a good deal from our students." The headmistress maintained her detached manner, and Rose Eileen suspected that under her tailored gray jumper was a cold heart.

"Her marks are outstanding," Marianna's mother interrupted brightly. "She's a natural student. She loves to read. She's curious. A good student should be curious, don't you think? Her teachers say she is way above average."

Marianna flushed. She had a feeling that her mother's flattery wouldn't help her in the least—and might actually hurt her. Without comprehending why, she sensed that with these women, reticence and understatement were the correct means of communication.

"What are your future goals?" asked the headmistress. "College?"

"I'd love to go if my family can manage—"

"It will be impossible unless Marianna has financial help," her mother explained. "She's an orphan. Her father died when she was small, and he left nothing—"

"The scholarship is based on need as well as scholastic standing. Of course, the family's financial position is kept in strict confidence."

"I think I'd like to write," Marianna said.

"You'll probably do better as a teacher." Liebschen turned to the headmistress, her smile placating. "Marianna loves to read—that's how writers start, isn't it? Any time you look for her, she's buried in a book—"

"Locust Ryse is not an experimental school. We emphasize the academic and the traditional methods of education. We consider math and science of utmost importance, since ninety percent of our girls go on to college. We suggest that our students have no social engagements during the week, and we emphasize the importance of home work and regular attendance."

Liebschen nodded her approval. "Girls need discipline. Unfortunately, I didn't have it; my mother was far too indulgent with me. As a result, I was an indifferent student. It plagued me when I was thrown on my own with a child to look after. It wasn't easy . . ."

She paused, and they all looked up as Mrs. Lovell's daughter, Allegra, came in. Clad in faded, patched jeans and a tee shirt, her dark, thick hair in two stubby pigtails, she stood at the door while a Kerry Blue puppy relieved his kidneys against the leg of a wicker peacock chair. Allegra acknowledged the introductions to the guests with a delicate grace, and then she and Marianna regarded each other warily.

The interview was abruptly over. Two young maids set the long glass table with casseroles, a bowl filled with salad greens, blue-and-white china service plates and heavy silver flatware. The yellow tea roses, spilling fragrance and beauty from their Chinese urns; the exquisite bowls of delicious lobster salad and the tiny hot biscuits; the crystal glasses of white rum and soda with a twist of lime—all this reminded Marianna of a Henry James novel.

Allegra, sitting beside Marianna, hardly touched her food. The puppy sat on the rug beside her, and she was more intent on feeding him than herself.

"He's cute," Marianna said, "but how can he see through those bangs?"

"He's used to it." Allegra set her dark glasses on top of her head like a crown.

"D'you raise them?"

"My mother does."

"Are there any more puppies? I'd love to see them." If she seemed obsequious, Marianna didn't care. She desperately longed for a response from this aloof girl.

"Okay, come along." Allegra pushed back her chair and hoisted the puppy to her hip.

"Perhaps Mrs. Dietrich might like to see the dogs," Prudence Lovell said, without making it appear that the committee was ready to discuss Marianna privately.

Liebschen followed Allegra and Marianna out of the side entrance toward the cluster of smaller buildings at the rear of the main house. Allegra opened the door to the kennels, where a half dozen puppies were huddled together beside their mother's belly, nuzzling and groping for food, while she lay there, a patient feeding station. Allegra knelt down, cuddled a pup in her palm and held him tenderly to her cheek, while he suckled the air, searching for the pump to which he'd been attached. She handed him to Marianna, who accepted him gingerly.

Marianna's mother showed great enthusiasm, although she disliked animals. "Who looks after them?"

"The kennel girl, mostly. I help weekends, when I'm here."

"They're adorable. D'you show them?" Marianna asked.

"Oh, yes. My mother does. We didn't do well at Westminster this year, but last year we had two Best of Show in other competitions," she said casually.

Marianna was more intent on watching than listening. Allegra's jeans were stained where the puppy had wet them, and there was a smudge of dirt on her cheek. Yet she looked so striking that Marianna was filled with admiration. After they inspected the runs and returned to the house to bid the committee goodbye, it was Allegra who walked them to the car.

Liebschen thanked her profusely. "I hope Marianna will be going to school with you. It would be a great privilege for her."

Allegra was polite to the older woman, but she turned to Marianna with a faint conspiratorial wink. "It's not all that great," she said. "You just met the chief warden, Mrs. Merritt-Jones. Wait till you see her slaveys, like Miss Caswell. . . . 'Hockey is a *running* game,'" she mimicked. "And compulsory showers after the game. With no privacy at all."

Allegra didn't know it, but at that moment she made a friend for life.

A slavey for life.

"You don't have a fighting chance." Liebschen was glum as she drove the balking Chevy toward the parkway. "You know what you did wrong? You didn't make them feel sorry for you. You didn't show how grateful you'd be—"

"I *won't* bootlick." Unable now to control her anger, Marianna stared straight ahead at the cars passing them.

"Paupers can't afford pride. I only wish Darlis had your chance. She wouldn't ruin it. She knows how to handle people."

Marianna thought that her mother was probably

right. The disappointment was shattering. But then, she asked herself, what made her think she deserved the honor? She was convinced that the other applicant was brighter, smarter, better looking. She herself was no welcome addition to any group—a nobody whom nobody wanted.

On Thursday evening of the following week, Marianna decided to go to the movies. The main attraction was an old Warner Brothers film that had just been reissued, and among its features was a song by Cristina's mother, Bonnie Rob Roy. Marianna hadn't seen Cris recently; her friend had taken a break from her tutoring.

She took a seat in the middle of the theater and watched people walking down the aisles—families with their children, couples, elderly women in groups, giggling adolescents. Feeling isolated, cut off, she thought that nobody could be more wretched.

"Marianna! Hi, Mari—"

Across the aisle, several rows closer to the screen, she saw Cristina, standing up, trying to attract her attention. "Hey, come sit with us—"

Stephen Terhune was standing beside Cris, wearing jeans and a white cotton turtleneck. She noticed his chiseled, tanned face and piercing gray eyes. His daughter didn't resemble him in the slightest. She swelled out of her jeans and tee shirt, and her short, jagged brown hair was brushed carelessly off her face, with its endearing irregular features.

"Where've you been keeping yourself?" Cris asked.

"I've been helping out at the store."

"I know. But that's no reason—I mean, I was waiting to hear from you."

"Cris, I didn't get the scholarship."

"You're kidding."

"The other girl got it."

"But Rose Eileen said it was going to be you. She had to leave early because she came down with a migraine. But she voted for you and she was sure the other women did, too."

"They didn't, I guess."

"Gee, it's a shame. It's not fair, leading you on—"

Marianna tried to sound noncommittal. "Well, that's the way it is."

"I was counting on us being together. It's going to be awful—those rules and uniforms. Maybe I could drop out and go to public school with you."

The lights were dimming and the audience settled in their seats. In a daze, Marianna was barely aware of the scenes drifting by until Cris clutched her arm and whispered excitedly, "Here's Mama. *Look—*"

Bonnie Rob Roy was in a cabaret scene. A petite woman, she was wearing a shapeless black dress that disguised her body, which resembled a teenager's, with only a suggestion of curves. Her dark hair, coarsened by dye and cut into a shag, emphasized the whiteness of her face. Her eyes were the showcase of her lost-child beauty, darkened by thick fake lashes and mascara and dominating her face.

Snapping her fingers, she began to sing. Marianna forgot who Bonnie Rob Roy was. She saw only a small, frightened young creature to whom she could relate, for they were both rejected, unloved. Caught up in an emotion familiar and painful, Marianna knew what the singer meant when she cried with hope that the end of the storm would bring the promise of the sun. Marianna didn't believe it—such goodness never brightened her life—but from the faith she heard in the singer's voice, she thought it might be possible. Perhaps after sorrow happiness finally did come . . .

The audience responded, intense with feeling, straining toward the screen. Marianna had never witnessed anything like it. She turned her head and saw Mr. Terhune, his elbow on the arm of his seat, his palm cupping his chin, his gaze fixed on the screen. That he was once married to Bonnie Rob Roy seemed highly improbable to Marianna.

And Cristina, sitting on the edge of her seat, eyes concentrating on the vision with love and awe—Bonnie was Cris's *mother*. In that moment, Marianna shared the adulation the audience had for Bonnie Rob Roy. She thought she now had some understanding of Cris's devotion to her mother.

"Isn't she *marvelous?*" Cris whispered to her. "You

must come to a concert. She's fantastic. Her fans treat her like she was Sarah Bernhardt. They carry her on their shoulders."

They sat in silence until the film ended. When the lights came on, they joined the lines crowding the aisles. "I can't wait to see Mama. We'll have a whole month together. Four weeks," Cristina said, gloating.

Her father was looking at her, and Marianna caught his sad expression. She had a feeling that he didn't approve of Cris's jaunts with her mother, that he'd be happier if she would stay home with Rose Eileen. But Marianna was to discover that Cris never stayed away from her mother too long. She was always marking time between visits.

Suddenly it occurred to Marianna that it must be quite difficult to be the *second* Mrs. Stephen Terhune.

The first week in September Marianna hitched a ride to Stamford. At Atlantic Square she hailed the bus to Shippan Point. Sitting behind the driver in the empty vehicle, she was aware of mixed feelings of anticipation and fear. She stared out of the bus window at the small shops along Main Street, observing people walking by sluggishly, touched by the heat of the sun.

Before long the bus left the busy streets behind, passed on the left the expanse of grass stretching toward the docks where small boats were anchored and moved at a faster pace toward the end of Shippan Avenue. Marianna got off the bus and headed toward the resplendent white stucco villa that was the main building of Locust Ryse, the stand of Australian pines, the great jars with their flowering burdens.

A little sentry box rested beside the great iron gates; an elderly guard was sitting inside on a stool, reading the *Daily News*.

Marianna paused before the guard, automatically respecting the sign that said PRIVATE. It was the story of her life, she thought—afraid to venture into rarefied atmosphere even when she was allowed.

. . . But she *was* allowed. She had first heard the news directly from Cristina, who had returned from her European trip earlier than expected. She had telephoned Marianna the morning she came home. Marianna hadn't seen her since the night of the movie.

"Mama has a new boyfriend." Cristina spoke so quickly that at first Marianna had trouble making out her words. "They took off for Italy. Mama wanted to include me, but I didn't feel like tagging along. A new love affair's good for her. She always sings better when she's in love."

Marianna was astonished at Cris's appraisal of her mother's talent and emotions. But Cris didn't dwell on the subject of Bonnie Rob Roy.

"I was going to ask Mama for your scholarship money, but she's broke. So I spoke to Rose Eileen and Stephen before I left. He's going to underwrite your expenses and tuition for one year. If you do well, he'll continue it. Isn't that *fabulous,* Mari? We will be together."

"I'm stunned. I can't believe it."

"Believe. *Believe.*" Cris's voice took on a comic note.

"How can I thank you?"

"Forget it. I'm purely selfish. I don't think I could survive without you. I met some of the girls before I took off. *Quels* snobs."

So Marianna Ellis was enrolled in September 1963 as a freshman at Locust Ryse . . . and she had a perfect right to be here, although school didn't start for another two weeks. She had a meeting this morning with the headmistress.

After the guard waved her along she walked down the circular driveway of crushed stone. On an impulse, she cut across the lawn, avoiding the sprinklers that sent rainbow sprays through the air, and headed for the rock-marked shore, where she sank down on a stone bench not far from the gnarled pines. Her eyes, touched with amber in the clear light, followed the stretches of water to Long Island, on the horizon.

Marianna hardly noticed the small sailboat that was moving slowly toward the dock. When it came near she saw that it had a single occupant, a young man. He made the boat fast, climbed the ladder to the dock and approached. His fair, sunbleached hair was clipped short, his face deeply tanned, his eyes covered by sunglasses. He was of medium height, and he wore white pants, a navy knit shirt and a white sweater over his shoulders, the sleeves looped like an ascot around his neck. He paused when he saw Marianna and smiled. "Hello," he said.

She nodded. "Hello."

"Are you a student?"

"Yes, sir."

"Freshman?"

"Freshman. My name is Marianna Ellis." Strange, she thought—she never said, "I am Marianna Ellis," but rather, "My name is . . ."

"I'm Marc Finley. You may be in one of my classes."

Her heart leaped. "What d'you teach?"

"English. Economics." He removed his sunglasses and rubbed his eyes, as though they were sensitive to the sunlight. His face was startlingly handsome, with a symmetry of brow, jawline and nose. His eyes were dark blue, not large but in proportion to his features. He was lean without being gaunt. The flesh was taut on the bones, and his skin gleamed with a burnished sheen usually found in men of darker visage.

"Are you going up to the school?" he asked.

"Yes. I'm due to see Mrs. Merritt-Jones."

"Do you know the way?" When she looked at him, he said, "Come along. Follow me."

She got up from the rock and nearly lost her footing, despising her clumsiness. His stride was swift and light, suggesting that he was naturally athletic. Marianna clumped through the sand to the lawn, where he was waiting for her. "This way," he said, walking across the grass to a small shadowed patio. She followed him, embarrassed by her hair, pulled back in a ponytail; her white blouse, wrinkled with the heat; her plaid skirt, bunched at the waistline, so obviously badly made.

Convinced that she didn't belong here, Marianna wanted to turn and run. She felt terribly inadequate —displeased with her ordinary appearance and her lack of talent, personality and promise. She was so involved in her misery that she failed to respond to Marc Finley's courtesy. Darlis, she thought, would be giggling, flirting, making points.

He held open the door to the building. "Mrs. Merritt-Jones's office is straight ahead," he said.

"Thank you—a lot."

Marc looked at her as if he was aware of her confusion and unhappiness. "Do you have transportation back to town?"

"The bus." She colored. "Thanks," she repeated.

After he left she stood a moment before the heavy Spanish door, trying to calm herself. Finally, in trepidation, she knocked.

Mrs. Merritt-Jones, in summer gray linen, was seated behind her desk. In the shaft of sunlight, Marianna noticed that her mass of carrot red hair was dusted with gray, and that her skin was prone to freckles, particularly on her flat cheekbones.

"You may sit down, Marianna," she said authoritatively. "I think we should have a talk before school begins, so you'll have an idea of what's expected of the new students."

"Yes, Ma'm." Marianna sat erect, hands in her lap, legs crossed at the ankles, forcing an air of dutiful attention. She listened while the headmistress extolled the academic achievements of earlier graduates and confided that she expected the same from Marianna.

"Remember, Mr. Terhune expects a great deal of you—as we all do. And Marianna, when I speak to you, look at me."

"Yes, Ma'm." Marianna's voice was soft, placating; she knew it was a mistake to look beyond the headmistress for a final glimpse of Marc Finley. She brushed a lock of tangled light brown hair off her forehead, where it stood up like a cowlick.

"I suggest you have your hair cut." Mrs. Merritt-Jones sounded concerned. "We expect our girls to look neat and well put together at all times. We expect you to conform to the rules and regulations. Effort and citizenship are called 'cooperation.' I hope you will work toward an A, which will put you on the Cooperation Honor Roll. These grades are determined by the Student Council and the faculty. We expect you to participate in athletics, which encourages our girls to develop their bodies and enjoy teamwork. Out rules and regulations are simple enough: You're not to make telephone calls. You're not to wear lipstick or nail polish. You're not to leave a study hall. Do you smoke?"

"No, Ma'm."

"Good. Our girls are discouraged from smoking or trying drugs. Talk in the library is forbidden. There is no communication during an exam. Study halls are proctored. The school emphasizes the Cooperation Honor Roll, study hall conduct, good sportsmanship, good behavior in classrooms, obedience to uniform regulations. These rules are set up as guideposts."

Listening, Marianna felt a fog of depression settle on her. The gold-touched lawns, the beauty of the Main House, the general air of charm and serenity—it all faded. She foresaw a future grim, stringent and ruthlessly disciplined.

"Marianna . . ." Mrs. Merritt-Jones stared with her pale blue eyes that seemed to penetrate skin and bones, to search out the secret hidden parts of her. "Are you *sure* you really want to come to Locust Ryse?"

Humiliation gripped Marianna's insides. She knew what the headmistress's motive was—to discourage her, so she'd lose heart and decide it was hopeless to live up to the school's social and intellectual standards. *You don't belong:* The message came through emphatically. *We already have our token scholarship student, and she's a black, which makes her perfect. Nobody can accuse us of a lack of social awareness . . .*

Gritting her teeth, Marianna took a deep breath. She even managed an ingratiating smile. "Why, Mrs. Merritt-Jones, I am looking forward to attending Locust Ryse. My public school advisor said I'd be getting the best education money could buy."

The headmistress relented a bit, smiling faintly. She stood up and said, "Well, we'll expect good things from you, Marianna."

"Thank you." Marianna wasn't fooled by the polite exchange of words. She knew how Mrs. Merritt-Jones felt about her, and she suspected the woman would give her a hard time. *She'll do her best to get rid of me,* Marianna said to herself. *Any mistakes and she'll ride*

the hell out of me. "You must prove yourself worthy
of Locust Ryse," she'd implied. Marianna felt like a
primitive youth subjected to cruel tribal rituals in order
to prove himself worthy of adulthood.

She was sorry, momentarily, that Stephen Terhune
had been so generous. But then she remembered Cristina and realized that through Cris's friendship and
support she would gain strength.

"About uniforms . . ." Mrs. Merritt-Jones was saying, in an afterthought. "We do have some used uniforms. Some of the parents turn them in after graduation. I'll speak to Miss Caswell, and she'll arrange for
you to have some."

"It won't be necessary." Oh, how fine Marianna felt
to be able to say that . . . "Mrs. Terhune is taking
Cristina in to be measured for uniforms, and she's
asked me to come along."

"That's very generous of her. You're fortunate, Marianna, that the Terhunes have taken an interest in you.
I hope you don't let them down, either." She nodded
and Marianna was dismissed.

In the great hall Marianna paused to collect herself.
It was over; there was nothing more the headmistress
could do. Instead of taking the door out to the terrace,
she ventured down the corridor leading toward the
Sound. The wall plaques were of vivid design—bright,
glowing flowers buried in masses of green, relieved here
and there by people; a bent brown peasant and his
donkey; a nun in black and white before gold-embossed
mission doors. The gleaming aquamarine tiles were
punctuated by flower-decked russet stone oil jars and
occasional tooled leather chairs spaced between the
arched window frames.

Marianna loved the beauty of the place in which she
would be spending most of her time during the next
four years of her life. She resolved to forget the headmistress's calculated effort to poison her with anxiety,
and her own fear that she wouldn't fit in.

Damn her, Marianna thought. *I'll make it. I'll surprise them all.*

CHAPTER II

ALLEGRA

In the late morning of the day following her graduation, Allegra Simon drove the red Jaguar to the Piano Store, parked in front and sauntered in, greeting Marianna and her mother with an insouciant wave of her hand.

"Hi, Mrs. Dietrich. Hi, Mari—" She approached the small side counter where Marianna was sorting a batch of records.

Marianna reflected, with justifiable pride, that in spite of Darlis's gloomy prediction, her friend had no intentions of dropping her. She noted that Allegra looked serene and elegant in her narrow black pants and white shirt. But she seemed rather washed out, Marianna thought, and no wonder . . .

Allegra approached Marianna's mother with a cajoling smile. "I've an errand to do in town. May Mari play hooky and come with me?"

"Of course!" Liebschen seemed flattered by Allegra's request. "May I ask what the nature of your errand is?"

"Cris needs a lift to the airport."

"Again? Where this time?"

"To Mexico. Bonnie Rob Roy's always combining performances with mini-face lifts. You know—a tuck here and there."

"Well, enjoy yourself." Liebschen opened the small cash box under the counter and took out two five-dollar bills. "Have lunch on me," she suggested grandly.

Marianna loathed taking money from her mother, who was obviously trying to impress Allegra. She knew that eventually Liebschen would remind her of what a drain she was on the family resources. Marianna had no intention of languishing in the store all summer while Darlis toasted herself and flirted with her adolescent pack at Cummings Beach . . .

She was following Allie out to the car when her mother called her back.

"Take a sweater, dear. The air conditioning—" Liebschen handed Marianna a white orlon cardigan and said in an undertone, "She's so sweet to come for you! Why don't you ask her for dinner soon?"

Marianna relaxed in the car, leaning against the black leather seat while Allegra drove skillfully out of the village and toward the Terhune house. On Ponus Ridge, they flew past the Towle family estate, secluded by the hedges of evergreens and laurel. Allegra didn't slow down.

"I suppose I should stop by and tell Grandmama I won't be home today," she said.

"Have we time?"

"Plenty. That's not the point. Once she sees me she'll start making plans for my future. I had enough of that crap this morning with my mother."

Instead she turned abruptly into the horseshoe drive of the Terhune house and parked near the entrance. She sounded the horn, and Cristina greeted them in a tie-dyed denim pants suit and a new choir boy's haircut that gave her round face a faintly oriental cast.

Cris flung her arms ecstatically around her two friends. "Gee, this is great of you! Rose Eileen's got a migraine, so she couldn't come with me. And the thought of sharing an hour with the houseman wasn't so splendid—I'd ask you in but Rose Eileen's miserable," she added with an uncommon touch of irony. "Rose Eileen always gets a headache when I'm going off to see Mama."

"Well, Rose Eileen loves you." Marianna felt very protective of Cris's stepmother, who was always so kind.

"Yeah, I guess she does. I love her too. But sometimes—" Cris shrugged, thinking how difficult it was to be the love object of two possessive women.

"Will your father be at the airport?" Allegra asked.

"I don't know. I doubt it. We said goodbye when he left the house this morning."

"He should see you off. He's *got* to." Allegra commanded, *"Call him."*

The houseman had put Cris's luggage in the Jaguar, and they were still standing by the car in the driveway. Cris shook her head. "I'd never bother him at the office. Even Rose Eileen doesn't unless it's an emergency."

"Well, this is an emergency. Go on, Cris, call him. Maybe he'll take us to lunch—the way he used to."

"You do it, Allie. You've got more nerve than Cris."

"But he's *her* father."

"I can't," Cris said.

"Oh, all right."

As Allegra walked toward the front entrance Cris caught her by the arm. "Not here, Allie," Cris said. "Let's stop on the road."

Before turning onto the Merritt Parkway, Allegra pulled into a gas station. The girls watched as she dialed.

To Cristina, this was merely another instance of Allie's daring. But Marianna, watching her through the glass door of the booth, saw the radiance in her face, heard her high, clear voice and thought, *"She's got a crush on Cris's father, just like the rest of us . . .*

"I'm calling for Cris," Allegra said to Stephen Terhune. "She wants to make sure you'll be at the airport . . ."

Evidently he wasn't planning to come, because Allegra extended the telephone receiver to Cris, who was standing by, visibly bored. "He wants to talk to you, Cris."

Cris spoke briefly and then told her friends, "Steve's sending someone to the airport with a check for me."

"How nice," Allegra said. "You can always buy a Mexican wedding dress."

"Mama's already got one. Wait till you see her. She looks marvelous . . ."

Cris's usual good spirits soared even higher when she spoke of her mother, as though the mere mention of Bonnie Rob Roy served as a shot of adrenalin. Marianna thought it was just as well that they were concentrating on Cris's trip. Without Cris's presence, she'd be tempted to question Allegra on a delicate and painful subject. A few months ago, Allie had confessed her plight to her, and Marianna had nearly forfeited the chance to graduate in a frantic effort to be of help—to save Allie from disgrace. Under the circumstances, Marianna felt she should broach the subject she had avoided mentioning to Allie three days ago.

Looking back, recalling Allie's agony over her pregnancy and her own attempts to help, Marianna felt sick. Had they done the right thing? Were they vulnerable to arrest if their actions were discovered? She had put the whole sorry incident out of her mind with ferocious determination. But then there had been a final horror. Dared she tell Allie that when she had returned to the hiding place beyond the Australian pines, where the new gym was to be erected, she could not find the tiny package? Had it been discovered, opened, examined? Or had it, she hoped, been carted away with the debris of cement, stone and mortar?

Marianna shivered. She glanced at Allegra, who was driving the Jag with such poise—the sweet little graduate, bound for an exclusive junior college and a debut. Half in admiration, half in anger, Marianna speculated on who the boy might be. Allie had not told her that, and naturally Marianna couldn't ask. But she wondered if it had happened the night they went to the Holmeses' with the boys from Choate, when there had been all that unpleasantness. . . .

"Rose Eileen's going to miss you," Allegra said to Cris, who was hunched up in the uncomfortable space between the two bucket seats. "Is there anything I can do for her while you're away?"

Cris smiled, her hyperactive eyes flickering behind her dark glasses. "Nothing, but thanks. Stephen's going to be home all summer, so she won't be alone."

"I wish you weren't going." Allie sounded disappointed. "We could have great times together. Drive up to Grandmama's cottage at Newport or just hack around here—"

"I wish you were coming to Mexico with us. Mama's such fun—"

Bonnie Rob Roy was waiting for them in the terminal. As they made their way to the First Class Lounge they saw her, surrounded by a half dozen wild-looking characters, all male. Bonnie waved a limp wave and came toward them with her small, rapid steps, her tiny waif's face crowned by a white straw cartwheel hat, her meager flanks in black pipestem pants, a black poorboy sweater clinging to her full breasts and a huge beige canvas shoulder bag weighing her down. Her eyes were hidden by owl sunglasses.

"Baby!" Bonnie opened her arms to embrace Cris, who was two inches taller and thirty pounds heavier than she.

Cris hugged her mother and introduced her to Marianna and Allegra. Bonnie held Marianna's hand and squeezed it. Then she took Allegra's and somehow managed to hug them both. Marianna now saw where Cris got her need for touching and clinging, why body contact was so necessary to her.

Bonnie Rob Roy introduced them, with humorous gestures of her fingers, to the young men who were standing around her like an indolent guard. They were a rock group called the Generation Dropouts and were on their way to South America.

While Allegra was talking to Cris and Bonnie Rob Roy, one member of the band started a conversation with Marianna. Emaciated, he looked taller than his medium height. His eyes were sunk deep in their sockets, and his cheekbones were prominent above the streaked brown mustache and thick, careless beard. His jeans and shirt, brought together by a silver-studded black suede vest, belonged in a ragpicker's collection. But Marianna saw something childlike in his clear blue eyes.

His group was friendly with Bonnie Rob Roy, and he asked about Cristina. Marianna told him about school and about the Piano Store. The old 78's seemed to interest him, and Marianna realized that he had a surprisingly sound knowledge of classical music.

Meanwhile Allegra was saying to Bonnie Rob Roy, "Cris tried to persuade Mr. Terhune to see her off, but he was busy—"

"He probably didn't want to see me," Bonnie replied offhandedly. "He doesn't approve of me, you know." She contrived to make it sound as though Stephen's disapproval was a compliment. Marianna noticed that she had a nervous habit of nibbling on the nail of her forefinger.

Cris stood by her, wide-eyed and happy, listening intently to whatever she said. Another of the Generation Dropouts, a scroungy-looking fellow, was attentive to Bonnie. His possessive hand was on her arm, and she obviously was enjoying it.

Near boarding time a tall, attractive man known to Bonnie and Cristina as the Duke arrived. While he kissed Bonnie, who clung to him even after the embrace and darted flirtatious smiles at him, Cristina explained to Marianna and Allegra that he took care of public relations for her father. The Duke was tall and big-boned, with the fair hair and vivid blue eyes of a Norwegian. He was wearing a blue-and-white striped cotton cord suit, an old-fashioned red bandana knotted around his neck and polished Gucci loafers.

He turned to Cristina and embraced her. When Cris introduced him to her friends Marianna noticed that he stared at Allegra, somewhat surprised—as if he had seen her someplace before. But Marianna figured that like most men he simply found Allie attractive. He was courteous to the Generation Dropouts, but they were hardly his type.

Taking an envelope from his breast pocket, the Duke handed it to Cris. "From your father," he said.

"I don't really need it," Cris told him.

"Darling, don't ever refuse money—from a stranger," Bonnie said sarcastically.

How can they be so lacking in appreciation? Marianna wondered.

"I've arranged to send photographs and copy to the club where you'll be singing," the Duke said to Bonnie, "and I'll be in touch."

"Will you check with my agents?" Bonnie asked. "I haven't received my first payment from the record company."

"Will do." The Duke was reassuring. "And if you're short right now—"

"I'll borrow from my daughter." Bonnie's laugh was raucous. "She's got a filthy rich father."

Once Allegra and Marianna were back in the car, Allegra said furiously, "Did you ever see such bad manners? How does Cris put up with her? How could Stephen have married her?"

She edged the Jag into the line of traffic leaving the airport. For someone who was often so muddled, Marianna thought, Allegra had remarkable coordination, whether she was driving a car or water skiing. Allegra opened her bag with her right hand as she guided the car.

"I'll get your cigarettes," Marianna said. She took out a cigarette, put it in Allegra's mouth and offered her the car lighter. "Where're we going?" she asked.

"I haven't decided," Allegra answered, giving her friend a familiar smile that suggested mischief.

It was soon evident to Marianna that they weren't returning to Connecticut, at least not immediately. They were crossing the Triborough Bridge into Manhattan.

After a prolonged silence Allegra said, "Cris is a damn fool."

"What d'you mean?"

"All her mother has to say is 'jump' and she says, 'How high?' "

Marianna, knowing how circumscribed her own life was, defended Cris. "Maybe she enjoys the glamour of her mother's life—all that travel and parties and meeting famous people—"

"Her father doesn't like it. He doesn't like it *at all*."

"How do you know?"

"How do I know? He told me."

Marianna was surprised that Stephen Terhune had

confided in Allegra. But he may have solicited her aid in dealing with Cris. He probably counted on Allegra's being discreet and close-mouthed, and she *was* that, Marianna reflected, when she chose to be. Marianna had learned in their four-year friendship that no one could pry a fact out of Allegra until she was ready to divulge it. She told you just enough.

Which was precisely what had happened two months ago . . .

In April, Marianna had noticed that Allie was acting curiously. She seemed absentminded, vague, almost elusive—and her schoolwork was suffering. At first Marianna thought it was an upset stomach, because Allie was always running to the Girls' Room.

Finally one noon, when they'd finished eating, Allie said to Marianna, "Come on—let's go out." When they reached the rocks by the shore, she turned away suddenly and heaved, losing her lunch in the bushes.

Her face yellowish in the bright spring sun, Allie said, "That lousy food—" She leaned against the tree. They were still wearing their winter uniforms, and she was perspiring.

Marianna took a Kleenex from her blazer pocket and tenderly blotted her friend's face. "Should I get the nurse?"

"Christ, *no*. There's nothing the matter—" She paused, then the words burst out. "Yes, there is. I'm pregnant."

Marianna stared, appalled. She knew such things happened; there was always talk about girls who went all the way and got caught. Of course, this had never happened to a Locust Ryse girl, since Mrs. Merritt-Jones kept her students in psychic chastity belts. Marianna remained silent.

Then Allie confided that she didn't know what to do. "I've got to get it taken care of," she said, her voice low and urgent.

"You mean an abortion?"

"What else? Worrying won't make it disappear. I've got to find a doctor who doesn't know my family."

Allie knew of a girl at the Yacht Club who was a

student at Fowler Prep. The headmistress there had arranged for her operation. She was sure Mrs. Merritt-Jones had an address, if they could only find it.

So Marianna—loyal, eager, devoted—put her future in jeopardy by breaking into the headmistress's office, finding Mrs. Merritt-Jones's address book. Just as she thought she'd found a doctor's name on the last page, she was discovered.

Marianna was terrified of repercussions, knowing how much the headmistress disliked her. Dear God, she thought, what would her mother say if she were expelled?

Allegra didn't seem to appreciate the awful chance she'd taken. She was simply vexed because of her failure. "Think of something, Mari," she'd begged.

"Let's ask Cris," Marianna finally suggested.

"You think we should?"

"Her mother might know." Marianna pounced on the thought. "I bet her mother has the name of a good doctor—"

Allegra was reluctant, but Marianna, while flattered that her friend wanted to share her problem only with her, insisted. So Cris was brought in and, true to her conditioning, she said matter-of-factly, "Sure, Mama will know. Mama has a good man for everything."

She telephoned Bonnie Rob Roy, who was in Vegas, and put the question to her bluntly. When Cris hung up, she had the name of a doctor who was patronized by the theatrical crowd. He was called the Abortion King. "He charges a minimum of five hundred dollars. Do you have the money, Allie?"

Allegra shook her head. Her allowance was less than that of the other girls, except Marianna. The Towles were conservative; they practiced a kind of Puritan discipline and self-abnegation.

"I could ask Stephen," Cris offered generously.

Allegra paled. "*No*. Please, don't ever think of it. I'll manage."

In the end Cris came up with two hundred dollars, Marianna withdrew a hundred dollars—which was practically all she had in her savings account—and

Allie sold two gold bracelets to a coin shop in Stamford. She had the necessary amount. . . .

Now, Allegra parked in a garage on East Fifty-sixth Street and they walked west toward Carnegie Hall. Marianna was surprised when Allegra led her into the Russian Tea Room.

She stared at the murals of the ballet on the walls, the bright red balls that gave the place the atmosphere of Christmas in July, the brass of innumerable old Russian samovars, the autographed pictures of celebrities, the crowded tables. Settling back in her seat, she remarked, "It's unlike any restaurant I've ever seen—not that I've seen that many. How did you know about it?"

"My father introduced me to it," Allegra said. "We used to stop here before the Children's Concerts. . . . He was Russian, you know."

"I didn't know. I mean, you've never spoken of him."

A shadow of pain darkened Allegra's face. She said nothing more, but turned to the captain to order their lunch. When the food arrived she scarcely touched hers, and Marianna wondered uneasily if she was still sick and too proud to admit it.

She wondered if Allie would ever tell her who the boy was.

On the way back to New Canaan Allegra was quiet. Marianna, sensitive to her mood, was equally quiet, yet questions were churning through her mind. If Allie had had an abortion in April, why was there this birth —this expulsion, or whatever it was that she had suffered only three days ago? Marianna knew enough about birth from physical education hygiene classes to appreciate the fact that when a child is born, there is something called the afterbirth. But two months later? She recalled the shred of humanity she had carefully wrapped and disposed of. It was a fetus, she was certain of it. Was this a *second* fetus?

At the Piano Store, Allie braked and let Marianna out of the car. "It's been fun," she said politely.

Marianna hesitated before she said, "Allie, I don't mean to pry—but are you *sure* you're all right?"

"Mari, you're repeating yourself. You asked me that twice in the restaurant. It's getting rather boring."

"Have it your way." Marianna slammed the car door.

"Mari," Allegra called.

Marianna went back to the car. Allie had raised her dark glasses over her forehead, and she looked vulnerable.

"I'm perfectly okay. And I do thank you for everything. You've been simply wonderful."

Allegra swung through the village in the direction of her grandmother's house. Had the impulsive visit to the Russian Tea Room been a mistake? She wondered. It had brought up images of other times, when she was taken there as a child by her father. *Daddy,* she thought, seeing him vividly in her mind—his gaiety and humor, his loving attention—*Why did you have to leave me?*

She shook her head and reminded herself not to dwell in the past. *Look, Allie, you've got to think ahead. Plan your moves,* she told herself. *Otherwise the family will overwhelm you.*

Her Grandmother Towle was in the garden inspecting the rose bushes when Allie parked the car in the garage and ran around to greet her. Grandmother Towle hadn't needed Rachel Carson's *Silent Spring* to warn her about the future of the earth. Her landscapers had been practicing organic gardening for years.

The old woman—still a formidable figure in her seventies—walked toward Allegra, favoring her left leg. Nobody would have dreamed that sciatica kept her awake many nights. She refused even to take aspirin for the pain. *That marvelous old stoic,* Allegra thought with affection. Her grandmother often took Allie's part, since she had for years disapproved of her daughter Pru's behavior.

"Will you be here for dinner?" she asked.

"Sorry, Grandmama. I'm going out."

"Where, may I ask?"

"To Cristina's. She's invited me for dinner and to spend the night—"

"I want to talk to you, Allegra. We haven't settled on plans for the summer."

"Oh, Grandmama, not *now*. It's just one day after graduation."

"We must make plans. It's already a bit late for your debut, although I've made some tentative arrangements."

Allegra looked startled. "If you'll excuse me—"

"Cook has some fresh cookies, the kind you're partial to. Iced tea?"

"I really can't wait, Grandmama—"

"Allegra, I'm going to go to the vault tomorrow. I plan to have some of my jewelry reset for you."

Instinctively, Allegra's hand rested on the Siberian amethyst under her shirt. "Thank you, but couldn't it wait?"

"If you're going off to Europe—"

"I'm *not* going."

"What will you do then?"

"My best friends are staying home for the summer. I'll probably spend most of my time with them."

Finally Allie broke away. She raced up the stairs to her bedroom and snatched a duffle bag from her closet and jammed it with clothes. Picking up her black Locust Ryse sports sweater, she dashed down and out to the garage.

Ten minutes later, she parked her car at the Terhune house. Rose Eileen was sitting in the solarium, working on a needlepoint pillow for Cris.

"Allegra!" She was delighted and kissed the young girl affectionately. "What brings you here—with Cris gone?"

"I figured you'd be lonely with her away, so I've invited myself over to keep you company."

"How very kind of you. I was rather dreading this evening, with Cris away and Steve leaving—"

"Where's he off to?"

"Just a conference in Washington. He'll be back tomorrow night."

"Wouldn't it be nice if he took us out to dinner?"

Allegra suggested. "Just to keep our spirits up. I mean, I miss Cristina, too."

"I'm sure you do. Well, we'll ask Stephen. It'll give us something to look forward to."

It surely will, Allegra thought. Happily.

Allie found it odd taking over Cristina's bedroom, which was so different from her own adolescent room at her mother's Greenwich house or at her grandmother's, with its antiques and New England comfort. How easy it was here to pretend she was Cris, blessed with a fascinating mother and an exciting, virile father!

Lying in Cris's bed, surrounded by the wicker and bamboo framed in luscious growing greens, Allie felt a strange restlessness. The floor-to-ceiling windows were open to the night, which exerted a magnetic pull. Without closing her eyes, Allie tried to imagine herself as a fully grown woman, with a woman's passions and responses.

The woman she admired was the clever seductress who glowed with innocence while wearing an undercoat of wickedness. What was so terrible about wickedness? she asked herself. In fairy tales, the wicked women always met with a bad end. But the biographies Allie had read proved otherwise.

When she was twelve she had read an unexpurgated story of Theodora, the courtesan who married the Roman ruler, Justinian. Theodora became her obsession, the lodestar of her fantasies. After a while, her reading had carried her into the Victorians, and she was enchanted with Lola Montez and the Edwardian beauty Lily Langtry. Behind the gilt mesh screens in her grandmother's library, she eventually discovered the biography of Jane Digby, the Englishwoman who rebelled against society and lived her final years, after glorious love affairs, with a devoted sheik.

Allie had read voraciously, fantasizing the lives of these women. What wife could elicit the adoration, passion and offerings of power that were tossed like bouquets of roses at their feet? . . . Now was the time, she felt, to live, to experience what the witty, uninhibited women before her had known. But where did one find a man strong and powerful enough to fasten her destiny to?

Stephen Terhune . . . ?

"I don't get it." Marianna's voice sounded puzzled over the wire. "You mean, you're staying with the Terhunes? But Cris is away—"

"That's exactly it." Allie knew she could not be overheard. It was the day after she'd arrived at the Terhune house and she was stretched out on a chaise on the terrace of the poolhouse. Rose Eileen was in her bedroom, taking the afternoon nap her doctor had pre-scribed for her high blood pressure.

"I don't get it," Marianna said again with the candor that sometimes antagonized Allegra. "What's your pur-pose?"

"To keep Rose Eileen company."

"Oh, come off it, Allie! You've got other reasons."

"Well, if you must know the truth, I'm fed up with my family—with Mommy and Grandmama. Let them cool off—and realize they can't order me around any-more."

"How long will you be at the Terhunes'?"

"I don't know. As long as Rose Eileen needs me, I guess."

The pause from Marianna's end was a stronger state-ment than anything she might have said about the sit-uation. "Well, let me know what happens."

Allegra returned the phone to the table. She leaned back on the chaise, her eyes closed in reverie. *I love it here,* she thought. *I belong here.*

"It feels like home," she had said earlier in the day to Rose Eileen.

"Please think of it as your home," Rose Eileen had replied. She was so appreciative of Allegra's thought-fulness, so delighted to have her as a guest, not only as a substitute for Cris, but as good company.

Yesterday, when Allegra had surprised Rose Eileen by her visit, she was determined to make the evening eventful, even though Stephen was out of town. They drove to Westport for dinner at a ramshackle inn that served delicious lobsters. Afterward, they went to a theater showing old films and saw *Orphans of the Storm* with Dorothy and Lillian Gish. Rose Eileen said Joseph Schildkraut, the hero, was prettier than the girls. "I used to have such a crush on him," she said with a sigh. "Of course, by the time I saw him on stage, he was middleaged. But what a beautiful man he used to be."

"Styles in men's appearances have changed," Allie commented. "I think your husband's awfully attractive."

"You should've seen Stephen when I first knew him. He was absolutely the *most* attractive man. He knew my older brother, who went to Boston University. One summer they both worked as hod carriers. I think that's how Steve first got interested in construction. My sisters and I were crazy about Steve. I always thought he preferred my older sister, Regina. When he turned to me, I couldn't believe it. I thought I was the luckiest girl in the world." She paused and added, "I still do."

"But you weren't married right away?"

"No. He and my brother both went off to California. Then he married Bonnie Rob Roy . . . and there was a long time lapse before he came back—to me."

"Was that an impulsive first marriage, d'you suppose?"

Rose Eileen didn't appear to mind the question, perhaps because she had settled the problem of Bonnie Rob Roy in her mind. "It probably was, and more's the pity. I think Stephen was hurt—he's so steadfast, you know. And he was concerned about Cristina. I suspect Bonnie needed him more than she realized. She still calls him when she's got problems . . . but a woman like that *would* destroy what was best for her."

At noon Stephen telephoned from Washington to let his wife know that he was taking the six o'clock shuttle and would be home for dinner. "I didn't tell him you were here," Rose Eileen said to Allie. "It'll be a surprise."

Now the late afternoon shadows were deepening. It was time to get ready for the evening. Allegra gathered herself from the lounge chair, picked up her paperback and sunoil and moved indoors. She mounted the broad curving staircase and walked past the room where Rose Eileen was resting, past the adjoining bedroom that was Stephen's.

In Cristina's bathroom she stripped and inspected herself for any suspicious stains. There were none. She was really damned lucky, though she still didn't understand why she had had an "accident" two months after her abortion. She had been terrified when it happened. Thank God Marianna was there, she thought—good, kind Marianna, always so helpful, always so discreet. Marianna's gratitude was something Allie knew she could count on forever, because she had taken Marianna's side when some of the snobbier girls were unkind to her during her first year at Locust Ryse. But not even clever Marianna could explain the expulsion. Could it have been twins? Allie wondered. She had screwed him once and come up with twins—and the doctor cleaned out one and left the other behind. My God, she thought, wasn't *that* a joke.

Allie stepped into a tepid shower—hot water might make her bleed, as it had right after the abortion. She dried herself carefully and put on a pair of brief panties, which she reinforced with a second pair. Her skin was moist and fragrant from the shower. She posed before the mirror on the door, left foot behind the right, hip slightly thrust out, left hand on her left hip. Her lustrous dark hair made a turban for her small heart-shaped face. The effect, she knew, was beguiling, and she hoped she would inspire an explosion of feeling in a lover who had never seen her nude.

Allie and Rose Eileen met at the staircase. She was in a simple white sheath with a tailored blue jacket, Rose Eileen in a multifloral caftan. Next to Allie, with her beautiful spare figure, the older woman, in spite of her fine coloring, looked ripe and overblown—a hothouse peach a bit too long on display. But Rose Eileen kissed Allie warmly, and the two of them, arm in arm, went out to greet Stephen, whose car was turning into the driveway.

"Oh Stephen—" Rose Eileen called out, her voice filled with joy. "It's good to have you home."

Allie's glance followed Rose Eileen's as he stepped out of the car. He was wearing a conservative English suit, dark with a pencil stripe. His rough, sandy hair grew in a V on his high, deeply lined forehead, and it had enough gray at the temples to suggest experience and character. It was clipped short, as it had been ever since Allegra first saw him in her freshman year at Locust Ryse. His face, like his body, was strong and finely proportioned. Under the bones of the brows, his dark gray eyes looked slightly dangerous. His was a year-round tan, more appropriate to a construction worker sweating on pipelines than to the president of an international company. When he smiled, as he did now, the folds deepened in his flat cheeks, giving him a disarming grace.

Stephen caught Rose Eileen's outstretched hand, leaned over and kissed her on the cheek.

"Steve, we have a guest," she announced proudly.

He was startled but quickly recovered his composure. "Allegra, good to see you. But you know Cris is away . . ."

Allie's smile was radiant. "I'm her stand-in."

"Isn't she a dear?" Rose Eileen said. "She was afraid I'd be lonely without Cris."

"We'll both miss her." He was walking between them into the house. "Have you heard from her, Rose Eileen?"

"Not yet, but she'll probably phone tomorrow—unless you'd like me to put in a call tonight."

He shook his head. After he went upstairs to shower and change, Rose Eileen confided in Allegra, "He worries about Cris's spending so much time with her mother. I tell him it's only natural for a girl to want to be with her mother, especially a mother like Bonnie—all the glamour and excitement of her life. . . ." She added sadly, "The headlines, too. It's not a good influence for a young girl."

Stephen was too tired to go out for dinner. After drinks on the terrace, they moved into the dining room for a meal of cold salmon and green sauce. Allegra was demure and quiet while Stephen and Rose Eileen talked, mostly about his meetings in Washington.

He excused himself when he had finished eating and bent down to kiss Rose Eileen again on the cheek. Then he went over to Allegra and touched her lightly, but she raised her face and he had to kiss her too.

"That's for Cris," Allegra said brightly, her pulse racing.

Shortly afterward Rose Eileen said, "I think I'll turn in. Is there anything you'd like, Allegra?"

Allegra stifled an impulse to reply, "Yes, your husband." *Another night,* she thought. But at least he was here in the house.

The wave of restlessness was worse tonight—aggravated, Allegra admitted, by Stephen's presence. She lay naked on the bed and closed her eyes but was unable to sleep. The musical clock chimed midnight, surprising her; she had no idea it was that late . . .

Allegra left the bed and stood immobile at the windows. A strange need was growing in her flesh. She ran her palms across her small, budding breasts and down her thighs, silken with the loving care inspired by the summer sun.

Without thinking, she groped for her short blue silk robe and pulled it over her shoulders. She opened the door to the hall, where a brass columned lamp shed an amber night light. Like a sleepwalker, she moved toward the end of the main wing, her bare feet digging into the deep pile of the carpet.

At the door, she paused. Her heart accelerated its rhythm; she felt it pounding in the veins of her throat. She turned the knob. Entering the room quietly, cautiously, she closed the door behind her. Her eyes saw nothing, but her ears heard his breathing. After a moment, as her eyes adjusted to the dark, she made out his body lying diagonally across the bed. He was hugging a flat pillow; the sheets were tossed over the end of the bed. His long, muscular frame was bare.

The repercussions of her behavior should have shocked her into action—to turn and leave the room. Should have . . . But the shape of the room was becoming clear in the night's light, and she thought of his taut body—the flat, long thighs, the powerful arms.

She dropped her robe to the floor. Taking one step slowly, then another, as though hypnosis was giving action to her wishes, she reached the bed. Carefully she sat down at the edge, where his back left a vacuum. She put her hand over his belly and gently, as a feather might fall, she let it rest on his flesh. And then, with equal delicacy, she molded her body to his back.

His flesh, cool in his relaxed sleep, suddenly took fire; his cock, under her delicate velvet touch, burst into a magnificent column. Still asleep, he turned around and clasped her to him, his mouth, hungry and demanding, groping for hers.

Sanity jolted him awake as she said softly in her young girl's voice, "Steve, don't move. Don't turn on the light." Her head went lower, exploring. "It's my surprise for you, darling."

"Good Lord, *no*." He sat up, his eyes looking for the clock's luminous dial. "Are you *mad*? Rose Eileen's in the next room."

"She took a sleeping pill," Allegra said confidently, as though that answered all problems that might arise. "Steve, you surely remember last time? I do. It torments my dreams. It's ruined all those silly prep school kids for me. I can't forget what it's like to have a *man*."

Aware of the potential danger, he swung his legs over the edge of the bed. She touched his thighs—such strength, she thought—but he moved away, demanding in a kind of puzzled anguish, "Why the hell did you come here?"

"Why do you think I'm here? To substitute for Cris? That's silly. I came because it's been so long and so much has happened that you should know about—and because I'm in love with you, and I want you to make love to me."

"Listen to me, Allegra." His fingers were cutting into her arms. "Get back to Cris's room and *stay there*."

She refused to budge. "There's something I must tell you. It concerns us—"

"Tomorrow."

"It can't wait until your wife's around. Darling, do you know what happened to me after our first time?"

"Allie, you've *got* to get out of here. You're driving me up the wall."

He was holding her hand, his other arm clasped around her shoulders so that her small breasts took on an unfamiliar swelling. He half-led, half-pulled her to the door, praying that the sounds wouldn't awaken Rose Eileen.

"I'll scream." Her voice was a low rasp. "I'll scream and yell that you lured me in here and tried to rape me—"

He slapped her. Hearing the sound of his palm on her cheek, he felt sick. He was aware of something wild and irrepressible coming to the surface—in himself and in her—and his determination to send her back to Cris's room crumbled. He loathed his lack of self-control. As he grappled to keep her quiet, his hands found her flesh moist, and he couldn't hold on to her. Somehow they stumbled together, and by some miracle fell to their knees in silence on the deep carpet. He held her, in a fury that was turning slowly into desire, and felt her response.

Her smooth fingers sought his armpits, his fine pectoral muscles, the strong stomach muscles leading down to his penis. She lay upon him like a young wrestler, and when he imprisoned her hands to quiet their temptation she covered his face and chest with quick cat-like licks, using the tip of her tongue rather than her lips.

It was a long time since he'd enjoyed a woman in a position above him. But this girl, so delicate and fragile, carried him along in a rush of freedom and excitement he'd completely forgotten.

Her exquisitely shaped fingers were avid, and he absorbed a tremendous surge of passion through her hands. Her small, busy tongue searched his crevices without shyness. Like a savage creature, she was teasing, nibbling, wanting to possess him within herself, shaking her hips against his until it was impossible for him to keep from peaking in a splendid explosion. He was losing himself in her, soaring beyond the limits of muscle and flesh.

He knew that she was no feminine vessel used merely for his pleasure. Exulted, his body shook until the veins in his temples grew as prominent as those on his cock. He grasped her waist and swung her over so that he was above her, and now her lips were coddling the nipples on his chest, which nearly made him crazy. He thrust himself into her sweet depths, and her feminine smell attacked his senses. The sheer physical reaction went far beyond that first time, when they had been swept together because of some hoodlums' violence.

In a state of frenzied joy, gripped by the spasms that raked his muscles and senses, he thought, *How can I ever leave her?*

The three of them had breakfast in the sunny solarium. Rose Eileen said she felt better; her migraine was completely gone.

As she and Allegra walked Stephen to his car, Rose Eileen said tenderly, "You look exhausted, Steve. Can't you take some time off?"

"I'll try," he said.

Just then Rose Eileen was called to the phone. Steve and Allie were alone. "No more of this," he said. "We were both out of our heads."

"Out of our heads on *us,* Steve. There was no danger, really."

"Oh no? Your reputation, my marriage. That's enough."

Her dark eyes mocked him, reminding him that he would never forget last night, nor would she. As to the risk of getting pregnant again, she didn't give it a thought.

CHAPTER III

MOTHERS AND DAUGHTERS
I: PRUDENCE AND ALLEGRA

Before the great Tudor house off North Street in Greenwich; before the Rolls Royce Silver Cloud and the collection of antique cars; before the Turner sunsets (inherited), the Sisley riverbanks and village roads, the Bonnard females and flowers, the Degas streetwalkers and the Chinese porcelains (acquired); before the kennels where she bred Kerry Blues that brought home blue ribbons; before the tiara she wore to the Metropolitan Opera galas on rare occasions (just often enough to prove it was hers and not on loan from Harry Winston); before the return to the formal trappings and the genteel brainwashing, Prudence had enjoyed a reputation that shocked her elderly parents, her Towle relatives and her many friends.

Prudence's parents were by birth and circumstance careful, never given to extravagant gestures. After the crash of 1929, when Prudence was five years old, they kept the full staff in the Manhattan townhouse and the New Canaan estate because it was their duty to look after their help. But the tenor of the times was reflected in their life style, which became even more modest than it had been. Prudence accepted it like a good Towle, stifling the bold impulses, the needs, the craving.

Until she met Pavel Simon.

In the spring of 1936 Prudence was about to make her debut. She was an heiress, although it was a word never associated with the family. It was too dramatic, too flamboyant for a lineage so conservative, discreet and very, very rich.

Prudence's father was head of a Wall Street investment house whose base rested on the vast Towle real estate holdings. The family's reputation was impeccable, if Yankee shrewd. They funded medical research, a section of the American wing of a Boston museum and various other lofty charities. The family was proud of their more recent ancestors—lawyers, physicians and teachers—but the present generation was dedicated to the preservation and enhancement of the Family Trust.

Prudence, an only child who had come late in her parents' marriage, had developed early into a singularly attractive girl. The family thought little of beauty, which they considered a form of female witchcraft. So Prudence was accepted as a tall, angular, agreeable young woman. She had an oval face and strange eyes, as black as her boyishly bobbed hair.

Prudence's mother somehow sensed that the odd, unpredictable streak in her daughter's nature wasn't limited to her occasional bursts of rebellion, like sleeping in the nude, sewing a scarlet silk lining in her conservative prep school blazer or wearing exotic turbans and flowing clothes, which Prudence copied from the movie beauties she admired.

"It's a stage she'll outgrow," her mother remarked. At least Prudence hadn't eloped with the family gardener or the groom, as certain rich girls had. So her parents gave Prudence leeway in small matters but exercised control in more important ones. They expected her to make her debut and then be married at St. Thomas's Church with six bridesmaids, a reception at the Plaza and a honeymoon abroad.

Not taking it all seriously, Prudence was agreeable. She came out at a tea at the New Canaan house. The only problem was her choice of a husband.

In the thirties, Prudence often said later, girls were brought up to depend on young men for ballast during "the year." A girl who couldn't count on at least two escorts for each ball was ready for a nervous collapse.

Her friends, whose mothers made elaborate plans for their debuts, invited her to their parties, and she was always included on the guest lists for the charity balls. But no matter where the girls and their escorts went, the last important stop of the night was, of course, the exclusive Stork Club.

Prudence was a favorite of Sherman Billingsley, the manager of the Stork Club. Sherman ran his place on the principle of snob appeal. He was dictator and arbiter, and anyone he excluded was doomed to spend the rest of his nights at the Manhattan Elba. Only the 21 Club carried greater prestige.

It was at the Stork Club that Prudence enjoyed herself the most. No patronesses were present to cast a disapproving eye on her dancing; she had no fear that news of her behavior would reach her mother. Prudence usually had the delightful problem of choosing between two or three escorts with whom she shared dances and champagne. She felt like a movie star or an opera *prima donna* or even Isadora Duncan, that mad, marvelous woman who typified what Prudence only sensed, but nonetheless yearned for.

The yearning—not yet a quest—was within her while she danced with bright young men to the tunes of Richard Rogers's "Mountain Greenery" and Cole Porter's "You're Delovely." She saw visions of herself in lovely apricot chiffon barely concealing her long body, draping herself to a man who was masculine and domineering, a savage yet tender lover—not like these Yale and Princeton boys.

When she was introduced by her friends to Pavel Simon at the Stork Club, she knew she had found her dream man.

Pavel reminded Prudence of the reckless Cossacks she had seen in films. He had a prominent forehead, high cheekbones, blue eyes, blunt chin, muscular chest, flat abdomen and powerful legs—and he wore dinner clothes with elegance. Prudence was aware of a sense of challenge, which she responded to. It would be fun to get to know him, she thought.

It was the time of the White Russian mystique. Movie stars eloped with Russians of dubious ancestry, and rich American girls married authentic White Russian aristocrats in reduced circumstances. Pavel Simon was not impoverished. He was a brilliant young mathematician with a sound background in economics. His people were Russian intellectuals, his father an economist with an international reputation.

That the elder Simon was a member of a secret revolutionary group was not discovered until the Revolution of 1918. He was killed by a splinter group of his own fanatic faction. Pavel and his mother escaped by the classic route: Her jewels opened the underground to Shanghai, where they barely existed during the boy's adolescence. Finally, with the aid of other White Russians, they reached Canada and found a haven with the elderly daughter of a famous Russian poet.

Pavel's natural gifts were sharpened by the efforts of survival. He attended McGill University, where he majored in business. When he and Prudence met he was established as a securities analyst in a distinguished brokerage house. He was able to provide handsomely for his mother and her close friends, who were all still living in the snug nest of the poet's daughter.

Pavel rented a small apartment on East Fiftieth Street, above a former speakeasy. He had a talent for understanding people as well as the stock market, and he adroitly combined business with his social life. He inspired confidence and trust. Among his many friends were men who knew the Towles, and since both he and Prudence frequented the Stork Club, it was inevitable that they would meet.

During Christmas week at the Towle estate in New Canaan, Prudence's parents greeted their daughter's latest fancy with courtesy but reserve. By the time they had coffee before the fire in the library, however, Mr. Towle's stiff, authoritarian manner had thawed, and Mrs. Towle, taking her cues from her husband, was gracious and friendly.

Prudence knew her parents well enough to appreciate the impression Pavel had made, for the Towles were unusually afraid of fortune hunters. Pavel, they could see, was *not* one of them.

With her family's reluctant blessings, Prudence and Pavel saw a good deal of each other. That summer they spent most of their weekends together, with his friends in Southampton.

One evening they were sailing on Long Island Sound. The yacht belonged to one of Pavel's business associates. It was a night of good wine, magic and calm waters. The moon was a wash of silver on the gentle waves. One of the guests, a young actress in a Broadway musical, was strumming her guitar and singing softly one of the production numbers.

Prudence, sharing a single deck chair with Pavel, felt the poignancy of the bittersweet lyrics, and she thought she would never be as happy as she was at that moment.

And Pavel, holding her with gentle hands, said it should all be forever; he'd have it no other way.

They became engaged.

Even before the wedding at St. Thomas's Church, the honeymoon on a yacht floating in the Aegean Sea, the apartment on East Sixty-third Street in Manhattan and the layette from Saks Fifth Avenue, Prudence was convinced that the man she loved had astute vision and would eventually elicit her father's respect. Pavel was well on his way to doing so.

The youngest member of the Family Trust, he was also the most aggressive and enterprising. Pavel described to the Board what he saw as the products of automation and automobiles: vast new shopping centers with tract houses nearby. Persuaded by the elder Towle, the Board decided to give Pavel his head. They allowed him to create a real estate syndicate—a spin-off of the Family Trust, of course.

Pavel explored all the tracts of land available on Long Island and across the Sound in Port Chester and Stamford. The Board was impressed with his enthusiasm and vision. They set up a subsidiary, a real estate investment firm, which was left entirely in his hands.

What nobody realized, not even Prudence, was that Pavel, the Wonder Boy, functioned best when the odds were against him.

Prudence adored Pavel for many reasons, not the least being his sense of compassion—a trait not characteristic of the Towles. And for his lovemaking.

And for his fierce loyalty, not only to new friends, but to his own people—Russian exiles—which amounted to an obsession. He enlisted the sympathy of his American friends, whose healthy checkbooks helped his worthy compatriots gain a foothold in the New World.

Prudence never questioned Pavel's loyalty for the refugees; nor was she jealous of the time he devoted to them. She was so grateful to be a part of his rich, stimulating life that she had only gratitude for him. Their marriage had given a new dimension to her world, and she blossomed.

As Pavel's wife Prudence was accepted, pampered and showered with affection. The emigrés looked on her as a generous, loving little mother and came to her with their problems, having faith in her ability to solve all. Her clothes were borrowed by young women who needed chic outfits to apply for jobs, to audition, to meet future husbands. Her furs were lent to an impoverished duchess, who was to have dinner with a Vanderbilt, and who had probably left behind in her St. Petersburg palace a collection of pelts far more valuable than Prudence's white ermine greatcoat.

Pavel took her to parties given by publisher Condé Nast, where she was introduced to the American and English stage and film stars, playwrights and novelists. She would never have met them at the family's evenings, which gathered only mere bankers, investment counselors and industrialists. Dullards.

By contrast, the Russian evenings, during which the emigrés entertained in a shabby railroad flat in a shabby brownstone, were even more stimulating. Drinking innumerable glasses of tea, they argued, speculated, consoled each other, made plans and traded suggestions, all the while laughing at their pain and humiliation. They were quick to anger, quick to forgive, quick to love, quick to separate and come together again.

Prudence responded to them with a thawing of inhibitions that would have shocked her parents. She hummed along as they sang their melancholy songs of Russia; she read great Russian literature. And always in their presence she felt so alive, balanced between laughter and tears.

With Pavel, life became a real fairy tale.

Allegra was a free spirit in her mother's womb. She was so active that the obstetrician could scarcely pinpoint her heartbeat.

"*Allegra*," Prudence's mother said with distaste just before the christening. "What an—unlikely name."

Her mother couldn't blame the name on Pavel. There was nothing Russian about it. Allegra, after Lord Byron's natural daughter, was a testament to Prudence's adoration of the Romantics—as exemplified by her own marriage to Pavel.

"There's more of *him* than the Towles in the child," said Mrs. Towle when Allegra exploded into a temper tantrum.

"Thank God for that," Prudence said. She had been eager to have a child by Pavel, and had wanted a son. She welcomed her daughter, but was from the start a little envious of Pavel's delight in the infant. From childhood, Allie was endowed with a reckless manner, a suggestion of sexual challenge that seemed to arouse a demon response in the male sex. As she grew older her demeanor suggested that she was vulnerable, even accessible, and that the control holding her in check could be conquered by a favored man.

Life among the family servants afforded Allie an education no school could offer. *Reality One,* she often called it in later years. Her parents, obsessed with each other, lived in elegance, enjoying life with an indulgence in sensual pleasures, but never to destructive excess. Prudence had dreamed of a perfect lover who would fill her life with fantasy, and this fantasy she received from Pavel. No matter how busy, he never neglected what he called "Pru's time."

During the first seven years of life Allegra—handed

from nanny to governess to teachers in a private school that emphasized French language and culture—found that her father seemed only peripherally aware of her.

But she was always joyfully aware of him. She waited in the apartment for the sound of his arrival, rushing to him as the door opened, a bright little tornado with glossy black pigtails, dark shining eyes and rosy patches in her cheeks, dressed in a pinafore and ruffled white blouse, short white socks and Mary Jane slippers. Her child's voice greeted him deliriously. "Daddy, Daddy—"

As she nuzzled against him, smelling the good odor of woolens, leather and tobacco, he asked, "Who's Daddy's little girl?"

And she responded in glorious ritual, "I am. I am, Daddy. Love me, Daddy—"

He did, depositing kisses on her cheeks and in the sweet folds of her neck, which tickled her until she broke into laughing hiccoughs. Once, she kissed him on the mouth—a full, unchildish kiss—and abruptly he pushed her away.

"Stop it, my little siren."

He took her by the hand and led her into the huge living room, and she was puzzled by his displeasure. Why was he annoyed? Mommy kissed him like that— she'd seen them when they didn't realize she was spying on them—so why couldn't she? Usually Daddy approved of her—certainly more than Mommy did, or Nana, her nurse.

Allie was now too old for her governess, who had finally been discharged when she found the child's behavior impossible to tolerate. But Nana had remained to do the sewing and mending, to look after Mommy, who didn't want a personal maid underfoot. Allie thought that Nana—small, wrinkled, mouth pursed, eyes shrewd behind her spectacles—made up stories that were to her advantage. When Allie was insolent Nana reported some awful lies to Mommy.

"Not true! Not true!" Allie shrieked. But who would believe her? Grownups, she knew, stuck together.

Nana said, "Allie will be what her mind wants her to be." And her mind, the old lady implied, was that of a rude, obstinate little girl who was determined to get her own way.

With Daddy, Allie was always adorable and adoring. He couldn't understand the complaints. "She's a healthy, lively little girl," he said. "Naturally she'll get into mischief. The Slav genes."

"You aren't like that, love," Mommy said.

"I learned self-control . . . for preservation," he confessed. "But Allie doesn't have to compromise. She can be herself."

Allie had mulled that over. What did he mean? Finally she cornered him with the question.

"Do what's best for you. Just as long as you don't hurt anyone else."

Mommy didn't approve. "You're much too indulgent with her. She'll go wild. We can't have it."

"Prudence, my love," he reminded her gently, "weren't you also a rebel?"

"I was. I am." She hesitated. "We should have another child—for Allie's sake. Perhaps it will quiet her down."

Prudence was unwise to suggest this in Allie's presence. "I'll kill it," Allie muttered. "I'll kill it with Daddy's gun."

But Allie didn't have to do anything to make sure that there were no more children to share Daddy's love. When she was in the second grade, Mommy was taken abruptly to the hospital, where she remained for nearly two weeks. Whenever Daddy came home after visiting her there he devoted the rest of the evening to Allie.

Allie was in heaven. She was so well behaved at home and at school that teachers and servants alike were puzzled, but pleased. Daddy read to her, or they listened to music together on the Magnavox or played Chinese checkers.

While her mother was in the hospital, Allie also spent more time with the servants. Listening to their gossip, she got secondhand information, including the truth about her mother's illness. One day she overheard Cook talking to the upstairs maid, and that night she had a horrible dream about her mother being sliced open with a huge knife, with blood all around her belly, and a baby, no bigger than a doll, being taken out of her. Dead. In her dream, it was naked, with a kidskin body like her doll's. . . .

"It'll be worse now, mark my words," Cook had said. "She'll never let him out of her sight."

"He's a handsome man," said the maid. "I bet lots of the missus's friends would like to make him."

"He's devoted to Miss Prudence. Nobody can say he married her for her money."

"They say he's making millions for the family— buying up land in Florida—"

"Mebbe. But Mr. Towle, he don't like it. He says the timing is bad. Mr. Simon, *he* says with all the GIs coming home—lots of them are gonna settle in the south. He says they got a taste of it when they was training and they like the climate. . . ."

According to Cook, there would be no more babies. When Mommy came home, pale and sad, she spent most of the day on her chaise in the bedroom, resting, taking no calls, making no plans. She even refused to see Grandmother and Grandfather Towle.

Allie, however, was always present. She was happy there wouldn't be another child and deliberately set about proving herself Mommy's darling. She offered to brush Mommy's hair; she brought in her own miniature English tea set to serve Mommy tea; she turned records on the record player, mostly Russian ballet music, which Mommy loved because Daddy loved it; she used her crayons and Mommy's Tiffany stationery to draw families—a daddy, a mommy and a little girl.

The trouble was that her parents seemed closer than ever since Mommy's return from the hospital. They often had dinner at a small table in their bedroom. At such times, the room was off limits to Allie. Nana usually hustled her to her own chamber.

But once Allie decided to trick Nana. She hid in the servant's bathroom, and while Nana was searching for her she tiptoed into the master bedroom. What she saw was so startling that she cried out. Daddy was on the bed in pajama bottoms, his chest bare. He was nuzzling

Mommy's neck the way Allie begged him to nuzzle her neck when he came into her room to say, "Good night, little one. Pleasant dreams."

Mommy became aware of Allie's cry first. Pushing Daddy away, she sat up. Allie saw her bare breasts, where her dressing gown had parted. Mommy said furiously, "What are you doing here?"

"I—I came to say good night." Allie was flustered, frightened.

"You said good night. An hour ago. Go to your room. Instantly."

Allie obeyed, with anger in her heart. They didn't want her around. Eyes stinging, she straggled toward her bedroom. She wondered if they were doing what the servants giggled about.

What she wanted above all else in the whole wide world was to have Daddy all to herself. But when Mommy went away, as Allie had wanted her to, Daddy went with her. Allie heard the staff discuss Mommy's health and the treatments she would receive in Switzerland, where Daddy happened to have business to take care of.

While Prudence and Pavel were savoring Geneva, Basel and Lake Como, an incident occurred in the Park Avenue duplex that changed Allie's life and brought her nearer to the realization of her fantasies.

The Pavel Simons, like Stephen Terhune a decade later, had a public relations man on retainer named the Duke. The title had been given to him by his clientele, the press and other important people as a form of recognition. Having graduated as a journalism major from the University of Nebraska, he had migrated to New York, leased an apartment at the Sherry Netherland Hotel and lived with a kind of casual elegance on the income from the Nebraska farms his family owned.

The Duke, who was then Nils Norstrand, was interested in public relations work. He found an opening as the assistant to a young woman who published a weekly information sheet that related the Manhattan visits of celebrities and where they could be reached. Since the scope of her sheet was limited by her lack of money, the Duke bought into the enterprise, and with the benefit of his money and enthusiasm the journal soon climbed in quality and circulation.

The time was ripe, he decided soon afterward, to launch his own firm. He remained a silent partner in the fact sheet, knowing it would be useful to him, and meanwhile he branched out. Through the Sherry Netherland, he met the P.R. heads of other first-rate hotels, and soon he was helping with publicity . . . and making friends with the new breed of Manhattan society—the new talent and the new rich, who came on like the wave of the future.

The Duke became something of a power, which delighted his ego and opened the doors of many pleasant bed chambers. He often combined love and work, and many of the rich and talented women who made copy in the outlets that counted to them—*Vogue, Harper's Bazaar, Women's Wear Daily*—owed their initial recognition to his efforts. The Duke was warm, kind and thoughtful, and he had a genius for bringing the right people together. He was a social Machiavelli—loved, adored and, on occasion, feared.

Just before Allie's parents flew to Switzerland, the Duke arranged to have the Simon apartment photographed by a magazine that published only the most interestingly appointed apartments and townhouses. The Simons had agreed to the project, and Pavel, having confidence in the Duke, signed the releases and forgot about the whole thing.

The 1955 Christmas issue of *Urban Life* offered a splendid journey into the tastes of the Pavel Simons, a blend of Art Deco, Russian bibelots and French impressionists. The photos showed white walls, white carpeting, upholstered white chairs and sofas, with touches of ebony . . . and for color, the collection of Russian icons and Fabergé Easter eggs. Drawing room, bedroom, library—they were perfectly decorated but rather unreal, like the stage settings for a play. There were no people in those rooms, nothing human.

Until the reader came to the dining room.

The picture showed polished woods and an expanse

of table glowing with hothouse fruits—purple grapes, peaches, nectarines—and rare Coalport china.

At the head of the table sat Allegra—seven years old, dressed in her school uniform, holding her head high, so the finely shaped head was outlined by the dark thick braids, her eyes lowered. A houseman in a white jacket stood behind her, holding a sterling salver with her poached egg, toast rack and glass of milk.

The Duke's young photographer had no aspirations as a social critic. The contrasts, however, suggested a fascinating photograph: the small girl alone at a table suitable for a château, the servant as the surrogate parent.

It was an effective commentary on the children of the rich during a period when the world was growing aware of the Have Nots.

In Switzerland Prudence and Pavel saw the advance copy of the magazine. Prudence was pleased; the apartment looked magnificent. Pavel, however, ignored everything but the image of Allegra.

"My God. She looks like a waif—like an orphan." The telephone vibrated with his anger. "The photographer—who is he? Some damn Communist? What does he want to prove—that luxury cannot give a child happiness?"

"He meant nothing of the kind." The Duke was defensive. "It was just a contrast."

"She looks so *lonely*," Pavel said.

The Duke asked quietly, "Isn't she?"

"Certainly not. She has the best of mothers. And I am devoted to her."

"I'm sure."

"How can we undo this? If Allegra understands this picture when she grows older, she's bound to hate us."

"Look, Mr. Simon. If you insist, there are several things we can do. We can photograph Allegra putting Christmas gifts for underprivileged children under a tree—you have one in your building, don't you? Or showing up at a children's wing in a hospital—"

"I don't approve of exploiting charities or holidays for personal gain."

"Then perhaps we can take a portrait of her and Mrs. Simon for *Town and Country*. We'll do pictures of the Russian Easter—"

At that point in her life, Allegra genuinely loved her mother, but unfortunately Prudence showed feelings only for her husband. She was fond of her child and was always punctilious about Allegra's physical care. But in her milieu children were turned over to nurses, tutors, boarding schools. The bond between mother and child, so strong in the inception, grew tenuous and weak. If Allie was sick, it was Nana who nursed her, who decided whether to summon a doctor. Cook listened when, over cookies and milk, Allie related her problems, and she counseled the girl, often badly.

Some of the surrogate kitchen parents were devoted to her, sorry for her, an emotion that convinced them that "money isn't everything." Others were cruel and malicious, including the tipsy one who declared she saw mice in the bathtub. Another was fired when Nana discovered, on her return from vacation, purple bruises on Allie's arms.

Once when Nana teased Allie about a boy in her dancing class, Allie shrugged her off.

"When I grow up, I'm going to marry my Daddy."

After Allie's parents came home from Switzerland Prudence was the same as before. But Daddy paid more attention to her. Small as she was, Allie now knew that when she turned to him he rewarded her with his full attention.

In his company, events took on a shine. Each outing became a holiday more festive than Christmas—the circus at Madison Square Garden in April; the children's concerts at Carnegie Hall; skating at Rockefeller Center; parties at the homes of his Russian friends, who bestowed affection on her lavishly. Daddy took her to lunch at the Russian Tea Room and several times at the Russian Bear, where she had borscht and little meat pies. Mommy was often busy Saturday afternoons, which Allie didn't mind at all. It was far more fun telling Prudence what they'd done than to have her share in their adventures.

Weekdays Allie could scarcely get through the hours from breakfast to dinner, when Daddy came home from the office. She was bathed, dressed in robe and nightie, her hair in plaits, her skin glowing with health. As he embraced her, Allie's world turned radiant. She felt herself bursting with love at the touch of his skin, his beard tickling her cheek, his smell—not like Mommy's expensive perfume, but a *Daddy* smell.

Allie's abundant capacity for love also revealed itself in her kinship with animals. She was allowed to have a dog in the Manhattan apartment—an elderly apricot poodle which she shared with her Grandmama Towle. Mary Twinkletoes was nine years old, arthritic, deaf, her eyes milky with cataracts. But Allegra cared for her; like many lonely children she was tender, solicitous, touchingly maternal with her pet. When she awakened from a bad dream at night and found the little dog's body next to her, she was comforted.

Whenever her parents went off for weekends now her father insisted on including Allie, and Allie insisted on including Mary Twinkletoes. The photographic essay had made its mark.

"Darling," Prudence complained, "we can't foist the child on our hosts."

Pavel said, "I treasure our life together, Prudence. It has made up for my early years. But I insist that we have Allie with us whenever possible. Our friends won't mind. Allie can join their children—"

So they compromised. If their hosts were close friends, they piled Allie and the poodle into the station wagon, along with their bags, golf clubs, sailing gear and other essentials.

Other weekends, she was shipped off to her grandparents' home in New Canaan, where she took swimming and tennis lessons, practiced conversational French with a weekend tutor and rode at Ox Ridge. She liked riding best—her father favored horses. Often, on weekends in New Canaan, Pavel would ride with her, and she loved the times when they galloped together along the bridle paths, shouting and whooping. Allie never became a finished horsewoman, which disturbed Prudence, who respected the classic style in sport. But Allie didn't care; the riders she admired were the Cossacks who put on a fiery display at Madison Square Garden.

Allie lived for the moments her father devoted to her. She resented her mother's sharing them, saying, "This is *my* time with Daddy."

In the winter she saw less of him, but he remained the hub of her existence. Her earlier affection for her mother was waning. Prudence thought the child's attachment to her father was unhealthy, and she assigned Nana the chore of keeping Allie in line. Nana saw to it that Allie was no bother to her parents.

When Allie complained to her father he said judiciously, "You mustn't depend on anyone but yourself. We never know what life parcels out."

It was advice he wasn't able to apply to his own condition. He was not prepared for his own catastrophe.

When the country was in a state of post-war chaos and new values were taking hold, Pavel Simon predicted the beginnings of a new time.

Gambling with cards, dice and the wheel didn't tempt him. Land was his gamble and his obsession. Where land was concerned in that post-war day, he discarded all restraint.

The first disquieting rumors came during a Sunday night Walter Winchell broadcast. Winchell, who had heretofore praised Pavel, did not mention him by name. He merely suggested that the real estate department of a solid Wall Street investment firm was in serious trouble.

After the newspaper headlines, the reporters, the lawyers, the confrontation between the elder Towle and his son-in-law; after Pavel's noncommittal statement to the press; after the terrible scenes between Prudence and Pavel, one shattering fact emerged: Pavel had helped himself to funds normally delegated for the family investment company, as well as monies from investors in the real estate branch, to expand his private holdings.

With reckless optimism he had promised generous profits to friends and clients. He had foreseen an America trekking to the Southwest, an America on wheels, its future governed by four-lane highways that would stretch endlessly across the country. He had a grandiose vision—huge shopping centers, ski resorts, second vacation homes in natural settings for sports and family playgrounds. He had borrowed money and repaid investors with such generous interest that they gladly reinvested, and gradually he had pyramided a top-heavy real estate empire. But the shopping centers, the vacation homes, the tract houses in Arizona for retired people hadn't materialized quickly enough. The country was in the post-war doldrums. To repay his loans, Pavel had to dispose of land at a loss. . . .

"The Charles Ponzi of Wall Street," the radio commentator branded him.

Seven-year-old Allie couldn't understand what was going on. Not only were the servants upset, unwilling to share gossip with her, but her family seemed to be in turmoil. Her mother was pale and distraught, and her father was often absent from home. Her Grandfather Towle, whenever he came to the apartment, appeared grim; he was usually accompanied by lawyers, and they shut themselves up in the library with her father, the talk going on for hours.

Allie saw the headlines in the *JournalAmerican,* the *Daily News,* even the *Times* and *Tribune.* "What did Daddy *do?*" she demanded of Cook.

"He took money that didn't belong to him."

"My Daddy wouldn't do that!"

"He took millions—he ruined people."

"You take that back!" The glint of the Tartar appeared in her deep, dark eyes.

The day Pavel Simon was sentenced to ten years in prison, his daughter grew up.

When Allie refused to go to school Prudence understood. It was equally painful for her to face the world. "Your father meant well. He never used a penny for himself."

The little girl burst into tears, tears as wild and explosive as her temper tantrums. Prudence held her, and they were closer then than ever in the past—or the future.

A few weeks later Allie saw a drawing of her father in a cell at Sing Sing. Next to it was an insert of her mother, in her tiara and ermine. And another of Allie herself on her pony.

The real estate syndicate was tottering. The claims of a recently widowed New Canaan investor named Mr. Finley, whose entire estate was involved, forced the syndicate into bankruptcy. Pavel had paid out fantastic sums for lobbying and influence peddling, and the total amount was so enormous that the family had no recourse but to allow this spin-off to go into bankruptcy.

Pavel had signed over the remainder of his estate, not to his wife but to his daughter.

Which would have left Prudence a pauper—were it not for the Family Trust.

The idea of a cell held a kind of morbid fascination for Allie. She thought of the cages at the veterinarian's office and how the animals hated them, whimpering to be let out.

Food lost its taste. A morsel would lodge in her throat and refuse to budge. "Swallow," Nana would command. "Allie, swallow."

The hurt was too big to swallow. How could she live without her father? How could she tell when it was time for supper, time for bed, time for weekends filled with music and riding?

The Manhattan apartment was closed. The furnishings, including Daddy's collection of art, were sold at an auction gallery. "We're going to live with Grandfather and Grandmama," Prudence said. "You'll like that, won't you, Allie?"

The afternoon before they were to leave the empty apartment, Allie took her savings out of the gold-and-enamel box her father had given her, put on her

English tweed coat and matching hat, and let herself out of the apartment.

The police in Ossining called her mother.

She never confided to anyone how she'd managed the journey—how she'd got a cab driver to take her to the address she wanted, which was the prison.

Her mother drove up to fetch her, accompanied by a man named John X. Lovell, who Prudence said was one of the family's lawyers. Allie expected a scolding, but John X. Lovell was very tactful. As he drove home, she sat in front between him and her silent mother. John asked, "Are you hungry, Allie? Shall we stop for a hamburger or a hot dog?"

She shook her head. She didn't know how to face what they might say to her. All she knew was that her beloved father was in a cell and couldn't get out, and she'd been so near him. Why couldn't they let her see him? She was longing just to *see* him. . . .

Pavel had asked Prudence not to bring Allie, ever, in the vicinity of the prison. He'd asked her not to come either, which Allie didn't know. But later that night, as she tucked Allie into bed, Prudence said, "Don't do that again, love. Daddy wouldn't like it." And then she held her close, whispering, "I thought I'd lost you, too, Allie. . . . I couldn't bear it."

Allie had nothing against John X. Lovell . . . except that he was free and her Daddy was not.

On the Towle estate in New Canaan there was a conspiracy to avoid Pavel Simon's name.

Allie saw little of her mother, but Grandmama Towle was always at home. The infirmities of age were evident only in her use of a cane to favor her arthritic hip. A month after Pavel was sentenced Grandfather Towle suffered a massive cerebral hemorrhage that left him totally paralyzed. When he died a few days later, Cook commented grimly that it was the fault of Allie's father.

Outwardly composed, Prudence kept her suffering locked within herself. She cringed when she recalled what she had said to her parents before bringing Pavel home to meet them. "The family is suffering from tired blood. A transfusion is needed, and Pavel is the donor . . ."

Prudence was aware of her mother's tacit conviction that a divorce was the only logical answer to her predicament. "But what about Allie?" she said. "Isn't she a living reminder of my—"

"Allegra is a Towle. She will be brought up as a Towle."

John X. Lovell was very supportive. He spent time with Grandmama Towle, and also with Prudence as she felt herself falling into a severe depression. Quiet, composed, dependable, he was a source of great strength to her. He was also attractive and well dressed, with an affable manner and a sound mind. But once Allie heard her mother complain, "If only he didn't look like all the men in the business section of *Time*."

Prudence conceded that Pavel had erred, had made foolish investments, had gambled with other people's money. Sometimes under the family pressures—which now consisted of her mother and John X. Lovell—she began to wonder if Pavel had married her for the family money rather than for herself.

What hurt her equally was that Pavel refused to see her when she went to the prison on visiting days. He cut himself off from her and Allie entirely.

Her depression worsened, and she spent three months at a private sanitarium. There she came to face the fact that she must make a choice.

She knew what a tragedy and public humiliation had done to Pavel, who had been revered by his friends. Dear Pavel, who felt he'd let everyone down, including his wife and child . . . Prison for a man of his nature was the final, crushing indignity. How could he ever return to the Towles, pretending all was as before.

A divorce was inevitable.

"You must arrange to provide him with funds for the rest of his life," Prudence told the family lawyers. "I cannot bear to think of him in need." She thought that, once free, he might leave the country for Paris. He loved France; he felt comfortable there.

While she was waiting out the guilt-ridden six weeks in Reno, John X. Lovell telephoned her.

Pavel was dead. In his cell. By his own hand.

As a model and trusted prisoner, it hadn't been difficult for him to obtain a knife to slit his veins.

He left the beginning of a letter to Allie, marked *"Pour prendre congé."*

Grandmama Towle and Nana gave the news to Allie. They showed her the letter and explained that the words meant "To take leave."

Prudence returned briefly to the sanitarium to avoid her daughter's hateful glances and to come to terms with this fresh trauma.

Six months later she married John X. Lovell, to the delight of her mother, her friends and to her own self-deception.

Allie sobbed at the wedding, which took place in Grandmama's house. Nana said it was because her dog Mary Twinkletoes, having had heart failure, was put down by the veterinarian.

But Allie cried, and cried, and the family doctor said such an endless display of grief was neurotic, after all; it was only an old poodle, and there were other dogs to be adopted. But Allie refused a substitute.

"Let her mourn," the psychiatrist suggested to Prudence.

Prudence wasn't sure *he* understood what the child was mourning for.

The house in Greenwich had eight bedrooms, ample for the large family John X. hoped for. But each time Prudence was ready to deliver, it was the emergency room that received her, not the maternity wing.

Allegra was therefore the sole heir to Grandmama Towle.

Allie was registered at Greenwich Academy, where she was miserable. By the time she was twelve, she was dropped by the school and accepted at Locust Ryse in Stamford, which was also academically first-rate.

She was growing into a young woman—prematurely perhaps, but the hormones were feeding the right signals to her body. Her face suddenly took on a pensive beauty and a childish touch of wickedness that could reduce a man to a bewildered state.

Prudence, remembering herself at Allie's age, could recognize a dangerous situation when she saw it. It was evident to her that her young daughter was mastering the art of seduction—on her riding master, her male tutor and any other attractive men who came within her range—especially older men.

II: BONNIE AND CRISTINA

After the debacle of Pearl Harbor, the universal hysteria, the draft, the three-shift war production, the food stamps, the gas rationing, the blackouts and the air raid wardens, a seventeen-year-old girl working the night shift in a California airplane plant discovered she had a voice. Whenever the brass called for amateur performers during lunch and supper breaks for bond rallies she raised her hand. Her name was Betty Oblanski, and she was a skinny, undernourished kid with long arms and legs, a gawky stance, a ragmop of tousled black hair and dark, sorrowful eyes. But she had bellows in her chest cavity and remarkable vocal chords.

Once in a while, someone in the crowd exclaimed, "My God, another Judy Garland!" or "An American Edith Piaf. The little sparrow."

A second-rate Hollywood producer, soliciting talent for an entertainment unit overseas, hired her. She was no Betty Grable or Rita Hayworth, but that little waif-like creature had a magnetic stage presence. She was a natural.

The star who emerged as Bonnie Rob Roy, with no past but a promising future, became the darling of millions of GIs overseas.

Success elated and terrified her. Would it last? Would she wake up to find it had all been snatched away? She worked obsessively, accepting too many offers with too little time in between for rest. She became a woman of uncontrollable urges.

During a weak moment, when she craved the security she'd never enjoyed in her orphaned childhood, she decided a young army sergeant named Stephen Terhune was her one true love. He wasn't as rich as the other men who courted her, but he was handsome in a rough, virile way—his body was a powerhouse. And he was someone she could confide in, lean on, depend on. She sensed this man could give her life structure and significance.

They were married and spent their honeymoon at a nightclub on Manhattan's West Fifty-second Street, where Bonnie was a smash.

Stephen had been a shy lover, but he was a satisfying husband. Bonnie, who'd never sampled more of love than a one-night stand, didn't know how to accept his outpouring of affection, consideration and respect. Their passionate nights were more to her understanding.

Manhattan clubs saw her through her pregnancy. She would emerge from the wings, with a sailor's walk to accommodate her bulging abdomen, so obviously pregnant that her audience feared they might have to serve as midwife. The idea of a pregnant entertainer was, after the initial shock, entertaining and original, even titillating.

Bonnie had a difficult birth and post partum depression. She celebrated her baby and her blues in a small adobe ranch house in Palm Springs. The nurse on duty attended her and Cristina while Stephen traveled throughout California, searching for building sites for his new construction company.

They both prospered, but not together. Bonnie—restored to quasi-health, with only her trembling, her flushes, her insomnia betraying her lack of emotional stability—went on the road with a sharp new manager. Cristina and a nurse accompanied her. The manager dominated her, and—it was rumored—sometimes slapped her around. Her earnings were impressive, but she was always in debt. Steve bailed her out when he could, but his business was still in its infancy.

"You're my security blanket," she told him on those

rare occasions when, after their divorce, they met on one of her tours so that he could visit the child. "I know you'll always be there when I need you."

He was reassured that she would do nothing drastic, that she would look lovingly after Cristina. He excused her behavior with a certain rationale: given her background—her early environment, the sudden shift from a nobody to a star—how could she act any differently? He tried to be understanding.

After her transcontinental American tour and her triumphs in England, France and Australia, Bonnie returned to the States and bought a Spanish stucco-and-tile mansion in Beverly Hills. She was scheduled to appear in a spoof of the old MGM musicals. When Stephen came to visit Cris he caught Bonnie and her third husband—a beautiful English boy—in a wild argument, complete with cups, ashtrays and vases used as ammunition.

Instituting a custody case was a last resort, a move he took with reluctance only after Bonnie refused to give up Cris. The case dragged out for two years, but finally, on Cris's fourteenth birthday, it was settled.

Henceforth Stephen would provide a home for Cristina during the school year, and she would spend her vacations with Bonnie. And henceforth, though Stephen didn't foresee it, Bonnie would use Cris as a weapon, a shield, an ace-in-the-hole. She knew that as long as Cris loved her and disliked Stephen, she wielded power over him. Above all else, he wanted Cris to be happy.

Stephen was careful to be generous with the visiting privileges in order to placate his ex-wife. And he reimbursed photographers, designers, physicians, restaurants and hotels. Bonnie, always extravagant, was indebted to them all.

Stephen soon heard that she was fortifying herself with drugs to keep up the unflagging, draining pace. He had invested a deep, unswerving love in his ties to Bonnie, and although they were now apart, he couldn't bear to see her destroy body and soul. He questioned young Cris about the drugs, but his daughter remained silent, whether out of ignorance or loyalty he didn't know.

From the time she was a small girl, Cris adored being alone with Mama. When Mama was home and relaxed she was like a big kid. They had such fun together, cooking if they were living in an apartment, going to a zoo if they were in cities, sharing stories about the famous people Mama knew and about her boyfriends.

The men who surrounded Bonnie Rob Roy were mostly musicians and composers who were younger than she. Gentle, sensitive and artistic, they got along beautifully with Cris. They pretended she was their child, and their devotion to her was touching. They took her to parks and museums, and Cris developed an easy, loving relationship with them.

As she grew older nobody knew the strange, secret life of Cristina Terhune. A miserable, fat, ungainly adolescent, Cris was always in Mama's entourage and in her shadow—even after she was introduced to sex by Bonnie's hectic, crazy life style when she was thirteen years old.

At the time she and Mama were living in Malibu with two of Mama's boyfriends. Mama planned to get rid of them when she flew East, but meanwhile it suited her to keep them as house guests. Cris knew that Mama never felt comfortable with her boyfriends for long. Somehow she would manage to cause fights, desertions, reconciliations and final breaks, and Cris had grown accustomed to the tears, slammed doors and even the threats of slashed wrists.

Mama was enjoying a *ménage à trois* with the two young men, whom she called A and B. They were beautiful beach boys with magnificent muscles, big shoulders and small asses. When Mama flew to San Francisco for a two-week concert tour, she left Cris in their care. She thought Cris would be safe with them; as far as she knew, they were interested only in wind and surf, gourmet cooking and interior decorating.

Mama was wrong.

A and B suspected that she planned to drop them, and they decided to take their anger out on Cris. They made the preparations dramatic. They opened all the windows to the California night and placed a shag rug outside on the sun deck. Then they both undressed Cris and stripped themselves of their shorts.

A, who was slightly shorter and narrower than B, flipped Cris over on her stomach and began to kiss her along her spine, while B took tiny bites out of her flesh. Suddenly the two men were entangled—she couldn't figure out how it happened. She was numb and a little uneasy; she hadn't thought sex would be like this, although she wasn't sure what she'd anticipated. She was thirteen, and men were somebody she trusted . . . people who attended her mother . . .

B was flipping his cock back and forth across her mouth. "It's divine," he said. She closed her lips tight, scared. His cock didn't start growing until A gave it a kiss—a long one. Cris was trembling, but not because of the way they were together. She had a sense that something terrible was about to happen to her. In spite of the cool air and the gentle wind from the shore, she felt herself grow sweaty from fright. Her face was buried in the rug and she twisted and groaned. But A had grabbed her and was chanting, "Open the door, Crissie," and he was handling her roughly, prying her backside apart and forcing himself inside her. She felt something tearing her skin and screamed. B said, "Use some Vaseline, old boy," which A did, first greasing himself and then shoving. She tightened herself, but his thrust was deeper and she knew she would faint; nothing could hurt like this, *nothing,* but she couldn't even moan because B had yanked her head back . . .

She wanted to die, and she passed out.

Cris didn't dare tell Mama about it when she came back from her tour. But for a long time afterward she was terrified of sex. Of men. Of her mother . . .

Sometimes the pressures of Mama's career were so great that she would tell Cris, "Don't ever be an entertainer. You'll be nothing but a slave to your fans.

They come and listen to you and get a charge. Then they drop you. And there's nobody around in the long, dark hours of the night . . . What do you plan to be, Cris darling?"

Cris said solemnly, "A nurse. I'm going to be a nurse."

Mama looked startled. "Every young girl wants to be a nurse. You'll change in a few years."

Cris hadn't changed. Cris at eighteen wanted passionately to take care of Mama when she was confused and sick from the drugs she was hooked on, to fend off her creditors, to cut the legal cords with her lawyers, agents and other leeches. She hated Stephen —whom she never called "Father"—for having taken her away from Mama. And now he wanted to keep Cris from protecting her—her poor, darling, unhappy Mama.

CHAPTER IV

The sixties were a time of skyrocketing affluence. The stock market was ascending. There was a fresh crop of successful young men, products of the new technology. Booming companies emerged with technical concepts that were a puzzle to the rich elderly widows whose bulging portfolios were zealously guarded by their long-time investment counselors.

Rebellion against the Establishment started in the high schools. Long, uncombed hair; dirty jeans; unwashed feet—a glorious revolt against nightly baths and electric toothbrushes . . . Young people hitchhiked to Berkeley, they abandoned Scarsdale for hippie communes. Nudity was in. Sex was in.

Not at Locust Ryse, of course, where the girls were protected from the rumbling of world events. But still, there was a subtle reminder of the times: The headmistress had her token black scholarship student.

When the girl dropped out after her second year, the headmistress was left with only Marianna to advertise the tolerance and generosity of Locust Ryse, conveniently forgetting that Stephen Terhune was underwriting Marianna's tuition.

The waves of rebellion—the violent marches, the passive sit-ins, the parades—swept through the campuses across the country. But Locust Ryse remained encapsulated, virginal.

Allegra, Cris and Marianna conformed, though their rebellion was also stirring. These girls, bred of the sixties yet curiously untouched by the cataclysmic events of those years, would in their time race into the seventies. And some would crash along the way.

"When I was a child, I dressed like a child," Allegra chanted. "Now that I am a woman, I shall, by God dress like a woman . . ."

Out went the bras, not much larger than the "training" bras she'd made her mother buy when she first attended Locust Ryse. Now, three months out of school, Allie wasn't burning her bras—a rather superfluous gesture, she thought—but tossing them into the waste basket.

"When the tits are unfettered," she told Marianna in her insouciant fashion, "there's a sexy feel to them. I've given lots of thought to my boobs—what there is of them. I've been fantasizing what it'd be like to have round, full tits—like yours, for instance."

"I hate mine," Marianna said.

"Well, I may use them as a model. Hormone shots or silicone implants—I've got to find out which are the best."

Allie was stepping into a new body stocking she'd just bought at Bendel's. She'd returned from a Manhattan shopping trip with boxes full of tight poor-boy sweaters, mini skirts and wide leather belts with military buckles. Her thick hair was combed back over her forehead, teased high, shoulder-length ends turned under. She wore a pale lipstick that Marianna found ghastly, but it was an improvement on the no-lipstick look required at Locust Ryse.

Allegra had invited Marianna for lunch at her grandmother Towle's on the Friday before Labor Day. She'd just spent a week in Newport, where her grandmother shared a cottage with a distant member of the Boston branch of the family. Allie had played tennis, danced, swum and sunned at Bailey's Beach and come back Indian-brown, slimmer than before, and bursting with sexual energy.

Mrs. Merritt-Jones had promised Allie's mother to use her influence at this late date to persuade Sarah Lawrence to accept Allie in spite of her inferior college boards. Sarah Lawrence, the headmistress said, was an ideal school for a free soul.

Allie had refused to consider it.

In desperation, her search fueled by another gen-

erous check from John X. Lovell for the school gym,
Mrs. Merritt-Jones prevailed upon Shaunton, a small
upstate college similar to Bard, to accept her.

Under considerable pressure, Allegra agreed to try
it. Meanwhile she had a fortnight to equip herself
for her new scholastic venture. She and Marianna went
to Best's, where their classmate, Hannah Byrd—the
sanctimonious former head of the Student Council—
was working as a college counselor, helping students
coordinate their wardrobes.

Hannah, whose dream was to be a woman preacher,
greeted them soberly, ready to equip them as well for
their spiritual destinies.

"Just for me," Allegra said brightly, pushing her
dark glasses onto her head. "Mari's skipping college.
She's got the most fabulous job in New York—"

Hannah was properly impressed. "I always knew
Marianna would be somebody. She's so smart. What
kind of work, Mari?"

Marianna looked bewildered.

"Tell her, Mari. Don't be shy." Allegra's eyes were
brimming with mischief.

Marianna caught up with her. "Why don't *you* tell
Hannah? Go ahead, Allie."

A pause. "Well—it's still a secret, but she's going to
be secretary to Bonnie Rob Roy."

"You mean the singer? Cris's mother?"

"That's the one."

"I hope you can help her." Hannah's bony face was
pious with concern. "I read she was busted in Mexico
City."

"Whatever for?"

"Drugs."

"Poor Cris. Why didn't she get in touch with
us?" Allegra went off on another angle. "I wonder if she
called her father. Should we check?"

"Mr. Terhune took Rose Eileen on a trip to Greece,"
Marianna answered. "They won't be back until next
week."

Hannah said, "It must be tough for Cris to put
up with her mother. I wonder if she has enough
faith—"

"She's a gutsy kid." Allegra was nonchalant. "She's handled her mother for years. Nothing fazes her—"

"And now with Mari present, she and Cris can work on her mother. And if they need help, I'd be glad to step in," Hannah offered.

While they were talking Hannah showed them the clothes that would be right for an elite college. Jeans were an essential, she pointed out.

"Great," Allie said. "I've got just the ass for them." Hannah colored.

Allie purchased flannel slacks, boots for winter, a parka lined with fleece, sweaters, shirts, skirts that looked like kilts, a new raincoat and penny loafers.

All the while she was helping them, Hannah was recalling the glorious ending to their Locust Ryse days. "You didn't come to the father-daughter baseball game," she chided Allie and Marianna. "How come?"

"We're both girls without fathers," Allie said innocently.

"But I thought John X. Lovell—"

"He's the stud who services my mother."

"Allie, you're incorrigible! I think Mrs. Merritt-Jones was shocked at the Senior Breakfast—"

"I don't know why." Allegra held up a beige sweater to gauge its size. "I brought her loads of flowers from my mother's garden. I went to the Trustees' Dinner for the senior class and their teachers, even though my mother thinks the Yacht Club food is atrocious. I went to Willing Afternoon and Class Day. I listened to the Class Prophecy—crap, if you ask me—"

"Why? Because they said you'd become a woman of influence and power through your husband?"

"Nope. Because they were talking through their collective hats. What do they know about the kind of man I'm likely to marry?"

"He'll either be a movie star or a president," Hannah said. "What do you think, Mari?"

"Allie will be what she wants to be," Marianna said. "But I think she hasn't decided yet."

I have, Allegra reflected. *If only I can make it* come true.

In spite of Allegra's loyal but phony buildup, Marianna had no job offer in Manhattan. With no prospect of any kind of work other than helping out in the Piano Store, she had enrolled in an accelerated six-week course at a Stamford secretarial school. She was now a good typist, but her shorthand bothered her.

Marianna had turned down a job as secretary to Evalina's rapidly growing music school, knowing she would turn into a drudge for both Evalina and her mother. But she had decided to help Allie's mother, who was momentarily without a secretary. Twice a week during the past month, Marianna had reported in the morning to the Lovell house.

When she arrived at nine o'clock, Mrs. Lovell was usually on the quilted chintz chaise in her sitting room, wrapped in a tailored striped silk dressing gown, while two or three Kerry Blue puppies wandered around playfully nipping each other. To Marianna, Prudence Lovell was in manner and appearance the essence of a great lady. She was fashionably thin and gracious, yet like Allegra she had a polite but distant manner. Although Marianna felt like a maid in the big Tudor house, she loved the mornings spent there, and she absorbed the atmosphere and enviable life style like blotting paper.

Mrs. Lovell made no small talk and was efficient in going through her mail—invitations for dinner; tickets for balls, musicals and benefits; requests asking her to sit on boards or become a patroness. Sometimes, however, she would talk to Marianna about Allie.

"I hope she likes the school she'll be attending," she said.

"I'm sure she will."

"One can never be sure with Allie." As Mrs. Lovell looked at her Marianna saw a shadow in the beautiful thick-lashed eyes, so much like her daughter's. "I wish I had as much influence on her as Mrs. Terhune seems to have."

Marianna thought that it was probably vexing for

Mrs. Lovell to feel Allegra preferred Rose Eileen to her, except everybody did agree that Rose Eileen exuded warmth and sunny affection. Once the Terhunes returned from their vacation in Greece, Marianna knew, Rose Eileen would mention to Stephen that she was available for part-time typing. Rose Eileen loved helping her young friends.

Meanwhile Marianna was counting the days until she could go out on her own. The daily abrasions of family life were wearing her down.

When she'd asked her mother if her family could manage college the response had been, "No way." Marianna's high marks and Mrs. Merritt-Jones's reluctant approval had brought two partial college scholarships. But they weren't enough, and freshmen weren't encouraged to take on jobs, which were considered too much of a strain during the period of adjustment.

Liebschen had said brusquely that the Dietrichs could not help her with books, clothes and all the extras. Although Marianna's four-year record at Locust Ryse was the best in her class, her mother wasn't impressed.

"It's not that you're so smart, but that the others are dumb," she said.

Marianna felt the sting of Liebschen's words. She wanted to scream, to tell her mother off: "What do you know? You're stuck in *True Confessions*. You're always saying, 'Between him and I.' And you pretend to play the piano when all you can do is bang a few chords."

Mrs. Merritt-Jones had suggested that Marianna would do well as a teacher—perhaps of retarded children. After all, the girl was so patient. But the truth was apparent: The headmistress lumped Marianna with misfits.

When Mrs. Merritt-Jones heard that Marianna had turned down her college acceptances and would attend night school, either at the City College of New York or the local community college, she was horrified. No Locust Ryse girl had ever attended those —institutions.

"Perhaps you should speak to Mr. Terhune," the headmistress had advised. "He was generous about giving you four years at Locust Ryse."

"I'm going to earn my way," Marianna said. This conversation had taken place after Mrs. Merritt-Jones had discovered her going through her address book. It was the only civilized talk the two had ever had. Marianna knew it was not kindness on the headmistress's part, but simply professional pride. The prospect of a Locust Ryse graduate—any Locust Ryse graduate—tossed among commoners offended her.

The Saturday following Labor Day turned into an unexpectedly delightful reunion for the girls.

Marianna was at Evalina Novak's studio, doing a cursory housecleaning job, when the telephone rang. Cris's voice, chirping with pleasure, greeted her.

"Hi, Mari, how are you?"

"Good. When did you get back?"

"Yesterday. But I stayed in town with Mama. I just came up to the country. Guess who's with me? Guess—" Marianna heard a conspiratorial note in Cris's question.

"You give up? Well, it's Vince! Remember Vince?" A pause. "The lead guitarist of the Generation Dropouts!"

Of course Marianna remembered him—that lean, hungry-looking fellow with cadaverous cheekbones and a scruffy beard in contrast to his innocent blue eyes. He looked *used,* she recalled.

"Let's all get together this afternoon," Cris suggested. "Where shall we meet? . . . Wait a minute—" She was evidently listening to Vince. "He's keen on seeing the Piano Store. He wants some of those old 78 records—"

"Is Stephen home?" Marianna asked.

"He and Rose Eileen are landing this afternoon."

"Have you talked to Allie?"

"Yes, she'll join us. Isn't it great, Mari? We'll be together again."

Marianna asked, "How did you enjoy Mexico City?"

"It was fab, especially after Vince and his guys stopped by on their way home—"

Evalina Novak waddled in just as Marianna hung up, and Marianna told her about Cris's call.

"Why don't you all come here tonight? I know the Generation Dropouts' records. This Vince is a bona fide musician."

Marianna was delighted and made the arrangements. They would have supper in the studio, with its floor-to-ceiling windows open to the night garden. Evalina gave her money to shop for the meal—cold cuts, salads, pastries, fruits, cheese and wine. Marianna found her mood lightened today. This was what life could be if she was on her own: music, friends, little suppers. The amenities of the good life.

After Evalina had dismissed her Saturday morning pupils, she came into the kitchen where Marianna was unloading the bundles from the delicatessen. Marianna, in brown shorts and a tailored blouse, her straight, fine hair combed off her face and clamped with a rubber band, her fair skin glowing with a post-summer shine, looked unusually happy.

"Is Vince coming with his boys?" Evalina asked, sampling a tiny ricotta cheese Danish, her tongue searching out the crumbs around her thick lips.

"Cris didn't say. Oh, I'm dying to see her!"

Marianna returned to the Piano Store when Cris arrived with her guest. Vince looked the same as he had at the airport. But Marianna could scarcely believe the change in her friend.

Cris's jeans and her white tee shirt outlined a new slender figure. Her dark hair was clipped short, with wings jutting out on her cheeks. Her face was thin too, so the olive eyes looked enormous.

"Cris, you look wonderful. You've lost so much weight. How'd you do it?"

When she smiled, Cris's nose wrinkled. "I didn't do it, Mari. Mexico did. With a little help from the *turista*."

"Are you okay now?"

"Just great. Mari, Vince wants to buy some old records—" Cris sat down in one of the corner easy chairs, legs tucked under her, and watched contentedly as Marianna and Vince went through Evalina's collection.

Vince picked up some Bach organ music: the Fugue in G Minor and the Passacaglia and Fugue in C Minor, recorded by E. Power Biggs at Harvard's Memorial Church. He told Marianna he collected Bach, and she showed him more of the collection of 78s.

Marianna felt the pleasure of sharing with him what was hers by proxy. When he mentioned casually that he had attended Juilliard, she was all enthusiasm. "Evalina Novak—she owns this place—do you know of her work?"

" 'Fraid not."

"She studied at Juilliard too."

Marianna was truly enjoying herself. Her only worry was that either her mother or sister would show up in the store. She liked the way Vince was listening to her, sitting on the floor in a Lotus position, his hands on his knees, his eyes closed. She felt herself drawn to him, which disturbed her. She knew she couldn't handle it.

When it came to sex she was eager but inexperienced. The boys in her public school days had generally ignored her. She felt herself one of the commonplace girls they found uninteresting. It never occurred to her to flirt in standard pre-adolescent manner or to start a conversation with a boy, even if he looked as though he might welcome it. Her mother's attitude toward sex had put a chill on her initiative. The curiosity, the burning in her loins, the hunger in her heart all confused and frightened her, but she could hardly turn them off.

During the Locust Ryse years, Marc Finley was the focus of her dreams. She had developed a crush on him that very first day they met on the school grounds, but his interest in her never went beyond a scholarly attention to her reading lists and advice on her "adjustment to life." All the girls were captivated by him; they talked about him, speculating about his love life. The music teacher was a eunuch, they decided. But not Mr. Finley. He came from one of the rich old Connecticut families that they read about in the social columns of the New Canaan papers.

Allegra had attended several coming out parties at which he was the debutante's escort. "Is he charming? Is he a good dancer? Do the girls go nuts for him?" Marianna had asked.

"I don't like him," Allegra had said, her voice unusually cold. She never gave a reason and Marianna didn't pry. . . .

In her fantasies she saw herself in white tulle, dancing at the Plaza with Marc Finley, dressed in tails and so handsome . . . Yet when a busload of boys arrived from Choate for a dance or a Glee Club concert, she was hesitant, staying in the background, keeping busy behind the punch bowl. She hated herself for her shyness, standing stiff, waiting for a boy to start a conversation before she allowed her lips to curve into a smile. They knew enough to stay away from her. She was a drip.

Allegra always knew how to act with the boys, perhaps because she didn't give a damn what they thought. She smiled and flirted and danced, her head always cuddled into a male chest, looking up into the male eyes, which wasn't always easy because she was so tall. But the play was effective and the boys responded. Mari wondered how long it was since Allie had begun to sleep around.

She dreamed of love and sex, and being innocent and idealistic she lumped the two together. Her friends, she felt, were infinitely more worldly than she. At least that was the impression she got from their talk during their secret afternoon sessions.

Allie, Cris and Marianna would sprawl on the hearth rug in Allie's room in her grandmother's house, postponing for as long as possible the tedious hours of homework. Always, after they had gossiped about the headmistress, about Miss Caswell, about despicable Hannah Byrd, teacher's pet and spy, they would turn to sex. Marianna admired Cristina's frank outlook acquired at the knee of a mother who took lovers as easily as happy pills. She had no idea what experience Cris might have enjoyed—Cris seldom contributed anything personal to the discussions—but she thought about it a good deal, especially during their sophomore year when Cris accompanied Bonnie Rob Roy to London and came back from spring vacation wearing mod clothes, carrying on about the Beatles, whom she'd met through her mother's manager.

Allegra was the object of Marianna's total, worshipful admiration. Allie had a sophisticated outlook on sex; she said airily that it was one of the necessities of life, to make a girl feel feminine and complete. From their sophomore year on, Allie often went to Harvard and Yale on weekends, dating sons of her family's friends, and she usually returned with fascinating stories about her free-wheeling, free-falling dates. Allie had tried pot, but Cris outdid her. At a discotheque in London she'd sniffed cocaine once, and once had been enough.

Allie would also talk about politics—the fury about the escalating war in Vietnam and the underground activities at Berkeley. Although she was quick to snub the political activities at Harvard, she managed to sample a kind of life style that was barred to the Locust Ryse girls. "We're surrounded by a moat," Allie announced. "Mrs. Merritt-Jones lives in an old world and she won't let us cross the bridge into a new one."

When Allie complained of their constricted life, what could Marianna say? She was unlike Allegra and Cristina and equally unlike the rest of their class. She didn't belong. She didn't know how to find her cues. She felt like putty, waiting to be molded into shape. . . .

Yet here was Vince, leader of the Generation Dropouts, showing an interest in her.

While Marianna was arranging for the buffet, Evalina and Vince were enjoying their musical shop talk. How lovely it was, Marianna thought, that they'd hit it off. Evalina sat on the piano bench, her compact figure stuffed into brilliant green silk pajamas, her solid neck hung with glittering gold chains and semi-precious stones. Vince didn't seem to mind that she was old enough to be his mother. They had Juilliard in common as well as an admiration for André Segovia, the classic guitarist, and an obsession for Bach. Marianna found it odd—and intriguing—that the leader of a rock group should have such a knowledge and love of classical music.

Before the others were scheduled to arrive, Marianna went home, showered and dressed. The sleeveless white blouse, the flower-sprigged mini-skirt and the flat black slippers looked fresh and pretty. She combed her hair off her forehead, pinned it in a topknot and foraged in Darlis's makeup bag for a pale pink lipstick. Although she never used perfume, she looked through the small bottles on her sister's dresser and found a flask of expensive Jungle Gardenia, which she knew was her mother's favorite. It was a bold, inviting fragrance, and she sprayed it on liberally.

Nothing could spoil this evening. This was her party, these were her friends and this fabulous rock group leader was here because he wanted to see *her*. Cris had told her so. By the time she returned to Evalina's, her face was flushed.

"Mari, you look *super*," said Cris, who had gone back to her house briefly and returned with a hamper of white wine. Allegra was coming in now, accompanied by a tall, lanky young fellow with shoulder-length hair who hid his eyes behind wrap-around aviator dark glasses. Like Vince, he was wearing patched jeans, a tee shirt and thick-soled, clumsy work-shoes. Allie was in her favorite pencil-thin black slacks and tight white poor-boy sweater.

Marianna recognized with discomfort that Allie's date was Tommy Holmes. It was during a wild party at Tommy's house in April that Marianna suspected Allie had got herself pregnant. If Tommy was the culprit, she thought wryly, he wasn't welcome here, and it was tactless of Allie to bring him . . . unless she was involved with him again.

The night of the party Tommy had taken LSD and run around naked and had to be driven to the emergency room at Stamford Hospital. Marianna prayed that Tommy had brought no acid with him tonight.

Allegra and Tommy sat on the sofa while Evalina, like a high priestess in her ladderback chair, had Vince at her feet. Cris and Marianna were on either side of him. The soft music coming from the stereo was by Glen Campbell—"Gentle on My Mind" and "By the Time I Get to Phoenix."

After a while the deejay played a new record by the Generation Dropouts. Cris jumped up excitedly. Pointing to Vince, she said, "And here he is, ladies and gentlemen, *in person*—"

Vince accompanied the record, singing the words he'd written: *"How long and deep the night without you . . ."*

The platters of food were neglected, the wine carafes drained, and then what Marianna had dreaded was happening. Like a magician, Tommy produced a pack of thin, wide white papers and a small envelope of marijuana, and began fashioning the joints. He offered the first one to Vince, who lighted it, inhaled and nodded his approval. Tommy passed the joints to the girls, even to Evalina, who said, "What the hell."

Tommy was now lounging on the floor, with Cris and Allegra supporting him, and they were all smiling. Vince pulled Marianna over to him, and she slumped against his shoulder, feeling his muscles through his shirt. The faint male smell of his body blurred with the sweet scent of the pot. She was floating—a strange, tempting sensation.

To Marianna, who'd always been in rigid self-control, the experience was like the song of a Pied Piper, urging her on, even though it promised danger. She tried to concentrate on the candles in their heavy brass holders, but her eyes were registering double, or triple —it reminded her of rockets on the Fourth of July. "Let go, let *go*," her senses were telling her. . . .

Vince raised her chin and looked at her in the gathering gloom of the studio. "You're a cute kid," he said.

Evalina was moving around the room, opening windows. "We better air the place well," she said.

Vince got to his feet easily and pulled Marianna up with him. "We'll fetch some air, Evalina. How many yards you need?"

Evalina waved him away with an expansive gesture. Vince opened one of the tall windows facing the rear, stepped over the low sill and lifted Marianna over, depositing her on the lawn. She was astonished at his strength; he looked so skinny and washed out.

Vince took her hand and led her into the garden. He was silent, but she was aware of the language of his body. His hand embraced her waist; his shoulder touched hers, and her response was a sudden, un-fettered joy. She was *grateful* for his attention, elated that he'd chosen to walk in the garden with *her*.

Almost hidden among the laurel was a marble bench, and Vince guided Marianna to it. The stone was cold to her bare flesh, unprotected by her short skirt. Vince was looking at her as they huddled to-gether, and she thought his eyes were like a cat's, measuring her. With a careless gesture he pulled the pins from her topknot and allowed her hair to fall over her cheeks. It was newly washed and smelled of Jungle Gardenia.

She wondered if her silence annoyed him, if she should make some gesture. But when she began to speak, he put his fingers to her lips and then sub-stituted his mouth, his tongue exploring until, in a breathless excitement laced with fear, she pulled away.

He said, "I've been thinking about you—since we met at Kennedy. You've kind of stayed in my mind."

"You're kidding." It was an adolescent remark and she regretted it, afraid it would offend him, turn him off. "It was so short. I mean, we didn't talk much—"

"Yeah, but you've got something. You turn me on."

Could she *believe* him? Common sense warned no. He was spoiled. She'd read about the groupies that tagged after rock stars the way camp followers used to tag after soldiers. Groupies were proud to give themselves to these musicians, even if only for a night's encounter. She'd heard Darlis rave about them; Darlis knew every rising star in the rock heaven.

She saw Vince bend down, his hands groping for something nearby. When he pulled it toward them she realized it was an outdoor mat, left here for sunning. He unfolded it, spread it full length and then turned to her again.

"What d'you say, kid?"

She was suddenly tense.

"You want to—don't you?" he said.

Her lips were parted in acquiescence. He explored her mouth, forcing it open again for his tongue, and then her breasts, now cradled in his palms. "I knew they were something. . . ." She felt the night air on her exposed breasts and his mouth again, working like an infant's, sucking the nipples until they were erect. And then, carefully, he eased her down on the mat, damp with the evening dew. She felt her head beyond the mat, digging into the grass, and she smelled the wet soil and greens.

He lowered himself beside her. "You're horny. You want it."

She moistened her lips, puffy from his vigorous embrace. "I don't know."

He ran his hand down her thigh and up again, between her legs. "Don't kid me. You're ready."

The sound of music drifted from the studio—the Fifth Dimension singing "Up, Up and Away"—and he laughed. "How's that for background music?"

Why couldn't she relax, accept, go along with him? Why did she have an urge to squirm away, to run back to the others? Yet a part of her, standing by, watching the two of them on the mat, was reminding her with scorn, "Grow up, Mari. You're nearly eighteen, for God's sake. It's time."

When Vince went at her with his hands, his demanding tongue, his groping body, a curtain came down on her mind and her feelings took over, the fluids in her body responding with abandon. If the preparations were clumsy, she was unaware of it. He pulled down her nylon briefs, then worked on his jeans, opening the buttons, and she felt, with a gulp of astonishment, the power of his cock jutting out in splendid demand. He whispered, "Come on, guide me," and his words brought her up, blushing and shocked and, at the same time, excited, her need growing to meet his.

He said, groping for her, "Don't get scared, I'll take care of you. . . ."

She felt her thighs torn apart, the intrusion, the widening of herself, a second of torture, a flash of searing pain followed by warmth and fullness. His voice was commanding, "Put your legs up around me . . . higher . . ."

As they rocked back and forth he groaned, pulled away and erupted with earthshaking force. And then he lay still, hazy, spent, his body glued to hers by the geyser of his sperm.

Feeling the sticky warmth, jolted rudely from her dreamy state, she heard him curse softly, and she thought, vaguely uncomfortable, vaguely unfinished, *Is this all there is to it?*

Was this how it had happened to Allegra?

Good Lord. She pushed him from her and sat upright. Was *this* how you got caught?

It was two in the morning when the party finally broke up and Allie sped off in the Jaguar with Tommy. Cris and Vince lingered awhile and finally took their leave. Marianna walked them to the station wagon, and Vince clapped her on her shoulder and said, "Good night, honey."

But his manner was different—rather remote, even bored, and she felt a twinge of anxiety. She was acutely sensitive to any change of tone, any sign that might suggest rejection.

She went back into the studio and began to close windows and pile dishes onto a tray.

"Let it go until morning," Evalina said. She rescued a cluster of grapes and popped one after another into her mouth, like coins into a slot machine. "Nice party."

"Yes, it really was." But Marianna's words were perfunctory; she was feeling low about Vince's treatment of her after they came in from the garden.

"Quite a musician, that Vince. I like his songs."

"What's he going to do with those Bach records?"

"Probably translate them into his own form—"

"Do you really think he's good?" She was trying to be casual.

"I think he's better than Bob Dylan—less introspective." Evalina drained a glass of Coke. "I saw a lot of rock groups in Vegas. Anybody with a guitar and a rhyming dictionary can call himself a rock expert. The woods are full of them."

Marianna thought it was an unfair judgment. But she was tired and couldn't wait to get home, to bed, where she could think of Vince, *and* what had happened to her. . . .

Marianna slid into bed, relaxing on the cool sheets. "You turn me on," Vince had said. They were beautiful words to a girl who didn't think she'd ever turn a man on. Beautiful. She hugged herself, and then hugged her pillow. He was leaving this morning, but she would hear from him. *Please, God,* she prayed. *Let him call me.* She'd never wanted anything so much since the scholarship at Locust Ryse. This couldn't be the beginning and so abruptly the end. She didn't care what Cris said about groupies. Vince was different.

She *would* see him again.

Their reunion took place sooner than she anticipated. Cris called at noon and said Vince had decided to take an evening train into New York. She asked Marianna to come over for a swim and supper at the pool, and Marianna couldn't have been happier.

Over French toast and maple syrup, she answered her mother's questions about the party the previous night. For once, Darlis was impressed. "You mean *Vince?*"

When Marianna nodded, Darlis asked, "You mean, he was *here*—at Evalina's? And you didn't tip me off?"

"You were out." Marianna was immensely pleased with herself.

"But he's still here. . . ."

"At the Terhunes'."

"Can I meet him? Can I get his autograph?"

"I'll ask him."

"You gonna see him again? Look, Mari, take me along. I'm dying to meet him. I've got one of his albums and everything—"

"It's not my party."

"Yeah, but if you ask Cris, she won't mind. She knows me."

When Marianna still hesitated, Darlis put on the pressure, her small girl's voice rising to a whine. "You're mean, keeping him to yourself. Mama, make her take me—"

Liebschen was fighting the sluggish effects of a sleeping pill with a brew of bitter black coffee. She was in no mood to act as conciliator to her daughters. It was autumn, and the prospect of winter depressed her. In the village the mistresses of the big houses were getting ready for the fall season, the sojourn to Palm Beach or Palm Springs. For her it would be another winter of coping.

In a way, her life had been more acceptable in Queens, where she was among people no better off than she. To be poor among the rich was exasperating. She couldn't shake off her anger at them, which was tinged with anger at herself. In this country, where opportunity was right around the corner, she had forfeited any hope for a bright future. She had had two losers: Each husband was a crummy loser. What hurt her most was that the women she saw in the village shops weren't prettier or sexier than she, but they were rich.

Marianna had had four years of Locust Ryse, and what did she have to show for it? *She's a loser, too,* Liebschen thought, concentrating her final hope on Darlis. Darlis had her own good looks and, thank heaven, she lacked Marianna's intellectual curiosity. She wanted what any normal young girl should want —a rich, eligible man.

Liebschen's reflections were interrupted by the girls' quarreling. Upset, Darlis had stopped eating. There was a dribble of maple syrup on her chin. Her tanned skin, Liebschen thought, was as brown

as the syrup—unusual for a girl with golden hair
and blue eyes—and now, at fifteen, she was probably
more attractive than she would ever be.

"I don't barge in on your friends," Marianna was
saying, "and you're not going to barge in on mine."

"I don't give a shit about them—that snobbish Allegra—but I want to meet Vince. I've *got* to, that's
all. If—"

"No way."

"If you don't take me I'll come over by myself.
I'll call Cristina."

"If you do—" Marianna got up, approached her
sister and put her hands on Darlis's shoulders, her
face muscles tense. "I'll tell Cris you invited yourself,
and that I don't want you around. Don't you dare
try it, d'you hear?"

Darlis pulled away, jolting the table. The pitcher of
syrup turned over and the liquid dripped down onto
the linoleum.

"Marianna, wipe it up!" her mother screamed.
"What's the matter with you?"

"Nothing's the matter with me. Why don't you ask
what's the matter with *her?*"

"Stop it, do you hear me? *Stop it.*"

"I'll stop. I'm fed up. That's all—" Marianna
marched out of the kitchen—not into her bedroom,
which was a rat's nest of Darlis's belongings, but into
the living room.

Her mother followed her there. "Marianna, I *insist* that you take Darlis with you."

Marianna flushed, but held her tongue. Inwardly
her anger began to steam until it clouded her judgment. "Mom—"

"Don't call me 'Mom.' You know how I hate it!"

Liebschen's words were a diversionary action,
meant to silence Marianna's outburst before it erupted.
Oh, her mother knew how to deal with her.

"Now, Marianna, you listen to me. I don't ask you
often to do something for Darlis. Four years you were
in Locust Ryse—did you invite her there *once?* It's
like you were ashamed of her. Or maybe—" the calculated cut "—maybe you were jealous of her. What-

ever." She paused. "Today, you will take her with you."

Marianna was gasping for breath. She couldn't speak.

"You'll take Darlis to meet your rich friends because you may not have them much longer now that school is over and you'll be going your own way. At least you'll give Darlis a chance to meet them. After that, she'll take over. She's smart. She knows what to do."

"Darlis is a kid—"

"Darlis is over fifteen and she knows more about some things than you'll know at fifty."

Marianna's growing anger exploded into fury. "I *won't*, and that's *that*."

"You'll change your mind, Marianna. Do I have to tell you that you're still dependent on us? That if it weren't for your stepfather you'd be waiting on tables? For four years he's fed and clothed you, while you had a chance to make something of yourself. You owe it to him and to me. Need I remind you that you still live here? You still sleep in our bed. You still eat *our* food—"

"I'm getting out as soon as I can—"

"That's beside the point. Today, your little sister is going with you."

Marianna broke. The tears flowed.

But in the end she took Darlis.

The Terhunes' poolhouse, with its wide open doors, its rattan furniture, its brilliant yellow-and-white striped canopy, made a striking backdrop for the pool. Allegra and an olive-skinned handsome young man were playing in the water while Cris sat on the pool's edge, stunning in a black bikini. Miss Greta, the long-haired shepherd, lay quietly beside her, raising her head occasionally to utter a friendly bark at Allie and the young man as they plunged into the depths. Vince, still in his faded patched jeans and tee shirt, was lying with his eyes closed on a canvas chaise in the shadow of the pool house. Over the stereo speakers Frank Sinatra was singing "Strangers in the Night." Rose Eileen was very big on Sinatra.

Rose Eileen, wearing a Hawaiian print mumu, kissed both Marianna and Darlis when they arrived and suggested that they change into bathing suits for a swim before lunch. Marianna introduced Darlis to Vince, who only nodded courteously. Allie, who was climbing out of the pool, sleek as a baby seal in her one-piece swimsuit, introduced them to her escort, a South American naval ensign she'd met in Newport, where he was assigned to the Naval War College.

As they were changing their clothes, Darlis whispered to Marianna, "That Vince—he's *something*—"

"Leave him alone." Marianna's voice was cold. "He doesn't like to be bothered."

Several housemaids served drinks, sandwiches and fruit. Allie ate beside her ensign, who was obviously much taken with her, though he was watching Darlis covertly. The young girl was sitting at the shallow end of the pool, wearing last year's swimsuit, which was too snug, short in the crotch and low in the bosom, so her plump breasts spilled over.

Marianna, in her practical Locust Ryse swimsuit, felt dowdy until she recalled last night. Although Vince's greeting had been casual, she wouldn't allow herself to be disheartened.

Before the others helped themselves to food she put two chicken sandwiches, grapes and a tall glass of iced coffee on a tray and brought them over to him. He seemed to be asleep. Looking down at him, she felt a melting; fear and hesitation vanished. She knelt beside his chair and said with gentle humor, "Vince, shouldn't you eat—to keep up your strength?"

He opened his eyes and looked at her, his brow gathered in surprise—recognition? And then a slow smile raised his lips. "How're you doing?"

"Just fine," she lied easily. "What about you?"

"Hangin' in there. Who's the kid with you?"

"My younger sister."

"Ah, jail bait." He grinned and rubbed his eyes with the flat of his hand.

She said, "When are you leaving?"

" 'Bout six."

"A tour?"

"Starting tomorrow. Philadelphia. Boston. The works."

She hesitated. The sun had coaxed beads of sweat to his face and there was the smell of him. She would forever after recognize it as a male smell—the sweat and the sweet aroma of pot.

"When will I see you again?" she asked. She regretted her words as soon as she had spoken them. What a stupid remark, practically *begging* him. How could she? Where was her pride?

He shrugged. "Who knows?"

The sickening lurch in her stomach . . . Well, she'd asked for it. Stupid, *stupid*. She turned away, aching, unable to hide the hurt.

Darlis climbed out of the water and shook herself like a puppy shedding drops around her. She pulled off her rubber cap, and her thick, fair hair fell over her shoulders. She trotted off to the dressing room and came back in shorts and a bandana.

Then, exuding youth and a kind of elemental, sexy beauty, she walked barefoot over to Vince on his chaise and said, "Move over." When he failed to comply, she sat on his stomach and lowered her head. She fastened her lips with passion and purpose on his.

CHAPTER V

In her cramped, expensive room at the Barbizon Hotel for Women, Marianna had too much time for brooding. Her window looked out on the rear of dreary, ugly buildings. She kept her shade lowered and stared at the blocked out space.

The images that passed through her mind, one after another without pause, were invariably about Darlis.

Why did Darlis have all the luck?

. . . Darlis, dawdling in the store that Monday . . . waiting? Vince had gone to New York the previous night . . . or had he? Why was she hanging around the store? Marianna wanted to lash out at her but kept her tongue. The little tramp. It was *indecent*. Had she slept with Vince? No chance; Marianna had kept them in her sight all evening at the Terhunes'. Tuesday Darlis went off to school with a bland secretive smile on her irresistible, golden face. The baby whore —Lolita. Marianna was sick with anger, jealousy and pain. And with disillusion. That last night Vince had acted as though nothing had happened between them.

"Be seeing you," he'd said.

Was this the way all men were? Was it possible that what had meant so much to her meant nothing to him? Was it just the pot? She couldn't understand, and the more she puzzled over it, the deeper the pain, the more stinging the rejection.

All week Darlis had stayed in the store after school, reading her movie and television fan magazines, blowing bubble gum—a picture of nubile invitation. Marianna resented her smugness, the smile that played around her lips.

The following Saturday Marianna was at Evalina's studio when Vince drove up to the store in a tan Bentley, elegant even by New Canaan standards. He had come to see Darlis.

Under the long hair, the patched jeans, the leather jacket, the Frye boots and the aviator's glasses was a nice boy from Bayonne, New Jersey, the youngest child in a wholesome middle-class Italian family. He had been taught classical music, particularly opera, but rock had turned out to be a profitable form of rebellion. Although Vince was suffering from overindulgence. Darlis intrigued him—particularly when she said, "Why don't you get lost?" at the Terhune pool, after her bold, tantalizing maneuvers to get him horny. Darlis—baby-fresh with her huge blue eyes that seldom changed expression, her tiny nose, her blond hair, her tight jersey top and hot pants—was the image of the glorious all-American girl, the baton twirler, the junior beauty queen who'd snubbed Vince in his junior high-school days.

He invited her to a rock concert at the White Plains County Center that night, and they slipped away before Marianna returned from Evalina's. Darlis had primed Liebschen not to mention it to her sister.

All during the concert Darlis remained aloof, polite but not carried away. It was very much her finest hour.

Vince managed to elude a demanding mob afterward, taking Darlis with him, intending to take her to the motel for a night of pot and sex. But she reminded him of her one o'clock curfew. In spite of his cajoling she persuaded him to bring her home. When he tried to screw her in the car she said, "If that's what you want, Vince, you've got your pick of groupies."

"What about you, Darlis?"

"You remember my name?" Her voice was a marvel of irony, in startling contrast to the pouting baby face. "How many chicks' names do you remember?"

"You're the first—in a long time." He nuzzled her neck, soft and moist from the drinks and the heat. She had a delicious little-girl smell. "How do you play, baby?"

"For keeps—it's all or nothing."

Had she really cared about him, her tactics might not have worked. Vince saw in her family a reflection of his own; he felt comfortable with the Dietrichs. Darlis's indifference was no put-on. She meant it. The challenge fascinated him. He couldn't wait to lay her.

Their marriage took place in Delaware, since she was under age. Liebschen willingly gave consent, although her father Jan was distressed. Darlis traveled with the Generation Dropouts in Vince's camper, and when she became pregnant, she went to stay with Vince's family in Bayonne. But she suffered a miscarriage and returned to Vince before a groupie could attach herself, like a barnacle, to him.

. . . Darlis, not yet sixteen, married to a success. What did it matter if he didn't bathe often, if he went for days without nourishment except pot and Coca-Cola? He could take "Sheep May Safely Graze" and turn the Bach melody into a rock-and-roll version that earned a gold record. That's what counted.

And all in so short a time. Perhaps that's what stung Marianna the most. For Darlis, her kid sister, it was the best time to be young.

For Marianna, it was the worst.

Now she was out of the family apartment, on her own, waiting to start a job with the Duke. It was strange, she reflected, that Allie had boasted to Hannah Byrd about "Marianna's fabulous new job," and here it had come true—except that it wasn't fabulous.

I hurt, she thought. Why did she hurt? Had Vince meant so much to her? Or was she, *finally,* beginning to grow up? Were these growing-up pains?

She looked around her little room in the hotel for women on their way—all this upward mobility and the beginning of equality for women in jobs, in life, in love—and she felt dispossessed. And lonely.

She couldn't wait for the job to begin.

It was a Monday in early November. In spite of a chill in the sparkling air, the city was at its best. The bright days spilled over into a cornucopia of delights:

first nights on Broadway, film premieres, the Metropolitan Opera, nightclubs, charity balls, dinner and galas. And all the hidden cafés where lovers met or fought or parted. It was a time for dreamers only if they were blessed with a driving talent for achievement.

Marianna was an outsider propelled by a desire to reach the status of the insider. She wanted to *be* part of the creators, the doers, who were eventually, inevitably, rewarded by fame and money. But who *was* she, anyway? she wondered. What talents did she possess? What skills?

The Duke, however, after their hour-long interview, seemed confident of her potential. "You've got a way with people," he said in his flat midwestern accent. "It can be useful in your work. You can go a long way with it."

So on that Monday morning, after waking early and lying in bed until it was nearly time to leave the hotel, Marianna—clad in a gray flannel jumper, a white shirt and a gray, black and white plaid jacket, her handbag straps over her shoulder—was on her way to the first day on the job. She looked fresh and scrubbed, the image of the ideal secretary as programmed by the secretarial school. She stood in the aisle of the Lexington Avenue bus, not minding the crush, bracing herself for . . .?

The Duke's office was a warren of cubbyholes. The partitions were at eye level, thereby keeping the staff members close together and breaking up the space of the once-elegant townhouse on East Forty-eighth Street, just off Fifth Avenue. The reception desk and switchboard were jammed into a foyer.

The Duke's personal habitat occupied the space in the high-ceilinged front room that overlooked the street. The magnificent old English desk was piled high with correspondence, releases, clippings, the *Social Register, Burke's Peerage, Who's Who,* the latest books by best-selling authors and scripts for plays and films that were potential investments for him and his rich friends.

The green leather desk chair had been constructed

to coddle the Duke's sensitive back, which had been injured in a sailing accident during the Cup Races at Newport a decade ago. All the walls of the office were painted flat white over walnut paneling, and they flaunted posters of plays, dance recitals and musical festivals in which his clients had reigned supreme.

The Duke was discriminating in his choice of clients, who included the socialite producer of sophisticated Broadway fare, the director of a state ballet company and the genteel female novelist who wrote blood-and-guts thrillers in her secluded Newport tower. His clients amused him and he served them with a casual air that didn't detract from his performance. Occasionally he took on one of the new millionaires, but of them all he continued an amiable yet businesslike relationship only with Stephen Terhune, whom he admired.

He had a gentleman's reticence about his private life and a Viking's lust for beautiful women. He had his choice of women and he sampled judiciously. Tomorrow's new star was often created as the result of his pleasures the previous night. Yet because of his courtesy, good taste and a real affection for women, the Duke continued his friendships with former mistresses, who had only glowing words for him. "He can make a woman bloom," they all said.

"He's a good boss," Laurie Cunningham told Marianna. "You just have to remember one thing—Cokes in the refrigerator. He doesn't drink, but he's sure partial to Cokes."

Laurie, an administrative assistant, was the first staff member that Marianna met. She was a recent Smith graduate, a Brooks-Brothers-sweater, skirt-and-raincoat type, with brown hair pulled back in a scarf-tied ponytail. She greeted Marianna with obvious pleasure, a smile on her round face. Marianna immediately felt comfortable with her.

Laurie introduced her to Flora, the office manager. A heavy women in a Lane Bryant shift, Flora had been with the Duke longer than the other employees.

"Where's my desk?" Marianna asked her.

"We didn't know where to put you," Flora said,

embarrassed. "Mr. Norstrand said for you to decide where you want to be and ask the super to fix it up for you." Evidently Flora didn't refer to the Duke by his socialite title.

Marianna was slightly upset, feeling as though she was an afterthought—or had been hired merely as a favor to Stephen Terhune. But she set about inspecting the premises in her search for a suitable workplace. She looked everywhere, from the Duke's office to a luxurious bathroom, which was now used primarily as a mail room.

Eventually she found a fair-sized closet that had originally served as a dressing room and was presently a storeroom. With the help of the elderly superintendent she spent the morning clearing out the cubbyhole and making it comfortable.

In the coming weeks Marianna enjoyed her work. While Laurie wrote press releases and Flora kept an eye on the daily routine, Marianna served in a kind of multi-capacity for the Duke. She saw to it that his suits went to the cleaners; she purchased gifts for his favorite hostesses and clients; she attended to the supply of Godiva chocolates which he had favored since he stopped smoking; she heated soup on the hotplate when he was tied up on the phone to the Coast or Europe. She kept a supply of small imported cans from Charles and Maison Glass, delicacies easy to prepare, which would appeal to him when he worked late.

She was, by nature and by school training, organized, and she dedicated herself to bringing order into the chaotic workshop. She cleaned the files, arranging them by names with cross indexes. Working with a list of past and present clients, she went through the Duke's collection of old newspapers and magazines, clipping and pasting. She took charge of the Duke's daybook, avoiding his careless habit of booking two appointments at the same time. She kept his Cokes iced, as well as Dom Perignon for guests; she began to balance his personal checkbook, which she found an interesting exposure to his private world. She penned in reminders for flowers; she kept track of his week-ends, so he wouldn't arrive in Tuxedo Park when he was due in Southampton.

During the Christmas season, when she often worked late, he insisted that she go to 21 or The Palm for dinner and charge the meal to him. But she felt ill at ease in such places and usually had a sandwich and coffee at the office.

One Friday evening in early December Marianna was working at her desk, going through old presentations. The others had left early—there was a radio alert for a snowstorm. It was quiet in the office, even snug with the lights on in early afternoon. Marianna was too busy to feel uncomfortable with the falling temperature. This was the kind of weather that was rough on Allie, who suffered from respiratory infections, and she wondered how her friend was doing—whether she was coming home for the holidays. Allie wasn't a faithful correspondent. From her brief notes, Marianna gathered she hadn't adjusted well to college, and weekend dates with Cornell boys just didn't appeal to her.

When the Duke came into the office she had just plugged in the hotpot. In the small refrigerator were the makings for a ham-and-cheese sandwich.

"Hey, what're you doing here? The office is supposed to be closed."

"There were a few more letters to type. And I proofed the material from the printers."

"That's nice, but really unnecessary. It's blowing up out there—you may not get home."

"I can always bunk here. There's room."

"I never had such a dedicated secretary," he said, visibly pleased.

Marianna saw that the wintry blasts agreed with him, bringing healthy color to his face. He was wearing a suede topcoat and boots, but his head was bare, the pale hair scarcely ruffled by the wind. His face was unlined, though Marianna knew he was nearly fifty. His blue eyes had faint shadows beneath them, the only suggestion of late nights and possible excesses.

"If you're game to brave the weather, we'll go out for dinner." He smiled at her.

She looked startled. She couldn't quite believe it. Was he serious?

"Get your coat," he said. "Do you have boots? The snow's pretty deep."

He helped her into her tan all-weather coat. She tied a wool scarf around her head, fished for her wool gloves in her pockets and slung the straps of her big bag over her shoulder.

The street was deserted, the snow pelting the world with thick cotton flakes. The only taxis in sight were those with Off Duty signs. The Duke took her by the arm to guide her across Madison Avenue and helped her jump over a slushpile. They arrived at the Four Seasons breathless, glowing with the damp cold.

After checking their coats they went up the handsome staircase. Marianna walked sedately, but she wasn't able to hide her delight at the display of simple elegance. Since the hour was early, they were shown to a table in the Pool Room, but Marianna suspected that the Duke would always command a good table whether or not he had a reservation.

Marianna, in a sweater, shirt and plaid skirt, felt distinctly out of place. But the Duke seemed pleased to be with her, and she schooled herself to composure. *Act as though you were Allegra,* she instructed herself.

But Allie was born to it, Allie knew instinctively how to behave, while she felt like an upstart. *Upward mobility,* Marianna thought. *Ha.*

"Will you order for me?" she asked the Duke, putting down the long, elaborate menu.

By the time their *quenelle* arrived, the room was filling up with pre-theater diners. A half dozen men stopped to shake hands with the Duke, and their beautifully dressed women kissed him.

The Duke made the introductions easily, and Marianna met the bodies that went with the names she read about in theatrical and gossip columns. "This could turn a girl's head," she said. "I feel so lucky working for you."

"Will you feel the same a year from now?"

"Oh, I think so."

"I'm frightfully disorganized."

"Once I get the files shaped up, there'll be no problem. Right now our problem is to locate whatever material you happen to be looking for."

He nodded. "Steve said *I* was lucky to have *you*. He's right."

She blushed with pleasure, too shy to meet his gaze.

He asked, "How do you happen to know the Terhunes?"

She explained, elaborating on Stephen's generosity.

"He's a great guy," the Duke agreed. "He's not the executive type that can be pre-packaged. He's one of the rare birds who made it big after Korea."

Then, relaxed and in an affable mood, he told her about his first meeting with Rose Eileen and Cristina five years ago.

"They were living in Newton, just outside of Boston, and Steve had just bought the New Canaan place. He'd hired me to do his PR work, and I suggested that it include his family. You know, they were all new to New York, and I figured that by helping them I could do a little extra for Steve.

"They drove in from Newton and registered at the Plaza. Steve and I met in the lobby, and when the headwaiter at the Edwardian Room showed us to the table I was startled. Here was one of the most beautiful women I'd ever laid eyes on, in a dowdy three-piece knit, with no makeup, and lower middle class written all over her. As for Cris, she was equally hopeless— fat and sullen. Well, I had my job cut out for me.

"Steve introduced me, and over lunch I talked about the pleasures of living in Manhattan—the museums, the art exhibits, the theater. You know, the whole bit. I even added the fashion shows, because those two really needed magic.

"Since Rose Eileen lacked star quality, I knew it'd take time and money to build her up. I refuse in general to help social climbers, and the town's crawling with them. But I liked the idea of playing Pygmalion to those two. Especially since Rose Eileen was clearly intimidated by the prospect of relocating and moving up into so-called Society.

"But you know—she refused my offer. She convinced Steve that she wanted the quiet and tranquility of the country, that jet-set activities would bore her. I've loved her ever since. She's a great woman. She's a good wife for him, although I'm not sure he's aware of it."

"Is his first wife still on the horizon?" Marianna knew it was bold of her to ask, but the Duke's easy manner encouraged her.

"Bonnie Rob Roy? She never lets go. She never loses contact with him. And when she's in trouble with the press she turns to him, and he turns to me. My problem with Bonnie is keeping her out of the papers. Her behavior generates more publicity than any performer needs." He paused, then added, "Damn shame Cris doesn't appreciate her father."

"Isn't it strange for such a strong man to have married two such different women—"

"But they're both clingers. I understand Bonnie was very sweet when they first met. And Rose Eileen is quite dependent, too, although she's a fine woman." He added impulsively, "Sometimes I wonder about Steve. He's at a crisis in his life, and he deserves a helluva lot more than he's getting—and that includes some recognition from Cris."

"Cris does seem more partial to her mother," Marianna said.

"Partial? She *dotes* on her. I understand Bonnie is opening in New York at the Copa on New Year's Eve. Cris plans to move in with her. . . ."

Marianna finished the last mouthful of chocolate mousse. The Duke, amused by her voracious appetite, said it was a pleasure to feed her—most of his dates were on nine hundred calories a day. He told her, with a mischievous look on his face, that he didn't like his women too thin.

Marianna thought he should have been an Olympic skier; she could see him swooping down a steep run, flying in the wind. She'd been too awed at first to evaluate her feelings for him. But now she could understand why women were so attracted to him.

She was grateful that he approved of her, that he liked the way she worked, that he found her dependable.

In a burst of emotion, she made up her mind—she would become indispensable to him.

By the time they had finished coffee and brandy, the storm was in full force, white, thick, diamond clear under the pale street lights. Most vehicles huddled at the curbs in their white blankets, and the first snow plows were trying to make headway against the drifts. It was dramatic, exciting . . . and a little frightening.

"We could wait it out with a couple of drinks," the Duke suggested.

"I don't mind the snow," Marianna said.

"Good. A Norse maiden. Reminds me of my Nebraska childhood."

He got their topcoats from the cloakroom. "Mari, will you be warm enough?" He raised the collar of her coat.

"Yes, plenty."

No cabs were available—not even a limousine for rental.

"Our best bet is to head back to the office," he said, tucking her arm under his. "What do you say?"

"You're right."

It occurred to her that the Barbizon wasn't much farther away than the office. But she stifled a giggle. If he had something in mind . . . No, it couldn't be! It was ridiculous even to think of it. But as they forged ahead through the white tundra, slipping now and then on the icy pavement, he kept her arm linked with his. The snow was blinding; the wind sneaked under her knit gloves, but somehow she felt snug and protected. Even happy. Was it right to feel frivolous and happy because her boss had taken her to dinner?

They leaped over snowbanks, ignored red lights. He said, "In a movie, we'd be throwing snowballs and wrestling in the snow."

She felt suddenly daring. "Want to try it?"

"I'm tempted."

They reached his office and he used the key for the downstairs door. He turned to Marianna, whose face was flushed and glowing with the melted snowflakes."

"Mari, you're a good looking wench."

"Flattery from the boss?"

"Well, I'll expect a raft of perfect letters tomorrow."

"Aren't your letters always perfect? Don't your newspaper pals always comment on your clear, properly spelled, well-typed copy?"

"They sure do. With my words and your spelling, we should go far together."

She knew his manner was light and teasing, probably the result of a fine dinner. But it lifted her spirits anyway. It seemed to her that he was including her in his staff—and he considered his staff his family.

In his private office he helped her off with her coat and then made her sit while he pulled off her boots.

"Can't have you taking cold," he said. "I can't do without you, Mari. You know how many secretaries I went through before Stephen suggested you?" He grinned. "If I tell you, you're apt to want a raise—"

If only she had some clever retort. She'd never been in this kind of situation with an older, sophisticated man, and she was at a loss. Here she was, out of Locust Ryse, nineteen years old and behaving like an amateur woman!

He sat on the deep tufted sofa opposite his desk. She looked around, wondering where she should sit.

"Here, beside me." He was evidently amused by her discomfort. "Isn't the wicked boss supposed to seduce his secretary?"

"Not when she's the best he's ever had."

His laugh was genuine, and he put his arm around her and hugged her. "This is one of the boss's perks. But let me tell you, it's *you*, not the girl on the job, if I'm making myself clear—"

He had the build of a big man, yet he was lean and muscular. She knew it would be easy for a woman to be carried away, to submit to him. She needed only to recall Vince, gaunt and dirty, to appreciate this healthy, vital man.

She felt a stirring of excitement, a puzzling, indefinable yearning in the private places of her body.

"Mari, are you a virgin?"

She blushed and shook her head.

"Your expression suggests it was not a happy event."

"It wasn't." Tears filled her eyes, unexpected tears of humiliation.

He said gently, "Would you let me make love to you, Mari?"

She held her breath. It was too much like a dream —a lonely girl fantasizing a lover she thought she would never have.

"Are you shocked?" he asked.

"Surprised," she admitted. "Flattered. I mean, so many women are taken with you."

She wasn't exaggerating. The handsome, rich women who came to consult him about charity balls and galas didn't hide their interest in him. Marianna was often in his office, taking dictation on one of these projects, when she saw the women's response to him. He was masculine, gentle and courteous, a rare combination these days.

He stood up and switched off the overhead light, leaving the faint ghostly afterglow of the muffled streetlights. He said that as a boy he had often sat by his window on the farm, watching the snow fall, and it had had a magical effect on him. He had wondered what it would be like to take off in the deep, windswept snow and walk into eternity.

"I was a crazy kid for a farm boy," he added.

He gestured for her to join him, and they stood at the window, arm in arm, watching the thick, white plush pile up.

"Wouldn't you love to fall into a snowpile?" she said.

"Or build an igloo. Think it might be fun to make love in an igloo?"

"With Eskimos as voyeurs?"

"Why not? Ice makes a good mirror."

"You're awful," she said, smiling, pleased with him,

pleased with herself. She adored being with him. The way it had come about—accident, impulse?—didn't matter to her. She was here with him, and it was evident even to her—so modest, with so little self-esteem—that he wanted her.

She allowed him to undress her, raising her arms as he took off her heavy sweater and unzipped her skirt. As it fell to her feet she shivered, standing in her bra and panties.

He went to his clothes chest, behind louvred doors, and brought out a cashmere cardigan. He draped it over her bare shoulders, first kissing them lightly.

She was shaking now, but with pleasure. He took other things from an upper shelf—a clean sheet and a beige-and-brown wool blanket, the sort used on hunting trips. He opened the blanket on the sofa and then added the sheet.

"Lie down, Mari," he said and covered her with the blanket. The fragrance of pine scent tickled her nostrils, and she sneezed.

"Still cold?" He was concerned, tucking in the end of the blanket so her feet were protected. Quickly he stripped off his shirt and pants and slid in beside her.

The sofa was not quite wide enough to accommodate both of them, so they were on their sides, facing each other. "We'll just have to keep each other warm," he said, "since those old radiators grow cold after midnight."

This is how it should be, she thought—not the groping of the young boys she'd met at Locust Ryse dances, or Vince, with his bony elbows and knees and his demands that a woman service him. . . .

The Duke had surely had a variety of sexual experiences. Yet his embrace made her feel special. She felt a sense of release as she gave herself freely to his growing passion, responding to her own desire. *Dear God,* she thought, *this is what love is.* This is what Allie had experienced, what Cris had enjoyed. She herself had been the last of the three, but it was beautiful with the Duke.

The blanket held them like a sleeping bag, and yet

she had no fear of the strange male body, warm and pulsating beside her. The strength of his muscles exerted a pressure that she found exciting. His arms were reassuring, and his lips were searching for her breasts, for her lips, quivering underneath him, yet she felt he was waiting for her response before he allowed himself to enjoy her.

She had no fear of what was to come—he made it all seem so natural and inevitable. She was aware of a joy that went beyond the fullness as he found his way between her silken thighs, slowly, carefully, asking softly, "Am I hurting you, Mari?" as though he knew her response.

The creamy fluids of her body were a new experience; her flesh was unaccustomed to the plunging, urgent demands of a male member. She tightened her thigh muscles instinctively, but his hands were soothing, and his lips gave her sensations she'd never known before. As their bodies blended he was not, to her, the man who had so much influence and authority during the daytime; he was a mysterious lover, a man from the north woods, from a world of silence and passion and beauty—yes, like her fantasies.

Her cheeks, her eyelids, were moist with tears.

"What's wrong, little love?" he whispered.

"It's so perfect. I never dreamed I had such feelings. . . . Shouldn't I thank you?"

"The other way around, Mari. It was wonderful for me. Just wonderful."

Later, when they were lying snug and warm, he said, "You know, I've always kept my business and social lives separate . . ."

Instantly she grew wary. Was he trying to tell her something, to warn her not to expect any more from this tryst than a one-night stand? The familiar ache of rejection swept over her, threatening her happiness.

"But then I've never had a woman like you," he added, "and I have a hunch we might both enjoy it."

As he kissed her nipples she knew it was just the beginning.

They fell asleep in each other's arms, and morning

came too soon. She opened her eyes to the streaks of pearl dawn. She heard the sound of water in the bathroom, and she got up, dressed quickly and went to the window to look out on the white magic of the city.

Until now New York had been a lonely place for her. But last night had changed that. She had a feeling that the Duke might take the place of the dream man in her life . . . Marc Finley.

There was a great deal of pre-holiday activity in the office. First the Duke's gifts were to be purchased —mostly jewelry from Tiffany's. Then there was the mailing of Christmas cards to friends and business associates all over the world. Finally freshly minted greenbacks were stuffed into the Duke's engraved envelopes and distributed to doormen, waiters, the chauffeur who drove him and the house servants of friends with whom he often spent weekends.

Marianna did much of the work, tackling with energy and enthusiasm the piles of messages, mail and gifts.

"My little office wife," the Duke said humorously when Marianna brought in to him a batch of beautifully typed letters for his signature.

In the few weeks after the snowstorm, he had taken her to the theater several times, once when a male client was substituting for the original star. After the performance they had had supper with the actor and then, without the Duke's even mentioning it, returned to the office for a night of love. Sometimes she wondered why he never invited her to his apartment, but then she cautioned herself to be thankful for whatever he gave her.

She was aware that he saw other women. But she was happy that he had chosen her, that having known so many beautiful, famous women, he found her satisfying. She suspected that he admired her freshness, her honesty, her simple and direct approach, and she reminded herself not to change if this was what he liked.

Marianna knew better than to make demands on the Duke. She waited for him to come to her, docile as a Japanese woman, attending to his needs. Yet some deep instinct, irrational perhaps, stirred powerful feelings within her. If her love for him was a compulsion, she didn't know how to handle it. Her self-confidence was shaky. She was scared that his interest in her would wane as suddenly as it had blossomed.

Somehow she'd counted on spending Christmas with him, which was totally unrealistic, of course. She was new in his life; he had old ties and obligations and would be flying to the Caribbean for the holidays.

Her mother wanted her to come home for Christmas and had actually telephoned to press the invitation. Darlis and Vince would be there too, for a special reunion.

Marianna had made a curt excuse. "Sorry," she lied. "I'm spending the day with friends."

"With Allegra, I suppose." Her mother didn't sound very disappointed. "Well, you'll probably have a better dinner than *I* can put on the table."

After the Duke left Marianna was still undecided about her Christmas plans. Laurie Cunningham had invited her for dinner with her family in Scarsdale, but Marianna had refused, feeling she might be an intruder.

Each evening she walked up Fifth Avenue. The crowds swirled around her, everyone appearing to have a destination—except herself. At the Barbizon Hotel, the girl next door knocked and asked if she'd join some of the other girls on the floor for a Christmas Eve party, but she had no wish to spend that evening with virtual strangers. Should she grab at anything in order not to be alone, she asked herself? Or should she steel herself and consider it another day that would pass, and then she would somehow go on . . . ?

On the morning of Christmas Eve the telephone rang as she was opening the Duke's mail. It was Allegra. She was on her way home to Greenwich, and she had just heard from Cristina, who'd asked her to come to the city for dinner.

"She'll be calling you," Allie said, adding, "it'll be nice to be together."

Marianna's spirits brightened. She knew Cristina had been busy, still living with Stephen and Rose Eileen but commuting five days a week to the American Academy of Dramatic Art in Manhattan. Marianna had lost contact with her in the past month, and so when her call came through she was grateful to the point of tears.

Not only did Cris invite her for dinner, but she added, "I'm staying with Mama at the Essex House for the next six weeks. She's opening at the Copa, and she's invited you to stay here with us. There's plenty of room."

Marianna said, "It's the best Christmas present I could get." She meant it.

Mrs. Merritt-Jones had been wrong about the kind of college that was suitable for Allegra.

Shaunton was an experimental institution, founded by a group of visionary teachers who encouraged individual thinking. But Allegra had no interest in student rebellion or world revolution; she thought that the Weathermen were all slightly demented and that any group who traveled to Cuba to help harvest sugar cane was too radical.

Allie's form of rebellion at Locust Ryse had been to develop friendships with Marianna and Cris, girls whom she knew Mrs. Merritt-Jones actively disliked. Here at Shaunton, however, she wasn't fortified by the adoration and support of her two best friends. The girls in her dormitory—originally a guest house on the old baronial estate on which the college was located—were not to her liking. They wore their hair short and favored granny spectacles and long skirts that were clumsy and antediluvian. They paired off with young men who let their beards grow and talked endlessly about their LSD trips. Some of the men had been members of the Peace Corps and were over-age for college; others were recent Vietnam veterans, bitter and paranoid.

The social life of the campus, with its political overtones, left Allie indifferent. She withdrew, making excuses that she needed more time for studies. She slept late, often cut class and didn't show up for SDS meetings.

The girls in her dorm soon gave up on her. They ignored her, giving her the kind of silent treatment that West Point cadets gave one of their number when he'd erred, according to their sacred code.

Sometimes, to repay the girls for their treatment of her, Allie flirted with their young men. In response, the girls didn't let her forget that her stepfather, John X. Lovell, was a staunch Nixon supporter.

The truth was that Allie suffered from ambivalence. She scorned the dropouts from comfort. Cold water flats and communes offended her sensibilities. She was a vegetarian only because it suited her; she loved animals and couldn't bear the thought of being a cannibal.

Yet tradition offended her too. But then why the devil, she asked herself, was she reading *Women's Wear Daily* and *Vogue*?

If only her father were alive to advise her . . .

Allegra piled her luggage into the red Jaguar which John X. had lent her to use at school. She added her favorite books, her stereo, records and tapes. The well-made furniture borrowed from the Greenwich house attic and the clothes she'd bought for school she left in her room. Her mother could send for them later.

She slid into the driver's seat, arranging her suede car coat around her thighs. Even in the cold weather she was in better spirits now, before Christmas, than she had been when she had arrived at Shaunton in October.

Allie had already braced herself for an explosion at home but she hoped to enlist her grandmother on her side. She took a final glance at the campus as she drove along the wide road, graced with two-hundred-year-old oaks. It was goodbye to the dorms, the labs, the gym and three months of boredom and misery. *Enough.*

She had no idea what her mother's plans were for the holidays. But one thing was certain: no debut.

Allie had been obstinate about it, and Prudence had finally relented, saying that she hoped college would give Allie a sense of purpose.

There was a spark of mischief in Allie's dark, glowing eyes when she imagined her mother's reaction to her plans—fireworks. . . .

She arrived in Greenwich in the early afternoon and found Prudence in the drawing room, kneeling on a Persian prayer rug, happily arranging gifts around the base of a beautiful Christmas tree. The air was rich with the scent of pine and fir, of applewood glowing in the fireplace and Prudence's costly perfume.

For a moment Allie had the curious feeling she was looking at an old photograph of her mother, not at the person. The difference between Prudence today and yesterday—the time of her marriage to Pavel —was so marked that even Allie found it painful to accept. All the joy that had given Prudence an extraordinary vitality while she shared Pavel's enthusiasm and sense of wonder had withered. Marriage with John X. had brought her back to the sensible world of her contemporaries. She sat on boards, worked with committees, entertained graciously. She was calm, passive —and as far as Allie was concerned, dead.

When Prudence saw Allie she rose with an easy, flowing movement, looking perfect, as always, in her wine-colored slacks and silk blouse. She kissed her daughter lightly on the cheek.

"Are you rather thin?" Prudence surveyed Allie casually, but with a maternal concern. "Are you still a vegetarian?"

"It agrees with me," said Allie, and there was a subtle warning in her tone: *Now, don't you start on me . . .*

"Have you had lunch? I waited—"

While they ate their toasted cheese sandwiches in the bay window seat, Prudence filled Allie in on family news. Grandmama Towle was failing. Prudence spent a good deal of time with her, and fortunately she'd found an excellent pair of nurses whom Grandmama liked.

"Is she growing senile?" Allie asked anxiously.

Three months ago when she'd left for college, the old lady, while infirm, was not incapacitated and still had a lively interest in the world around her.

"Physically, perhaps. But her mind is sharp." With a touch of wry humor, Prudence added, "The Towle women don't go off their rockers. They survive. And endure."

The houseman came in and asked, "About the records and the hi fi, Miss Allie . . . Are those staying here or going to New Canaan?"

Before Allie could answer her mother asked, "You brought your things home?"

"Everything I wanted." Allie braced herself.

"Isn't it excessive to cart your belongings up and back?"

"I'm not *going* back."

Prudence set down her coffee cup carefully. Her thin, sculptured face became a mask. "I'm sure I misunderstand—"

"You don't misunderstand. But I'll make it clearer. I'm not going back to Shaunton."

"Isn't this rather impulsive?"

"Perhaps it sounds impulsive to you. But there's no way I can stay there. *No way.*"

"Need I remind you that you'll have difficulty finding another school?"

"I'm finished with school. I've had all I want. And all I can take."

"What do you plan to do?"

"I don't know."

Prudence said deliberately, "Your father would be very disappointed."

"I don't think you should speak of my father. If anyone would have disappointed him, it's you."

"*Allegra—*"

Allie ignored the warning in her mother's voice. The moment was ripe; all the suppressed anger spilled over in a rush of ugly accusations. Allie said that it was Prudence who had persuaded Pavel to marry her, had persuaded him to join the Family Trust even though he wasn't suited for it, had pressured him into living the way she wanted . . . and then had turned her back on him when he desperately needed her.

"He *killed* himself because of you," Allie shouted, her voice breaking. "He didn't have to die. If you hadn't ruined his life he'd be alive today—"

"How *dare* you accuse me of hurting your father. He meant *everything* to me." Prudence's words didn't come out as she had intended. She wanted to tell Allie how miserable she was, what a calamity it had been for her to desert Pavel, but that it had been, after a fashion, Pavel's doing. He couldn't return to her and face the family and his Wall Street friends. His pride drove him to destruction.

"Allie, listen to me . . ."

"Daddy made a new woman of you—and when you left him and married John you shriveled up. Well, it serves you right. You destroyed him, but you're *not* going to destroy me. Daddy wouldn't be upset if I dropped out of a school that bored me. He would encourage me to lead my own life. To take a chance. He always said life was risk. He always said I had a right to do what I want with my life—"

"And what do you want to do?"

"I don't know. But I mean to find out. I do know that I won't settle for being a Greenwich wife—like you." With those words Allie stalked out of the room, out of the great hall, out of the front door.

By the time Prudence reached the door, the Jag had screeched out of the driveway. Prudence shuddered, thinking of the awful accidents that occurred during Christmas week.

"Allie, come back," she wanted to call out, but she found herself thinking:

Pavel, come back; come back. We need you. . . .

Allie manipulated the car with demon haste, the speed easing her anger. When she arrived at Grandmama Towle's house she let herself into the hall. A motherly woman in white came down the stairs to greet her.

"You're Miss Allegra," the woman said.

Allie nodded and asked, "How's my grandmother?"

"She seems to have a little more strength today. She's been looking forward to seeing you."

"May I go up now?"

"By all means."

The nurse followed Allegra up the stairs to the master bedroom, where Grandmama Towle was half-sitting in bed, propped up by several large pillows. Her gray hair was sparse over her pink skull, and the heavy Towle chin seemed sunken, as though the flesh could not anchor the bones. But her eyes, Allie saw, were alive.

"Grandmama—" Allie hid the disbelief, the horror at the change in the old woman, who had always been such a supportive friend to her. She knelt beside the bed, holding her grandmother's withered hands, so cold and dry to the touch. She raised them to her lips.

"Sorry . . . Allie . . . this is a poor holiday for you . . . They won't allow me downstairs . . ."

"It's not important, Grandmama. We'll celebrate tomorrow in your room."

"But this evening—"

"Don't worry about me, Grandmama. Cristina invited me to her mother's apartment for a late supper—"

"Your mother—?"

"Oh, I imagine she and John have made plans for the evening." She snuggled her face against her grandmother's violet-scented bed jacket. "Would you like me to stay here tonight? I can call Cris—"

"Nonsense. You go and enjoy yourself. You should be with young people."

"I'll probably be late. I may even sleep over, if they have the space."

With a sense of foreboding Allie left the sickroom. She got into the car and switched on the motor. Yet once the Jag was warmed up she didn't budge. She stared at the old-fashioned house, at the surrounding regal oaks which had been saplings during the Revolutionary War. And suddenly she had a vision of this familiar place abandoned, the gardens overgrown, the flower beds gone to seed, vines everywhere.

There was no assurance, she knew, that the house —or the Towle way of life—would survive. By inheritance the house would come to Allie if she wanted it. But she couldn't see herself as the mistress of such an establishment.

Unless the man in her life was Stephen Terhune ...

Marianna found the suite number and pressed the button. The door was flung open by Cris, dressed in a white cashmere jumpsuit, a purple-and-gold sash around her meager waist. She threw her arms around Marianna, dislodging the box of Plumbridge chocolates from her friend's hands.

"Mari, *hello*. It's terrific to see you. ... Come on in. Mama's anxious to see you again—"

What her managers, directors, agents and fans thought of Bonnie Rob Roy was reflected in the gifts that made a sumptuous boutique out of the living room. On the end table by the sofa a small silver tree glowed with scarlet baubles of tiny jewel lights. Delicacies were scattered on chairs and tables around the room: fruits from Oregon orchards, nuts from Georgia groves, chocolates from Godiva and Blum's, scarlet and white poinsettias, yellow tulips in clay pots and fragile hothouse tearoses.

The scent of an expensive French perfume preceded Bonnie as she emerged from the bedroom, wafer thin, boyish in black slacks and knit turtleneck sweater, her face whitewashed with powder, her dark eyes luminous.

"Marianna, so *good* to see you. How pretty you look." Bonnie hugged Marianna impulsively, as though her daughter's friend was her dearest kin, and Marianna responded, flattered, touched.

"You're coming to stay with us while Mama's in New York, aren't you, Mari?" Cris said.

"It's a very generous invitation, but I'm not sure. I mean, I don't want to be in the way—"

"You'll not only be welcome," Bonnie said frankly,

"but you'll be a great help to us. If you're here, living with Cris, her father won't make a fuss. He'll feel that she's safe." She smiled wryly. "He doesn't approve of me, you know. He thinks I'm a bad influence on my child."

"Now, Mama, don't get upset," Cris begged. "Whenever you mention Steve, you get so *down*—"

"Allegra's included in the invitation," Bonnie added. "The three of you can raise a little hell while I'm singing for my supper."

"Allie'll have to go back to school," Cris said.

"I haven't heard from her since Thanksgiving," Marianna said. "Does she like it?"

"Hates it. The only men she sees are the Cornell boys, and she says they're one huge bore."

"I hear Vince made your kid sister legal." Bonnie lit a tipped cigarette, inhaled deeply, coughed and snuffed it out. "What'd she want with that nature-boy?"

Marianna managed an airy smile. "Upward mobility, I guess. And putting it over on his groupies." *Or getting away from Mama,* she said to herself.

"Maybe she can keep him in line. He's a hit-and-run lover."

Marianna wanted no cloud to ruin the evening. She was glad when more guests arrived and Bonnie was caught in the whirlpool of admirers, musicians and old friends who'd heard she was staying at the Essex House and somehow managed to sneak in.

Bonnie was equally gracious to them all, lavish with drinks and Beluga caviar. She was chatting animatedly with a reporter from one of the trade papers, but she broke away to greet a disc jockey who'd helped her last album make it to the Top Ten. Cris watched her proudly.

"I suppose I should circulate," Cris said to Marianna, "but I'd rather stay with you. Mari, what's new? Any special boyfriend?"

"No," Marianna answered. She had told no one about her affair with the Duke. Cris wouldn't understand anyway; as far as Marianna knew her friend hadn't had a real lover, though she *seemed* sexually experienced.

"I'm going to school nights, beginning next semester," Marianna said, avoiding the subject of men.

"Great! Where?"

"The NYU College of Business."

Cris looked puzzled. "What courses?"

"Journalism, public relations, maybe some areas of television—things that will help me with my job."

"That's marvelous. Maybe you'll end up working for Mama. Wouldn't that be *super?*"

Marianna smiled politely. The Duke had once mentioned the number of press agents who had acquired ulcers as members of Bonnie's ever-changing entourage.

The room was crowded now with guests who were waiting for Bonnie to sing. In the past few months she was at her best performing for her friends. It was then that they heard the heartache, the yearning—the qualities that made her unique.

Friends and fans alike agreed that her recent concert appearances, even her nightclub acts, were not quite Bonnie at her best—that it was a shame what liquor, drugs and men were doing to her. How many comebacks were there in one set of vocal cords? they wondered. They said, in corners at Sardi's, in dark bars on West Forty-fifth Street, that if she wasn't rushing headlong into a breakdown, then she was at least schizoid. Everyone was interested in seeing how she'd manage this New York appearance.

Bonnie beckoned to Cris. "We're running short of food. Could you call a Chinese place and have them rustle up some spareribs and eggrolls?"

"Will do."

"Good party." Bonnie was happy, youth and enthusiasm breaking through the makeup that didn't quite hide the lines around her blazing eyes and trembling mouth.

"You going anywhere next week?" a fan asked hopefully.

"I'm staying in town," said Bonnie resolutely. "Rehearsals with the band, interviews—" She shrugged. "The usual before an opening."

"I hope Mama doesn't overdo it," Cris said to Marianna, concerned.

"She's a night person."

"True. But there're so many demands on her time. Sometimes she forgets that her body can take just so much."

"Does she ever relax?"

"Not if she can help it."

Just then the telephone rang and Cris answered it. It was Allegra, saying she was on her way from Greenwich. She told Cris that she had just informed her mother that she was leaving school.

Marianna and Cris talked in the bedroom until Bonnie came in with a muscular young athlete who was a member of the U.S. Olympic swim team.

She waved airily to them. "Run along, my darlings."

They left, closing the door behind them. Marianna was embarrassed by Bonnie's behavior, but Cris didn't seem to mind. She chattered excitedly about Allie's news.

"It's funny," Marianna said. "I'm going back to school just as Allie's dropping out."

CHAPTER VI

MARIANNA

They were not to spend another Christmas together for several years. But they kept in touch, by letters or by phone, and they saw each other occasionally.

Marianna knew Allegra was in Paris, studying gourmet cooking at a school connected with a famous restaurant. Cristina was still enrolled at the American Academy of Dramatic Art, although she had dropped out for a semester to spend time with her mother. Cris had confided in Marianna shortly after the Copa opening that Bonnie was often sick and wasn't sleeping well.

In the spring Marianna began her evening studies at New York University. The city girls who attended classes with her were friendly, but they couldn't understand why a student from a posh prep school like Locust Ryse would pass up an elite college in favor of the Washington Square campus. They found Marianna's satisfaction with their school puzzling: It was like buying at Mays' on Fourteenth Street when you had a charge account at Saks Fifth Avenue, they said.

The young men were equally uncertain about her; they could relate better to the local girls who were in class less to get an education than to find a husband.

Marianna's life continued to revolve around the Duke and her job. Their intimacy had developed into a comfortable love affair. Her devotion flattered him: She was loving, even passionate at times, and she had taught herself to hide her jealousy of the other women in his life.

Several weekends in May he took her to Southampton. Then, just before Memorial Day, she had to take a leave from him—her mother had had a hysterectomy and was in mourning for what she called her "lost femininity." Marianna spent the next month of weekends with her.

On every visit Liebschen gave Marianna bulletins about her daughter who had married a famous rock star.

"And who never comes to see you," Marianna reminded her.

"She can't get away. After all, Vince is on the road constantly. And he wants her with him," Liebschen said.

"I'll bet." Marianna's tone was dry; she was angry with herself for swallowing the bait.

One Monday in June Marianna arrived at the office to find the Duke in great spirits. It seemed he'd met a Hollywood PR girl at a party, and she was settling in New York. Since she sounded knowledgeable and had good contacts both on the east and west coasts, he had suggested that she call him.

"I want you to talk to her," he said to Marianna. "I think we can use her." He leaned down and kissed her on the cheek, a gesture that didn't relieve her anxiety. She went into her office and tried to concentrate, but she had a feeling something wasn't quite right. Perhaps the Duke was beginning to take her work for granted.

But he had been infinitely kind to her. He'd sent her to a top hairdresser, who had streaked her pale brown hair with gold and taught her how to use color pencils on her face to soften the small bump on her nose, emphasize the slant of her eyelids and exaggerate her full lips. And the Duke had suggested that she wear clothes with soft colors and easy lines that showed off her beautiful round breasts.

If Laurie and Flora were disturbed by the boss's interest in her, they hid it. Marianna was warm and helpful; they liked her. And Marianna herself was so happy and well adjusted in her little nest that she had no intention of having it disturbed.

After she checked the morning mail she put in a call to her sister. Darlis reported she and Vince had leased a loft in Soho, which they were remodeling, and that she was busy taking a photography course.

"I'm calling about Mama," Marianna said coolly. "I've taken care of her every weekend. Now it's your turn."

"Sorry. No can do." Darlis said Vince expected her to go on the road with him. And his manager had been in touch with Bonnie Rob Roy about a concert at Carnegie Hall.

"Darlis, you've got to make time for Mama."

"She's always complaining about something, Mari. You take her too seriously."

Marianna hung up, defeated. But she was damned if she'd lose the Duke because of her family.

Her name was Winifred. "But everybody calls me Winnie," she said to Marianna over lunch at a posh Swiss restaurant.

Winnie had fortified herself with two double Scotches and a hearty lunch. She was a small, shapely girl who was probably older than her makeup, dress and manner suggested. The stamp of Hollywood was evident in her long blond hair, bold brown eyes behind oversized sunglasses and perfect capped teeth. One thing she certainly had, Marianna quickly decided, was *chutzpah*.

Back in the office Marianna reported to the Duke. "She has a good background, if her résumé is honest. She's brash, so I think she could get along with certain types of people—"

"Let's try her for a month," he said. "If she doesn't work out we'll let her go."

Marianna had the feeling that if Winnie the Pooh, as Marianna had dubbed her, got through the door, she'd end up running the place, but she chided herself for her insecurity: After all, the Duke loved her.

She had a right to her fears, however, as she soon discovered when she stopped at the office unexpectedly one Saturday afternoon.

The Duke had told her he was going to Newport

for the weekend. But when she entered the bathroom Marianna found him there, stretched out on the massage table, naked, with Winnie the Pooh's head buried between his legs. Her blond hair was covering her face and her busy mouth, and the expression on the Duke's face made it clear that she was doing a commendable job.

"Marianna, I want to talk to you," the Duke said.

"There's nothing you have to say to me."

They were in his private office. He had wrapped a terry robe around his body after Winnie had fled, expecting perhaps a hair-grabbing match with Marianna.

"You're right, Mari. I'm glad you understand." The Duke put his arm around her shoulder and looked tenderly into her stricken tear-strained face. "We have an open relationship, right, Mari?"

She closed her eyes. The tightness in her throat traveled down to her chest.

"You must understand, Mari, that I've been around a long time. My tastes may be more corrupt or more sophisticated—whatever you choose to call it—than yours. This woman did something for me I'd never ask you to do."

"You're damn right," she said.

And so she learned to compromise. But that was what life was about, she knew—one grew by learning to make the best of things.

Marianna found it odd that Winnie bothered her while the Duke's elegant, fashionable ladies did not. She saw that he was drawn to the girl, commonplace though she was. A temporary aberration? Maybe. Perhaps, like many men experiencing a mid-life crisis, he was scared, and he needed cheap, easy goods like Winnie to perk him up. . . .

When Marianna worked with Winnie during the newcomer's first few weeks, she found that Winnie picked her brain and then presented Marianna's ideas to the Duke as her own. Marianna realized that she was no match for this creature, who would clearly stay on longer than a month.

How much loyalty, she wondered, did she owe the Duke? Was it loyalty, or was it love? Reason suggested that if he wanted an open affair with her, it left her with the right to make her own life. There were many attractive men around. She decided she would date them if they asked her.

The Duke took his cue from her aloof manner. He seemed relieved but uneasy. Her respect for him wavered, her contempt increased, and yet she did love him, and she was in agony every time he screwed Winnie—or Winnie screwed him.

Meanwhile she assumed the smart Manhattan career-girl style. Sometimes when she passed a shop window she didn't recognize herself. What had happened to Marianna of the Locust Ryse flannels and sensible oxfords?

She now carried herself with the grace of the well-born: her slender feet in elegant French boots, her gold-streaked hair teased and brushed off her forehead, then caught in a ponytail with a small signature scarf. She bought her clothes in Saks and Bonwit's. The Duke often sent her to lunch with his designer clients at the Frog Pond, and she was a replica of every stylish young woman in the place.

The Duke found that Marianna brought enthusiasm and excitement to every publicity campaign. She was full of ideas, and many of them, though sounding far-fetched, were workable. Her instinctive grasp of what women wanted—to watch, to read, to wear, to enjoy—was uncanny. When he complimented her on this talent, she was surprised. "I just think of what I'd like to have happen to me," she said.

The Duke had begun to turn over to her his more temperamental accounts. "Mari'll take care of it," he'd say, confident of her tact and patience.

Yet the Duke seemed aware of her shyness and tried to help her overcome it. He took her to parties and encouraged her to circulate. "Once everyone realizes who you are and that you have a pipeline to the columnists, they'll fall all over themselves to be nice to you," he told her.

On a Saturday afternoon in the last weekend of

July he invited her to a cocktail party at which fifty
people would be meeting to discuss plans for a children's art exhibit. The proceeds of the show would
underwrite country vacations for underprivileged city
children. Marianna had found that the Duke gave
generously of his time to causes he considered worthy.

Marianna was excited about going out with the
Duke—they hadn't been together often in recent weeks
—and had bought a new dress for the occasion. It
was white linen, double-breasted and outlined in black
silk braid.

When the Duke picked her up in the Barbizon
lobby he expressed his approval of the dress. He himself was well tanned from his last weekend in Southampton and looked handsome in his English gray
flannels and dark blue blazer with gold buttons.

The gathering was at the apartment of Regina Latham, wife of a popular state senator who was running for reelection. They took a cab to the beautiful
pre-war building on Park Avenue near Eightieth Street.

Marianna thought the apartment exquisite, particularly the living room. The French furniture was
delicate: chairs and sofa upholstered in antique watered
blue silk; rare vases filled with silk flowers in varie-
gated colors; twin mirrors on one wall reflecting a
collection of French Impressionists on the other.

Regina Latham, a small, animated woman wearing
white silk pajamas, spied the Duke and waved to
him. She crossed the room and took him by both
hands, hugged him and allowed him to kiss her on
the lips.

Learning who Marianna was, Regina greeted her
warmly and then introduced her to the guests nearby.
After shaking hands with politicians, city officials, re-
presentatives from the United Nations, well-known
actors and a literary agent, Marianna met the guest of
honor, film producer Saul Cohen.

Marianna chatted with the producer, his wife and
Regina until a serious young man joined them. He
seemed different from the other men, who were flirting with attractive women as they drank. He was of
medium height, too thin for his flannel trousers and

corduroy jacket. His face was long and angular, the features well placed, and he wore his brown hair cut short, close to his skull, in a style favored in the 1950's.

"You and Noel should have much in common," Regina said to Marianna. "Noel's just back from England, where he was a Rhodes scholar. He's starting work at the Third Network next month—in the editorial news department."

She described Marianna's duties at the Duke's office while Noel Osborn listened attentively. Then he asked Marianna a few questions about public relations and she elaborated, thinking that the desire to please a man had never deserted her. In spite of any rejections she may have suffered, she automatically responded to a man—any man—with fawning enthusiasm. Yet in this instance she didn't mind her reactions. Noel was so attractive in a quiet way that she wanted to impress him, to arouse his interest.

Regina moved on to her other guests and Noel went to fetch Marianna a fresh drink. He returned with two puff pastries filled with caviar.

"Thanks. I'm starved." Marianna licked her finger.

"Will you have dinner with me?" Noel asked abruptly.

She blushed. "I wasn't fishing for an invitation."

He laughed.

"I can't. I'm sorry. I came with my boss."

When he looked at her knowingly she quickly said, "Oh, it's nothing like *that*. . . . I'm clumsy and getting in deeper. What I mean to say is *yes*, I'd love to have dinner with you—if the Duke has other plans for himself—"

"Will you ask him, or should I?"

As it turned out, their hostess had planned a buffet dinner. The Duke noticed Marianna and Noel Osborn sitting together at one of the many small tables set up, and seemed pleased. He devoted his time to Regina and the producer's wife, who was obviously impressed with him.

Normally, Marianna would have been thinking,

Here comes another account. But she was too taken with Noel Osborn to be aware of anything but her own feelings.

 Dear Allie,
  I wish you were here to advise me. Or to guide me. Or whatever. You manage people, particularly men, so beautifully. I've always tried to learn from you but I've seldom had anyone to practice on.
  I do now, and it gives me the jitters.
  I'm terrified I'll say the wrong thing or make the wrong move. You'd think I was back at Locust Ryse, waiting for the busload of Choate adolescents to arrive—palpitations, sweaty palms, the whole bit!
  I keep asking myself: Why should a man like Noel Osborn find me attractive?
  Let me tell you about him. We met yesterday afternoon at the home of Senator Barney Latham. The columnists were there—Louis Wolfe and Suzy among them—several photographers, a smattering of TV people, business executives. Anyway, somebody introduced me to this very attractive young man who looked English (which he isn't). He's in his mid-twenties, a Princeton graduate and a Rhodes scholar. He was working in the British Broadcasting Company—a very minor job, he says—when he received an offer as assistant producer on the Third Network's new morning news show. Six months with the Duke has prepared me to deal with clients and to feel reasonably at ease with them. But Noel got through to me, right from the start.
  He's from the South—his father is a professor of philosophy at one of the Southern colleges—and he has a blend of Southern and English manners . . . without sounding pretentious, I must add. Anyway, we talked and talked! He likes the prospect of television, mostly because he has great confidence in his boss, who's planning a series of broadcasts on our future relations with Russia.

Noel will be flying to Moscow to do the legwork. He speaks Russian and is studying Chinese dialects, which should make him very useful to the network.

The Duke signaled to me that he was ready to leave, and Noel said he would ride down with us. I had the feeling he didn't want to part with me, which was super.

We were all sandwiched in one elevator: Saul Cohen and his wife, Noel, Louis Wolfe, the Duke and I. When we walked outside the sun was in command, but by seven o'clock its golden haze was blending into the lavender shadows. (Romantic, eh?)

Saul Cohen said to all of us, "Can I give you a lift?" The chauffeur drove up in the Cohen limousine, and we all crowded in—Noel and I used the jump seats. The chauffeur turned east, along Eighty-sixth Street. We realized he was driving us to the mooring on the East River. We were to use the Cohen yacht, which is pretty impressive; the Duke says it's almost on a par with the Revson yacht. . . . It was all pretty grand for me, as you can imagine. We boarded, the stewards offered us drinks and off we went.

We sailed around the tip of Manhattan. It was like an old MGM movie, with the little secretary suddenly lifted out of her plebeian role. The Cohens and the Duke were talking about the producer's new film, Lorenzo the Magnificent. *Louis Wolfe was making notes for his Monday column, and Mrs. Cohen had fallen asleep in her deck chair. There was something peaceful in the air in spite of the river traffic—the ferries, the small cruisers, the ungainly freighters.*

Noel and I were standing on deck at the rail. The breeze was whipping my hair, loosened from the silk scarf, and Noel caught a slender strand and curved it behind my ear. He was smiling.

"This is nice," he said. "It's nice being with you."

We stood in absolute silence, but with a kind of communication I'd never felt before. I wanted to sail on forever . . .

But soon we were mooring the yacht at the West Side Basin, and the Cohen limousine was waiting, having driven crosstown. Louis Wolfe was dropped off at his apartment. The Duke had a date and excused himself, after making sure Noel would escort me back to the Barbizon. We thanked the Cohens, who were very gracious and told us they wanted to see both of us again. And then we found a path on Riverside Drive and walked slowly as dusk deepened. It was incredibly romantic, and when Noel and I reached the Barbizon he held my hands in his as though he wanted to keep me with him.

"I'm sorry I can't ask you up," I said. "It's forbidden."

"Tomorrow?" he said. "Lunch?"

"Okay."

"Dinner?"

I must have shown surprise, because I didn't think he was the impetuous type.

"Dinner?" he repeated.

Girls hurrying into the hotel gave him a lingering glance. He looked so attractive.

"Dinner," I agreed.

He leaned to kiss my cheek and he remained there on the pavement until I was safely in the lobby. I was floating: such a perfect day, such a wonderful man. . . .

I do wish you were here, Allie. To keep me from sounding too eager. To keep me from making a mistake that might alienate him. You know, after four years in that nunnery I really am not yet comfortable with men. I don't know how to behave. I defer to them, I'm flattering—behavior my mother taught me, at least by osmosis.

I'll keep you informed.

> Love
> Marianna

After she finished the letter Marianna realized that she hadn't mentioned her affair with the Duke. She wondered if he would be jealous. . . .

Noel called her the following morning at the office. "Would you like to have lunch in Central Park? Or would you rather brown-bag it? There's a good deli around the corner from my apartment."

"Let's compromise. We'll eat our sandwiches in Central Park and then visit the zoo."

He called for her at the office and they walked to the park. Noel shared her enthusiasm for long strolls and people-watching. They went deep into the park, found a deserted bench and shared their feast with the squirrels. They made up stories about the people passing by. When it was time for her to return to the office, they lingered in front of the building. Each time she made an effort to leave him, he remembered something he wanted to tell her.

Laurie and Flora wanted to know everything about him. She told them as much as she knew, which was impressive. They thought he was handsome, his manners flawless.

During the afternoon his image remained in her mind. She loved his hazel eyes. He had a way of looking at her, intent but with a touch of something she couldn't define. Sadness? No, his mouth turned up with a friendly, optimistic smile. Yet somehow it seemed as though all the sides of his personality weren't integrated. But then, she asked herself, whose are?

Over dinner at the Carlyle Café he told her about his youth. It had been rather idyllic; he was a kind of Tom Sawyer of the respectable middle class. He had three younger sisters who'd gone to Randolph-Macon College, but each was married before her junior year. They were comfortably settled in North Carolina, members of the Junior League, volunteering at the local hospitals, showing specimen plants at the Annual Flower Show of the Women's Club. He said he had been in love with a girl who was a friend of his sisters, but when he imagined what his life would

be like if he settled down in his home town, he knew
she wasn't for him. That was the extent of his emotional involvement, he said.

"Wasn't it difficult to break off?" Marianna asked.

"Not when I thought of the alternative. It was better to clear out—before she was hurt."

She felt a shadow of something—a premonition.
But his smile reassured her.

They spent the week together, sharing lunches and
dinner every day. He was eager to visit the art galleries, and although he'd had enough theater in London, he wanted to see what New York had to offer.
They went to a number of Off Broadway plays. Just
as she'd learned about modern painters from Saturday
afternoons spent with Cris and Stephen Terhune, just
as she'd learned from the Duke about celebrities and
how to get along in Manhattan—a kind of primer for
single-girl city living—she learned from Noel about
drama, the technique, the importance of absorbing the
classics and then discarding them and writing with
freshness and emotion.

He offered her charming, unexpected gifts. Once,
when they were about to eat at a new restaurant on
Madison Avenue, he asked her to wait and dashed
into a florist's shop. She expected a rose or a yellow
orchid. He brought out a bouquet of lilies of the val-
ley, and their fragrance gave a kind of glory to the
evening. He was disappointed that she didn't care for
Emily Dickinson and bought a book of her poems
for her. It was as if he wanted her to accept his
favorites, to like what he liked. She thought that was
a good sign . . . the best.

He had barely touched her during the lovely hours
they had spent together. At the Sutton Theater he had
put his arm around her shoulders, but casually, as
though to rest it. When they strolled up Madison
Avenue, looking at galleries and boutiques, he held
her hand, and a feeling of desire traveled through her
body. Everything was leading toward a climax. But it
couldn't be "Your place or mine?" because she still
lived at the Barbizon, and he was sharing an apartment with a friend.

She prepared carefully for their Saturday night date: a delicate lotion after her shower, which left her skin satin to the touch; her face scrubbed until it gleamed, pale bronze, enhanced by sun oil; no makeup except some lip balm; her hair loose, flowing as she moved her head; a brief white linen shift with a low V, suggesting the swell of her firm young breasts; and Estée Lauder bath oil, used as perfume, at the pulse points, as Allie had taught her.

They met at seven in the lobby, crowded with young men waiting for their dates to appear. Noel smiled, that odd, lopsided smile she'd learned to interpret as approval. He kissed her on the cheek and they went out into the humidity of the street.

"I start work on Monday," he announced.

"Oh." She felt a sense of loss. How could that be, after only a week? Yet so much had been crowded into seven days. . . .

She forced herself to sound lighthearted. "Shall I be a cockeyed optimist and hope—"

"Oh, I'll be around," he said. Impulsively, she linked her arm through his and he pressed it to his body.

"What would you like to do tonight?" he asked.

"Couldn't we just go somewhere quiet—and talk?"

He nodded. "I know just the place."

He took her to a half-century-old Italian restaurant off Washington Square, originally a speakeasy and now a meeting place for second-echelon politicians. The scampi and pasta were superb. But Marianna wasn't concentrating on the food; even the bottle of wine failed to stimulate her appetite. She needed to etch this evening in her memory, to remember its flavor.

She noticed that Noel seemed tense. He was disturbed, she decided, because their lovely week was ending. She wondered if he would speak of it, tell her how much he'd enjoyed it and how he hated for it to be over. *Need it end?* she wondered. Even if he was working hard the next few weeks, before taking off for Russia, there would be time to meet. Perhaps to make love?

Marianna was impatient for dinner to be over, but not the evening. She was keyed up . . . and nervous about the next step.

Noel was telling her about his new job again. She listened intently, delighted that he enjoyed talking to her although he was repeating himself.

"How long do you expect to be in Russia?" she asked.

"Depends on how much cooperation we get from the Russian government. Anywhere from six weeks to three months."

"It makes me sad to think of you so far away." Instantly she knew it was the wrong admission. She added hastily, "I suppose it's partly envy. Any women in your company?"

"I doubt it. But I don't think the whole crew's been firmed up yet."

The evening wasn't turning out as she had anticipated. She felt a sudden chill, and the last sip of wine turned sour in her stomach.

"What would you like to do?" he asked when they left the restaurant.

It was, she felt, an unspoken suggestion, a request he was reluctant to put into words. She said gently, "Whatever you say," and their glances met in tacit agreement. His smile was boyish, without any of the wariness she sometimes sensed in him. Perhaps, she thought, he'd been afraid of rejection.

He helped her into a cab and gave the driver an East Side address. "My friend is out of town for the weekend," he said to Marianna.

As the driver parried uptown traffic, Noel put his arm solicitously around her shoulders. "Are you warm enough?" She nodded, and he held her closer, his hand creeping up to open the fasteners of her dress and reaching for her bare midriff. She shivered, and his mouth touched hers lightly before he buried his face in her hair, silken and fragrant. His embrace tightened, leaving her breathless.

They hurried from the taxi to the lobby of a large high-rise. The furniture in his friend's one-bedroom apartment was modern, the colors deep blue and green.

Noel said, "Take off your dress, Mari," and handed her a blue velour robe. She followed him into the bedroom, which was as lacking in personality as the living room. She took off her dress, hung it in a closet and shrugged herself into the robe, tying the belt snugly around her small waist.

He was smiling, obviously pleased with himself. "Why is a girl in men's clothes such a turn-on?"

He led her into the bathroom. They took a shower together and she responded to his touch as he ran his hands over her body, making small patterns of soap suds. *Let the Duke have his casual love affairs,* she thought.

He wrapped her in a thick terry robe and dried her face gently. "You don't need makeup. You should never use it. Your skin has a natural radiance."

Noel helped her off with the robe, his glance admiring. She lay down on the bed and he joined her, turning on his side, his elbow bent against the pillow, his cheek in the palm of his hand as he observed her. He wasn't erect yet, but it took only a moment before she felt his strength against her. He proved the master of the erotic kiss; there were no private places within her that he failed to explore.

"Are you taking care of yourself?" His voice was low.

"What d'you mean?"

"Are you on the pill?"

"Yes, yes, *of course.*" The Duke had insisted that she be protected.

His tongue played against her flushed skin, but oddly, he wouldn't allow her to reciprocate. "No," he said, "I'll come too quickly."

He was intent, absorbed, almost as though he'd forgotten her in his quest for pleasure. When he spread-eagled himself over her moist body he covered her eyelids, her temples, with faint kisses, like the touch of butterfly wings.

She led him into her secret place, holding her

breath, aware of a sudden exquisite pain as he entered her. His movements were tentative in the beginning; he withdrew and gently entered again, watching her expression in the shadowy light.

"Open your eyes," he whispered urgently. *"Look at me."*

She overcame her shyness and stared into his eyes, and the pace of his thrust increased, culminating in a full, rapturous peak.

He rolled over on his side, his breath labored.

"I know why the old movies always show a wave spending itself on the rocks," she said, wanting to amuse him. But he lay with his back to her, exhausted.

Soon after they dressed, and he put her in a taxi, giving the driver a bill.

"Do you mind if I don't take you home?" he said. "I've got some work that has to be finished."

"Will you call me tomorrow?" she asked, feeling it was a reasonable request.

"If not tomorrow, Monday."

"Good night, Noel."

" 'Night." He waved to her as the cab drove off.

She had the uncomfortable feeling that he was relieved to see her go. But she told herself that she was being ridiculous: They had been in each other's arms; their bodies had invaded one another. How much more intimate could any two people be?

That night she slept uneasily; her dreams were fitful and frightening, and she was glad when morning came. But Sunday was no better.

At last it was Monday morning and she could go to the office, where she could turn her attention to something besides what had happened with Noel— and what was going to happen. She managed to look busy when Laurie drifted in and made an excuse when Flora tried to talk to her. "Later," she said. "I have to finish these letters for the boss."

Each time the phone rang her palms dampened with anxiety. And each time the call wasn't for her. She didn't go out to lunch for fear that she would miss Noel's call.

Watching the clock was torturous. She made excuses for him: He was due at the network this morning; no doubt he was tied up in meetings. Probably he and his colleagues went out to lunch to continue their talks; it often happened.

But couldn't he spare two minutes for a call?

He'd telephone later, she was sure of it; it was his pattern to communicate with her every day.

Please call, Noel. Please, she prayed.

She remembered that sometimes, when she was thinking about Allie or Cris, the telephone would ring. "I've just been thinking about you," she'd announce triumphantly.

She concentrated on Noel the rest of the afternoon, while she typed the Duke's letters and drafted releases on some of his Hollywood actors who were visiting New York. Finally during a coffee break, when her shoulders ached with tension and her fingers were sore, she read the *Daily News*. Sure enough, there was a mention of the Latham party in Louis Wolfe's weekly column and what Wolfe called the "Daylight Excursion" on the Cohen yacht. Among the guests he mentioned the Duke and his beautiful secretary and Noel Osborn, who was an authority on Russia.

At five o'clock she gave up. He wasn't going to call, but she had an excuse to call him—to tell him about the Wolfe item. Since he was new in town, he might not read the columnists.

Alone in the front office, she braced herself and dialed the Third Network. She asked for Noel and added that he was probably in the news center. She was afraid they might have trouble tracking him down.

"Who do you wish to speak to?" the network switchboard operator asked again.

Marianna had an impulse to hang up. "Noel Osborn," she whispered nervously.

"One moment, here's Mr. Osborn."

She heard his voice, sounding rather British: "Osborn here."

"Noel, it's Marianna."

"Oh, yes."

A pause. She wanted to ask why he hadn't called, to tell him she had waited all day.

"How did your first day go?" she asked lamely.

"Like all first days. Briefings, meeting with the crew."

"Noel—"

"Yes?"

"Did you see the mention in Louis Wolfe's column?"

"Yes. It was brought to my attention. Very decent of him."

Did she have the right Noel Osborn? she wondered. Or was this a part of him she'd not met before?

"Are you planning to call me later?"

"If I have time. The evening's pretty well tied up."

"Oh. Well, I'll be home all evening."

"Right. Thanks for calling."

He hung up.

She stared at the mouthpiece, feeling humiliated and abandoned.

She found his note at the hotel Tuesday afternoon. He'd evidently mailed it after their talk.

"I'm sorry," he wrote, "but it's no good. You don't make stars for me."

She had hated her small, gloomy room in the hotel. Until the rejection.

Now, shattered and confused, she found the room a burrow, a shelter for the heart. Was it possible that only a week ago she'd had her feelings in control, no outside forces having the power to destroy her? In seven days Noel had moved into her life, taken possession of her being, so that she awoke each morning with a single joyous thought: He was making up for the pain the Duke had inflicted on her . . . and all the hurt of her past.

. . . Or so she'd believed. *Dear God, what went wrong?* she asked herself again and again.

She remembered Allie once explaining that men weren't very attentive after they'd had sex. Orgasm not only drained them but left them shaken, eager to get away.

She wished again that Allie was home, so she could hear her faintly sarcastic analysis of the death of an affair. She had written Allie such an ecstatic letter; she couldn't bear to follow it up with the sad ending.

And so she thought of writing a letter to Noel, demanding an explanation; he did owe her that. But she knew it would be a mistake to insist on seeing him—he was so obviously disappointed in her. She hadn't measured up to his dreams.

Looking inward, she admitted she didn't deserve him.

Laurie and Flora knew she was distraught. She took on more than her share of the work load; she never went out for lunch but had a container of yogurt at her desk; she looked wan and had lost weight.

"Honey, you look down." Flora had brought in Danish pastries to share with Laurie and Marianna. "Come on, baby. Nothing cheers you up like a delicious goodie."

"I'll eat it later," Marianna said, attempting a smile.

"That's what you said yesterday about the chocolate chip cookies. But they were on your desk after you left. I thought you *liked* chocolate chips—"

"I do, Flora. I love them. But—" She turned away before tears flooded her eyes.

Laurie tried to help her too. She invited Marianna to a new restaurant that served a dozen kinds of home-made soup, but Marianna made an excuse.

She couldn't, however, turn down the Duke when he said one Friday evening, "Mari, I feel like seafood tonight. Join me. I have some business matters to discuss with you."

As they sat facing each other in a booth, Marianna realized for the first time that he looked tired. The lines around his eyes and mouth were more pronounced in the mahogany tan. He'd been involved in an important campaign that concentrated on the upcoming wedding of a young actress and a duke. He began to discuss the project but broke off, seeing the far-away look on Marianna's face.

"Mari, I've noticed in the last couple of weeks that you aren't yourself. Let me be Big Daddy—"

She looked down at the menu and then held it up

so its double spread nearly hid her face. The waiter was patient, poised for her order.

"Mari—"

"I'm sorry. I can't seem to decide."

"The lemon sole? The broiled striped bass?"

"Just a salad."

"Lobster? Crabmeat?"

"Lobster, I guess."

When the waiter left the Duke took her hand in his. He seemed genuinely concerned. The two sides of him puzzled her—the good friend and the casual lover.

"Mari, are you pregnant?"

She was startled. The thought had never entered her mind. Yet to her horror, she found she couldn't remember the date of her last period. She stared at him. Was he thinking of himself or Noel?

"I'm not. At least, I don't think so."

"Good, although I do know of a good abortionist. Look, Mari, when I said we might try an open love affair, I didn't mean for you to go overboard on a mad, passionate fling—of how long, may I ask?"

"One week. One absurd week."

"Brief enough."

She was aware of his concern, although he was not passing judgment on her. Perhaps, she thought, men wanted open love affairs for themselves but drew the line when their women tried to do likewise. . . . Yet because he was her friend she longed to unburden herself. Maybe he could analyze her weakness as a woman.

"I don't know what I did wrong," she said.

He leaned back against the tufted leather of the banquette. He said slowly, "What makes you think you did something wrong?"

Without a word she took Noel's letter from her straw handbag, and in spite of her embarrassment she handed it to him.

He read it and returned it to her. "You're shifting the blame to your own shoulders . . . as though you expected it."

"I suppose I did," she said reluctantly. "His interest

in me was flattering. I just couldn't believe it—he was so charming. He's had such a brilliant academic background—"

"And he came on strong," said the Duke.

"*Did* he." For the first time, there was a suggestion of anger in her voice.

"And quickly, within what—a week? And then—curtains. Does it occur to you that he might be afraid of being found out? Or found wanting?"

She was astonished. "I never thought of it. I mean, well, it wouldn't go with his character. He seemed so confident—so sure of himself."

"Which made you take the blame. When the calls stopped, you thought it was your fault. Even when he made excuses like, 'I'm busy. I'll call you later.' " The Duke shook his head. "Why are women such masochists?"

She was numb. For a moment she thought bitterly that he contributed his share to female masochism.

"He's probably a mixture of pride and inadequacy, the kind who won't commit himself because he hopes something better will come along. The kind who thinks, 'She can't be much, if she's fallen for me.' He may be good at pitching the news, but he may not be much as a man. To protect his ego he lays the blame on you —and you go along with it. He's perfect. You're flawed. . . ."

"Mari," the Duke went on, "when I suggested we feel free to have other affairs I didn't want you to get hurt. There's a freshness about you, a kind of streak of the primitive woman who wants to love her mate completely—which is the reason I think you should have more experience. You may be attracted to me one day, to Noel another. But you should know all kinds of men, learn what makes them tick—which may have *nothing* at all to do with you." His voice was warm, almost loving. "Too bad wisdom comes at the price of unhappiness."

He talked about the various types of men and their differing needs and desires. She listened gratefully, forgetting her jealousy, forgetting even her pain, but needing to absorb his knowledge. The Duke, for all of his indiscretions, had an honesty and dependability which comforted her. If she could understand what men needed, perhaps she could get over Noel.

After they left the restaurant they walked down Park Avenue in the soft, balmy night. Marianna said she would take a cab home.

The Duke stopped and looked at her with a strange expression: not lust, but something she'd never seen before.

She shook her head.

"Mari, we must make up."

"Sorry." She flagged a taxi. "See you in the morning."

She was proud of herself, even in the midst of her confusion, and felt an unexpected surge of strength.

When she arrived at the office the next morning Winnie the Pooh was clearing out her desk. "I'm going back to the Coast," she said brightly. "It's my kind of town."

Have I really won out? Marianna wondered. How would it be the next time?

Right now she found it easier to forget Noel. The Duke had given her the armor she needed to combat the hurt of rejection.

"The Duke wants you," Flora said several days later while Marianna was at the Xerox machine. On her way to his office, she picked up a sheaf of letters for his signature.

"You're looking better, Mari," he said when she walked in.

"Thanks. I have some letters—"

"Leave them. I'll sign them later. Right now I want to talk to you." He gestured her to a chair.

"Oh, oh. What did I do wrong?"

"Mari, for God's sake, will you stop being so self-deprecating? You've done *nothing* wrong and *plenty* right. You're a great asset here; you have a future in communications, and when the time is right I won't hold you back."

She was touched, yet she wondered what was coming next.

"I understand from Flora that you've had three years of French. How would you like to practice what you learned in school?"

"D'you have some letters to be translated?"

"No, my innocent. I'm asking if you'd like to see Paris."

"Would I!"

"As a member of the wedding party."

She could scarcely believe her ears. He was referring to Faith Alcott, the Boston-bred actress who was touted as a young version of Katharine Hepburn. After making an auspicious debut in an artistic film, Faith had attracted the attention of one of France's most eligible young noblemen and was engaged to him shortly afterward. This was not a Cinderella story, however; Faith was well-born, of a family comparable to her suitor's. Under any circumstances the wedding would have sparked stories on all the society pages. But with Faith's sudden recognition as a film star the publicity had mushroomed into hysterical demands from the press, radio and television—all of which the Duke was handling with his customary talent.

"I'll fly over for the wedding," the Duke said. "But I can't leave here until the day before the ceremony. You'll be my stand-in, arrange all details, meet the press, just as you do here."

To his surprise, she hesitated. "For how long?"

"Two weeks. You can chaperone the honeymoon. Expense account all the way." He paused and then said, bluntly, "Just what the doctor ordered, Mari. We'll be together—"

She was suddenly resolute. "Great. I can't think of anything nicer—except being the bride. When do I leave?"

"Next Monday morning. With the wedding party. You'll be staying at the Ritz."

"You're a good boss, *Monsieur le duc.*"

He laughed. "You'll be meeting the real thing in the bridegroom. He's quite a guy. He and Faith will restore the public's belief that romance isn't dead."

Elated about her asignment, Marianna made her first call to Mrs. Lovell. She asked for news of Allegra, who hadn't answered her last letter.

"She's been touring," Mrs. Lovell said. "At the moment, I believe she's in Provence. Write her in care of American Express." She added reluctantly, "When you see her, Marianna, do ask her to write to us. She's been a disappointing correspondent."

Her second call was to Cristina, who was ecstatic about her news.

"That's fabulous. You've been so darned good, working so hard. What about clothes?"

"I haven't given them much thought; I've been too busy."

"Why don't we meet for lunch Saturday? And then go to Bloomie's—"

"Not this Saturday. I'm due at New Canaan."

"How *is* your mother?"

"Pretty well, I guess. She's having more tests today and tomorrow. . . . How is Bonnie Rob Roy?"

"Super, at the moment. She's got a new boyfriend. He's going to write music for her." Cris laughed, but there was a strained note in her voice. "Mama can't live without love. Period."

Marianna promised to keep in touch and then went back to her work. She typed up the bride's schedule for the week and made her own list of press and magazine contacts. And then, with Laurie and Flora, she pored over guidebooks and maps of Paris. She still couldn't believe she was going.

Saturday morning, on her way to Grand Central Station to catch the train to New Canaan, Marianna stopped at the Liggett's drugstore on Forty-second Street and looked through the paperback shelves. She bought a couple of paperbacks on the psychology of women—what she really wanted was information on what makes men tick. She was still suffering from the end of her affair with Noel, but in the rush of the week's events she had thought less about him. She hoped that her trip would help heal her wounds.

After she paid her bill she cut through the store

and opened the rear door that led directly into the station. She seldom used this entry; the waiting-room seats were usually occupied by strange, furtive-looking men. Near the men's toilets she saw a few young fellows in jeans and windbreakers, and older men more carefully dressed in suits and soft felt hats.

Then she spotted him. He was seated at the end of the bench, a folded copy of the *Post* in his hands. She stopped, wheeled back and faced him.

"Noel, what're you doing here?"

He looked up startled. It was the first time she'd seen him wearing a hat, and it was pulled down low over his forehead. Although the weather was warm he was wearing a raincoat, and he looked sad and listless. What was the matter with him?

"I'm waiting . . . for a friend," he said.

"I hear you're leaving Sunday." She was trying to make small talk, not knowing how to act or what to say. "Did you know that I'm flying to Paris Sunday morning?" She went into details about the wedding party. "It's all very posh—Faith Alcott's family, very much the Boston Brahmins, and his family, very old French lineage, and her Hollywood friends, very new crowned heads. I'm supposed to keep the press in line and act as companion to Faith. . . ."

Noel was polite but distant. They stood silent for a moment, and then he said, "Well, good luck. I must be going," and turned away.

She hurried through the waiting room to the station to make her train.

She found a middle seat, between two executive types who were absorbed in reading the stock market and business columns. The air conditioning wasn't working and she leaned back against the seat, conscious of her rapid heartbeat. Something nagged at her mind. Why did he look so unhappy? Had he lost his job? No, that couldn't be it; the Duke had told her Noel was on the Moscow party. Why was he sitting there among those odd-looking men and the bold, handsome young fellows?

Suddenly she knew.

No wonder she hadn't made stars for him.

Oh, Noel, she thought, more in compassion now than in anger, *you poor man.* . . .

At nine o'clock that evening Marianna called the Duke's apartment. His answering service told her he was in Southampton.

"Will you give me his number there, please? This is his office. It's urgent that I contact him."

It was nearly eleven o'clock when she reached him. He and his hosts had just come home after a dinner with friends.

"I don't know how to tell you this," she began nervously, "but there's a problem."

"What's up, Mari? For Christ's sake, spill it. Has Faith changed her mind or has her fiancé jilted her?"

"Nothing like that. It's just that I can't go to Paris."

"This is a helluva time to tell me. What happened? Your boyfriend make up with you? Are you going to Moscow with him?"

"You aren't funny." Her voice was anguished. "It's my mother."

"I thought you said she was coming along well—"

"She was. But they've found a lump in her breast—"

"Good God."

"They're operating Monday morning. They'll take a specimen and send it down to the lab for a frozen section while she's still under anesthesia. If it's malignant —which they think it may be—they'll do a radical mastectomy."

He was speechless for a few moments. "Can't you hire private nurses?" he said finally.

"She wants me there. She's very emotional about it. This may be her second major operation."

"It's a shame. I hoped this trip would be the Yellow Brick Road for you, Mari."

"I appreciate it," she said. "But I'm hamstrung. I can't turn my back on her."

"Isn't there anybody else in the family—?"

"My sister's on the west coast with her husband. Even if I locate her, she won't come. She never allows anything to interfere with her life."

"What's the next step?"

She pondered his question. "Laurie?"

"I guess so." He didn't sound very optimistic. "Think she can manage?"

"Oh, yes, She's competent. I'll get back to the city tomorrow afternoon and give her all my notes. She'll get along well with Faith. They're both Smith graduates."

"What about you, Mari?"

"I can't walk out on my mother. Flout your duty, and guilt takes over—"

"It's a damned shame. I'm sorry, Mari. I'll make it up to you some other way."

"Thanks." She knew what he meant but hung up before he could hear her sobbing.

Four hours of surgery. Then the recovery room. While Liebschen was coming out of the anesthesia the surgeon went into the fourth-floor lounge to speak to Marianna and her stepfather.

"I think we got it all out. She came through surgery nicely," the doctor said, "and I think she'll do well." With a reassuring nod he left them.

Marianna turned to her stepfather. Jan Dietrich's aging, sensitive face was briefly free of anxiety.

"Liebschen will be upset," he said. "She set great store by her—breasts."

"You'll have to explain it to her," Marianna said. "It was her breast or her life."

"Marianna, I'm truly sorry." He made a helpless gesture. "Your trip—"

"Forget it, Jan. I'll have to go back to the city for a couple of days but I'll be back here each evening. And once Mama is allowed to come home I'll take a few days off to help her get settled. But what about you? Will you be able to manage?"

"Yes, yes. Don't worry about me. I will take care of everything—the shopping, the preparation, even the cooking."

"What about the store?"

"I will speak to Evalina. Perhaps one of her students

might want to earn a few dollars—he could stay in the store. Otherwise we will close it until Liebschen is restored to health."

"We'll manage. And she'll be okay. You heard what the doctor said."

"You don't think he was just . . . how shall I say it . . . reassuring us? Kidding us along?"

"I doubt it. He'd be more apt to tell us the truth. Not to Mama perhaps, but certainly to us. I believe him; Mama will recover and she'll be as good as new."

"She will take the surgery badly. Mark my words."

Marianna went home with her stepfather. Liebschen had come down from the recovery room on a rolling stretcher, with two nurses lifting her onto her bed and then putting up the guard rails. She drifted in and out of a drugged sleep, and since the floor was short of nursing staff, Marianna got permission to stay with her for the night.

Now Liebschen was stirring. She had pulled away her blankets, and Marianna, moving softly to the bed to cover her, was shocked by the swathe of bandages around her chest. In the dim light her mother looked like a stranger, her blond hair off her forehead and ears, her face clean of makeup, faint bruises under her eyes. Marianna felt a surge of pity deepened by love.

She reached down over the guard rail and touched her mother's cheek with her fingers. She was praying for her recovery. *I'll never be impatient with her again*, she resolved.

The next evening, while Jan sat with Liebschen, helping her sip her tea and spoon her jello, Marianna stepped out of the room to go down to the coffee shop for a sandwich and a soda.

On her return she paused a moment outside the half-open door.

"Look what Marianna gave up for you." Her stepfather's voice was reproachful, which meant Liebschen had been complaining about something.

"She *owes* it to me," Liebschen said irritably. "I gave up plenty for her."

Marianna could have stood it all—looking after her mother at home after the stay in the hospital, helping her bathe, finding books she would enjoy, preparing food to tempt her appetite . . . keeping in touch with the office by telephone, giving instructions to the temporary secretary who was taking her place.

But what hurt—and hurt terribly—was the news that Laurie had met an Englishman at Faith Alcott's wedding and was about to marry him.

"*We'll be living in London most of the time,*" she wrote Marianna in her meticulous boarding school script, "*. . . using the family flat at the Albany and spending weekends at their place in Sussex, where we plan to redo the gardener's cottage. . . .*"

It could have been me, Marianna thought. *It should have been me.*

CHAPTER VII

ALLEGRA

Allegra found the latest Locust Ryse Newsletter among her messages and mail at the American Express office in Paris. Curious, she turned to the Alumnae News for the Class of '67. The corresponding secretary was Hannah Byrd, bless her gossip-mongering little heart!

Allegra Simon left Shaunton. She is in Paris, studying the culinary arts with Maxim's or the Cordon Bleu, or one of those posh schools.

Allie, the total vegetarian! Does she abstain from those culinary delights?

Allie, when you come home, your former class-mates expect you to put on a gourmet spread.

Marianna Ellis is apprenticed to a famous public relations figure, which means she gets to see all the Broadway shows, attends all the posh parties.

Well do I recall the day Allie and Marianna were shopping in Best's, where I was a college counselor, and Allie tipped me off to Marianna's fabulous new job.

Cristina Terhune is no longer at the American Academy of Dramatic Art, but is taking private voice, dancing and dramatic lessons. Will she follow in her famous mother's footsteps?

Now for the rest of us: Our lives may seem humdrum compared with those of our glamour girls. Four of our classmates are married and

*two engaged. The class can now boast two moth-
ers....*

Clutching her mail, Allegra turned into a small
café. The outdoor chairs were tilted, their backs resting on the edge of round tables. She went inside and
sat at a table near the tall glass windows that kept out
much of the February cold. She ordered a croissant
and *café au lait* and remained there for half an
hour, thawing out, watching the never-ending rush of
pedestrians.

Winter was wretched in Paris.

The stones of the ancient buildings reflected the
muted grays of the sky. The chestnut trees were in
hibernation; steam clouded the glass of café windows.
It seemed to Allie as though all of Paris was melancholy. She knew she had made a mistake by agreeing
to come here.

The school her mother had chosen for her was run
by an elderly aristocratic Frenchwoman. Madame was
thin and beak-nosed, with artfully dyed hair squared
in a chignon and quick eyes that missed nothing. Despite her reduced circumstances she wore magnificent
clothes, willingly given to her by St. Laurent, Chanel
and Patou, to whose salons she directed her young,
rich charges.

Madame and her staff aimed to educate high-born
girls in the essential art of gourmet cooking and the
selection of fine wines. The five-month course cost
three thousand dollars and included tickets to the opera, ballet and theater; field trips to the Louvre and
Versailles; and weekend tours to the countryside, where
the students stayed in the homes of titled French
families.

Most of the girls lived in Madame's establishment,
a beautiful old stone house not far from the American
Embassy. Allegra, who had arrived after the class
started, chose to register at a small family hotel, which
met with Madame's grudging approval. The pension,
favored by knowledgeable tourists, was located across
the street from the rear of the Ritz.

Allegra was obliged to attend classes four days a week. During her free time she would walk the streets alone, wishing that Marianna and Cris were there to share her impressions. But more than that, she wished her father could have been with her . . . Paris had been his favorite city.

Dressed in layers of clothes before the style became fashionable, Allie was never completely warm. But her long walks were a kind of obsession with her, enabling her to cast off her dark moods. She went alone to Notre Dame but joined a group of American sightseers, feeling more comfortable in their midst. On the Left Bank she met American boys, most of whom were backpacking across Europe on their way to Afghanistan or India, where they could smoke dope and dream like the old Chinese in their opium dens. She had no interest in them.

Allegra was losing weight—not deliberately, but just by passing up the meat and fowl dishes prepared by her classmates. Occasionally she had a salad or an egg dish, but she was never hungry. Her morning croissant and coffee sustained her until dinner, which she often ate at the hotel. Her room was spacious and overlooked a garden, and often on Sundays, when she was too tired to stir, she'd sit at the window and gaze out at the barren trees and shrubs, wishing that spring would finally come.

She longed for warm weather, hoping the sun would bake out her wretched cough. Madame had told Allie that she found her habit of clearing her throat offensive. She wanted her to see a doctor, which Allie thought was ridiculous. Nothing was wrong with her, except the everlasting chill in the air, so bone-penetrating.

One Saturday late in March she decided to visit the Louvre by herself and she made a leisurely tour, listening to the cassette she'd rented. She recalled the lovely Saturdays spent with Stephen Terhune, who had taken her, Cris and Marianna to the art galleries in Manhattan. Thinking of Stephen made her miserable; she'd botched *that* up with her big mouth and her dramatics.

She felt empty, purposeless and considered flying home, but she had no idea what she'd do there.

Then something happened that relieved her increasing depression. The Paris *Vogue* was photographing Madame's culinary school and its students for a double-page spread. The photographer was an American expatriate named Arkady, who invited the girls to visit his studio on the Left Bank.

Well in his seventies, Arkady was spry and agile. Except for his thick brush of white hair, his too-pale blue eyes and his fleshy mouth, he looked like a man two decades younger. The girls, chaperoned by Madame, found his quarters very bohemian, and all of them ordered extra copies of the prints that would appear in *Vogue*.

After her classmates bade Arkady goodbye, smiling prettily, Allegra waited. When he took her hand the photographer said in an undertone, "I'd like to do some portraits of you. You have the most magnificent eyes I've ever seen. Will you sit for me?"

Allegra's eyes met his in cool, detached understanding. They would have a photographic session, but that wouldn't be all. *The old goat* she thought, feeling amused for the first time in months.

The following Saturday she returned to his studio, where he photographed her surrounded by fresh flowers. The result of the sitting was his famous *Girl With Tulips*: the nude with only an amethyst gem in the hollow of her lovely throat.

After Allegra had posed for him in the seductive manner that was natural to her he wrapped her in a fine woolen shawl and led her over to the couch. She knew what was coming, but it didn't matter. She was passive rather than docile.

Looking down at her thin body, the curving thighs, the flat ribcage and small, almost non-existent breasts, he said, "Do not fear, Allegra. I shall possess you only in spirit. My body no longer obeys the desires of the flesh."

He kissed her gently and held her in his arms, and somehow she found his embrace comforting. She thought it strange that there was no stirring of passion in her body. She wanted only to be held, to be stroked, to be a child again, seeking and receiving sustenance.

Arkady took her to see plays by Genet, Beckett and Ionesco. He escorted her to restaurants on the Left Bank that she, as a student, would never have discovered. She loved the attention the restaurant keepers gave to the dogs that came with their patrons and told Arkady about her mother's collection of Kerry Blues and the poodle she'd loved as a child.

"You're refreshing," Arkady said. "You have a small child's candor and a sophisticate's capacity for pleasure. What are you doing taking culinary lessons? Why aren't you studying at the Sorbonne?"

"I'm lazy. I seem to be trapped in a kind of 'I-don't-care' mood."

"Eat your fish, Allegra. Don't toy with it. *Eat.*" He was trying to persuade her to give up her vegetarian diet.

"You're too thin. And I don't like that cough."

"It's a Paris cough," she said. "From all the dampness."

"I think you should have it checked."

Adroitly she changed the subject. "Why do you stay in Paris when your work can command higher fees in New York?"

"Shall I tell you? . . . I'd be uncomfortable in a country that votes Nixon into office. Or in a country where law and order is in such a sad way. Or where low-cal soda is a kind of beer and sports figures make more money than Picasso. In this age of nuclear over-kill, a Paris garret is one of the last holdouts. . . ."

Arkady flew to Egypt in March to take fashion shots for a new British picture magazine. He invited Allegra to accompany him, but she refused. She still felt tired, and her cough seemed to be getting worse. She wondered if her illness was somehow connected to the abortion. . . .

She would never forget that day. She had taken the train to Manhattan and had hailed a cab outside Grand Central Station.

When she gave the driver the address he regarded her carefully, as if he was aware of what she was about to do. She was wearing a beige-and-white tweed jacket, neatly buttoned to her neck; a jumper of camel's hair; English walking shoes from Abercrombie's; and a brown beret on her head. Girls dressed like that didn't go to the Lower West Side to go shopping, the cabbie probably knew.

Allie sat at the edge of her seat, her white-gloved hands neatly folded together to stop their trembling. The driver turned toward the Hudson River where there were dingy parking lots, dark-faced taverns, elderly women sitting on the stoops, janitors carting out refuse.

The cab drew up to a building that looked newer than the adjacent decrepit brownstones—a dirty orange-brick apartment house.

Suddenly Allie felt terribly lonely—and scared. What if something went wrong and she bled to death? *Dear God,* she thought, *I'm terrified.* But she knew it was wrong to pray to Him under the circumstances. . . .

She gave the driver a large tip.

"Look, miss—"

She turned away, embarrassed.

Allie squinted at the names alongside the row of push buttons, looking not for the doctor's name, but for another, which she'd been instructed to do. The buzzer sounded, the front door clicked and she went tentatively into the lobby, shadowy even in daylight.

One flight up; the door to the rear. She knocked. It opened partly on a chain latch, and she caught a glimpse of a blond Hollywood-type beauty. Then the door opened, revealing a starched white uniform, a chunky body and thick sexy legs in white stockings. The blond was the nurse on duty.

"I have an appointment." Allie wet her lips, barely able to whisper.

The nurse nodded and led her into what looked like a makeshift waiting room. It was furnished with a blue sofa, several Windsor chairs and a table on which were recent women's magazines and several ashtrays —nothing more.

The nurse sat down at the table, which served as a

desk, and asked Allie for her name and address. The woman scribbled the information on a card and then looked at her expectantly. Allie removed the wallet from her pouch and took out four hundred dollars, mostly in tens and twenties.

The nurse showed her into a dressing room and asked her to put on a white hospital gown and to leave a urine specimen. Allie moved mechanically, piling her clothes neatly, more neatly than usual, trying to postpone the inevitable.

Finally the nurse looked in. "Doctor is ready," she said briskly.

Allie followered her like a sleepwalker into the little operating room where the doctor was waiting. He was a heavyset man with spectacles guarding his eyes, his face hidden by a dark beard and mustache. He was wearing a white coat, and his hands were red from scrubbing and antiseptics.

He nodded. The nurse pointed to the examining table. "Sit here, Miss."

The nurse fastened a cuff on her upper arm, squeezed the bulb until it tightened and then watched the reading. She seemed puzzled and looked up at the doctor.

"I'll take it," the doctor said. He got a similar reading. "Are you on any medication?" he asked Allie.

"No."

"Your blood pressure is a bit low."

"I'm anemic, I think." Seeking to reassure him, she added, "But I'm very active. I ride and swim and water ski. . . ."

He asked her about school, and she told him that she loved French and Spanish and was bored with Ethics, and she was supposed to go to college in September, although she wasn't looking forward to it. Her mother was hoping for Mount Holyoke.

"Isn't that too close to Smith? The boys spread themselves pretty thin."

The doctor had a sense of humor, Allie thought, which made her feel better. "Well, they date Smith. But they marry Mount Holyoke."

While she was lying on the operating table he gave

her a whiff of something. She was semi-conscious, but she hoped she made a good impression, which was her aim in the presence of any man. But her legs were doubled up, her feet thrust in the stirrups like a helpless animal. . . .

What would her mother say if she could see her now? she wondered. Prudence wouldn't make a scene; she was too cool and distant. Allie's behavior had at first confused then infuriated Prudence. Not so with Pavel. "My little firebrand," her father used to call her. . . . Allie felt a sharp twinge in her midriff and uttered a soft moan.

"It's finished. Now you'll lie down and rest," the doctor said. "That wasn't so bad, was it?"

Lying on the couch in another room, she tried to block out of her mind what sex had done to her. . . .

Several hours later when she was ready to leave, the nurse helped her dress, gave her a few instructions and then handed her a wad of bills.

"The doctor cut his fee in half for you." The woman was visibly annoyed.

Downstairs Allie hailed a cab and directed the driver to Tiffany's, where she ordered a heavy gold bracelet, engraved with two sets of initials—AS and ST. She paid cash for it and still had enough money for her taxi to Grand Central.

She was feeling shaky by the time she got on the train and her thighs felt wet. She went into the washroom and stared at herself in the mirror. And then it hit her: *My God,* she thought. Stephen's baby. . . .

At five o'clock in the afternoon Stephen Terhune went back to the Ritz after a meeting with an international banking group.

Paris wasn't showing its best face. Rain pelted the streets, and he was relieved to reach his room and strip off his damp clothes. Then, clad in a blue robe, he poured a drink from the bottle of Scotch on the small end table, and leafed through his correspondence. There was no mail from Rose Eileen, but he had received a message from Allegra Simon.

"Please call me," the note read. "I am staying on

the Rue Cambon, just across the street from you. It is *most* urgent." She had written down her telephone number.

Stephen had known she was in Paris; Cris had mentioned it before he left the States, but he preferred not to see Allegra again. In New Canaan he had carefully avoided her whenever she visited the house.

The second time with her had been a terrible blunder on his part, he thought. And for the life of him, he couldn't figure out why it had happened. He was no cradle-snatcher. The women who intrigued him were for the most part sophisticated, knowledge-able and much nearer his own years. Rose Eileen was different, of course; she had a magnetic beauty and a warm, loving heart, and his affection for her was lasting. But there were moments when he found her dull, and he hated himself for his feelings. The wild night with Allegra remained to torment his memory . . . and stir his blood.

The telephone rang.

"Stephen—"

He recognized her voice, even though it sounded hoarse.

"I'm so glad I got you," Allegra said.

"What's wrong?" he asked. "You don't sound right—"

"I'm sick—I'm burning up—I don't know what to do—"

"Where are you?"

She gave him the name of the hotel. He asked for her room number, promised to come over immediate-ly and got into dry clothes. When he knocked at her door ten minutes later, she called, "It's open—come in."

She was lying in bed, the covers drawn to her chin. He realized she was feverish, but at the same time she was shivering.

He took her hand. "How did you know where to find me?"

"Cris wrote you'd be at the Ritz."

"How long have you been sick?"

"Oh, on and off for weeks. I can't seem to shake it, and yesterday when I went to class I got *soaked* . . ."

She told him about the culinary school. She'd skipped today's class because they were going to cook a rabbit.

She was talking nervously, rapidly. When she ran out of breath she began to cough, a rough, rasping sound.

"We'd better call a doctor," Stephen said.

"No, it isn't necessary. I couldn't *bear* a French doctor; they're all so indelicate—"

"There's the American Hospital," he said. "They must have American doctors."

"No, no. I'll be okay. If you'll just stay a little while—I'm kind of scared to be alone—"

He pulled up an armchair, looking at her flushed face, wondering whether to override her refusal to see a physician.

He decided to go out to get some food. When he got up she clung to his hand.

"I just want to bring some fruit," he said. "Look, have you any aspirin?"

"Plenty. I've slallowed tons of them."

He came back with oranges, Perrier water, cough syrup, a thermometer, tissues and other sundries. Her eyes were glazed, and he removed the thermometer from its case, shook it and put it under her tongue.

She seemed to have trouble breathing. Her bluish lips were parted, but he closed them gently to get a correct reading. He was concerned: She was obviously in need of a doctor. Her temperature registered four degrees above normal. She was much thinner than he remembered, and he didn't like the flush spots on her cheeks.

There was no spoon in the room to measure the cough syrup, so he poured the liquid into a glass, and she drank it. Suddenly she was sick to her stomach, and before she could reach the bathroom she vomited on herself and the carpet. She was gasping now, dry heaves shaking her frail body. When he tried to help her she turned away.

"Don't be ashamed," he said. "I've taken care of Cris when she was sick. Here, let's remove your night-gown—"

He helped her into a fresh gown, which he found in the bureau drawer, and then he dampened a towel, bathed her face and got her back into bed. He cleaned up the mess and sat beside her again until she drifted off.

Quietly he went downstairs and spoke to the concierge. He asked if an American physician had registered at the hotel.

They were fortunate, the concierge said. An American doctor was staying there, but he was out for the evening.

At midnight, the young doctor rapped on the door. Stephen let him in, apologizing for the late hour. The doctor examined Allegra and suggested that she be taken to a hospital.

"She's had bronchitis most of the winter," Stephen explained.

"It's evidently developed into pneumonia. She needs antibiotics and better care than she'd get here. . . ."

Stephen and the doctor wrapped Allegra in her fur coat and a blanket and helped her downstairs into a taxi.

Allegra roused herself. "Don't leave me, Steve—"

"I won't," he promised. "I'll be right here with you."

"They've taken enough blood to put Dracula into business," Allegra reported when Stephen came to visit several days later. He was loaded down with gifts: silk nightgowns, books, magazines.

"I understand you're woefully anemic," he said, "so I'm not so sure Dracula would find you suitable. . . . How come, Allegra?"

"I've been a vegetarian for a couple of years," she said.

"You aren't getting enough protein. Your body has been feeding on itself."

"Stephen, did you call the school?"

"I did. Madame was sorry to hear of your illness. She looks forward to your return."

"Must I go back? I *loathe* it."

"I suspect that's between you and your family."

"You haven't written Cris I was sick?"

"Not a word."

"Thank you. You're a good man, Stephen Ter-hune."

He saw the first sign of humor, the first wicked gleam in her eyes.

Within five days she was allowed to return to her hotel. Stephen felt it was too soon; he was due in London for a few days and he didn't want her to be alone. But she was determined, and he arranged with the concierge to see that her meals were sent to her room and that she had enough eggs, fish and cheese to compensate for her protein deficiency.

Later in the afternoon, when he stopped by to say goodbye, he found her sitting in a chair by the window. She was freshly bathed, her gleaming hair brushed off her delicate face. She had on a long night-dress and a lace bedjacket.

He told her about the London meetings.

"But you'll be back?" she asked anxiously.

"I'll be back. And I expect you to have gained a couple of pounds in that time."

"Stephen—" She stood up, raised her arms and embraced him. "How can I ever thank you?"

He smiled. "My pleasure."

Was he mocking her? She put her cheek to his, searching for his lips, but he moved away.

"Don't tempt me, Allegra."

"I just want to kiss you," she whispered. "To show my gratitude."

"Your gratitude got me into trouble once before," he said. "We don't dare risk it again."

"You don't like me—"

"Quite the contrary. I like you too much."

Before she had told him about her abortion, after they had made love in his bedroom ("I carried your sons," she'd said), he'd taken for granted that nothing had happened to her. Now that he knew about the consequences of the operation he was even more disgusted with himself. *Good Lord,* he thought. *What the poor kid went through.*

He wondered how he could make it up to her . . . without getting involved again.

It had been an accident—Stephen would swear to it. The chauffeur, off for the night, had left the station wagon at the railroad station for Stephen, who had a set of extra keys in his pocket.

Stephen had taken the nine o'clock express that stopped at Stamford before New Canaan. His late afternoon meetings had gone badly; he was tired and frustrated. He was scanning the evening paper, sitting alone in a narrow seat meant for two, when he heard her voice.

"Is this taken?" He glanced up, and she said, "Why, Mr. Terhune, I didn't realize it was you."

Cristina's school friend, Allegra Simon, slipped into the seat beside him. She was wearing a little red jersey shift and a short fur jacket. Her face, with its strange, high cheekbones, had a distinctive beauty that was at odds with her girlish manner.

They made polite, idle talk—about Locust Ryse, graduation and the senior class's plans for the future. He recalled that Cris adored this girl; she was always talking about her with the most extravagant praise.

Cris said the boys were keen on Allegra, who called them twerps and cared only for her dogs and horses. And older men, Cris added . . . But then all girls were crazy about father figures, Stephen thought.

Except his own daughter.

An hour was a long time to spend with an immature young girl, particularly that evening, when his day had ended on a sour note. He was distracted, thinking that he'd never been a company man and never would be.

A Depression kid, he had been brought up to appreciate the value of a dollar. Whenever he felt he'd come on too strongly in a deal, that his proposal was less forthright than he'd have liked, he always made up for it with an impulsive act of kindness to assuage his conscience. He was responsible for the organization "Give An Older Worker A Break," which helped find jobs for workers who'd been forced into retirement. Scholarships were available for the children of his staff, both in the States and abroad. He had a streak of compassion—often a fatal flaw in a man of power, he knew—but it was shored up by an elemental drive for power. Financial writers called him the last of the rugged individualists.

Allegra was chatting away. He forced himself to listen patiently, though the new construction plans that were the subject of the day's meetings were giving him a headache.

At the station he asked if anyone was calling for her.

"I'll take a cab," she said.

Naturally he wouldn't think of it. She said she was going to her grandmother's house, and he offered to drive her there.

The night was dark, the sky covered with brooding clouds that threatened showers. Stephen took short cuts with which Allegra was unfamiliar—secondary roads, narrow and curving. He drove easily, pleased that he'd met Allegra and had her in the car.

Suddenly, she cried, "Mr. Terhune, *stop!*"

They were on a long stretch of deserted road. He stepped on the brakes as the headlights revealed a roadblock of some kind—either wire strands or rope stretched across the road from one side to the other. As the station wagon came to a jolting halt, a couple of young fellows in leather jackets approached the car and lounged on either side, watching Stephen's reaction with a defiant air.

He lowered the car window and asked them to move the block.

They whistled; they jeered. Then they tossed a few empty beer cans at the window.

Stephen opened the glove compartment and took out a gun. Allie was shocked. He put his hand on the door handle, and she pleaded, "Don't go. They look vicious."

"We can't let them bully us. When I get out of the car, you lock the door so you'll be safe. Okay, I'm going—"

He walked out, his heart beating crazily, knowing there was no alternative. The six burly youths were gathered beside the wagon. Stephen suggested in a calm voice that they let him drive off. They remained motionless, insolent, sizing him up. Then they began to circle him, reminding Stephen of the Indians who surrounded Conestoga wagons in western movies.

He said quietly, "I am armed. I have a permit to carry a gun. It's loaded. And I won't hesitate to use it."

They were eager to challenge him, the alcohol they had consumed obviously burning in their veins, and they saw the face of a pretty girl in the station wagon. They moved in, and he stood fast.

When they were upon him, he fired the gun, aiming for their kneecaps. Two of the hoodlums doubled up and fell screaming; one, who was swinging a heavy chain, let it go and it hit Stephen in the shoulder, momentarily numbing his arm—but not before he had sent another shot at the fellow's knees. Since Stephen was in motion, the bullet caught his assailant in the groin. His scream was unearthly. The others turned and fled into the bushes.

In the distance, Stephen heard the wail of a police car siren. He jumped into the car, locked the door and drove off. His shoulder throbbed painfully.

When he reached the woods adjoining the Towle house, he turned into an old wagon road. He switched off the lights and took a deep breath.

"You okay?" he asked Allegra.

"Yes. But I almost died when they ganged up on you—"

"Good thing I had a gun in the car."

"Do you really have a permit?"

"Yes. It's often necessary in my travels."

Her breath suddenly exploded in short gasps, and he realized she was sobbing—a delayed reaction to the attack. He dreaded to think what could have happened to her.

Suddenly she was in his arms, clutching him. He responded in a surge of feeling that astonished him. He held her, kissing her lips, exploring her tiny breasts, her satin-smooth thighs. He hadn't experienced such a wild, uninhibited rush of passion in years. It was a violent, clumsy embrace—a release from a moment of danger.

They lay in the back of the station wagon, disheveled, spent. He was holding her fiercely, even afterward, as though protecting her from the marauders ... or perhaps from himself.

Before morning he called his lawyer, and they met at police headquarters. The incident was suppressed; Stephen lodged no complaint against the hoodlums and arranged for his lawyer to pay their bail.

It was an accident, Stephen repeated to himself now, recalling that night. As he nursed Allegra through her illness, he swore it would never happen again. He hadn't been able to resist temptation when she had come to his bedroom, but *this* time ...

He called for her early on a Monday morning. She wore a pale blue cashmere sweater dress that accented her flat ribcage and narrow chest. Over it, she had draped a raincoat with a wool lining, the collar raised jauntily. Her dark hair, brushed off her pale face, was held in a gold barrette. As always she was wearing sunglasses. And as always she moved with flair.

His rented Mercedes was parked outside. He put her overnight bag next to his own on the rear seat.

"Where are we going?" she asked.

"No place in particular. I thought we'd drive south and let each day take care of itself."

Her heart leaped. Dared she hope they were embarking on a journey during which they would open their hearts to each other and explore their shared passion without shame or secrecy? That he had arranged this trip, no doubt taking leave from pressing business affairs, was, she thought, a sign of his growing love for her.

She looked at him from behind her glasses, aware of his strong profile, the deep folds in his cheeks when his lips were pressed together. He wore a gray pullover, a striped sports shirt, gray pants, and a worn brown tweed jacket. She was proud of how handsome he was.

He said they would travel between the Loire and Rhone valleys, unless she had other preferences.

"I haven't. I'm just happy to be here with you."

She wondered whether her voice betrayed her ecstacy.

They were beyond the outskirts of Paris, and Stephen was consulting the Michelin maps. They had left the main highway now and were wandering on old wagon roads, past great stretches of meadowland, past farmhouses where chickens, geese and sheep dotted the landscape.

In the evening they stopped at a manor house which Stephen said often had rooms available for guests.

They had dinner with the owners—a middle-aged doctor, his wife and two grown sons. Allegra didn't need coaxing; she allowed herself to enjoy poached chicken in a velvet-smooth sauce over rice, the lettuce served as a separate course with a goat cheese. She was pleased that she could converse with their hosts in French. Stephen, she noticed, spoke French but not faultlessly; he was aware of his errors and didn't seem to mind them.

After dinner they went to their two bedrooms, which were in a guest house that had been converted from a *pigeonnier*, its round walls covered with a thick mat of ivy. The night was clear, the air sweet with the promise of spring.

She took a deep breath. "Oh, Stephen, it's been such a *perfect* day . . ."

"Tomorrow, another perfect day," he promised. In the small foyer he kissed her lightly on the forehead. "Sleep well, Allegra."

Then he closed his door. She was puzzled. He was attracted to her; he wanted to sleep with her. Why, then, was he so aloof?

As she put on her silk nightgown she paused before her door. Should she make a move? Was he waiting for a sign from her? She was in a quandary, but suddenly she felt a draft from the half-open window. She slipped into the narrow bed and covered herself, and before she knew it she was asleep.

The following days were for her like the pages of a picture book leafed through too swiftly. She and Stephen had breakfast at the inn or guesthouse where they had slept before they explored the surrounding countryside. One morning they climbed through rough, abandoned paths overgrown with vines to reach the ruins of an old chateau, where they shared a lunch of French bread, cheese and a wine of the region. In the afternoon, they crossed a Roman bridge and lingered in the nearby village, admiring the stalls of sausages, cheeses, vegetables and honey. Then they climbed the bell tower of the village church and looked out at the rolling landscape, marked by stone houses with private walled gardens.

Sometimes, as they were driving, he talked about Cristina. He said he didn't believe Cris wanted show business; she was merely imitating her mother. She was dating men Bonnie Rob Roy had introduced her to, and they weren't the men he'd choose for her.

"But she won't listen to me," he added, "and it's useless to confront her mother."

He had kind words for Marianna. "She's gone as far as she can in the Duke's office. It's inevitable that she'll step out on her own."

Friday came too quickly. After breakfast he turned the Mercedes toward Paris.

The trip had ended. But she felt restored. Her appetite had improved, and the antibiotics that had cleared her chest also seemed to have cured the low-grade vaginal infection that had troubled her for so long. She was aware of her lust for him, but each night they had gone to their separate rooms. He had given no indication that it would be different any time in the future.

They spent Saturday together in Paris. He had another wonderful day planned for them: galleries, bookshops, dinner in a three-star restaurant. When finally he took her back to the lobby of her hotel he told her he was flying to New York early in the morning. He made her promise to take care of herself and said that when she returned to the States, he expected her to be completely healthy again.

Then he took her hands in his. His eyes searched her face, but his lips were thin with self-control. He said, "Goodbye, Allegra."

"Stephen, it's been *wonderful*. You've saved my sanity." Tears gave a strange luster to her dark eyes, which she knew betrayed her pain. "I'll never forget this. *Never*." She pulled her hands away, draped them around his neck and kissed him on the mouth. He responded with a passion that sent a tremor through her body.

He had restrained his urges for so long that now the offer of her lips was too much for him. He held her close.

"Please, Stephen—please, come up to my room. We'll say goodbye there."

"We'd best say goodbye here," he said.

"Stephen, *please*—it doesn't feel right to end it this way."

"It's right, Allegra. And it's the only way."

He looked at her intently, and beyond his stern expression she saw a gleam of tenderness, of caring, that reduced her to tears. How could they part so abruptly after five heavenly days? It was cruel. . . . What had she to look forward to? Who *cared* about how to make a puff pastry or a pâté? She'd been waiting all of her growing years for someone like Stephen. To lose him would mean the dashing of her dreams, of her ambition to attach herself to a great and powerful man.

She would not give him up, she decided. But wisely, without another word, she let him go . . . for now.

Two weeks later Allegra received a transatlantic call from her mother. Prudence said that Grandmama Towle had died in her sleep. Allegra was expected home for the funeral.

Prudence also told her that she had inherited the bulk of her grandmother's estate. . . .

Allegra was saddened by the death but exultant that she was now completely on her own. None of her family—neither her mother, her stepfather, nor the other family trustees—could keep her from doing what she intended to do next.

CHAPTER VIII

MARIANNA

I seem to be addicted to my male teachers, Marianna thought.

First there had been Marc Finley, who had shown only a teacher's interest in her. When his contract at Locust Ryse wasn't renewed, Marc had gone back to Harvard for graduate work. Later he was drafted by the President for his Economic Council. His photograph often appeared in *Time, Newsweek* and the business pages of *The New York Times*. Marianna had clipped the material and sent it to him with a note congratulating him and bringing him up to date on her own life. Marianna's letter had initiated a casual correspondence between her and Marc—but nothing more than that.

Then Ted Ballin, her communications teacher at night school, had come into her life.

Early in his course she had become interested in him. She knew he was a graduate of City College and was now working toward his Master's degree at NYU. He was of medium height, but so thin that he looked taller. In his mid-twenties, he had the appearance of a street-smart city kid—a full head of curly brown hair resembling an Afro; a beetle brow under which his dark eyes were small, darting and all-seeing; and a face that was just short of being handsome. He was careless about his clothes, looking more like a student than an instructor; his shirts were usually wrinkled, and his chino pants or jeans had the right amount of wear.

Once, before class began, she heard him discussing the tragedy of Kent State, where the National Guard had killed four innocent students. He sounded so bitter that she decided there was a heart and a cry for justice under his rough exterior. She found the blend of his brilliant mind, uncouth manners and wiry body oddly attractive, as did many of the other women who took his class.

Marianna had fully recovered from her disastrous affair with Noel Osborn. Her obligations to her job—and to her mother, who was recuperating slowly from surgery—kept her so busy that she had little time now for brooding or introspection. She felt that for once she was able to regulate her life. Having a successful career wasn't the answer to a rich, meaningful existence, she knew, but at least it was an exercise in survival.

She kept reassuring herself this was a great time to be young and female. The Pill and her job had given her independence. Unlike the women of a generation ago, she didn't have to pine by the telephone, waiting; she could call a man and suggest a date without feeling that he would think less of her. She didn't have to flatter him or hang on his words. An equal companionship was possible.

Why, then, was she suddenly so marriage-conscious? So hung up on Ted Ballin?

"You interest me, Marianna Ellis," he'd said one night after class, when the course he taught was nearing its end. They began to date, going Dutch on dinners, tickets to Off Broadway plays, even bus fares. She could understand and cope with his lack of funds. What disturbed her was his unconcern about it. She expected him to be embarrassed or apologetic, but then she decided it was an old-fashioned criticism on her part—Locust Ryse versus New York University.

One evening in late October, as they were walking on lower Park Avenue, a fine rain began to fall. "What'd you say we have sandwiches at my place?" Ted said. "There's a deli on Forty-second Street . . ."

His look was urgent, intimate. She longed to respond, yet some instinct held her back. Something about Ted, in spite of his adoption of today's easy life style, told her that he would think less of a woman who slept with him. She put herself on an alert. *Food,* she thought, wryly, *but no screwing.*

His apartment was in a building in the mid-Fifties. It was a bad neighborhood, with papers floating in gutters, uncollected garbage and broken whiskey bottles in doorways of empty stores. Old characters roamed the pavements: winos staggering from store fronts to curb; old bag ladies with rheumy eyes and mottled faces; and packs of teenaged marauders.

The front door of the old building had no lock. "Let me go first," Ted said. "Sometimes you can get unpleasantly surprised here."

The wooden stairs were worn and bare; the sound of their heels reverberated. There was no ventilation in the hall, which had a stale, heavy smell.

He unlocked the door to his apartment, let her in and switched on the light. His furniture consisted of a bare electric bulb, a card table, a couple of chairs and a day bed. *How dreary and depressing,* she thought. How could he live here?

They sat at the table and ate their corned beef sandwiches. When they had finished he leaned toward her and said, "I know this isn't your bag, Mari. But you're a helluva good sport."

He had been testing her. But she didn't know it then.

When Marianna wouldn't sleep with him, Ted assumed she was a virgin.

He asked her to marry him. The sooner the better.

"We're legal now," he said on the cold December day they took the subway to City Hall for their license.

But she still held out. Abstinence seemed to give her strength. Her work improved; a new spirit gripped her. She was cheerful, obliging.

This was what she'd hungered for: the total commitment of one man. She'd be his lover, his companion. She'd help him by keeping him comfortable and free of financial worries until he received his Master's and Ph.D. Then she fantasized them in residence at a college—preferably in New England—with a beautiful campus and a fine library, and he could teach and write textbooks. . . .

Their wedding guests were mostly Marianna's relatives and friends. No invitations went to Ted's family. His parents were no longer living, and he'd had nothing to do with his brothers and sisters for years.

Evalina Novak had arranged for the reception to take place in her studio, following a City Hall ceremony in New York.

Marianna's mother was still in delicate health, but she did order a wedding cake for the couple. Rose Eileen and Stephen Terhune sent roast prime ribs, a baked ham and a houseman to carve and serve. The Lovells provided champagne and caviar.

My friends, thought Marianna, too moved to express her appreciation. They were all here, the people she loved.

The Duke arrived early with Flora in a station wagon filled with pots of white chrysanthemums and a case of white wine from his cellar. Wearing his brown English tweeds and ascot tie, he helped Evalina and Flora arrange the flowers to create a temporary altar. He had told Marianna that he wasn't pleased about the marriage, and now he behaved impeccably, as a friend of the bride should.

Evalina, recently thinned down, was wearing a becoming azure crepe dress with a revealing neckline.

"You should be going back to Vegas," Marianna told her.

Evalina embraced Marianna, crushing the white cotton-and-lace Mexican wedding dress. "Another twenty pounds and I'll make it," she said. "There's a nostalgia trend, you know. People are dying to see old favorites."

Allegra drove up in a vintage Studebaker, one of her stepfather's new acquisitions.

"Allie, you look gorgeous." Marianna hugged her. "It's been so long. . . ."

"Is Cris coming?"

"Yes, with Rose Eileen and Stephen. I'm so happy we'll all be together again."

She stared at Allie. "You look different—"

Allegra was in a cashmere dress that clung to her bosom, which was exquisitely rounded. She whispered in Marianna's ear, "Breast implant. Isn't it terrific?"

"Please come meet Ted," Marianna said, feeling uneasy. "He knows all about you."

Ted had bought a dark blue suit for the occasion but had balked at a white shirt and tie and was wearing a turtleneck. Marianna thought he looked handsome, although rather pale and nervous. She introduced Allie and Ted, beaming at both of them, holding her hands over theirs, wanting them to love each other— her husband and her dear friend.

"Allie made my years at Locust Ryse bearable. She just wouldn't let anyone bully me."

Allie laughed. Before she could respond to Marianna's praise, they heard the sound of a car. "That must be the Terhunes. . . . Excuse me," she said.

Ted watched her walk out, her rounded buttocks tense and outlined by the delicate cashmere.

"She married?" he asked.

Marianna shook her head.

"She'll wind up as the mistress of some important character, like the Secretary of State. She looks snooty, but there's invitation written all over her body. She's available, like Marilyn Monroe."

Marianna perched on the arm of his chair. She smoothed the curly brown hair off his forehead. "You don't mind this *too* much, do you?"

"Well, I feel like an inmate in a zoo."

"But these are my closest friends. I wanted them to meet you."

"Where's your folks? Or aren't they coming?"

"Of course they're coming. So is my sister and maybe my brother-in-law. But it takes Mama quite a while to get ready."

Allegra walked to the door to greet the Terhunes. As Rose Eileen embraced her, Allie found herself thinking, *What have you done to make him happy? Nothing . . . He'd be with me where he belongs, if he weren't such a gentleman. . . .*

She kissed Rose Eileen, bundled in ranch mink,

and Cris, who Allegra thought looked thin and wan.
And then she included Stephen in her welcome. He
greeted her courteously but with caution. She prayed
that he was aware of her body's rich scent, the way
her hands touched the back of his neck—all her messages of love and desire.

He was wearing a double-breasted blue suit with
pin stripes. As always, the sight of him—long, lean,
sunburned—filled her with desire to be near him, to
touch him, to look into his face and read the feelings he
sought to control.

Marianna talked to Cris for a while. "When Ted
and I settle down, we must get together. How long
has it been?"

"A couple of years," Cris said, "but it feels much
longer."

"We mustn't let it happen again."

"Where's the groom?" Stephen asked, and Marianna
went to call Ted, who was in Evalina's office.

By the time the bride and groom returned to the
studio Marianna's family had arrived. Darlis had come
without Vince. Her outfit was outlandish, Marianna
thought—high black kid boots, full flowered skirt, tight
black sweater and embroidered red felt vest. She wore
her long, curly blond hair unfettered, with a band of
floral print tied Indian-fashion around her forehead.
Immediately she started snapping pictures with her
camera, like a child with a water pistol.

Holding onto Jan's arm, Liebschen looked delicate,
breakable. The weight loss which resulted from her
illnesses had burned away the layers of fat, and her
brown pants suit hung on her frame.

Everyone was making small talk, waiting impatient-
ly for the minister from the Friends Meeting House
who would conduct a second wedding ceremony,
which Marianna had wanted for her parents' sake.

When the minister arrived Evalina went to the piano
and began the first notes of the "Wedding March."
Marianna and Ted stepped into the studio and walked
slowly toward the altar.

Ted looked uncomfortable, but Marianna, her head
crowned with a wreath of white roses, was radiant.

After the ceremony was over, Liebschen held her lips together, but oddly, Marianna's stepfather had tears in his eyes.

The Duke managed to hide his sense of loss.

CHAPTER IX

MARIANNA AND ALLEGRA

Marianna never tried to be the Housewife of the Year
. . . nor, for that matter, the Sexpot of the Month.

Which was what Ted seemed determined to make
her. Morning and night, he was insatiable. But something about their wild, passionate moments between
the sheets left her with disturbing suspicions, which
were confirmed when Ted talked casually, even flip-
pantly, about his former bedmates.

Marianna unhappily concluded that it was impossible for Ted to respect a woman he slept with. It
seemed that the more available a woman was, the
more he loathed her—including his wife.

"Every guy feels this," he said one Sunday as they
got up from bed to dress and go out to dinner. "I
suppose it stems from the basic hostility between the
sexes." He added pontifically that he thought the power struggle between the sexes ended up as a struggle
in the social, political and business world. And maybe
the Germans were right: Women *did* belong in the
kitchen with their kids. Marianna listened to this general putdown without really believing it. In the early
months of marriage, she was still enchanted with her
status as Ted's wife and continued to pray that a sense
of intimacy would develop between them, although
Ted seemed to hold himself apart from her. He loved
her and yet he had a need to demean her.

Marriage had quickly changed him. The qualities
she'd found so engaging seemed to have coarsened.
His attempts at tenderness were usually a souce of

embarrassment to him, but she loved him enough to accept the darts of quasi-humor without showing hurt. She told herself that he was like a street urchin, defying her to love him when he was bad.

In December, when she had first moved in with Ted, bringing her clothes and books, she had scoured the two rooms, sprayed for insects, painted the woodwork and the doors and cleaned the windows. To buy a few pieces of furniture she had wanted to go to Bloomingdale's, but Ted said, "Nothing doing." They were not in the same class as her rich friends, he reminded her. So they shopped in a couple of thrift stores for used furniture. In a Japanese store Marianna bought a blue corduroy spread, bright patchwork pillows and white china.

"Doesn't everything look nice?" she asked after the chairs, table and small loveseat were arranged in their bed-sitting room. "So bright and cheerful."

"That it is," he agreed grudgingly. "Just like a girls' dormitory."

"But Ted, I asked you to come with me and help me choose colors—"

"I don't have time for that crap," he said. "You arrange it the way you want; it's okay with me."

"But I *want* you to be pleased. I *want* you to be happy . . ."

He looked at her and lowered his head. Abruptly he grinned and swung her into his arms. "You know what makes me happy, kid."

Don't make waves, she cautioned herself.

The summer months were hot and trying. The city suffered in the midst of a heat wave; children turned on fire hydrants to cool off, creating a water shortage. The heat in their two small rooms was stifling. Finally Ted bought a secondhand electric fan, which made the bed-sitting room bearable at night.

They always slept close together in the spoon position that pleased Ted, even in the summer. He clung to her and called her name again and again in his sleep. She knew his dreams haunted him from his outcries and the way he thrashed around, kicking his legs out. He obviously wanted her support, though he often said proudly that he didn't need anyone; he was an independent soul. But he *did* need her.

Ted was an early riser; he petered out in the evening and was always grumbling about his night classes at Washington Square. Sometimes, looking at him bent over a book—his hairy torso bare except for a pair of shorts, his curly brown hair kinking with sweat, his virile face with a five o'clock shadow—she wondered what was the heart of him, what he really felt: Was it what he said or left unsaid? It seemed to Marianna as though they were groping toward each other in a fog, but as they reached out they missed each other. She had been more at ease with him during their curious courtship. Why had she married him? To forget Marc Finley? To show the Duke and Noel Osborn that other men wanted her?

No, she decided. She *was* attracted to him, and she had been happy and stimulated when she dated him. She wondered whether she had been hoping that a total commitment would help her become a fulfilled woman.

Ted was such a contradiction. . . . When he criticized a new play or book, belittling her enthusiasm for it, he would suddenly soften and say, "I didn't mean to spoil it for you, Mari. But I get so damned annoyed when it's merely second-rate. . . ."

In some matters, the intellectual ones, his standards were high and demanding. But in the practical matters of everyday living he was a slob. She went to a nearby laundromat every Thursday evening with a bundle of sheets, towels, his shirts and jeans. She washed his socks with her own nylons in the bathroom, although he always complained about things hanging over the shower rail. She did the marketing unless she was obliged to work longer hours than usual, in which case Ted substituted for her, always reminding her that it was an unmanly task and a nuisance.

She tried always to be pleasant, amenable; to honor his needs. Between her job with the Duke and her role as Ted's wife, she expended all her energy.

But after nine months of living with Ted she was disappointed . . . and disillusioned. On the weekends,

after she returned from her visits to her mother and
stepfather in New Canaan, he was always grumpy,
and she spent that evening coaxing him into good
humor.

The one thing holding them together was sex. When
she awoke in their dingy apartment, lying beside Ted,
his rump nestled into the curve of her flat belly above
the mound of silky pubic hairs, she felt full of happiness and desire. Ted himself always awoke with an
erection; all his vigor centered in his raging penis.
He assured her this was perfectly natural for any
normal, healthy male.

She still carried over from her Locust Ryse days,
when she and her friends had speculated endlessly
about sex, a purely romantic vision of sex: the perfumed night; the veil of moonlight; the lover's passionate, undying devotion.

But the passion Ted aroused in her was different, a
deep, primal response that was overpowering. Once
when they were in bed, she had felt like a strange
creature with uncontrollable urges and she had cried
wildly, "Fuck me, Teddy, *fuck me!*"

He had pulled away from her. Resting on the palms
of his hands, he was so shocked by her demand that
he lost the strength of his manhood.

"You sound like a two-bit whore!" He was furious.
"If I didn't marry you, you'd probably end up like
one!"

He got up, dressed and stormed out of the apartment. She wondered whether to go after him. But
something held her back. *Why is he so angry?* she
asked herself. *What have I done to upset him?*

Somehow, in recent weeks, whatever she did annoyed or offended him. *How did we get into this
state?* she wondered, refusing to admit that the problems had begun as soon as they had been married . . .
and she had never really known him before that.

Whenever they fought, or rather when he sounded
off, annoyed with her, he would retreat into a sulky
silence until she made the first peace offering. She
had learned to be careful not to attempt reconcilia-
tion too early. The third day was the best; by that

time Ted's anger had subsided and his sex drive would cause him to remember that there was an attractive young woman in his bed. Available, too . . . she couldn't refuse him, although she was beginning to hate herself for her submissiveness.

He didn't like Marianna to show any response; he wanted her lying flat, looking helpless. He expected her to rest her legs over his shoulders and then he grappled, scarcely touching her soft, yielding flesh, until he penetrated. Recently his sexual overtones were marked by an impatience that made her feel he wasn't aware of her, except as a receptacle for his needs. Their sex was over before she was aware of it, after a ferocious peaking. And then, weak and exhausted, he turned away from her, as though she'd siphoned off his strength.

Bewildered, unhappy, unfulfilled, Marianna ceased to believe this was the way sex—and marriage—was supposed to be. Her couplings with Ted excited her initially but failed to satisfy her. She wanted to suggest to him that he try to control himself a little longer. But when she tried to speak of it he shut her off with an angry gesture.

By autumn their marriage had reached a low point. She didn't know whether Ted was aware of her acute suffering. She felt like the ultimate failure.

I am nothing, she thought in a wave of depression. *I cannot hold a man or make him happy.* Because she was ill at ease with him she placated him, as one would a vicious enemy, with delicate, polite words. Brilliant, clever Ted; of *course* he was superior to the other teachers; no doubt they were jealous of him. She felt so duplicitous, acting differently from the way she felt. . . . She thought she had gone beyond her need to flatter men, but she was Ted's twenty-four-hour-a-day puppet.

What hurt most was Ted's contempt for her friends —for the Duke, Allegra and Cristina. Marianna was working very closely with her boss. As much as she tried to regulate her time, her hours were uncertain. If she happened to be late to prepare dinner, Ted would explode.

"You're a goddamn weakling. . . . You've got no spine. . . . You let that phony public relations guy exploit you. You toady to your mother, trying to win her love, which is a farce. She thinks more of your sister—that cheap little slut—than she ever will of you. You're a slavey for your friend Allegra—and that other little screwball. Cris is probably on drugs, trying to make it in her mother's footsteps. . . ."

Her silence was no longer passive but filled with bitter anger at him that their love had gone sour. Yet they slept together; they had breakfast and dinner together; they spent Sundays together when she wasn't in New Canaan. They *seemed* like a civilized young couple, each working hard toward the future. But she was hiding her misery from the world.

Marianna awoke one morning in mid-November reluctant to get out of bed. She felt cold; there was never enough warmth in the radiator.

Ted groaned in his sleep and turned to face her, wrapping his arms around her slim waist, his head buried in her bosom. "How about a quickie?"

"There's not enough time. I've got to be at the office early today."

"The hell with time. Come here, Mari."

Even though she usually responded immediately to his demand, she felt there was something degrading about it. Sex was always enjoyed at *his* convenience and *his* desire. He took for granted that she would give him what he wanted.

He was absorbed in the pleasure of kneading her firm breasts, sucking the pink-brown nipples. His cheeks, rough with the night's stubble, were like sandpaper.

"What're you mumbling?" he demanded.

"My period."

"What about it?" He paused, glaring at her.

"I'm late."

"How late?"

"I'm not sure. I forgot to mark my calendar. Maybe it's because of the stomach bug I had a few weeks ago."

She took the Pill regularly, but her bout of vomiting and diarrhea might have left her unprotected.

"You're supposed to take care of yourself." He moved away from her, sitting up on the edge of the bed, his upper torso naked, his hips covered by the shorts he wore while sleeping.

"I *am* taking care of myself. But the Pill isn't infallible. Nothing is."

He fumbled for a cigarette in the pack lying on the small rug beside the bed. "We can't afford a kid." His erection vanished.

Each subsequent morning and night he hoped for some sign of her period. He didn't touch her, although they still shared the bed. After her period finally arrived he went back to using condoms, complaining that they dulled his pleasure.

By that time, Marianna no longer cared.

Ted's problems, she realized, could not be overcome. In spite of his brilliant mind, which drew his students to him, he was unsure of himself with anyone who had more money and position than he. He had a rigid, old-fashioned concept of marriage, not allowing for any change in a man-woman relationship. And she was convinced that he was a born loser.

She ached with compassion, but she saw no way of helping him. She had tried to introduce him to some of the television producers she knew, but he refused to honor the appointments she made for him. He seemed to feel it would be a sign of weakness to depend on her for his progress. Yet when it came to household expenses he was perfectly agreeable to her paying for food and incidentals.

She found her dreams often of Marc Finley, who had encouraged her never to settle for less . . . which was exactly what she was doing.

Marianna and Ted were on their second year of marriage. One night in early January they were having their first dinner guest—Allegra, who in the past year had gone off to Palm Springs and Beverly Hills to visit some film people she'd met on the Riviera. She had now leased a Manhattan apartment from a friend.

Allegra was due for dinner at 7:30.

Marianna rushed home from the office and put the chicken she had poached the previous night in the oven. She started the wild rice and set the table with the sterling silver service Allie had given her as a wedding gift.

Ted sat on their easy chair, watching her as she prepared a salad. Although he'd met Allie only once, at the wedding, Marianna had filled him in with anecdotes about her. Whenever Allie was mentioned in a social or gossip column or her photograph appeared in *Vogue, Harper's Bazaar* or *Urban Life*, Marianna always brought the clipping home to show Ted.

"She looks like a typical rich girl," Ted usually replied.

"You musn't judge Allie by her manners. She's a truly great friend. Very supportive."

"That's a generous commendation."

"Well, I owe her a great deal. I was the only poor kid in that snooty school. When the girls in our class tried to ride me, Allie put them in their place. She took Cristina and me under her wing. The creeps in our class were scared stiff of her. Her family had more money than theirs and social position from way back when . . . ."

The small round table was bright, the candles ready to be lit, the aroma of food rich in the air. She sat on their bed waiting for Allegra to arrive. Ted, coming from the bathroom, flopped beside her. She was smiling at him, pleased with the occasion. He had dampened his hair, trying to smooth it down, but it was already curling on his square forehead. The black, wiry hair sprouted on his chest at the opening of his sports shirt. He looked handsome, the heavy brows adding a brooding look to his dark eyes.

Marianna needed only to catch his glance, so unabashed in its desire, to feel a similar need. She could scarcely curb the longing to sit on his lap, to fill his mouth with her tongue, to run her fingers through the hair on his chest and then down, to loosen his belt buckle and feel the throbbing flesh.

"Mari—" His response to the invitation in her gaze

was electric. His arm crushed her ribcage, his lips nuzzled hers, searching for the sweetness she offered. Her thighs responded, conditioned by thirteen months of his bruising demands and the satisfaction that came afterward . . .

It was with considerable effort that she drew away from him. "Not now, Ted. Assignation at midnight, yes?"

"A promise?"

"A promise."

"Maybe she'll leave early," he said.

That didn't seem likely, for at nine o'clock there was still no sign of Allegra. Ted was annoyed. He was right, he said: She was a rich, thoughtless brat.

"There must be a reason." Marianna was making excuses. "Maybe I should call—"

"Don't you *dare*. Forget it. Drop her, which is probably what she's doing to you."

"Oh, no. She'd never do that."

"Let's eat and get to bed."

The ringing of the phone broke up the incipient argument. It was Allegra.

"Whatever happened?" Marianna asked. Listening, she tried to interrupt. "But Allie, everything is ready. We're waiting . . . what? Oh, well, just a minute—" She turned to Ted. "Allie wants us to come over to her place."

"What about all this food?" he asked, displeased.

"She suggests we keep it until tomorrow. She says there's a marvelous Chinese restaurant in her building, and by the time we get there, the food will be ready . . . ."

Eventually she persuaded him to go. Allie opened the door of her apartment, which was on Park Avenue and Sixty-fifth Street. She was in red Chinese silk pajamas, her hair piled high on her head and speared in place by two amber pins. As always her features were dominated by her dark glowing eyes with their thick lashes and her exotic cheekbones.

"Here you are! I've been *longing* to see you . . . ." She embraced Marianna warmly.

Then she clasped Ted's hand firmly and said in her

gentle voice, "I'm so happy to see you again, Ted."

She led them into the living room, all leather and lucite and neutral woven rugs. "I'm sorry I couldn't get down to your place, but I had an unexpected visitor." Her gaze was on Ted but she was speaking to Marianna. "Stephen Terhune."

"Oh? Something wrong with Cris?"

"Well, he seems very concerned about her."

"Her mother again? Or a new man?"

"Both, I gather. Bonnie Rob Roy is evidently bored with her latest and has decided to foist him on Cris."

"Isn't that Cris's problem?" Marianna said. "After all, she's twenty-three years old. She should know what she wants."

"Well, you know how her mother influences her. I thought girls of our generation were supposed to be able to break away. But poor Cris is hooked." She went to a small glass bar with a collection of liquor, ice and glasses. "By the way, Marianna, how's your mother?"

"She's recovered. She's finished her chemotherapy. But she's very depressed."

Allegra got up from the sofa to answer the door chimes. A Chinese waiter in a white jacket wheeled in a cart set with covered dishes.

"Good," said Allegra. "I'm starved."

"That doesn't sound like you, Allie," Marianna commented. "Are you off your vegetarian kick?"

"Definitely. That's way behind me."

They used the Lucite cocktail table. The waiter opened the covered dishes and served them deftly. After he left Allie sampled a lobster dish.

"You're using chopsticks." Marianna was impressed.

"I had a Chinese lover." Allegra's shone with wickedness. "They're really the best kind."

"*Allie.*"

"Do I shock you, Mari?"

Marianna looked at her husband; he was intent on finding lobster morsels on his plate.

"Not really," she replied. "It's just that I never know whether to take you seriously."

"I don't fib, do I, Mari?"

"You don't. But sometimes I think you exaggerate
—just for effect."

Ted looked up. "What makes a Chinese man superior?"

"His appreciation. His sense of gratitude toward the
woman. In his way, he's really quite a stud."

Marianna had been out of touch with Allie for the
past year while Allie was wandering, visiting luxurious
watering holes, throughout the world, and apparently
sharpening her feminine guile into an irresistible mag-
net. Marianna was aware of Allie's raw physical mag-
netism for the first time, and it scared the hell out of
her. Did Allie have to practice her seductive skills on
Ted?

Watching her best friend and her husband, Marianna
grew puzzled and upset. Without agreeing on any subject they managed to engage in a subtle fencing match.
They seemed less and less aware of Marianna. A painful memory stung her senses; once again, she saw
herself ignored, the outsider wistfully looking in . . . .

Ted, who usually turned in early, seemed in no hurry
to leave. In fact, he suggested that they drop in at a
new discotheque on Third Avenue. Allegra seemed interested, but Marianna said bluntly, "I hate to break
up this lovely evening, but I've got a breakfast meeting with one of the Duke's clients."

She got up to leave, but Ted made no move. Allegra
reached for his hand. "There you go," she said, treating him with the indulgence a mother might give a
spoiled child.

"It's been an experience," he said as they moved
toward the door. In the hall, Allegra pushed the elevator button, then stood in her doorway with her most
dazzling smile. She kissed Marianna on the cheek. "See
you soon, Mari." She seemed about to kiss Ted too
when Marianna tugged at his arm.

"The elevator," she said.

Out on the street Ted said, "Your friend's a born
hooker."

"I don't want to talk about her," Marianna replied
coldly.

"Who'd she say was there—before we came?" he persisted.

"Stephen Terhune."

"She'd been laid. She had the look."

"You're mistaken. Stephen is Cris's father."

"No matter. She had the look. I've seen it before."

Marianna suddenly realized he was right. She wondered if Cris knew . . . .

Their assignation after midnight was wild and impassioned. He was consumed by his needs, but Marianna found no pleasure in their coupling. She knew that his fantasies were of Allegra, not herself.

Allie. A great wave of resentment came over her although she told herself that Allie was unaware of her effect on Ted.

Stop being so damned understanding . . . , she said to herself. For the moment, she hated both Allie and Ted.

The following week the Duke asked Marianna to fly to Florida. Madame Tanagra, the cosmetic queen who was an intimate friend of his, had just bought a villa in Palm Beach and was about to launch her social career. She was not yet accepted by either the old guard or the new money. But she was a courageous woman who had escaped when the Nazis overran Poland. Her vast cosmetic empire had been built on a single item: an extraordinary perfumed bath oil.

"The only way she can gain a foothold," the Duke said, "is to make herself indispensable to the aging ladies who rule Palm Beach."

The Duke had got into the habit of brainstorming with Marianna, whose ideas were always sound. He felt she had long outgrown her job with him, that her only reason for staying was somehow connected with her marriage, which he suspected was in trouble.

Marianna looked forward to the week's trip—her first experience traveling on the job. Madame Tanagra had invited her to stay at her villa on the edge of Lake Worth. She packed some of her dresses and cardigans from two years ago—she couldn't afford any new clothes.

She was excited about the assignment. But when she told Ted about her plans, he was annoyed.

"What are you, his errand girl? Why can't he go himself?"

"Ted, you don't understand—"

"I understand that you put your job above our marriage—"

"Oh, for God's sake, Ted. Don't make a production. I'll only be gone a week." She added, "You can manage without me—"

He glared at her. "You're damned right I can. For *good.*"

She couldn't believe it. She said quietly, "If that's the way you want it."

She finished her packing, closed the suitcase and picked up her lined raincoat.

"Where the hell d'you think you're going?" He looked up from his book.

"There's no sense of my staying here."

"You're not going anywhere. You're staying right here—where you belong, despite what that boss of yours thinks." He pushed back his chair, shoved aside the book and approached her, his eyes blazing with anger.

Momentarily afraid, she dropped her coat.

"Okay. I'll stay."

He made love to her later as they lay sleepless beside each other. She hated it, hated him, hated her body for responding.

The next morning she left for Palm Beach.

Allegra didn't expect to hear from Ted, in spite of the obvious lust in his face when he and Marianna had visited. Yet ten days later when he phoned and asked to see her, she wasn't really surprised.

"You mean now?" she asked. It was early evening.

"Tonight."

"With Marianna, of course."

"Marianna isn't here. She took off for Palm Beach."

"You sound as though something is wrong."

"It is."

"Did Marianna suggest you talk to me?"

"Christ, no. I need to talk to somebody, and I figured you'd be understanding—seeing that you're old friends—"

"Ann Landers in the flesh. Come along."

She changed from a terry robe to a mauve chiffon caftan, brushed back her hair to the nape of her neck, sprayed her heavy perfume in front of herself and then walked through the mist. The bell rang too soon. He must have been in the neighborhood, she figured, annoyed that he was so sure of himself.

But once Ted reached the apartment, he seemed more ill at ease than on his first visit. Instead of leading him into the living room, Allegra switched on the lamps in the small library.

He refused a Scotch and settled for a Coke. He gulped it down and chewed the ice cube, which set her teeth on edge. She regretted having allowed this creep to come here. And yet . . . there was something about him that intrigued her. He had a short fuse, probably an explosive temper. No matter how much she tried she could never ignite Stephen's temper. The idea of a man totally out of control appealed to her.

"D'you think I'm the right man for Mari?"

"Do you want to be?" she parried.

"Hell, yes. Why do you think I married her?"

"Why *did* you?"

"Because she's unique. I figured she'd make a great companion—"

"Doesn't she?"

"Not as long as she holds on to that job."

"Why don't you suggest she give it up, then?"

He was silent.

"If it's a choice between you and her job, which would she take?" Allegra was enjoying goading him.

He squirmed. She suspected he'd come to see her on an impulse and was in deeper than he'd planned.

"What do you want me to do, Ted?"

"Well, talk to her—maybe she'll come to her senses."

"Convince her your well-being is more important than her job?"

"That's it. Next year I'll have my Master's and then

my Doctorate. I'll get a decent job. I'll take care of her."

"Does she know this?"

"Of course she does. But it's been no good for a while."

He leaned toward Allegra and she sensed his intention, even before he did.

He said bluntly, "I think you're bad for her. For me, too."

"Why do you say that?"

"Because I can't get you out of my mind." He stood up, scowling, his eyes as fierce as an animal's. "Sounds like one of those corny songs, but it's the truth, damn it. I wish to God Mari had never brought me here," he said angrily.

He reached out and pulled her to her feet. The caftan fell open to her waist, revealing the round perfect breasts she was now so proud of.

"You shouldn't be allowed loose." His lips were drawn back from his teeth. "You belong in one of those cribs. I want to make love to you—no, that's too fancy. I want to screw the hell outa you."

Under the Ph.D. candidate she saw the gutter-sharp kid. Fascinating. She felt the warmth and the stirring in her loins as his hands grasped her waist beneath the caftan.

"Where?" he demanded. "Here?"

She shook her head and led him into her bedroom. He lost no time. He quickly removed his jeans and shirt and stripped her caftan, leaving her bare, her body a carefully tended vessel made deliberately for pleasure.

He made no effort to seduce her, to get her ready for his taking. He was over her, wild, rough, probing, in an abandon that frightened her. Before she was prepared for him, he had wasted himself.

He moved away from her, cursing softly to himself.

"Is it always like this?" She lay on the bed, her thighs together, a frown on her face.

He nodded.

"Doesn't it take you any longer to build up for a second go-round?"

"Once is enough."

She reached for her robe. "I didn't intend to be my best friend's surrogate." Her voice was soft yet touched with acid. "But there's what's wrong with the two of you. No girl likes to be left high and dry." She sat up, her hair loose and falling over her high cheekbones, her arms, thighs and legs golden from the Caribbean sun.

He got into his clothes with clumsy haste. Embarrassed, he began hunting for a cigarette. She motioned to a Limoges porcelain box.

"Do you really want my advice?" she asked.

"Shoot."

"She smiled. "Rather inappropriate, my dear."

"Don't play games." There was a sudden anguish in his voice.

"I understand you're a genius in your work. But you lack insight into a woman's needs. You've got a real problem, Ted. I presume you know the cause?"

He glared at her, either too humiliated or too hurt to speak.

"You don't really like women, Ted. Oh, I know most men are ambivalent. It's often a love-hate relationship between a man and a woman. In your case, you peak and leave a woman unfinished, frustrated: the ultimate punishment. Poor Marianna. Or should I say, 'Poor Ted?' "

He pulled her up from the bed. Then, with the palms of his hands, he pushed her back again. She fell awkwardly, but he didn't wait. He was on her, straddling her, scooping his bulging cock from his jeans. This time his penetration was bolder, eased by the semen he'd deposited in her moments earlier.

He took her with a savage, mindless rhythm that was compounded by fury and lust. His sweat had a rich, male smell that fired her response. She let herself go, welcoming his vigor, holding him in the smooth brace of her arms and legs, joining with him in a climax of sensation só intense that for a moment she passed out.

As she lay back, relaxed, her perspiration mingling with his, she realized with surprise that it had been damn near perfect.

She smiled, her eyes shining with their wicked gleam. "Treat Marianna like this and she'll never leave you."

His face darkened with disgust. He raised himself from the bed. For a moment she was afraid he was going to hit her.

Then, deliberately, he spat in her face. And left.

Good God, she thought. *If Marianna stays with him, he'll destroy her.*

When Marianna returned from Palm Beach with Madame Tanagra's lavish gratitude, she filed for divorce.

Then she had a nose job. And with the Duke's encouragement, she began to do free-lance writing. Her brief, pungent articles appeared regularly in magazines, and she soon acquired a devoted readership.

Many of the articles were interviews with celebrities, but she grew bored with this sort of work. She decided to move on to reporting the opinions of psychologists, sociologists and marriage counselors on relationships, love and sex in the new age of women's liberation. She herself needed some counsel, for she was deriving little satisfaction from her casual postmarital affairs, most of which she herself put an end to—for a change.

In one of her articles Marianna wrote:

What a woman does is not what she is.

How do you become a fulfilled woman? It has to come from inside of you.

You can release those forces by the climate you create around you. The body can offer you guideposts if you listen to what your body tells you.

The feelings must come from your acceptance of yourself as you are.

Awareness is like a switch that releases the force which guides you to the solution of your problem.

She knew it was guidance she needed more than her readers did.

Marianna left the Duke when a television network executive who admired her writing offered her a job as a commentator. She was given a fifteen-minute slot just before the six o'clock evening news.

In the past three years young women had started to make a dent in the shell of an industry that restricted them to consumer tips, household shortcuts, beauty aids, and interviews with lesser film luminaries. Marianna felt she was in the right place at the right time. Networks were on the lookout for bright, articulate women like her. Though her contract was modest, the possibilities for her future were limitless.

Her daily segment was meant to be a relief from the reports of arson, murder, political corruption and worsening world affairs. She interviewed interesting personalities in the theater, the arts and contemporary affairs.

"Listening to Marianna Ellis," the critics reported, "is like reading a bright hip piece in *New York* magazine."

One Wednesday afternoon during an early autumn snowfall in New York Marianna answered the telephone at her desk in the television newsroom and heard that her sister, Darlis, was in the reception room.

Her first reaction was that something had happened to her mother.

But Darlis reassured her that Liebschen was all right. Taking the armchair at the right side of Marianna's desk, she slouched back, her white lambskin coat open to reveal a flowered challis skirt and a knit shirt that did justice to her full breasts. As always she wore a kind of printed band around her forehead, Indian style. Marianna saw that she looked even more beautiful than ever. No wonder all the newsmen were staring. Darlis, Marianna reflected, had the same allure as Allegra—an allure that seemed to say, "Take me, if you can, and I'll be yours."

Instant availability.

"Have you been out to see Mama?" Marianna asked.

"Not lately. I've been busy. My photography is going to pay off now."

"Oh." Marianna lifted her brows. Darlis hadn't come for a social call, she thought wryly. Now that she was in television her sister probably wanted some special favor.

"Everything okay with you and Vince?" Marianna asked.

"Well, our life depends on the charts. If one of Vince's records is high on the charts he's high. Otherwise . . ."

"There are more lows than highs?"

"Sure enough. All you have to do is look at *Billboard*—"

"What about the groupies?"

"They don't bother me. They're like rats. They know it when a group is down."

"And your place in Soho?"

Darlis chewed her gum industriously, an infuriating vision of pink-and-gold innocence. "We had to let it go. No money."

Marianna was tempted to ask, "What do you want from me?" but she held back. She resented Darlis—a girl with a pretty face could have everything . . . .

"Where're you living now?" she asked politely, thinking Darlis expected it.

"On Park Avenue and Eighty-sixth Street."

"That doesn't sound like Vince's cup of tea. I should think he'd prefer the Lower East Side."

"Oh, I'm not living with him."

"Where is he? On the road?"

"No. He's holed in with some freak in East Village. . . . Marianna, listen I need help—I mean, he needs help. You've got influence. Could you get him into that place in Connecticut—Silver Hill?"

"I don't know. Is he on liquor or drugs?"

"What does it matter? He's freaked out all the time. His group left him. He'll freak out for good if he doesn't get help."

"Can't you stay with him, or make some arrangements—"

"My boyfriend doesn't want me to get involved."

"Your boyfriend?" Marianna thought, *This is unbelievable.*

"Yes. He's simply great. He's got this thing for me . . ." She mentioned the name of a man who had written the lyrics for a recent Broadway hit. "The only thing is, he doesn't believe in marriage. So I figured out how to hook him—" Her smile was gleeful. "I've moved in with him. I'm going to let him get me pregnant."

For the first time in her life Marianna pitied her sister.

It was not until two years later that Grandmama Towle's estate was finally settled. Allegra had lived in Paris again, gone on safari in Africa and spent her summers in Newport and Seale Harbor with friends.

She was in Beverly Hills when she had received John X. Lovell's summons to come to New York for the settlement. Now, waiting in the reception room of the Family Trust for her mother and stepfather, Allegra wondered how they would react to the revelation of what she had planned to do with her inheritance since the day her grandmother died. She suspected they would disapprove, but of course they couldn't stop her from doing what she wanted.

Her mother and stepfather came in, Prudence in a classic Chanel blue suit, John X. in a Brooks Brothers gray that had seen years of wear.

"Allie, I hope we haven't kept you waiting for too long," John X. said. He looked as though he meant to kiss her, but she held out her hand coolly. Prudence seemed uneasy, Allie noticed.

Her stepfather's private office was conservatively furnished with oak cabinets, a black leather sofa and an antique desk, bare except for a pen and inkwell and a tan leather portfolio, which John X. now opened.

Allegra said, "Before we discuss anything, I want you to know what I intend to do with Grandmama's money."

Her mother was watching her intently, a shadow of pain on her handsome face.

John X. said, "Go ahead, Allegra. We're listening."

"A great number of people lost their savings because of my father's well-intentioned investments. They turned out badly, and people lost their money. I should like to pay them back."

Her stepfather was startled. "It would be difficult to track down people. Many were his friends and neighbors in New Canaan, you know. And the statute of limitations would be in effect—"

"I want to clear his name," Allegra said with determination. "I see no other way to do it."

"Even if it straps you?"

She nodded.

John X. turned to Prudence. "Pru, that's a noble gesture, don't you think?"

Prudence was silent, a mask on her face.

John X. said, "I think we have news for you which will brighten your efforts to clear your father's name."

He said that some of Pavel's investments in land that had seemed so unrealistic after World War Two were suddenly showing life and value in the present land boom. He said it would take months, perhaps years to straighten everything out, but he understood Allegra's sense of obligation and applauded it. The Trust lawyers would try to unearth those investors who were still alive, or their families.

"One of my teachers at Locust Ryse lost out in my father's dream—Marc Finley. Do you remember him?" Allegra asked Prudence.

"I do indeed. He gave up graduate work for a year to support his mother, who'd lost a good deal. He must hate us—"

John X. excused himself to check on the Pavel Simon files, and Allegra and her mother were alone in his office. They weren't looking at each other.

Finally Prudence said, "His name will be cleared ... at last."

"He'd like that," Allegra said quietly.

Her mother looked at her and saw the lovely old amethyst on the chain around her neck. More than anything else, it brought back to her the image of Pavel ... her adored Pavel.

Tears filled her eyes.

She and his child had both lost something precious,

a fine human being. In their world there would never be another like him.

Allegra got up from her chair and went over to the sofa, where her mother sat, pale and stricken. She took out a hankerchief and wiped her mother's cheek. So Prudence grieved too. . . . She had never forgotten. . . .

"It's all right," Allegra whispered. "He would be pleased with us."

CHAPTER X

Cristina Terhune wanted to continue studying music and acting. But whenever she started a class at the Academy or studied with a private teacher, she had to drop everything because of a change in Mama's plans.

Mama was getting worse and there was nowhere Cris could turn for help.

Certainly not to Stephen. Bonnie would be furious; she'd cry and scream that Cris was betraying her. But Cris wished she could speak to him; after all these years, he was the only man Mama was really afraid of.

Mama was between engagements now and doing the town. Her latest boyfriend, Gary Dupré, was taking her to the new discos—Studio 54 and New York, New York—and they wouldn't get home until dawn. Cris would lie in her bed, tossing, anxious, wondering if Gary was selling Mama the uppers that had caused her so much trouble.

Like many of Bonnie's boyfriends Gary was a young homosexual composer. His work wasn't recognized, and he supported himself playing the piano and singing in a second-rate bar. He was in his mid-twenties, but *this* one Mama wasn't trying to palm off to Cris. She wanted him all to herself. And he obviously knew a good thing when he saw it: Mama still had a dozen more comeback tours in her.

Cris was usually delighted when new boyfriends attached themselves to Mama. They were like comforting, protective brothers to her. But there was something peculiar about Gary that Cris couldn't put her finger on.

He'd taken Bonnie to a rehabilitation house for

people coming off drugs, and now she had decided to do a benefit concert for the place. Cris felt that Gary was insidiously taking over Mama's life.

Late on a crisp autumn afternoon Cris walked up Fifth Avenue toward Fifty-ninth Street. She looked like a dynamic young debutante, her brown-black hair falling in feathery tufts around her gamin face and her boyish body in pipestem pants, a tight sweater and a beat-up English raincoat.

The suite at the Essex House was vacant, since Mama and Gary had gone to Pound Ridge the day before to talk to a producer about helping with the benefit. Cris welcomed the quiet. When Mama was in residence the stereo was always playing some of her old songs, which had made the Top 40 consistently in earlier years.

She opened the door to the living room. And stopped dead. Sounds were coming from the large bedroom—sounds of a woman crying, screaming, shouting . . .

Terrified, Cris ran to the bedroom door. She pushed it open.

Mama was naked, her skinny little body bare, her hands shielding her face against the blows Gary was inflicting on her with his fists. His shirt was torn, the tails coming out of his pants.

"Mama!" she screamed, *"Mama."*

Bonnie was moaning, huddled on the carpet, and Gary was now kicking her mercilessly in the ribcage with his boots.

"Stop it!" Cris begged.

He ignored her. She looked around frantically. Empty liquor and soda bottles stood on the dresser. Without knowing what she was doing, she picked up a bottle.

She didn't mean to hurt him. She wanted only to stop him from beating Bonnie. But she swung too hard. The bottle hit his skull. He paused as though startled, unbelieving, and then he crumpled to the floor.

Bonnie stared at Gary, who was half-conscious and bleeding. She yelled at Cris, "Look what you've done! You've *killed* him . . ."

Cris was immobile; in a daze she protested, "But he was hurting you—"

Bonnie stood up, naked, bruised, bleeding, her dark eyes glazed. "So *what*—whose business is it but mine—"

"But Mama—"

"Mama. *Mama.*" Her voice was jeering, raucous. This was a Bonnie Rob Roy Cris had never seen before.

"Who asked you to interfere? What the hell are you doing here anyway? Why can't you leave me alone? Wherever I am, you're around. I can't get rid of you. I'll *never* get rid of you. I'm boxed in—first by that fucking father of yours and now you. You're just like him, damn it. Always wanting to run my life—Get out . . . *Get out,* d'you hear me? I'm sick of the sight of you."

Stunned, Cris backed away from the tawdry tableau. She turned around and went out of the suite. In the corridor she began to shake. She didn't wait for an elevator but rushed toward the heavy door that opened on the stairs.

Marianna now lived near Gramercy Park, in a beautiful marble-and-limestone building with a twenty-four-hour-a-day doorman.

Her apartment, decorated with fine antiques, was oddly reminiscent of the New Canaan house of Allegra's Towle ancestors. It was often the background for high-fashion pictures used in the Sunday papers, and *Vogue* had done a three-page layout of the home of the young career woman who combined yesterday with tomorrow.

On a Friday afternoon, her show taped, Marianna was working at home on one of the Duke's charity projects—a benefit for the Rehab House. They were often involved in similar causes, although Marianna was now out on her own. They worked well together, better than ever before. Their love affair had ended long ago, but they still enjoyed each other's company.

Marianna was expecting the Duke at about nine o'clock. When the doorman announced a visitor she was surprised to hear it was Cristina.

"Cris, I was just thinking of you. As a matter of fact, I was going to call you. I'm working on the Rehab House benefit, and you can help me out with Bonnie—" She stopped when she saw the anguished expression on her friend's face. She was clutching her shoulder bag with trembling hands.

"My God, Cris—what's up?"

"I killed a man—I think—"

"You—*what?*"

"Mama's boyfriend . . . he was beating her . . . and I tried to stop him—"

Marianna took Cris by the arm and led her into the living room. She tried to remove her raincoat, but Cris held on to it, as though it gave her security.

By the time the Duke arrived a half hour later, she had Cris in a robe and had quieted her down.

The Duke listened quietly and then said, "Our best bet is to call Dr. Hayden. He's the medical director of the Rehab House. I'm sure he'll know what to do."

Dr. Douglas Hayden agreed to come to Marianna's apartment after he saw Bonnie and Gary at the Essex House. While they waited for him the Duke held Cris in his arms and assured her that the assault would not be mentioned in the newspapers or on television. He had clout, and he intended to use it.

An hour later the doorman called to say that Dr. Hayden was on his way up. Marianna hadn't expected the physician to look so young. He was bearded, and he wore jeans, a knit shirt and a suede jacket. But there was a quiet authority about him; he seemed judicious without being stern.

Dr. Hayden told them that Bonnie was resting in her suite. It seemed that she had called a plastic surgeon who had operated on some of her friends. The surgeon said he would fix Gary up without reporting the incident to the police—Cris hadn't used as much force as she'd feared. Bonnie's injuries were mostly bruises; she would be fine.

Marianna felt greatly relieved. She had confidence in Dr. Hayden and was certain that everything would work out, though there would undoubtedly be some problems.

After a time Cris was able to talk freely. She looked at her friends—the Duke, Marianna and now Dr. Hayden—and said, "I'm so glad I thought of Marianna . . . . Even at school we always turned to her. I kept walking the street . . . . I even went to the Bus Terminal. But it seemed silly to run away at my age—"

"People run away no matter how old they are," Dr. Hayden said, "and for lots of reasons. But Cris, your time for running is over."

She whispered, "What will happen to Mama?"

"She'll survive. Gary was with us at Rehab House for a while, trying to straighten himself out, and he picked up just enough know-how to dazzle a woman like Bonnie. They'll go off on her next tour and he'll play your part, Cris. But, she'll collapse one day. And maybe she'll accept help."

"What about me?" Cris asked. "What will happen if all this gets out?"

"I told you it will be hushed up," the Duke said, "in all areas. I expect all you'll be responsible for, Cris, is the cost of Gary's plastic surgery."

His remark was calculated to amuse her, to ease her tension, but her laughter turned to tears and she couldn't stop sobbing.

Dr. Hayden took over. "Cris, if you really want to be of help, we'd be grateful if you could help out at the Rehab House. We're always short of volunteers."

It was his way of telling her that if she felt a need to atone for what she'd done, this was a way to do it.

Marianna served coffee, and Cris said slowly, "Isn't it strange that through Gary Dupré I should meet you."

She was talking to the doctor, but the Duke replied for him.

"You go where you're needed, Cris, And the kids at the Rehab House need you more than your mother ever did."

The Duke's hunch proved correct.

Cris moved in with Marianna. Each morning she got up at seven, made her breakfast and went to the Rehab House, where she put in an exhausting but constructive day.

The house was run like a commune, with each individual doing his share. Dr. Hayden was tough but fair, and gentle when necessary. Cris developed skills in working with the patients, who ranged in age from eleven to eighteen. Surprisingly there were more girls than boys. She made herself useful teaching drama and dance. At first her work was an obsession with her. But gradually she came to realize that her need to give, to nurture, had been transformed into a skill that could be useful and satisfying.

She saw Rose Eileen and Stephen often and sat at their table when the Rehab House benefit was launched at the Waldorf. Unfortunately Bonnie Rob Roy was unable to attend, but the star of a movie musical had performed.

When the orchestra was playing its last number Cris danced with Dr. Hayden.

"I've been waiting for this break," he told her genially, "after watching you teach the kids."

"Why don't you join my next class?" Cris said, smiling. "It's all on the House." She'd been wanting him to ask her to dance all evening.

As Cris became involved in her new world, Allegra and Marianna were thrown together—by friendship, but also by the fact that they now moved in the same social, cultural and political circles.

Allegra was dating K.C. Burkett, a handsome, notorious womanizer who was the son of a Palm Beach real estate tycoon. K.C. had invited her to fly to Palm Beach on the Burkett family's Lear Jet, and from there to cruise the Bahamas on his yacht for a week.

When Allegra, chic in a sable-lined raincoat and a honey-colored cashmere dress, saw Marianna already seated, she let out a whoop of delight. Later, as they exchanged gossip over drinks, Marianna told her she was going on the cruise to gather information for a section of a forthcoming television documentary on the new American royalty. Marianna was writing and editing the script.

Marianna looked terrific, Allie conceded, half out of pride, half out of jealousy. Few young women had made it as Mari had. While Allie looked outstanding, like a fashion model in *Vogue,* Marianna had managed to acquire the chic of the successful career woman.

K.C.'s father, known as Senior, had great plans for his only son in a family of five daughters. He had already begun to use his power to see to it that he got what he wanted: K.C.'s election as a New York State Senator from Manhattan, where the Burketts maintained a cooperative apartment.

It was Senior Burkett who had arranged with the President of the network Marianna worked for to give her time to spend with his son. He wanted K.C. to be included among the young American aristocrats who took their inheritances seriously. Senior also knew that it was important for K.C. to publish a book on a serious theme—something like *The Greening of America.* Writing a book was an excellent way to launch his son's future among influential intellectuals, and Senior wanted K.C. to have the help of a man who had both knowledge and prestige. He had invited Dr. Marc Finley, a distinguished economist, on the cruise, thinking that perhaps the young man could even be persuaded to ghost-write the book.

An important young PR man named Rod Bailey had been included among the guests as well. He was a genius at making people look good on television and had already made a political star out of a clumsy nobody.

Marc Finley had accepted Senior Burkett's invitation for a double reason. He wondered what the old brigand was after, and he thought it might be interesting to see Allegra Simon again. Her gesture to make restitution for her father's behavior had surprised him; it had been his first experience with a rich person who would willingly part with a nickel.

He didn't remember Allegra very well. The one Locust Ryse student who remained in his mind was Marianna Ellis, the scholarship student sponsored by Stephen Terhune. She was a sort of colorless girl, but there was a quiet intensity about her that had intrigued him.

He had first heard about her television program from some of the Radcliffe girls in his classes. They liked her because as an interviewer she was honest. She wasn't coy; she didn't behave like an actress. She simply asked questions and let the subject save or hang himself.

She had written him several notes asking him to appear on her show, and he regretted that they had been unable to settle on a date. Now, on the Burkett yacht, sitting on deck with a drink, he saw her and Allegra coming aboard. And he realized that the shy young girl he remembered, all angles and dreams, wasn't there. This was an attractive, self-assured woman who had just enough of a touch of the seductress to engage his interest.

He wasn't looking at Allegra at all.

K.C. greeted Allegra with a kiss on the lips, a pat on the fanny and a sense of proprietorship.

"Are you married?" Allegra asked Marc after they shook hands. "No? The saints be praised. Mari's been brooding all the way down here. She's sure you're married and have a flock of little Finleys."

"If he were," K.C. said, "he wouldn't be on deck, Allie. This is a trip for singles only."

Marianna and Marc just smiled at each other.

Every morning Allegra, Marianna, Marc, Rod and K.C. had breakfast on the sun deck. They spent the next few hours sunning themselves and generously anointing one another with tanning lotion. It was the most proper cruise K.C. had ever hosted, but it was for a good cause.

After lunch, served on the afterdeck, they all talked about politics and K.C.'s potential. Only Allegra remained silent as she lay on a chaise in a white bikini bottom, her lovely implanted breasts bare, the nipples lightly touched with pink blusher so they wouldn't burn.

Marianna was enjoying the iridescent blue of the water, the brilliant sun, the shimmering moonlight. The only thing that wasn't perfect was that Marc hadn't made love to her. He was friendly and humorous; he

beat her at backgammon; he asked questions about her
interviews with well-known political figures.

Once, when they were standing on the deck, he put
his arm around her, which filled her with hope. The
touch of his sinewy body made her conscious of what
she'd felt for years. She thought he looked just as he
did the first time she'd seen him on the shore at Locust
Ryse.

He and Allegra had similar family backgrounds, and
yet they were totally different in character, she thought.
Marc's humor was dry, his judgment unwavering when
it came to decency and honor. He had accepted the
money Allegra had offered him, he told Marianna, because he felt his family deserved recompense, and he'd
used it to set up a trust fund to aid needy students.

"You're quite a remarkable man," Marianna said,
"I hope you don't mind my gushing, but I was in awe
of you at school and I'm still the same. Can you
stand it?"

"I suspect that you still see me as your sainted
teacher at Locust Ryse. I'll have to put a stop to that?"

His embrace was strong and unhurried. She never
knew that a kiss could so arouse her.

"I've wanted to do this for a long time," Marc said,
"but I couldn't see myself seducing a schoolgirl. . . .

In her narrow stateroom she lay naked on her bed,
her body silken from sun and oil, pulsating as she
watched him in the moonlight. She had dreamed of
this for years—that one day he would discover her as
a woman. *God,* she thought, *what a beautiful man he
is.* His skin was sun-smoothed and rippled with muscles. When he eased his body beside her on the bed she
felt as if she was about to make love for the first time.

The range of his passion, the first touches that sent
shudders through her, the mounting pressures, the
strength of his body as he took over, astonished her.

"Mari, my darling . . ." She heard his voice, hoarse,
slightly breathless, and her body accepted his; her hips
and pelvis were vibrant and alive, and she thought,
This is how I've always wanted it to be.

It was after midnight when he got up and put on his

pants and shirt. She was lying on the crumpled sheets, looking he said, like a houri.

"If Mrs. Merritt-Jones could see us now," she said, smiling.

He knelt beside her and kissed the tendrils on her cheeks. "I can't figure out who's the teacher and who's the pupil. We'll have to decide this a little later," he said. His face was serene, but the depth of feeling darkened his eyes.

"Goodnight, teacher."

He got up. "Goodnight, scholar. Tomorrow we'll discuss Lord Keynes's theories . . . ."

My darling, she thought when he closed the door behind him. *Marc, my darling.*

She didn't brood about whether this was a one-night affair, a result of the yacht, the sun, the moon, the aphrodisiacal tropical air. If she had got this far with Marc—so far beyond her fantasies—there was hope.

The cruise was nearing its end. K.C. let Marc and Rod discuss a strategy for his political future. He meant to enjoy himself. Twice a day and once more at the witching hour he made love to Allegra.

She was always prepared for him. She loved sex, loved the fact that he could maintain an erection for hours. And she had helped him . . . her gentle, knowing fingers had moved down to his withered scrotum while his cock penetrated her.

"I'm always getting raped by the right people," she said after he had finally come—the one time he had been able to on the yacht.

She was the only one who understood, K.C. thought . . . the only one who made him feel his slight physical deformity was an asset instead of a flaw.

CHAPTER XI

Senior Burkett thought that his son should concentrate less on beautiful women and more on politics. He did realize, however, that a proper wife was a tremendous asset to a politician. Naturally she should come from a good family; she should be attractive, articulate, ambitious and well-mannered.

When Senior met Allegra he was impressed. But being a practical, farsighted old man, he had her checked out. Her background and financial status were excellent, although it was possible that an opponent might bring up the scandal about her father. Still, Senior figured cynically, with so many jailbirds these days, K.C. might get votes from unexpected sources. The school Allegra had attended wasn't on a par with Miss Porter's or Foxcroft, but Locust Ryse did have a good reputation. And certainly Allegra was endowed with the social graces so useful in Washington.

K.C.'s mother, who had met Allegra at the Saratoga Golf and Polo Club, thought she was most attractive. And the five Valkyries, who were K.C.'s sisters, admired her ability on the tennis court and at the dog shows. Their baby brother could do worse, they conceded.

Meanwhile Allegra's mother and stepfather—concerned about their jet set daughter's life as a rich, independent nomad—were relieved when Allegra informed them blithely that she was having a passionate go-round with K.C. Burkett.

K.C. was a tall man with broad shoulders and a ruddy complexion who looked, Allegra thought, like the Marlboro Man. He amused and intrigued her. He was not one of the third-generation rich who resented his family fortune and the way it had been accumulated —in the Burketts' case by the sale of bootleg liquor during the Depression. K.C. enjoyed the money for the indolent life it afforded him. He spent two days a week in the Burkett offices that controlled real estate ventures throughout the country. But he was bored with his work, and politics seemed like a good alternative.

He had met Allegra in Acapulco, and since then their couplings had always been marked with a sybaritic pleasure. They both enjoyed the senses; they experimented with sex, and Allegra found him satisfying, if somewhat exhausting. She'd heard from one of his men friends about his debauched weekends in Las Vegas, during which he used up an entire chorus line of girls.

And yet, Allegra thought, they were good for each other. If he was to get somewhere in Washington he needed her, and she needed him if she was to be allied with a man of power. K.C. had charisma, brains, money and good looks. What he lacked, Allegra concluded objectively, was a cause.

She spoke to Marianna about K.C. and his "destiny," ("Quote, unquote," she had said) and Mari, bless her, came up with an answer although Marc Finley, her new man, had decided not to help with K.C.'s campaign.

"Let him follow Bobby Kennedy's vision," said Marianna. "It was a worthy one."

With a cameraman, Marianna took K.C. and Allegra to visit a family on welfare who lived on Park Avenue, beyond the line that divided the haves from the have-nots. For the first time in his life K.C. saw cockroaches, rats, cracked ceilings and toilets that didn't work. And he heard the squall of ten people of assorted ages living in two ugly rooms.

He was startled. Shocked. Indignant. He decided that the whole welfare system needed overhauling. Marianna assured him that she'd heard it before; however, if he could use his mind and family resources to implement his ideas, he'd get strong backing.

Meanwhile, K.C. and Allie saw each other often.

When some of Arkady's photographs were scheduled for a Manhattan showing at a Madison Avenue gallery she persuaded K.C. to attend the preview with her.

"I didn't know you were interested in photography," he said, as they moved through the small, crowded gallery.

"I'm not. But I have a reason . . ."

They went from photo to photo, each one a Parisian street scene of great beauty. When they came to the series of nudes Allegra's heartbeat accelerated. So the old goat had included her picture—just as she'd anticipated.

There she was in a full-length nude, her head turned away, her body lithe, boyish, with just enough curves to give the picture a subtle sexual lure. Her thick hair was covering part of her cheek, and not enough of the face showed to reveal her identity.

K.C. looked steadily at the photograph and looked at her mischievously. He touched the Siberian amethyst on the chain around her neck, his fingers resting there briefly. As he looked at her, offering her delicious promises, she was titillated.

"How many know about it?" he asked.

"Just you. And Arkady, the man who took it."

"Your lover?" There was nothing jealous about his manner, just curiosity.

She didn't answer. He looked down at her face, his prominent eyes intent. "Any way we can buy the print? Take it out of circulation?"

"I don't know."

"Did you sign a release?"

"I didn't sign anything."

"It would be rather embarrassing if someone recognized you. Allegra—two things." A new timbre in his voice remended her of Senior. "Are you on the Pill?"

"You know I am."

"Okay. Two things must go—the picture and the Pill."

That was the way he proposed to her.

Later that evening she telephoned Stephen to give him the news. She no longer hoped to arouse his

jealousy; she merely wanted him to know. Her en-
gagement gave her an excuse to speak to him—she
hadn't seen him in months. She didn't know whether
she'd lost her appeal or whether Rose Eileen's physical indisposition kept him faithful to his wife. Allegra
had heard that Rose Eileen was being treated for high
blood pressure.

"I thought you'd rather hear it from me than read it
in the *Times* on Sunday," she said to Stephen. She
knew that whenever she closed her eyes, responding to
K.C. or whomever, it would be Stephen's image before
her.

"I'm glad you called me, Allegra." He sounded
calm, in control.

She paused, her lips trembling. "Then you approve?"

"He can go a long way—with the proper direction.
You can go with him."

'Do you think that's the reason I'm going to marry
him? Oh, Stephen, you're so wrong!"

"Allegra—Allie—" Now there was pain in his voice.
"No matter what the reason is, that's the way it's got
to be."

Oh, Stephen, she said silently, *it's all a poor substitute for you.*

K.C.'s mother put her faith in God, but she wasn't
sure that He'd guided her son into the right marriage.

By the time K.C. and Allegra returned from their
honeymoon and spent some time with the Burketts in
Palm Beach while their Manhattan apartment was being put in order, Mrs. Burkett suspected their marriage
was a misalliance. Allegra passed most of her days
secluded in her bedroom, seldom joining the family for
a sail or lunch. Why this obsession with privacy? Mrs.
Burkett wondered.

When she came to the Burkett house Allegra was
always polite and deferential to her in-laws. She exchanged sallies with K.C. and even included the Burkett daughters in her conversation. Yet Mrs. Burkett
was aware of the distance Allegra put between herself
and the family, and she feared there was serious trouble
between the newlyweds.

K.C.'s mother admitted to herself that she and Senior had been too indulgent with their only son. She wondered whether Allegra had discovered his need for so many women. Mrs. Burkett was afraid K.C. would remain a womanizer—like his father, who had flaunted his succession of beautiful young mistresses until prostrate cancer put an end to his excesses. But Mrs. Burkett loved her son fiercely—not only because she came from a family that valued sons above daughters but because, for all his rugged manliness, he was flawed. His "problem" was never discussed and was hidden from sight, even among the intimate family.

Her husband was not sensitive. The physical image of his son pleased him. He had no inkling of what the boy had endured because of his glandular illness.

But Mrs. Burkett understood him and how he reacted to pressure and stress. Decisions were a torment to him; he was often afraid to act. He relied too much on his advisors, including his revered but feared father. Mrs. Burkett wondered why K.C. needed all his women—to prove himself a man in his father's eyes? To convince himself that he was desirable despite his malformation?

K.C.'s mother badly wanted to explain her son's nature to Allegra, so she wouldn't lose patience with him. If only she'd give him time . . . he was coming into his own, with the aid of his new political acquaintances. Allegra's friend Marianna Ellis was teaching him about the plight of the inner city and the dispossessed.

Allegra had concluded that politics was a boring, disreputable vocation. The only politician she found attractive—if not overly persuasive—was John Lindsay, and he was no longer in the spotlight. She abhorred crowds, noise and obnoxious people whom she had to entertain simply because they shared a political banner with K.C. She also disliked huge family gatherings, which were to her no better than political rallies. All the Burkett relatives, dozens of them, gathered too often in an orgy of feasting and boasting.

One afternoon, when Marianna joined a family clambake, she said soberly to Allegra, "Eating people isn't nice."

Allegra wanted to hug her. K.C.'s healthy, handsome relatives were indeed cannibals.

"I feel like a Christian in the arena," she said. "Their intensity devours me."

K.C., Allegra knew, had a reputation for devouring his women. It hadn't diminished since their marriage, although he had less time now to devote to his fancies. But his campaign office was staffed with beautiful young college graduates who'd majored in political science and who vied for his attention.

Allegra seldom visited K.C.'s headquarters. But now, settled in their elegant East River apartment, she was the dutiful wife. She was a gracious hostess, bringing together people who would be helpful to K.C. She relied a good deal on Marianna for leads, and Mari introduced her to many influential people in business and the arts.

"He's got to make it," Allegra confided in Marianna one evening. Her schoolfriend was a frequent guest at Allegra's parties. "It's the only way this marriage can survive."

They were in Allegra's dressing room. The small, circular space was like a jewelled *boîte* with its full-length mirrored panels, its closets spilling with colorful clothes, shoes and furs. The air smelled of bouquets of flowers and Allie's perfume, which she sprayed in the air.

Marianna thought Allegra had never looked more striking but was far too thin, and her dark eyes seemed to have lost their gleam. Too often they had a far-off gaze, almost a blankness.

"Allie, you sound as though it's rough," Marianna said.

"Not rough. Just *nothing*."

"Isn't there something you can do?"

Allegra shrugged. She was busy with her jewels, the amthyst earrings and bracelet K.C. had given her to go with her Fabergé necklace.

"It will turn out right if K.C. is elected."

"Isn't that strange?" Marianna said. "Everyone has always felt you should be the woman behind a famous man. It's come true."

Allegra smoothed her dark hair behind her ears. "We'll see." Something in her voice disturbed Marianna. Were her words a promise or a threat?

Marianna put her hand on Allegra's bare shoulder. They made a striking contrast, Allegra in white satin from St. Laurent in Paris, Marianna in a black knife-pleated Fortuny gown from a Fifty-seventh Street thrift shop.

"Hold on, Allie. As his wife, you'll go places. *Make it work*, even if you decide to have an arrangement."

A shadow passed over Allegra's face. "I'm hanging in. What else can I do?"

Marianna, eager to do an explosive show, had decided to interview Dr. Walter Rapf—the King of Abortionists who had performed Allegra's operation when she was at Locust Ryse. Dr. Rapf had just been released from Danbury prison, where he had served five years after being convicted of illegal medical practices.

"My guest today," Marianna said when she went on the air, "has a medical degree from John Hopkins University. He is a Board Certified surgeon, though not in the field that is his specialty.

"He is a man to whom thousands of women have reason to be grateful.

"He has for thirty-two years—not counting the five he recently spent behind bars—defied authority to come to the aid of women who desperately needed help.

"He has never lost a patient.

"He is known—to the police, to politicians who berate him in public and ask for his help in private, to other doctors who would not defy an unjust law—as the King of Abortionists.

"Welcome, Dr. Rapf."

The doctor sat in the easy chair opposite her, a stocky, aging man in a brown suit and white shirt and tie. His neatly trimmed gray hair and beard and his old-fashioned heavy-rimmed spectacles gave him the appearance of a modest middle-class professional man, possibly a teacher or a public accountant.

Dr. Rapf smiled, his cheeks puffing up, touching the lower part of his glasses. "I'm like a child, learning to communicate by words," he said. "It's not traditional for an abortionist to be kept in solitary confinement, but the prison made an exception for me. I don't think the warden approved of me."

"Dr. Rapf," Marianna said, "has the Pill reduced the need for your services?"

"On the contrary. Today, more young girls experiment with sex than we'd have believed possible a decade ago. They start young. They are uninformed. Or so unrealistic—though they call it romantic—that they won't use precautions. They're involved in adult situations which they handle like children. Then there are young women who become pregnant by accident or rape. And young wives who cannot afford more children. Contraceptives aren't one hundred percent safe. There's *always* a chance. . . ."

"Doctor, the former image of the abortionist was of an evil man in a hidden office who treated his patients quickly and often carelessly—either out of ignorance, because he wasn't a bona fide doctor—"

He nodded. "They're still around, there aren't as many as there were before. A woman needn't hemorrhage or die of septicemia today."

"When you were in medical school did you consider abortions as your specialty?"

"I planned on a family practice. I happened to consider abortion an integral part of it."

"Would it be forward of me to ask how you started doing abortions?"

"Not at all. After I graduated I came to New York and got a chance to serve my residency here. Then I opened an office on the Lower East Side, near Bellevue Hospital. My standard fee was two dollars a visit. But this was during the Depression, and not many of my patients could afford even that. Naturally I treated them whether they could pay or not. What the devil—we were all starving together.

"Then one young girl came to me. I'd been treating

her father, who had a stroke, and her diabetic mother. The daughter was her parents' sole support. Well, she was in love with a young man and they didn't have enough money to get married. She asked me to help her, but I was afraid of getting in trouble with the law. So I turned her down." He lowered his head, looking as though he was reliving the painful incident.

"You can guess the rest," he went on. "She asked a druggist or a friend to recommend someone, and she went to a woman who called herself a midwife. When she began bleeding the woman threw her out of the apartment. By the time she got home and her mother called me, it was too late . . . .

"After that I never turned away any woman in need. I made no bones about it."

"Which didn't sit well, I take it, with the law or your fellow physicians," Marianna said.

"Right. The Park Avenue gynecologists who aborted their rich patients wanted no publicity about the practice. The Church was violently opposed to it, and a good many of the policemen and judges were Catholic.

"I've helped out many women—from the wives of fellow physicians to the mistress of a judge who pronounced one of my jail sentences. He was a good fellow, though. I served less than a year."

"And went right back to doing what you had decided to do?"

"Definitely. But they were watching me like vultures—waiting for me to lose a patient or make a mistake."

"About how many abortions have you performed during your career—or is that a secret?"

"No secret. I'm rather proud of my record." His tone was touched with irony. "You might consider me a champion. At least three thousand. Possibly a few more or less."

The interview was going well. Marianna was pleased. Dr. Rapf was articulate and made no attempt to hold back information or to applaud himself or his actions. He was, she reflected, a forthright, dedicated, compassionate man.

"So many? Do you ever hear from any of the women?"

"Not unless they need my services again." He took a handkerchief from his breast pocket and wiped the sweat from his forehead.

"I spent the morning at a local abortion clinic," Marianna said, "and they explained their procedure to me. I wonder—what is your method?"

"It varies, depending on the length of the pregnancy. I usually do a dilation and curettage, and afterward administer a heavy dose of antibiotics. I prefer whenever possible to keep the patient overnight. And I always offer information on birth control. You'd be surprised how often it's rejected."

"That *is* surprising," she agreed, recalling guiltily the chances she herself had taken.

He leaned forward in his chair, his face suddenly stern. "When I began my practice, women were thought of as breeding animals. Unwanted pregnancy was a woman's problem. How did she solve it? You've read about the atrocities . . . .

"I've spent thirty-five years battling anti-abortion legislation. I've been arrested. I've spent days in court, used my earnings to hire good lawyers. Even my wife gave up on me. To her I was in the same class as a shyster lawyer—an ambulance chaser. She didn't see me as a fighter for women's rights."

He stood up, overcome by his memories. But he shrugged them off and said more quietly, "I've lived to see the day when a woman can come to a legitimate clinic, receive proper care by a reliable physician, pay a fair fee—or nothing at all if she's broke—and emerge from the experience without physical trauma or much emotional shock."

"What are your plans for the future?"

He smiled. "To continue the fight. It'll be much easier now. I have the support of Women's Lib."

The program ended on an optimistic note, stressing the hope that today every woman had the right to decide her own future as a mother.

Marianna's producer, who had made a meal of his

fingernails throughout the broadcast, approached **Dr.** Rapf and thanked him. After some small talk, she walked her guest to the elevator.

"I can't thank you enough, Doctor."

"Thank you, Miss Ellis. If there's ever anything I can do for you . . . ."

"I'll remember," she promised.

She returned to her office in a glow of achievement and concentrated on the stack of letters and messages on her desk. The director dropped in unexpectedly.

"That was a bit of a risk," he said.

"I thought you liked it."

"What I may like and what we put on the air aren't necessarily in accord," he said solemnly. "You can be mighty persuasive, Mari. But I was considering substituting another one of your tapes—"

"You *wouldn't!* I'll appeal to Planned Parenthood and the Civil Liberties Union and my lawyer—"

"The network president won't like it. I'll wager the switchboard will be swamped."

"So—"

"That means trouble. You're supposed to be provocative but not provoking." He kissed her on the cheek. "It's tough to have to censor an ambitious broad. Take it easy, Mari. You'll last longer."

When she returned to her apartment she heard the phone ringing. It was Marc, calling from Washington.

"Marc, did you hear it?" she asked.

"I did."

"Was it any good?"

"First-rate. It carried a punch. Much better than if you'd merely made a sermon of it."

"If the studio gets many protests, I'll be in a jam."

"Don't worry, Mari. I'll bail you out. But listen to me . . . I don't want you ever to go through this. If you're pregnant, let me know."

She was silent.

"Mari—did you hear me?"

"I did, Marc. Yes."

"What're you thinking?"

"That it's the darnedest offer I've ever heard."

"But it stands, Mari. Remember that."

She held the telephone to her bosom even after he hung up. He was serious; she had sensed recently on his weekly trips from Washington that he had something on his mind. She'd been afraid at first that he was getting tired of her, but now she knew how important she was to him.

The next call she received was from Allegra, who had big news: She was pregnant.

It was a good year for K.C. Burkett. He was elected to the State Senate by Manhattan's Silk Stocking district, and he became a father.

Allegra, having time on her hands, had listened to Marianna interview a gynecologist on the LaMaze method of natural childbirth. Since K.C. was occupied with staff meetings, it was Marianna—and sometimes Cris—who accompanied Allegra to the classes for pregnant women and helped her with the exercises. In a way, it was like old times.

Marianna was in Washington on an assignment when Allegra went into labor. In spite of her fear, Allegra carried her small bag down to the street and took a taxi to the hospital. When she was being wheeled on a stretcher to the obstetrics wing her pains increased. She was whimpering by the time the nurse helped her undress.

"The doctor is here," the nurse said, "and they're trying to locate your husband—"

When they got her on the new table that had come from France and was supposed to help during labor, Allegra was pale and sweat-streaked. None of the exercises she'd learned in class seemed to help.

"You aren't cooperating," her doctor chided her gently.

In the haze of pain that was convulsing her body, she moaned that she was being lacerated. Then suddenly she saw K.C. standing near the bed; his dinner jacket was hidden by a hospital gown. His face was masked except for the prominent eyes, which seemed larger than usual as he watched his wife writhe in agony, her face distorted with pain. She was begging for relief, something to see her through the ordeal.

K.C. was against it. He knew his wife. She was a good sport; she'd be able to give birth naturally.

The nurse reported his objections to the obstretrician, who said between taut lips, "Get his ass out of there."

When Allegra had received her medication and was gathering her strength for the delivery, she heard one nurse whisper to another, "The young wives think I'm cruel because I'm against LaMaze. But I can't see any unnecessary suffering. With a little anesthetic, it's over so much more quickly."

Marianna, visiting Allegra two days after the birth of Patricia Simon Burkett, walked out to the nursery with K.C. He strode with a triumphant air, Marianna noticed. She wasn't sure of her feelings for him. He was proving to be an able politician. He had the Kennedys' polish and charm, and his audiences, when he spoke, adored his sharp wit.

"She takes after her daddy," Marianna said as she looked at the infant.

K.C. straightened up, and Marianna was aware of an expression on his face she'd never seen before—sorrow, regret? She couldn't quite make it out.

"Be sure and tell that to her mother," he said. His tone was bitter.

Allegra had decided that Patricia—or Tish, as she called her daughter—would have two godmothers . . . Marianna and Cris.

"What's going on between Allie and K.C.?" Cris asked Marianna after the baptism.

"Nothing much," Marianna said softly. "They've got the perfect image, and it will carry them on to fame and fortune—"

"Allie doesn't look happy." Cris sounded concerned.

"She's got the *post-partum* blues."

"K.C. isn't much help to her. You know the talk about him and some babe he's taken on as an assistant. An absolutely beautiful black woman who used to model and who now feels the time is ready for black women to get politically minded . . . ."

Tish, a beautiful curly-headed, round-eyed baby, was just celebrating her first steps and words when her father was killed in an automobile accident that also took the life of the young woman who was in the car with him.

After the autopsy, from which certain facts had been carefully omitted, K.C. Burkett was buried next to the church in which, three years earlier, he had taken Allegra as his wife.

Allegra was in the front pew, with her mother and stepfather, all the Burketts, K.C.'s senatorial staff and all of their friends. Marianna, Cris and Marc Finley sat quietly in the back.

I feel so vulnerable, Marianna thought. *We're all so vulnerable. Death is only a second away and still we don't embrace life. What will happen to Allie now? Is Tish enough?*

"She'll need us," she whispered to Cris, who nodded solemnly, her face red and puffy with grief for her friend.

It never occurred to them to wonder why Stephen wasn't present . . . or Rose Eileen.

After the hymns and the organ music, Marianna and Marc, who had recently become engaged, told Cris goodbye and walked to the corner to hail a cab.

"I've got the jitters," Marianna said as Marc held her hand. "I'm scared. I'll worry all the time you're on a plane." He was about to fly to San Francisco.

"I'll call you as soon as I get in," Marc said, gazing at her with tenderness. "I know how you feel, darling. You want to hold tight, to clutch, because it's all over in a flash—"

"Marc, you aren't going to take the San Francisco job?"

"Not permanently. Nor the New York one, either. But the farthest I'll go is Washington again."

"That would be reassuring. I mean, we could see each other every weekend—"

"Certainly. There are lots of two-career marriages,

and many of them are working." He kissed her and then turned toward the waiting taxi.

She watched him step into the cab, feeling not like the experienced career woman she was but like the vulnerable young girl who had loved Marc from the day he walked up the beach from his sailboat and was her first kind encounter with her new school and her new world.

Dear Marc, she prayed, *let's make our marriage work.*

Two weeks after the funeral Allegra appeared at the offices of the Burkett family's lawyers for the reading of her late husband's will. He had been generous with her. But most of his fortune he had left to his daughter, Patricia.

Senior Burkett knew that he could break the will if he so chose. He suspected, but was not certain, that for several months Allegra had been having an affair with Stephen Terhune.

CHAPTER XII

Allegra left her apartment at eleven in the morning after leaving a note for the maid that she wouldn't be in for lunch. The new English nanny was looking after Tish.

She was in a hurry, eager to bring Stephen her news. He'd be surprised. And pleased. "Steve," she'd say, "it's just as I hoped. The Burketts are going to be reasonable." That obsessively proud and ambitious family had decided—perhaps following the advice of their lawyers—to be charitable.

They had made the right decision, Allegra thought. She was reluctant to expose K.C.'s memory to the lurid press a year after his death, but she might have had to do so if the Burketts had followed through on their vicious plan to deprive Tish of her inheritance.

Stephen had been deeply concerned for her during her marriage to K.C.—a marriage of public glamour and private anguish. He was more than her lover, as he'd always been. He was a friend, confidant, advisor. Stephen was as well informed about legal matters as most lawyers, and had—through some power ploy and a considerable amount of money—gotten hold of K.C.'s autopsy report, which indicated that the young Senator hadn't been wearing pants at the time of his fatal accident. Allie smiled, thinking that everyone had a guru these days; hers was Stephen. Thank God for him . . .

She stopped at a restaurant and picked up two box lunches. Then she set out crosstown, enjoying the walk and the destination while deploring the environs. The only time she ventured this far west—a few blocks from the Hudson River—was to rendezvous with Stephen at their hideaway. She had little fear of seeing a familiar face in this run-down neighborhood.

Allegra turned toward the brownstone. Its exterior was clean, the walk refuse-free, the basement protected by a black iron grille. Stephen owned the building, which would eventually be part of a highrise complex.

She ran up the stairs to the front door and then to the second floor, where she inserted the key in the double lock of Apartment 2-A. The musty air and the whine of steam heat welcomed her.

She unfastened her coat and tossed it on the forest-green sofa. The glass-and-chrome cocktail table was piled high with artbooks, several volumes of poetry and a porcelain cachepot of yellow chrysanthemums. The bright colors of the apartment were much more to Allegra's taste than the dark browns of her Sutton Place duplex, furnished with antiques provided by the Burkett family.

The alcove beyond the living room was devoted primarily to a large brass bed. It was bare except for the mattress—she always stripped it before leaving and piled the used sheets in the bathroom, where the superintendent's wife would collect them.

She pulled off her turtleneck sweater and smoothed her hair in place. Walking to the linen closet in her lace bra and her skirt, she took out sheets and pillowcases and then made the bed.

Finally she stationed herself at the window, indifferent to anyone who might glance up at her. She couldn't wait to make love with Stephen . . . "Are you pleased?" he always asked afterward. "Was it good for you?"

My love, she thought, with a rush of feeling, *we're so lucky to have found each other . . . After all this time, when others are breaking up, we're just coming together again.*

She saw him approaching the building, a lean, well-muscled man who kept himself in superb physical condition by playing tennis and exercising. A minute later she heard his footsteps in the hall and heard the sound of his key in the lock.

"Steve!" She ran toward him with the exuberance of a young girl, unashamed of her joy. "Oh, Stephen . . ."

He scanned Allegra's exquisite face—the curved cheekbones with hollows beneath them and the dark, glowing eyes that still reflected a girlish innocence. Life had bruised her, he knew, but her sense of wonder hadn't dimmed. In another woman the childish quality would surely have irritated him, but in her he found it irresistible.

"Allie, my dear—"

He embraced her, holding her tight.

He led her to the sleeping alcove and drew the shade over the window. With a practiced ease he cupped her small, firm breasts in his palms, and brushed the nipples with his lips. She shivered, her smile secretive. Her long, thin body was no rounder than when he'd first savored it, then a schoolgirl's body. Her skin was smooth, perfect except for the stretch marks of pregnancy.

He lay on the bed, his eyes closed, thighs together. Smiling, he scooped her to him so she was above him. She touched his lips and eyelids, the thick, light hair on his chest. She nibbled and flirted gently, pretending shyness as she retreated before his growing need.

He was strong, demanding, searching for her, and she accommodated him, although it was not her favorite position—she preferred the weight and power of his body on hers. His drive seemed strained, his smile rueful, and yet as they were joined she felt an extraordinary reaction, a surge of trembling, waves of sensation that were somehow for her alone.

In climax, she was completely self-centered, her cries of ecstasy for herself, and it was strange, even unsettling, because always before she was aware of his needs, much more than of her own.

He collapsed against the pillow, gulping air, his breathing rough, like a runner at the finish line. She was surprised, but since he had such great strength she didn't question it. She was content to lie beside him, letting the air dry her body as she waited for the renewing passion to recharge him. It was always wonderful the second time around, when imagination and tenderness took over after the initial desire had been satisfied.

After a moment he got off the bed and went into the bathroom. She heard the rush of the shower. He came back, his body still damp, a towel wrapped around his middle.

"Must you get back to the office?" She couldn't hide her disappointment.

"Not until later. But I'm due at the Athletic Club at three."

"For tennis?"

"Yes." He slapped his flat abdomen. "I'm getting flabby."

"Let me fix you a drink. I've got a delicious lunch for us." Allegra sensed that something wasn't right, but she couldn't pinpoint it. It wasn't like Stephen to dash off—and for tennis, of all things. Their routine was out of kilter. Usually they made love after bathing, and then, wrapped in robes, they ate and shared their experiences since their last meeting. Today, however, he dropped the towel and put on his clothes.

He sat on the Eames chair, easing his back while he knotted his tie. He tasted the wine she had poured for him, nodded approval and found a cigarette in the silver box on the cocktail table. He wasn't interested in the ratatouille, the crusty bread, the unblemished pears, the Brie cheese she had brought.

"Steve, you aren't eating."

"In a minute, Allie. I want to talk to you."

Her spirits sank, the way they did with the onset of the blues. "What about, darling?"

"The Burketts."

Perhaps, if she gave him her news first, he wouldn't be angry with her. "Steve, I meant to tell you—they've changed their tactics. They're coming around—"

"The Burketts didn't come to power through fair

dealings. The old man was always vicious and corrupt. He's worse now, with his only son dead and so much money involved in K.C.'s will."

She was silent, twisting the corner of her robe.

"Did you agree to some legal arrangement?"

"It seemed best, Steve. As much as K.C. hurt me, I'd hate to have his reputation bandied about in the press. I've got to think about Tish. I don't want her growing up and learning from others what her father was like."

"Why didn't you get in touch with me?"

"Steve, it all happened so suddenly. Their lawyers called on me and assured me that the Burketts want no misunderstandings or trouble."

"What about K.C.'s will?"

"I imagine it will be settled now."

"I'm not convinced. Marianna told me somebody has been making inquiries about you."

"A reporter, I suppose."

"Or an investigator. He was asking her about your days at Locust Ryse."

Allegra's face clouded. "What's of interest in my prep school days? That I had a C average with what my teachers called an A-plus mentality?" Despite her words, she was frightened.

"What matters is that someone is curious about you. How long since K.C. died? Thirteen months? You've not given an interview since then. Silence has built up curiosity about you that candor never could. If the Burketts try to break the will, you'll be fodder for every front page and column—"

Oh, how stupid of her! She seemed to grow smaller, hugging herself with her arms as though she'd never feel warm again.

"Steve, what shall I *do?*"

"First, no more meetings here."

"What do you mean?"

"We must give up this place. Before they're on to it."

Only this little nest had meaning to her now . . . . She couldn't speak.

"We'd best not see each other again, Allie. We can't risk it—for your sake. It's been perfect, but I should have known better—"

"Nobody knows about it. Or us—" There was an imploring note in her voice.

"I hope not. But we can't be sure."

Something happened to her then. Her love for him drained away. Stephen was suddenly an enemy, along with the others who'd hurt her. She said quietly, "So you want out?"

"What the hell are you talking about?"

"Is this your way of ending it? Poor Allie, I'll let her down easy. If she thinks the Burketts are at fault, she'll accept our breakup—"

"Allie, you're out of your mind." He caught her in his arms. "I'm thinking of your welfare."

"My welfare! I *detest* people who think of my welfare." She was lashing out at him in fury, trying to get him to release her.

"Allie, listen. I'm not 'people'—I'm the man who loves you. I don't want a split any more than you do. Remember how far back we go? We've shared something special, something given to few people to experience. We can't allow it to be stained by scandal."

When he raised her chin she had to look at him. His expression was tender, with an air of concern that went beyond the emotions of a lover. She forced herself to speak rationally.

"Steve, I'm sorry I blew up. But it's a sore spot with me, you know. I've got to believe the Burketts' intentions are decent—for their son's sake."

"In their case, propriety and greed don't go together. K.C. left you and his child a substantial amount of money. He appointed you a trustee—"

"You know why he did it?" she paused.

Stephen waited for her to continue.

"Not for love of me. K.C. didn't know what love meant. He could sleep with me and the next day have a matinee with a couple of call girls. I told you about his weekends in Vegas—when he went down the chorus line and left three girls with cracked ribs." Her voice broke in her agony. "Making me a trustee was simply a way to get back at his family—at that goddamn domineering father of his and those impossible sisters."

"Whatever the reason, we mustn't use this place again—"

"For how long?"

"Until the estate is settled, and they can't cause you any more trouble."

She fervently wanted to believe him. Without Stephen's support she'd waver and collapse. But the most precious moments of her life had been spent here . . .

"Steve, why can't we be together—not hiding but out in the open. The Burketts wouldn't dare attack me if I were your wife." Desperation had brought her to her plea.

He was rigid. What was going through his mind? she wondered. The image of Rose Eileen, whose insecure temperament didn't live up to her glorious beauty. . . . and whom Stephen treated with a gentleness and courtesy that Allegra felt she alone deserved from him? Stephen, who was a financial wizard, had once confided bitterly to Allegra that in his personal life he was a two-time loser.

"We'll talk about it another time," he said.

"But the time is *now*."

"Don't push me, Allie." He glanced at his wristwatch. "I'm late."

"Well, if a game of tennis is more important to you than our relationship—" She was indignant, hurt.

"Oh, for God's sake!" He picked up his jacket and stalked from the room.

She fell back on the sofa, her face buried in her palms. After a time she looked around the room, not yet composed but needing an outlet for the anger burning inside of her. She picked up an expensive celadon vase from the table.

Slowly, methodically, she began to destroy everything in the apartment.

She didn't hear about Stephen's collapse until Marianna telephoned her at home.

It was the lead story on the ten o'clock news: "Stephen Terhune, President of Terhune International, was stricken with what appeared to be a heart attack during a game of tennis at the New York Athletic Club, at four o'clock this afternoon.

"A physician from nearby St. Bartholf's Hospital was playing on an adjacent court. He was able to resuscitate Terhune and give him emergency treatment, continuing his efforts during the ambulance ride to the hospital.

"According to a hospital spokesman, Terhune was admitted to the Coronary Care Unit and is now in guarded condition."

When Cris got to the hospital waiting room Marianna, Allegra and Rose Eileen were already there.

Rose Eileen was standing by the window where the draperies were parted, facing the street. Cris ran to her.

The older woman turned, opening her arms to embrace her. "Oh, my dear—"

"He'll be okay, Rose Eileen. I'm sure of it."

Rose Eileen bent over her stepdaughter as Cris clung to her. Even in the moment of great stress, Rose Eileen had an unaffected beauty. Her figure, in a simple sweater and skirt, was rounded and womanly.

Watching Rose Eileen as she stood with Allie and Cris beside her, making an effort to be positive in order to raise their spirits, Marianna thought, *What will happen to her if Stephen doesn't make it?*

She was relieved when the Duke came into the room, evidently having been called away from a party or dinner. He was wearing a tuxedo, and his pleated white shirt front reflected the pallor of his face.

The Duke spoke to Rose Eileen and held her hand, comforting her. Like most people who were involved both professionally and socially with Stephen, the Duke felt a deep respect and affection for him.

"Marianna—" He kissed her on the cheek. "Any news?"

She shook her head.

"How bad is it?"

"He's survived the crucial first half-hour after the attack. I understand that's encouraging."

"Rose Eileen asked me to call Dr. Levy, Stephen's physician. He's at a medical meeting in Houston. Once we contact him I'll ask him to recommend a local cardiologist."

"I wish Doug were here," Cris said, "but he's in Chicago visiting his parents. He'd know the best doctor . . ."

The telephone on the end table rang. Marianna handed the phone to the Duke. He took charge, answering the first inquiries from the press, business associates, friends and finally asking the switchboard to hold further calls.

A few reporters had drifted in and were standing around, smoking and sipping coffee from cardboard containers Marianna had brought in from the vending machines downstairs.

Cris was now at the telephone, calling Bonnie Rob Roy. She was reluctant to contact her mother, whom she hadn't seen since the horrid scene in the bedroom of the Essex House suite. But she thought Bonnie should be told about Stephen's condition. When she couldn't reach Bonnie in her Los Angeles hotel room, she asked the hotel operator to check some of the local nightclubs, explaining that it was an emergency.

Suddenly she felt a firm hand on her arm. She looked into Rose Eileen's face.

"I'm trying to get Mama," Cris explained. "She'll want to know."

"Hang up," Rose Eileen said softly. "Don't leave a message."

Cris froze, the telephone in her hand. This stern woman was not like the Rose Eileen she knew. The lovely face was devoid of its usual tenderness.

"But Rose Eileen, she *depends* on him. She'd be *furious*—"

"If she comes East against my advice, she will not be allowed to see him. You may tell her that if she calls you."

Cris shook her head. "I don't understand—"

"I'll make it plain later, when we can talk, when we know how Stephen is doing. But perhaps it is enough to tell you now that if he comes through this attack there will be no more leeches in his life. Cris, I have been his wife for fifteen years and with God's help I'll be with him for many more. I know his merits and his faults. In order to make it he needs me."

Rose Eileen turned away. Stephen's biggest fault, she knew, was that he felt he had to help everyone. But there were some people she would see to it he no longer helped.

Cris uneasily replaced the telephone on its hook. . . .

Rose Eileen's attitude hurt her. She sat alone in a corner of the waiting room. Mama had a right to be here—in spite of the divorce. Mama had priority, no matter how Rose Eileen felt . . . Not that she blamed her stepmother, Cris's loyalty to Rose Eileen ran deep—

"It's pretty awful, isn't it?" Allegra's voice. Darling Allie, who was always there when Cris needed her.

Allegra put an arm around Cris's sagging shoulders to support her. Cris recalled the many moments at school when she'd had the blues and Allie had brightened her spirits. How kind of her now to assume a place among them, almost as though she was one of the family.

"It's meant so much to me . . ." Cris's voice was barely above a whisper, "having you as a friend all these years. I've often wondered why you picked me."

Allie looked directly at her. "You're Steve's daughter," she said. "And besides, damn you, I happen to like you."

Cris stared at her, shaken. Allie loved him. *Allie loved him* . . . the confession suddenly made her see Stephen as he was—a man women adored, a man *Allie* adored . . .

After K.C. Burkett's death Rose Eileen had felt the need to go to a retreat. Nobody would ever connect his death with her need, but in her mind the two were inseparable. She knew Allegra's widowhood posed great danger for her future.

The purpose of the retreat was not only to know God but to know herself—to make friends with herself, to evaluate herself and make certain that she was worthy of Stephen.

She had learned a great deal while she was away, but it had taken this crisis—Stephen's life at stake—to bring out the strength she'd been nurturing.

She was allowed only five minutes every two hours in the Coronary Care Unit. *Family only*, she reminded herself. She was glad for that . . .

Stephen was lying in his bed, guard rails up, like a man in a science fiction movie, manipulated by wires that attached him to a machine that monitored his vital systems. Pain gripped her heart when she realized how much smaller his powerful, virile body looked.

Dear God, give him life, and I will change, I will do my share, she prayed.

The night nurse motioned that her time was up and she obeyed. All of her life Rose Eileen had been accustomed to obeying orders. Perhaps that was the flaw in her marriage, she thought. She had listened to Stephen and obeyed him, and when she was hurt she suffered silently.

Her steps were lagging as she returned to the waiting room. It was deserted now except for Allegra, who was smoking nervously. Marianna and Cris had gone out for some sandwiches.

"Did you see him?" Allegra's voice was hoarse.

"They let me look in on him."

"And?"

"He was sedated . . . Allegra, I want to talk to you."

Something in Rose Eileen's voice disturbed Allegra, sent out warning signals. "Yes, Rose Eileen. What can I do?"

"You can leave Stephen alone."

"What do you mean?"

Rose Eileen's face was a mask. "I mean, for good. Forever."

Allegra felt her strength draining away. She was suddenly frightened and helpless, and Rose Eileen, who had always been a friend and defender, loomed as an enemy. "I don't understand what you're getting at—"

"You understand. You've understood for a long

time, but you thought if you continued fooling me, lying to me, betraying me, you would finally win. You won't, Allegra. Take it from me, you won't."

"But Rose Eileen, I'm your *friend*—"

"Since when, Allegra? Since the night you came to stay with me because you said you were a surrogate for Cris— and you spent the night in my husband's room, making love with him?"

Thinking back to that horrible night, Rose Eileen closed her eyes. How stupidly *trusting* she'd been! She had slept restlessly that humid night. She'd been worried about Cris, accompanying her dreadful mother on another reckless jaunt.

When she had first become aware of the sounds outside her room she thought it might be the long-haired shepherd. She had opened her door a crack, but the night light showed no sign of the animal. She listened again and carefully opened Stephen's door a crack. She had thought he might be having a nightmare.

The sounds coming from the rug by the window had been sounds of love . . . .

"You were so kind, staying with me when Cris went off—so you could seduce my husband—"

Allegra's eyes narrowed. She was calm now as she stood up to face Stephen's wife. "I never heard of anything so far-fetched. Are you all right, Rose Eileen? Are your tranquilizers upsetting you?"

"I'm in control of my faculties, thank you." Even as she looked at Allegra, whom she'd once admired and loved like a daughter, Rose Eileen found it difficult to believe that this confrontation was taking place. But the recollection of what she had heard that night in Stephen's room was enough to build her strength.

"I want you to leave Stephen alone. You are *not* to see him again."

"I can't believe you're saying this to me—"

"I'm saying it, Allegra." Rose Eileen's voice was thick with emotion. "I'm saying it for all the feelings that have been stifled in my heart all these years. If Cris can't appreciate her father, it's sad. But that's the way it will have to be. If Stephen comes through this siege, I'll make sure you don't see him again. Even if I have to reveal your long affair with him."

Allegra was aware of a wave of nausea. She remembered Stephen's anxiety that morning and his decision to make their split permanent. Had he suspected Rose Eileen knew of their affair? Allegra had thought that he was only worried about the Burketts.

"You'd create a scandal?" she whispered.

"I'd create a scandal," Rose Eileen repeated. "I know K.C.'s father, not well, but well enough to appreciate his greed. I've heard about the Burketts' plans to break K.C.'s will because they don't want his child to inherit his millions—if indeed, she is his child."

"If you insist on slander, disguised as truth," Allegra said furiously, "you may as well know that once the suit is settled and I am free to marry again—it will be Stephen."

Rose Eileen didn't flinch. "How long have you planned this?"

"Since the first time I saw him. I knew that some day he'd be mine—lover first, husband later."

"It won't work, Allegra. Stephen is my husband and will remain—"

"But you can't give him a child."

Rose Eileen said coolly. "He has Cris. Perhaps some day she'll shape up. and perhaps . . . your child, too?"

Allegra didn't answer, and for a moment Rose Eileen forgot that this poised, glamorous young woman was her adversary. She thought of her and Cris and Marianna, three schoolgirls, boisterous one minute and moody the next, hating school, loving it, shy about boys, eager to meet boys.

Was Stephen an obsession with the schoolgirl Allegra? Did she have a father-fixation?

Well, he was an obsession with his wife too . . . and she'd never let him go.

"You'd better decide, Allegra, whether you really want the Burkett millions for yourself and the child. Because I have evidence about you and Stephen and your little hideaway that I won't hesitate to use."

Allegra was too stunned to speak. She knew beyond doubt that the child was Stephen's. But she would never tell anyone—not even Stephen—because she wouldn't allow her daughter to be branded as illegitimate. Allegra wanted to make sure Tish would have as much money as she herself had had before she gave away most of her Towle inheritance to her father's creditors.

"My child will get whatever is due her from the Burketts," Allegra said quietly after several moments, "and you'll never know whether my little Tish is K.C.'s or Stephen's . . . ."

Stephen felt a band around his upper arm, but it didn't feel like the pressure that had nagged at him the past few days. He opened his eyes, his lids still heavy with sedation, and watched a nurse squeezing a small rubber bulb. She released the pressure, unfolded the cuff and wrote something on a slip of paper.

Then she pulled his covers to one side. He was wearing a hospital johnny coat, he noticed, and his legs were encased in rubber stockings, which she was removing.

"What're those?" he asked. They were his first words since the attack.

"Anti-emboli stockings. I'm going to take them off for a half hour during this shift."

"What time is it?"

"Eight A.M."

"How long have I been here?"

"Since yesterday afternoon."

"Does my family know?"

"Yes, they're in the waiting room."

"Can I see them?"

"Let's ask Dr. Hassan. He should be here any minute."

"What happened to me?"

"Dr. Hassan will discuss it with you," she said.

"Did I have a heart attack?"

She left the cubicle without answering him and he thought the whole thing was ridiculous. A heart attack? Absurd . . . He was in top shape, and although he was no longer an excellent athlete he had respect for his body. He kept his weight down, he seldom drank too much, and he'd been cutting down on cigarettes. He smoked now only when he was under a great deal of pressure.

He had recently had an EKG that indicated his heart was sound. It it wasn't his ticker, what could it be?

Anxiety about Allie? Fear that she was about to go into a storm that would wreck her future?

A doctor entered the room. Stephen assumed this was the Dr. Hassan the nurse had mentioned.

"Good morning, Mr. Terhune," the young physician said. He was a slender, well-built man with dark, short hair, who looked as if he came from India or Pakistan. His manner was gentle, almost courtly.

"How are you this morning, Mr. Terhune?"

"What do you think, Doctor?"

"It is an oriental trait to answer a question with a question." He leaned over Stephen and listened with his stethoscope to the heart sounds. When he was finished he stood up, folding the stethoscope, smiling at Stephen. It was a smile that skillfully hid everything he knew except what he wanted his patient to know.

Stephen wasn't fooled. "All systems are shut down."

"Not quite."

Stephen's sense of hopelessness was total. He had a sudden despairing conviction that he'd never leave this hospital bed. The doctor made a move to leave the room, then appeared to change his mind. He returned and sat down on the one easy chair next to the bed.

"How bad is it?" Stephen asked although he didn't really want to know.

"Dr. Preisinger will discuss your condition with you."

"Who's that?"

"The cardiologist. He was recommended by your physician."

"When will he be here?"

"At noon, I believe."

"When can I get up?"

"He'll tell you. By tomorrow you should be able to sit up and dangle your legs."

"You make it sound like a great achievement."

"It is."

Stephen was not convinced. He felt he'd betrayed himself and all those who counted on him. "I'd like to see *The New York Times*," he said.

"It is preferable that you have a few days' rest before reentering your world of finance."

"Was my—my illness announced?"

"In the press and on television, unfortunately."

"I must know if it affected the price of our stock."

"That must wait, sir."

"It *can't* wait. Let me make one call—"

"I'm sorry, Mr. Terhune. The telephone isn't connected."

"Get my secretary. Get Norman, my assistant—"

"Please calm yourself, sir."

"Who's in the waiting room? The nurse said there were people in the waiting room."

"Your family, I presume."

"Please have my wife come in."

"Mr. Terhune, visitors will be forbidden if you cannot control yourself." The doctor was looking at the oscilloscope, where the lines recording Stephen's heartbeat were lengthening. "I'm afraid you must remain quiet, sir, until Dr. Preisinger arrives."

The young resident left, and a nurse came in with a capsule and a cup of water.

"Are you knocking me out again?" Stephen asked.

She smiled enigmatically.

He lay back exhausted, watching the oscilloscope. They had him by the short hairs; there was no way he could outwit them. A moment ago he had wanted Rose Eileen, knowing she would do what he wanted, even if it was against the doctor's orders. He had wanted to contact his office. But at this moment, bereft of energy, he thought of Allegra.

Of all his obligations, he was most concerned about her. Knowing her, loving her, he had a sixth sense about Allie, and he suspected she was heading for trouble. He had to protect her, not only from her in-laws, but from herself . . . .

That dark cold night in Paris . . . so long ago that he saw it played out with two people who were Allegra and Steve and yet were not. Her bed was no invitation to passion; the sheets and blankets wrapped around her body testified to her high fever, aching bones and bronchial cough. He was sitting beside her, close to her bed, holding her burning hands in his, talking to her, although he wasn't sure his words penetrated her confused mind.

"Allie, you'll make it," he had said, "because we're together, we're fighting this together . . ." And she *had* made it.

And now, he wanted her beside his bed, wanted to hear her whisper, "You'll make it, Steve, because we belong together. In spite of everything, we belong to-gether."

But he wasn't sure that she would give him that promise—because times changed, situations changed; because he felt old and crushed, old and defeated. What would a young woman want with a man over the hill?

In early January New York was in the grip of a raging storm that threatened a new Ice Age. Wild winds roared around the highrise buildings, whipping dirt and litter in the face of helpless pedestrians. Slick, unsanded pavements and frozen gutter slush tested the balance of the unwary.

Wrapped in a blue robe, Stephen looked down at the desolation of Park Avenue.

"It is advised," said the radio announcer, "that anyone with a pulmonary or cardiac problem remain indoors."

He switched off the bedside radio, reached auto-matically for a cigarette and let his arm freeze halfway. "You do without," the doctors had said.

He had done without many things, and now he was scheduled to be in Milwaukee at the end of the week to undergo open heart surgery with a prominent cardi-ologist who performed miracles with bypasses in the heart.

"Steve, once you can climb a couple of flights without panting, you'll be okay in the sack," the doctors had assured him . . . .

For Rose Eileen, that dear undemanding woman.

But not for Allegra. When he'd said they must not see each other again he had meant until after the lawsuit he was certain the Burketts planned to institute. But now he would not see Allegra again because his appreciation and loyalty belonged to Rose Eileen.

He turned his head as his wife entered the bedroom, carrying a tray set with English china, crystal and silver.

"Darling, your lunch," she said.

He looked at the tray, which she had placed on the table by his wingchair and then looked at her.

Rose Eileen managed a smile, but her eyes were misty. "It's not very exciting for a meat-and-potatoes man," she conceded, "but you'll be eating what you enjoy—in time."

She had prepared a meal of dry toast, chopped meat patty broiled without fat and decaffeinated brew. Rose Eileen got down on her knees beside him. "I know it's tough, darling. You're marking time—"

He didn't answer. She felt a flow of affection, thinking of his suffering, his stoic acceptance, and suddenly she wondered if he was afraid. It wasn't like him, but still . . .

"Stephen, are you —I mean—"

"Afraid? Yep, I'm scared out of my mind. I hear that when you wake up it feels as if a Mack truck has crushed your chest."

"But your heart will be new. That's what counts. You'll be as good as new. Maybe better." She took his hand and kissed the dry, cold palms. "But will you be satisfied with an old lady like me?"

"I'll think about it," he said.

They smiled at each other. Both knew the answer to her question.

It was Commencement Day for the Class of '77 at Locust Ryse.

World affairs were in a state of chaos, but little had

changed at the school—at least on the surface. The graduates still marched toward the platform in their white dresses, carrying sheaves of scarlet roses, but their number had multiplied. There were now fifty-five seniors, and only a third of them had been accepted by Seven Sister Colleges. The others would be going to the men's Ivy League colleges as well as to the big universities and less prestigious institutions.

As the guest arrived the junior class girls ushered them to their seats. Four hundred people were expected. The wooden seats fanned out around the platform, with the new gymnasium as a backdrop. The gym had been completed through the generosity of Stephen Terhune. At the suggestion of the Board of Incorporators, it had been named for Mrs. Merritt-Jones, who had found the gesture very touching.

Among the first guests walking across the freshly mowed lawn was Stephen Terhune and his wife. For a man who had recently undergone heart surgery, he looked healthy and youthful. There was a spring to his walk, since he jogged a minimum of three miles every day. Rose Eileen was thinner than she had been, and the nervous flush caused by her high blood pressure had faded. The serene expression on her face emphasized her great beauty.

Rose Eileen shifted in her chair to watch the crowds flowing in.

"Don't worry," Stephen reassured her. "They'll be here any minute. You know Dr. Hayden is always punctual."

"Stephen, do you think there's anything serious brewing between Cris and Dr. Hayden?" Rose Eileen asked.

"Well, she hasn't run off since she's been working with him. I understand she got mad at him one day and walked out—and reached the second block and turned around and apologized. Hayden is good for her. I guess he's the kind of father she needed."

"He's awfully young and attractive to be a father-image."

His gray eyes grew lighter as he saw Cris moving down the aisle, her stride swift and impatient. She was wearing a loose, flowing crinkled muslin dress with poppies on a creamy background. Her short, boyish haircut looked becoming with her feminine dress. She was thin, energetic and eager, the qualities Stephen had admired in her mother. But Bonnie had destroyed her talent by cultivating the vices—liquor and drugs—that had eventually done her in. She had been in and out of sanitariums for the past few months.

At least Bonnie hasn't destroyed Cris, Stephen reflected. It was ten years since the day in 1967 that he had stood on the platform and handed Cris her diploma. How young and vulnerable she'd been, and how ruthlessly Bonnie had used her—as Bonnie used everyone.

"Hi!" Cris said joyfully. "Well, here we are. Doug, just look at him. Less than four months out of surgery. Doesn't my father look marvelous?"

My father. Stephen was grateful for his dark glasses. It was the first time she'd called him "father" since she was a child.

My God, he thought, *this may be the beginning.*

Rose Eileen pressed her hand over his. She knew; she was sure. Bonnie Rob Roy had given birth to Cris, but Stephen realized that Rose Eileen had given her the love and understanding that made her the fine young woman she was.

"Has Allie come yet?" Cris asked, looking around eagerly. "She was taking the shuttle up from Washington."

Stephen felt his heart lurch.

"I understand she's leading a very busy life there." Rose Eileen's voice was expressionless.

"Yes. She's closed the Sutton Place apartment and bought a house in Georgetown." Cris grinned. "She said she wouldn't miss this for anything. She just wants to see Mrs. Merritt-Jones's face when Marianna steps out on the platform . . ."

Organ music filled the air. Behind parents and grandparents, the contemporaries of the graduating class were filling the last rows. Coming down the outer aisle were the Dietrichs. Evalina Novak and Marianna's sister Darlis were both dressed in summer silk prints. Darlis—her makeup subdued, her blond hair in a chignon—no longer behaved like Vince's wife, which she was now only in name. Liebschen, fully recovered from her operation, walked happily beside her husband.

"Here she is!" Cris called out. Allegra and her escort were moving toward them, smiling as Cris waved and motioned to the empty seats she was guarding.

Stephen appeared to be listening to Rose Eileen, giving her his full attention.

Allegra looked magnificent, as always. Her white gauze two-piece dress accentuated her slim, tanned figure. She'd never been so thin, almost one dimensional, and the effect—with her dark hair piled high on her head—was dramatic. The only jewelry she wore was the amethyst necklace her father had given her.

She was accompanied by a young man, the son of a southwestern politician who was destined to take his father's seat in the Senate. Stephen had read about Robert Morris. He was an attorney for Ralph Nader's organization and for the Legal Aid Society.

As Allegra made the introductions Cris decided she approved of Robert Morris. Like the late K.C. he was tall and broad-shouldered. His gray worsted summer suit was well-cut, his jacket three-buttoned, his tie carefully knotted.

Allegra had gone a step beyond K.C., Stephen thought, but she was still the same Allegra.

Marianna, Stephen recognized, had made it on talent, ability and drive. She was the woman of the seventies —generous and loving, but very much her own person. Stephen knew about her marriage to Ted and her long love affair with the Duke, and he reflected with admiration that experience hadn't harmed her, but had brought out her latent strength. Marriage for her would be a genuine partnership. He looked forward to attending her wedding next month.

Even his Cristina, Stephen decided, had learned to channel her capacity for giving. And if she needed the support a good man could offer her, it seemed to Stephen that Douglas Hayden was a fine choice.

But Allegra, he knew, would grow only through a man. Whether it was a kind of indolence or a lack of will, whether it was the trauma of her early years—which was nothing compared to what Cris had experienced—Allegra would never make the effort to shine on her own. She would always be in a man's shadow, but hopefully, a powerful man who deserved such a lovely, golden shadow.

Stephen was pleased that she'd listened to reason and had settled the Burketts' lawsuit out of court. Her little girl, Tish, would be far richer than Allegra herself ever was.

We need only to wait, he thought, *and time does the rest—one way or the other . . .*

The sun was a spotlight, spilling its gold on the platform as the graduating students and the faculty fell into line for the Procession. Mrs. Merritt-Jones was at the head, with Rabbi Joseph Greenbaum, who would give the Invocation, beside her.

Behind the Rabbi, Marianna Ellis walked with Marc Finley. Most of her former classmates who were at Locust Ryse for their tenth reunion, barely recognized the slim, fashionable young woman with the gold-streaked hair.

After the Invocation Mrs. Merritt-Jones stood up and went to the lectern. "Our guest speaker today is not a teacher or a businesswoman. Yet she is a woman of the world, since her face and voice are familiar to everyone who watches television. We have watched her progress with great pride . . ."

As Mrs. Merritt-Jones lauded her accomplishments Marianna recalled the moment a decade ago when she had come up to the headmistress to accept her awards and had shuddered, thinking about how she'd nearly lost out . . . .

Was Allegra's friendship worth the danger and the risk? Yes, Marianna reflected, *friendship is worth it.*

That was one of her traits that Marc appreciated: her loyalty and devotion to her friends.

Dear Marc, she thought. When she was his student he had told her never to settle for less. With Marc, she felt she had the best there was.

Mrs. Merritt-Jones was finished with her introduction and Marianna stood to a burst of applause, feeling strange to be on the other side of the lectern.

She told the graduates that they were about to face a new world with no guideposts along the way . . . that a woman made her mistakes and then picked herself up, having learned from them, and went on . . . that Marianna herself and her classmates of 1967 were nearing thirty, and they were still learning. Finishing school didn't finish; preparatory school didn't really prepare. But the time did come when a woman was able to combine all the instructions and criticisms, all the learning and yearning, and make a capable, valuable human being out of the fragments.

When Dr. Marc Finley stood up after Marianna had finished, Mrs. Merritt-Jones was again lavish in her praise. Before he was one of the economists on whom the President called regularly, she said, he had been on the Locust Ryse staff. Very graciously, he had returned to participate in commencement exercises . . .

Marianna saw Marc's courteous bow as he approached the lectern. *Maybe we both owe Mrs. Merritt-Jones something,* she thought. *If she'd treated us decently we wouldn't be here today . . .*

She looked down at her friends sitting together and singled out Allegra and Cris, both so proud of her.

Then she looked up. While Marc was handing out dilpomas to the girls in white with red roses, he was smiling. At her.

And she remembered . . . remembered what he'd written in her Locust Ryse yearbook all those years ago . . . "Live as though you intend to make your life a work of art."

ABOUT THE AUTHOR

ANN PINCHOT has been publishing fiction and nonfiction both in magazines and books for many years. She is the author of numerous works, including *52 West, Vanessa,* and *Weep No More My Lady: The Life of Judy Garland.* A former model for Saks Fifth Avenue, she has also been a feature writer for Hearst newspapers and a senior editor for a major book publishing house. She now makes her home in Stamford, Connecticut.

A Special Preview of
the powerful opening section of
the phenomenal bestseller

THE RIGHT STUFF

by

Tom Wolfe

Although this is the story of America's heroes—
the first flyguys in space—it is also the story of
their wives. While the hero was aloft, his wife
faced harrowing uncertainties and still had to be
a performer with the whole world watching.

Within five minutes, or ten minutes, no more than that, three of the others had called her on the telephone to ask her if she had heard that something had happened out there.

"Jane, this is Alice. Listen, I just got a call from Betty, and she said she heard something's happened out there. Have you heard anything?" That was the way they phrased it, call after call. She picked up the telephone and began relaying this same message to some of the others.

"Connie, this is Jane Conrad. Alice just called me, and she says something's happened . . ."

Something was part of the official Wife Lingo for tiptoeing blindfolded around the subject. Being barely twenty-one years old and new around here, Jane Conrad knew very little about this particular subject, since nobody ever talked about it. But the day was young! And what a setting she had for her imminent enlightenment! And what a picture she herself presented! Jane was tall and slender and had rich brown hair and high cheekbones and wide brown eyes. She looked a little like the actress Jean Simmons. Her father was a rancher in southwestern Texas. She had gone East to college, to Bryn Mawr, and had met her husband, Pete, at a debutante's party at the Gulph Mills Club in Philadelphia, when he was a senior at Princeton. Pete was a short, wiry, blond boy who joked around a lot. At any moment his face was likely to break into a wild grin revealing the gap between his front teeth. The Hickory Kid sort, he was; a Hickory Kid on the deb circuit, however. He had an air of energy, self-confidence, ambition, *joie de vivre*. Jane and Pete were married two days after he graduated from Princeton. Last year Jane gave birth to their first child, Peter. And today, here in Florida, in Jacksonville, in the peaceful year 1955, the sun shines through the pines outside, and the very air takes on the sparkle of the ocean. The ocean and a great mica-white beach are less than a mile away. Anyone driving by will see Jane's little house gleaming like a dream house in the pines. It is a brick house, but Jane and Pete painted the bricks white, so that it gleams in the sun against a great green screen of pine trees with a thousand little places where the sun peeks through. They painted the shutters black, which makes the white walls look even more brilliant. The house has only eleven hundred square feet of floor space, but Jane and Pete designed it themselves and that more than makes up for the size. A friend of theirs was the builder and gave them every possible break, so that it cost only eleven thousand dollars. Outside, the sun shines, and inside, the fever rises by the minute as five, ten, fifteen, and, finally, nearly all twenty of the wives join the circuit, trying to find out what has happened, which, in fact, means: to whose husband.

After thirty minutes on such a circuit—this is not an unusual morning around here—a wife begins to feel that the telephone is no longer located on a table or on the kitchen wall. It is exploding in her solar plexus. Yet it would be far worse right now to hear the front doorbell. The protocol is strict on that point, although written down nowhere. No woman is supposed to deliver the final news, and certainly not on the telephone. The matter mustn't be bungled!—that's the idea. No, a man should bring the news when the time comes, a man with some official or moral authority, a clergyman or a comrade of the newly deceased. Furthermore, he should bring the bad news in person. He should turn up at the front door and ring the bell and be standing there like a pillar of coolness and competence, bearing the bad news on ice, like a fish. Therefore, all the telephone calls from the wives were the frantic and portentous beating of the wings of the death angels, as it were. When the final news came, there would be a ring at the front door—a wife in this situation finds herself staring at the front door as if she no longer owns it or controls it—and outside the door would be a man . . . come to inform her that unfortunately something has happened out there, and her husband's body now lies incinerated in the swamps or the pines or the palmetto grass, "burned beyond recognition, . . ."

My own husband—how could this be what they were talking about? Jane had heard the young men, Pete among them, talk about other young men who had "bought it" or "augered in" or "crunched," but it had never been anyone they knew, no one in the squadron. And in any event, the way they talked about it, with such breezy, slangy terminology, was the same way they talked about sports. It was as if they were saying, "He was thrown out stealing second base." And that was all! Not one word, not in print, not in conversation —not in this amputated language!—about an incinerated corpse from which a young man's spirit has vanished in an instant, from which all smiles, gestures, moods, worries, laughter, wiles, shrugs, tenderness, and loving looks—*you, my love!*—have disappeared like a sigh, while the terror consumes a cottage in the woods, and a young woman, sizzling with the fever, awaits her confirmation as the new widow of the day.

The next series of calls greatly increased the possibility that it was Pete to whom something had happened. There were only twenty men in the squadron, and soon nine or ten had been accounted for . . . by the fluttering reports of the death angels. Knowing that the word was out that an accident had occurred, husbands who could get to a telephone were calling home to say *it didn't happen to me*. This news, of course, was immediately fed to the fever. Jane's telephone would ring once more, and one of the wives would be saying:

"Nancy just got a call from Jack. He's at the squadron and he says something's happened, but he doesn't know what. He said he saw Frank D—— take off about ten minutes ago with Greg in back, so they're all right. What have you heard?"

But Jane has heard nothing except that other husbands, and not hers, are safe and accounted for. And thus, on a sunny day in Florida, outside of the Jacksonville Naval Air Station, in a little white cottage, a veritable dream house, another beautiful young woman was about to be apprised of the *quid pro quo* of her husband's line of work, of the trade-off, as one might say, the subparagraphs of a contract written in no visible form. Just as surely as if she had the entire roster in front of her, Jane now realized that only two men in the squadron were unaccounted for. One was a pilot named Bud Jennings; the other was Pete. She picked up the telephone and did something that was much frowned on in a time of emergency. She called the squadron office. The duty officer answered.

"I want to speak to Lieutenant Conrad," said Jane. "This is Mrs. Conrad."

"I'm sorry," the duty officer said—and then his voice cracked. "I'm sorry . . . I . . ." He couldn't find the words! He was about to cry! "I'm—that's—I mean . . . he can't come to the phone!"

He can't come to the phone!

"It's very important!" said Jane.

"I'm sorry—it's impossible—" The duty officer could hardly get the words out because he was so busy gulping back sobs. *Sobs!* "He can't come to the phone."

"Why not? Where is he?"

"I'm sorry—" More sighs, wheezes, snuffling gasps. "I can't tell you that. I—I have to hang up now!"

And the duty officer's voice disappeared in a great surf of emotion and he hung up.

The duty officer! *The very sound of her voice was more than he could take!*

The world froze, congealed, in that moment. Jane could no longer calculate the interval before the front doorbell would ring and some competent long-faced figure would appear, some Friend of Widows and Orphans, who would inform her, officially, that Pete was dead.

Even out in the middle of the swamp, in this rot-bog of pine trunks, scum slicks, dead dodder vines, and mosquito eggs, even out in this great overripe sump, the smell of "burned beyond recognition" obliterated everything else. When airplane fuel exploded, it created a heat so intense that everything but the hardest metals not only *burned*—everything of rubber, plastic, celluloid, wood, leather, cloth, flesh, gristle, calcium, horn, hair, blood, and protoplasm—it not only burned, it gave up the ghost in the form of every stricken putrid gas known to chemistry. One could smell the horror. It came in through the nostrils and burned the rhinal cavities raw and penetrated the liver and permeated the bowels like a black gas until there was nothing in the universe, inside or out, except the stench of the char. As the helicopter came down between the pine trees and settled onto the bogs, the smell hit Pete Conrad even before the hatch was completely open, and they were not even close enough to see the wreckage yet. The rest of the way Conrad and the crewmen had to travel on foot. After a few steps the water was up to their knees, and then it was up to their armpits, and they kept wading through the water and the scum and the vines and the pine trunks, but it was nothing compared to the smell. Conrad, a twenty-five-year-old lieutenant junior grade, happened to be on duty as squadron safety officer that day and was supposed to make the on-site investigation of the crash. The fact was, however, that this squadron was the first duty assignment of his career, and he had never been at a crash site before and had never smelled any such revolting stench or seen anything like what awaited him.

When Conrad finally reached the plane, which was an SNJ, he found the fuselage burned and blistered and dug into the swamp with one wing sheared off and the cockpit canopy smashed. In the front seat was all that was left of his friend Bud Jennings. Bud Jennings, an amiable fellow, a promising young fighter pilot, was now a horrible roasted hulk—with no head. His head was completely gone, apparently torn off the spinal column like a pineapple off a stalk, except that it was nowhere to be found ...

In keeping with the protocol, the squadron commander was not going to release Bud Jennings's name until his widow, Loretta, had been located and a competent male death messenger had been dispatched to tell her. But Loretta Jennings was not at home and could not be found. Hence, a delay—and more than enough time for the other wives, the death angels, to burn with panic over the telephone lines. All the pilots were accounted for except the two who were in the woods, Bud Jennings and Pete Conrad. One chance in two, acey-deucey, one finger–two finger, and this was not an unusual day around here.

Loretta Jennings had been out at a shopping center. When she returned home, a certain figure was waiting outside, a man, a solemn Friend of Widows and Orphans, and it was Loretta Jennings who lost the game of odd and even, acey-deucey, and it was Loretta whose child (she was pregnant with a second) would have no father. It was this young woman who went through all the final horrors that Jane Conrad had imagined—assumed!—would be hers to endure forever. Yet this grim stroke of fortune brought Jane little relief.

On the day of Bud Jennings's funeral, Pete went into the back of the closet and brought out his bridge coat, per regulations. This was the most stylish item in the Navy officer's wardrobe. Pete had never had occasion to wear his before. It was a double-breasted coat made of navy-blue melton cloth and came down almost to the ankles. It must have weighed ten pounds. It had a double row of gold buttons down the front and loops for shoulder boards, big beautiful belly-cut collar and lapels, deep turnbacks on the sleeves, a tailored waist, and a center vent in back that ran from the waistline to the bottom of the coat. Never would Pete, or for that matter many other American males in the mid-twentieth century, have an article of clothing quite so impressive and aristocratic as that bridge coat. At the funeral the nineteen little Indians who were left—Navy boys!—lined up manfully in their bridge coats. They looked so young. Their pink, lineless faces with their absolutely clear, lean jawlines popped up bravely, correctly, out of the enormous belly-cut collars of the bridge coats. They sang an old Navy hymn, which slipped into a strange and lugubrious minor key here and there, and included a stanza added especially for aviators. It ended with: "O hear us when we lift our prayer for those in peril in the air."

Three months later another member of the squadron crashed and was burned beyond recognition and Pete hauled out the bridge coat again and Jane saw eighteen little Indians bravely going through the motions at the funeral. Not long after that, Pete was transferred from Jacksonville to the Patuxent River Naval Air Station in Maryland. Pete and Jane had barely settled in there when they got word that another member of the Jacksonville squadron, a close friend of theirs, someone they had had over to dinner many times, had died trying to take off from the deck of a carrier in a routine practice session a few miles out in the Atlantic. The catapult that propelled aircraft off the deck lost pressure, and his ship just dribbled off the end of the deck, with its engine roaring vainly, and fell sixty feet into the ocean and sank like a brick, and he vanished, *just like that*.

Pete had been transferred to Patuxent River, which was known in Navy vernacular as Pax River, to enter the Navy's new test-pilot school. This was considered a major step up in the career of a young Navy aviator. Now that the Korean War was over and there was no combat flying, all the hot young pilots aimed for flight test. In the military they always said "flight test" and not "test flying." Jet aircraft had been in use for barely ten years at the time, and the Navy was testing new jet fighters continually. Pax River was the Navy's prime test center.

Jane liked the house they bought at Pax River. She didn't like it as much as the little house in Jacksonville, but then she and Pete hadn't designed this one. They lived in a community called North Town Creek, six miles from the base. North Town Creek, like the base, was on a scrub-pine peninsula that stuck out into Chesapeake Bay. They were tucked in amid the pine trees. (Once more!) All around were rhododendron bushes. Pete's classwork and his flying duties were very demanding. Everyone in his flight test class, Group 20, talked about how difficult it was—and obviously loved it, because in Navy flying this was the big league. The young men in Group 20 and their wives were Pete's and Jane's entire social world. The associated with no one else. They constantly invited each other to dinner during the week; there was a Group party at someone's house practically every weekend; and they would go off on outings to fish or waterski in Chesapeake Bay. In a way they could not have associated with anyone else, at least not easily, because the boys could talk only about one thing: their flying. One of the phrases that kept running through the conversation was "pushing the outside of the envelope." The "envelope" was a flight-test term referring to the limits of a particular aircraft's performance, how tight a turn it could make at such-and-such a speed, and so on. "Pushing the outside," probing the outer limits, of the envelope seemed to be the great challenge and satisfaction of flight test. At first "pushing the outside of the envelope" was not a particularly terrifying phrase to hear. It sounded once more as if the boys were just talking about sports.

Then one sunny day a member of the Group, one of the happy lads they always had dinner with and drank with and went waterskiing with, was coming in for a landing at the base in an A3J fighter plane. He came in too low before lowering his flaps, and the ship stalled out, and he crashed and was burned beyond recognition. And they brought out the bridge coats and sang about those in peril in the air and put the bridge coats away, and the Indians who were left talked about the accident after dinner one night. They shook their heads and said it was a damned shame, but he should have known better than to wait so long before lowering the flaps.

Barely a week had gone by before another member of the Group was coming in for a landing in the same type of aircraft, the A3J, trying to make a ninety-degree landing, which involves a sharp turn, and something went wrong with the controls, and he ended up with one rear stabilizer wing up and the other one down, and his ship rolled in like a corkscrew from 800 feet up and crashed, and he was burned beyond recognition. And the bridge coats came out and they sang about those in peril in the air and then they put the bridge coats away and after dinner one night they mentioned that the departed had been a good man but was inexperienced, and when the malfunction in the controls put him in that bad corner, he didn't know how to get out of it.

Every wife wanted to cry out: "Well, my God! The *machine* broke! What makes *any* of you think you would have come out of it any better!" Yet intuitively Jane and the rest of them knew it wasn't right even to suggest that. Pete never indicated for a moment that he thought any such thing could possibly happen to him. It seemed not only wrong but dangerous to challenge a young pilot's confidence by posing the question. And that, too, was part of the unofficial protocol for the Officer's Wife. From now on every time Pete was late coming in from the flight line, she would worry. She began to wonder if—no! *assume!*—he had found his way into one of those corners they all talked about so spiritedly, one of those little dead ends that so enlivened conversation around here.

Not long after that, another good friend of theirs went up in an F–4, the Navy's newest and hottest fighter plane, known as the Phantom. He reached twenty thousand feet and then nosed over and dove straight into Chesapeake Bay. It turned out that a hose connection was missing in his oxygen system and he had suffered hypoxia and passed out at the high altitude. And the bridge coats came out and they lifted a prayer about those in peril in the air and the bridge coats were put away and the little Indians were incredulous. How could anybody fail to check his hose connections? And how could anybody be in such poor condition as to pass out *that quickly* from hypoxia?

A couple of days later Jane was standing at the window of her house in North Town Creek. She saw some smoke rise above the pines from over in the direction of the flight line. Just that, a column of smoke; no explosion or sirens or any other sound. She went to another room, so as not to have to think about it but there was no explanation for the smoke. She went back to the window. In the yard of a house across the street she saw a group of people . . . standing there and looking at her house, as if trying to decide what to do. Jane looked away—but she couldn't keep from looking out again. She caught a glimpse of *a certain figure* coming up the walkway toward her front door. She knew exactly who it was. She had had nightmares like this. And yet this was no dream. She was wide awake and alert. Never more alert in her entire life! Frozen, completely defeated by the sight, she simply waited for the bell to ring. She waited, but there was not a sound. Finally she could stand it no more. In real life, unlike her dream life, Jane was both too self-possessed and too polite to scream through the door: "Go away!" So she opened it. There was no one there, no one at all. There was no group of people on the lawn across the way and no one to be seen for a hundred yards in any direction along the lawns and leafy rhododendron roads of North Town Creek.

Then began a cycle in which she had both the nightmares and the hallucinations, continually. Anything could touch off an hallucination: a ball of smoke, a telephone ring that stopped before she could answer it, the sound of a siren, even the sound of trucks starting up (crash trucks!). Then she would glance out the window, and a certain figure would be coming up the walk, and she would wait for the bell. The only difference between the dreams and the hallucinations was that the scene of the dreams was always the little white house in Jacksonville. In both cases, the feeling that *this time it has happened* was quite real.

The star pilot in the class behind Pete's, a young man who was the main rival of their good friend Al Bean, went up in a fighter to do some power-dive tests. One of the most demanding disciplines in flight test was to accustom yourself to making precise readings from the control panel in the same moment that you were pushing the outside of the envelope. This young man put his ship into the test dive and was still reading out the figures, with diligence and precision and great discipline, when he augered straight into the oyster flats and was burned beyond recognition. And the bridge coats came out and they sang about those in peril in the air and the bridge coats were put away, and the little Indians remarked that the departed was a swell guy and a brilliant student of flying; a little too *much* of a student, in fact; he hadn't bothered to look out the window at the real world soon enough. Beano—Al Bean—wasn't quite so brilliant; on the other hand, he was still here.

Like many other wives in Group 20 Jane wanted to talk about the whole situation, the incredible series of fatal accidents, with her husband and the other members of the Group, to find out how they were taking it. But somehow the unwritten protocol forbade discussions of this subject, which was the fear of death. Nor could Jane or any of the rest of them talk, really *have a talk,* with anyone around the base. You could talk to another wife about being worried. But what good did it do? Who *wasn't* worried? You were likely to get a look that said: *"Why dwell on it?"* Jane might have gotten away with divulging the matter of the nightmares. But *hallucinations?* There was no room in Navy life for any such anomalous tendency as that.

By now the bad string had reached ten in all, and almost all of the dead had been close friends of Pete and Jane, young men who had been in their house many times, young men who had sat across from Jane and chattered like the rest of them about the grand adventure of military flying. And the survivors still sat around *as before*—with the same inexplicable exhilaration! Jane kept watching Pete for some sign that his spirit was cracking, but she saw none. He talked a mile a minute, kidded and joked, laughed with his Hickory Kid cackle. He always had. He still enjoyed the company of members of the group like Wally Schirra and Jim Lovell. Many young pilots were taciturn and cut loose with the strange fervor of this business only in the air. But Pete and Wally and Jim were not reticent; not in any situation. They loved to kid around. Pete called Jim Lovell "Shaky," because it was the last thing a pilot would want to be called. Wally Schirra was outgoing to the point of hearty; he loved practical jokes and dreadful puns, and so on. The three of them —*even in the midst of this bad string!*—would love to get on a subject such as accident-prone Mitch Johnson. Accident-prone Mitch Johnson, it seemed, was a Navy pilot whose life was in the hands of two angels, one of them bad and the other one good. The bad angel would put him into accidents that would have annihilated any ordinary pilot, and the good angel would bring him out of them without a scratch. Just the other day —this was the sort of story Jane would hear them tell—Mitch Johnson was coming in to land on a carrier. But he came in short, missed the flight deck, and crashed into the fantail, below the deck. There was a tremendous explosion, and the rear half of the plane fell into the water in flames. Everyone on the flight deck said, "Poor Johnson. The good angel was off duty." They were still debating how to remove the debris and his mortal remains when a phone rang on the bridge. A somewhat dopey voice said, "This is Johnson. Say, listen, I'm down here in the supply hold and the hatch is locked and I can't find the lights and I can't see a goddamned thing and I tripped over a cable and I think I hurt my leg." The officer on the bridge slammed the phone down, then vowed to find out what morbid sonofabitch could pull a phone prank at a time like this. Then the phone rang again, and the man with the dopey voice managed to establish the fact that he was, indeed, Mitch Johnson. The good angel had not left his side. When he smashed into the fantail, he hit some empty ammunition drums, and they cushioned the impact, leaving him groggy but not seriously hurt. The fuselage had blown to pieces; so he just stepped out onto the fantail and opened a hatch that led into the supply hold. It was pitch black in there, and there were cables all across the floor, holding down spare aircraft engines. Accident-prone Mitch Johnson kept tripping over these cables until he found a telephone. Sure enough, the one injury he had was a bruised shin from tripping over a cable. The man was accident-prone! Pete and Wally and Jim absolutely cracked up over stories like this. It was amazing. Great sports yarns! Nothing more than that.

A few days later Jane was out shopping at the Pax River commissary on Saunders Road, near the main gate to the base. She heard the sirens go off at the field, and then she heard the engines of the crash trucks start up. This time Jane was determined to keep calm. Every instinct made her want to rush home, but she forced herself to stay in the commissary and continue shopping. For thirty minutes she went through the motions of completing her shopping list. Then she drove home to North Town Creek. As she reached the house, she saw a figure going up the sidewalk. It was a man. Even from the back there was no question as to who he was. He had on a black suit, and there was a white band around his neck. It was her minister, from the Episcopal Church. She stared, and this vision did not come and go. The figure kept on walking up the front walk. She was not asleep now, and she was not inside her house glancing out the front window. She was outside in her car in front of her house. She was not dreaming, and she was not hallucinating, and the figure kept walking up toward her front door.

That the preacher had not, in fact, come to her front door as the Solemn Friend of Widows and Orphans, but merely for a church call . . . had not brought peace and relief. That Pete still didn't show the slightest indication of thinking that any unkind fate awaited him no longer lent her even a moment's courage. The next dream and the next hallucination, and the next and the next, merely seemed more real. For she now *knew*. She now knew the subject and the essence of this enterprise, even though not a word of it had passed anybody's lips. She even knew why Pete—the Princeton boy she met at a deb party at the Gulph Mills Club!—would never quit, never withdraw from this grim business, unless in a coffin. And God knew, and she knew, there was a coffin waiting for each little Indian.

Seven years later, when a reporter and a photographer from *Life* magazine actually stood near her in her living room and watched her face, while outside, on the lawn, a crowd of television crewmen and newspaper reporters waited for a word, an indication, anything—perhaps a glimpse through a part in a curtain!—waited for some sign of what she felt—when one and all asked with their ravenous eyes and, occasionally, in so many words: "How do you feel?" and "Are you scared?"—America wants to know!—it made Jane want to laugh, but in fact she couldn't even manage a smile.

"Why ask *now?*" she wanted to say. But they wouldn't have had the faintest notion of what she was talking about.

Anne, as well as the other wives of the potential astronauts, were thrust into the spotlight. They were forced to take their own risks as their husbands embarked on adventures more thrilling and dangerous than anything previously attempted.

Read the complete Bantam Book, available October 22, 1980 wherever paperbacks are sold.

THE LATEST BOOKS IN THE BANTAM BESTSELLING TRADITION

Bantam Book Catalog

Here's your up-to-the-minute listing of over 1,400 titles by your favorite authors.

This illustrated, large format catalog gives a description of each title. For your convenience, it is divided into categories in fiction and non-fiction—gothics, science fiction, westerns, mysteries, cookbooks, mysticism and occult, biographies, history, family living, health, psychology, art.

So don't delay—take advantage of this special opportunity to increase your reading pleasure.

Just send us your name and address and 50¢ (to help defray postage and handling costs).